STRINGS
ATTACHED

First published in Great Britain in 2019 by Trapeze,
an imprint of The Orion Publishing Group Ltd
Carmelite House, 50 Victoria Embankment,
London EC4Y 0DZ

An Hachette UK company

1 3 5 7 9 10 8 6 4 2

A CIP catalogue record for this book is
available from the British Library.

ISBN (Paperback) 9781 4091 8577 2

Typeset by Born Group

Printed and bound in Great Britain by Clays Ltd, Elcograf S.p.A.

MIX
Paper from
responsible sources
FSC® C104740

www.orionbooks.co.uk

STRINGS
ATTACHED

Erin Reinelt

For Anna,
My favourite person and
greatest champion.

Chapter One

'Wheelie bin races tomorrow afternoon!' Charlie exclaims with the easy joy of a small child, as he takes in a chalk sign outside the door of the Three Horseshoes. He parks the Mini convertible haphazardly across two spaces, before opening Jean's door with a flourish. 'I knew there's a good reason this is my favourite pub.'

'We have the post-nuptial brunch tomorrow,' Jean reminds him, lurching out of the car and patting her hair back into shape. The neat chignon she'd fixed that morning has blown flat and sideways, like a bad toupée.

She eyes the thermos bottle lying on Charlie's seat suspiciously.

'Ah, but brunch is at eleven! The races start at two,' Charlie says, swooping her off the gravel into his arms and carrying her through the entrance to deposit her in front of the barman. Jean used to giggle when he did this, at the ostentation. The old-fashioned chivalry! But for some time now she has suspected his motive is to be served as quickly as is humanly possible.

'I thought you'd never been to Kent! How can this be your favourite pub?' Her knees wobble as she leans against the bar. She had been holding them together, vice-like, throughout the swerving drive.

'A boozehound never tells,' Charlie says, tapping his nose with one finger over an impish grin. 'But I'll give you a clue: proximity.'

Jean rolls her eyes. The mirror behind the bar, scuffed as it is, does not paint a flattering picture of them as a couple. Charlie's longish black hair stands at a seventy-five-degree angle from his scalp; his suit is askew, one white shirt end flapping over his trousers. Jean's lilac dress brings out a sallow tone to her skin. Her face is a mottled puce, with red splotches high on her cheekbones.

They both look like they've been spat out of a tornado.

'Two pints of lager and three whisky chasers, my good man!' Charlie orders with a twinkle in his eye. 'Maybe four. Jeannie?'

'Charlie, the ceremony starts at five!' Jean protests, checking her watch. It was nearly 4 p.m. 'And don't call me Jeannie.'

'The venue is only five minutes away,' Charlie says, turning his huge, brown, melting puppy gaze at her. That look still has the power to twist Jean's heart, even as his irises are increasingly swamped by ballooning purple eyebags.

'I haven't seen Sarah in almost a year. I don't want to be rude!' Jean hates the shrill edge that has been creeping into her voice, more and more of late. She can't help it. It has become as natural to her as shallow breathing and anxiety.

'Pish tosh! Grown men don't take orders from confectionary.' Charlie smiles, fluttering a layer of her pleated dress with his fingertip.

Jean inspects herself, wounded. She can see now that the multi-layered maxi style the pushy saleswoman had insisted was 'Timeless, seventies' looks exactly like a stack of upside-down cupcake wrappers. Not so long ago, she would have found this funny. Today, it makes her want to cry.

'It's timeless and seventies,' Jean says defensively.

'You can't be timeless *and* seventies,' Charlie points out.

'Here you are, mate,' the bartender says, passing over the tumblers almost flirtatiously. Charlie always had this effect on people. Whether it was his slightly fey manner or air of adventure, every stranger became an instant friend. If Charlie were a perfume he'd be called: What Larks!

As soon as the glass touches wood, he necks two of the whiskies in quick succession, and Jean motions to the barman for the bill. She pays before Charlie has a chance to order another round. On their first date, Charlie had merrily described himself as a 'bedwetting alcoholic first, journalist second' and so, fairly warned, Jean never took him to task for his drinking. More of a liability than a mean drunk, his occasional buffoonery had seemed a small price to pay for his undeniable charm.

Unfortunately, on special occasions, she had to watch him like a hawk.

Jean sips her pint and turns her agency iPhone on.
Shit.

'Five missed calls . . .' Jean says, her heart pounding. 'Jez is going to kill me!'

'Tell him to fuck off!' Charlie says, somewhat bitterly. Of late, his own work has been drying up, a touchy subject. And increasingly, his advice seems geared towards getting her fired. 'It's Saturday.'

'It might be an emergency,' Jean says, dialling back nervously.

Charlie snatches the mobile from her hands.

'It is never an emergency. *And* it's your best childhood friend's wedding. What's her name again?'

'Sarah!' Jean reminds him for the fifth time, wrestling the phone from his hands. 'I'll be two minutes.'

It's Charlie's turn to roll his eyes.

3

Her boss calls at any hour of the day or night, no matter the occasion. Jean even left her grandmother's funeral early, after Jez feigned a heart attack to lure her to the office. To be fair, working for the best political PR firm in London means 24-7 availability, and that had been during a top-secret crisis with the Prime Minister's dodgy uncle.

'Why does everyone have a dodgy uncle?', Jean wonders aloud to herself, as the phone rings.

'What the hell are you on about,' Jez says by way of hello.

'Oh, you know,' Jean laughs the tittery social laugh she has developed listening to the comedy of MPs. 'Weddings! Weird uncles abound. Is something wrong?'

'Have you not read Twitter?' Jez shouts down the line.

Jez always referred to Twitter as if it were a work of great literature she could be shamed into consuming.

'My phone is low on battery! We were in a rush,' Jean cringes, gulping her pint for Dutch courage.

PR had been much more fun before social media turned into a dragon eating its own young. When she'd started out it had been a heady mixture of parties, policy and power. Unmissable conversations happened in real life and her clients appeared to actually want to improve the lives of the people. Over the past few years, however, her list had been overwhelmed by despotic overgrown schoolboys.

'Lord Kinder was picked up cruising on Hampstead Heath!'

'That's recoverable!' Jean says, breathing a sigh of relief. Yes, the Tory MP with his pearl-clutching appeals for family values would find this personally humiliating. But post #MeToo, a bit of anonymous cottaging was practically twee. 'Tell him to whack himself in the eye and we'll go for the confused-after-mugging excuse. Does he have a dog?'

'I don't bloody know! That's your job! So do it!'

He hangs up abruptly.

'I'll get in touch with the papers. Have a great weekend! Thanks, I will. Bye bye,' Jean says calmly to no one, pretending to have been treated with normal conversational etiquette in front of Charlie.

Jean had quickly adapted to Jez Addington's aggro-dictator style when she'd started at Addington Media Agency fresh out of university. She found it strangely comforting, perhaps because Jez was so similar to her father. And it was a good buzz, the scandal and panic, or rather the re-framing of scandal and the calming of panic. On her good days, it made her feel strong, capable, almost magic. Like if Glenda the Good Witch helped sex perverts to keep their constituencies.

On her bad days, which were becoming more frequent, she worried that her only life skill was clearing up cluster-fucks left by grown men.

'I told you to put your foot down. He'll never respect you if you don't assert your boundaries!' This coming from her boyfriend of three years who has never respected her boundaries, and is now patting her on the shoulder patronis-ingly as Jean rapid-emails her contact list.

'Not now,' Jean shrugs him off.

'You're not still in a huff about those shoes, are you,' Charlie said with a pout, poking her playfully in the ribs.

Jean looks up with a glare. 'I hadn't been. Until you reminded me.'

These days it wasn't uncommon for Jean to wake up alone in the flat they shared in Peckham, only to find Charlie passed out on the doorstep. Brewer's droop had murdered their sex life, but at least the bedwetting had actually been a joke. Charlie always made it, if not to the actual toilet, at least to a potted plant or the closet. As Jean kept her shoes placed in cardboard boxes, neatly folded in tissue paper, they had mostly gone unscathed. Except for those brand spanking new velvet stilettos she had been planning to wear today.

'What's happened to you? I said I'd replace them,' Charlie says, finishing off his pint. 'You never used to be such a bore.'

In Charlie's world, this was the worst possible thing someone could be accused of. Lie to his face, rob him blind, piss on his shoes – all would be forgiven if you made him laugh.

And Jean used to make him laugh, all the time.

Her throat constricts against a sudden knot. What *has* happened to her? Is it attending the wedding, her third this year? Is it her age? Is turning thirty the tipping point where you transform into a nag-shrew with shit clothes and no sense of humour? Her older sister had offered to buy Jean a course of colonics for her birthday, and she had been very excited about it. Until she realised it was a cruel joke about her anal-retentiveness.

Jean looks down at her phone again. She finishes off her correspondence. She enjoys the satisfying swoosh of emails sent. The only reliable part of her life. Technology.

Jean had decided that this weekend, she would turn off her phone and be fully present. She and Sarah hadn't seen much of each other in recent years, and Jean was touched at the invitation. Also, Sarah's family made her nervous. They were the sort of people to cut you forever dead in Waitrose if a ringtone disturbed a speech. Not that being ignored in a supermarket is the cruellest punishment ever, but to the Kent bourgeoisie, it is equivalent to pistols at dawn.

Jean turns off her mobile resolutely. The act makes her heart pound.

'We're late,' Jean says, finally looking up.

The barman sets down two more pints before them.

'Charlie!'

'What? You were on your phone. We could be here for hours!'

Jean takes Charlie's arm and steers him towards the door. He wriggles out of her grasp and trots to the bar.

'Jean, don't be mad. What's five more minutes? I'm just trying to have fun! Like we used to. Have fun. Remember that?' He raises the glasses in Irish handcuffs, sipping from them simultaneously and giving a saucy wink.

Jean couldn't tell any more if she was over-reacting or under-reacting to Charlie. She had lost sight of what was normal behaviour. But she could sense herself morphing into the kind of girlfriend she used to see bitching out their men at the pub, when she was young and foolish enough to pity the boyfriend.

'We can have fun. At. The. Wedding!' Jean yells. The barman coughs to hide his laughter. Sensing an audience, Charlie sets down the pints, drops to his knees and recites, hand on chest.

' "Never give all the heart, for love will hardly seem worth thinking of to passionate women if it seem certain! And they never dream that it fades out from kiss to kiss—" '

Yeats. It had been a favourite of Charlie's since his mother told him she was leaving his father for their gardener, three months ago. 'I'm an adult child of divorce!' he had wept piteously in her arms. 'You're certainly an adult child,' Jean had responded, fondly at the time.

Jean puts her head in her hands. When she looks up, she catches a girl staring at them from across the room, smirking.

You wouldn't think him so charming if he'd pissed all over *your* goddamn shoes, thinks Jean. She considers shouting the sentence, but restrains herself. Because she is not feral. She is a grown woman, in control of her life and boyfriend.

'We will have fun at the wedding,' Jean states again, calmly this time.

She collects herself and walks out to the car, Charlie trailing behind her. She gets in the passenger seat and looks out the window, arms crossed over her chest. Her body jerks as the Mini barrels forward onto the main road.

Charlie sips from his thermos as they speed towards Mount Ephraim Gardens, the ends of his satin bow-tie flapping wildly behind him. Jean resists the urge to cross herself. She wonders again if it is actually filled with coffee, as he insisted. He wouldn't do that to her, surely? There was a vast difference between stopping at the pub before a five-minute jaunt down a country lane, and drunk-driving the A2 all the way from London.

'Could you please slow down?' Jean says, the seatbelt digging into her flesh through her dress. 'I'd rather be late than dead!'

'Nearly there! We'll be bang on time,' Charlie says with self-satisfaction. He sets the thermos aside as he takes a left turn towards an enormous country house.

As he pulls into the parking lot, Jean takes the thermos from the cup holder. Charlie freezes. Jean sips. It isn't coffee. It isn't even an Irish coffee.

Straight vodka.

Charlie parks the car. She can see his hands trembling a little as he lets go of the steering wheel.

'I never drink in the mornings,' Charlie says defensively, before Jean has the opportunity to accuse him of anything.

'No,' Jean smiles wryly, 'that would require waking before noon.'

Jean necks what remains.

'I'm sorry,' Charlie says, head down, his eyes peeping up at her under dark lashes like a shamed little boy. But he wasn't a boy. He was a thirty-five-year-old man. And she was his babysitter.

'I'm not sure it's a good idea if you come any more,' Jean says, looking into the distance. She can see a wooden sign painted with 'Sarah and Toby's Wedding' in gold calligraphy, pointing towards a path leading into the woods.

Jean knows she should be upset that Charlie has endangered both their lives on the drive down from London, but oddly, she's not. Neither is she surprised. It is one in an endless list of things she has let slide. She looks down into her lap, fingering the cheap lilac chiffon. She had chosen this man. This sick man. Mystifyingly, she had also chosen this dress. This hideous dress.

It's funny the things you notice when a part of your life is ending forever.

'I'll behave, I promise, Jean. I love you,' Charlie says, pathetically.

The thing was, he did love her. She never doubted that. He would declare it, loudly and wildly, when he brought her toasted crumpets with Marmite in bed and read to her on lazy Sundays in the park. When he brushed her hair when she was unwell and teased her back to good humour when she was feeling down.

But who wouldn't love the woman who bit her tongue, held back, never told you off, and let you be exactly who you wanted to be, holding her cheerful façade together so perfectly you had no idea she was crumbling under the weight of it? Jean's fate, should she stay with Charlie, and what she once thought of as her reward, was to be loved as a falsehood of her own design.

'I don't know,' Jean whispers, suddenly blinking back tears. 'I just don't know any more.'

'Jeannie,' Charlie's voice cracks. 'Don't do this to me.'

'Take our bags to the hotel. We'll talk things through later tonight.'

Jean stumbles out of the car towards the garden path, her vision blurred, hearing the sound of wheels crunching gravel behind her. She searches her bag for a mint to disguise the cheap vodka on her breath, as she follows a trail of balloons tied into the foliage with ribbons.

And to think this weekend she had hoped they might reconnect sexually, after a year of coitus-toodrunktofuckus.

'Jean! My god darling, it's been ages!'

Jean looks up, mournfully.

Sophia, Sarah's cousin, quite literally barefoot and pregnant with a garland in her hair, waves from across the bridge. Her whole body wiggles with the movement, in an ecstasy of excitement better suited to an electrocuted custard. While there is no other word for her than adorable, her jolly-hockey-sticks-on-crack-itude is just the thing to tip Jean into true, bleak despair.

'I *love* your dress!' Sophia says as she waddles near. She will be the only person to say this and mean it, and somehow this makes Jean's sense of futility weigh on her all the more.

'Thank you! It was in the sales,' Jean says, through a strained smile.

'Oooh, I do love a bargain. Isn't it so happy! Like a springy spring cloud!' Sophia beams. 'Lovely colour. Like cupcake icing!'

Sophia's most endearing and most annoying quality is relentless good cheer.

'Is this number . . .?' Jean asks, motioning in the direction of Sophia's bulging belly. Two? Three? Six? Even as a child, Sophia always seemed to have small children underfoot. Jean's vaguely proffered hand is grabbed and pressed hard against the pit of Sophia's groin.

'Four! Can you believe it? Oh, he was just kicking a moment ago,' Sophia says as Jean gently prises her hand away. Even when her best mate Tess was pregnant with her son Fynn, Jean had struggled not to find The Bump a bit disturbing. Luckily, Tess never became one of those miracle-of-life types. She had described giving birth as 'Like *A Texas Chainsaw Massacre* and *Alien* mash-up in your goddamn pum.'

'I hope we're not late! How far is the ceremony?' Jean says, turning to look anxiously over her shoulder. Why did she have to almost break up with Charlie *before* the twenty-four hour stretch of politely bumbling small talk interspersed with dad-dancing that she knew was to come? She had seen Sarah and Toby sporadically over the years, but she hardly knew their friends. If ever there was a time to get absolutely hammered with your alcoholic lover, it was now. In fact, it was expected.

'Oh gosh, you are right, mustn't dawdle. I had to make a dash for the loo. Third time in an hour! Sarah is running behind. *Disaster* coiffure. Her favourite stylist was booked and his assistant did this vertical layered jobbie that looked most odd. All very nineties apparently, but one doesn't want to look like a "Grunge" on one's wedding day!'

'Quite right,' Jean smiles, feeling guilty about her impatience towards a woman so completely harmless that she took grunge to be a noun.

Sophia takes Jean's arm and shepherds her through the trees to a manicured expanse of rolling lawn, at the top of which stand red brick stairs beneath a wrought-iron gate. Eggshell blue tents peak in front of the mansion, the alfresco dinner protected from the chance of summer rain. Guests in sorbet frocks, suits and swooping hats sit on a row of white chairs lined up before a bespoke altar, garlanded with pink roses.

The vicar stands beneath it, all kindly beneficence. Toby waits beside him with the groomsmen, vibrating head to toe with nerves. A white grand piano perches on a stage. The pianist plays Chopin, wearing a lilac linen suit the same shade as Jean's dress.

It must have cost a bomb, and Jean hasn't even seen the banquet yet.

'Beautiful,' Jean murmurs as they approach the ceremony. She casts around the crowd for familiar faces. Apart from the best man, Sean, and Toby and Sarah's parents, she doesn't recognise anyone. Jean's family had moved out of Kent after primary school and Sarah had preferred to visit her in London, finding the fresh air dreary and the rolling hills stifling. She seemed happy to stay in the countryside now, however. Aga, Range Rover, accountant hubby. Tick, tick, tick, dream life sorted.

'Yes, but what a grey, grey day!' Sophia sighs tragically. 'But look! A hint of sunshine through the clouds!'

There is no hint of sunshine, not a sliver of a fragment of a ray, but Jean supposes that Sophia can't bear to be construed as having said anything negative.

'I'm sure it will brighten up in no time!' Jean agrees, wishing she could say the same about her future. If only Charlie could control himself.

Of course, if he could control himself, he wouldn't be Charlie. Wasn't that what had drawn her to him in the first place? His flagrant excess and flouting of convention, so different from Jean's square, efficient duty. He comported himself like a seventeenth century wastrel-lord, and she was his devoted valet.

If only she didn't still love him.

As the tune changes to the Bridal Chorus, Sophia squeezes Jean's hand and wiggles in her happy Labrador way to join her family near the altar. Three cherubic heads turn to greet her. Jean looks for a seat.

The only empty space is at the very back, next to a man who is crumpled in his chair, as if half-hiding. A man who turns to stare up at her, hopefully.

Charlie.

Bugger it all.

Jean laughs, despite herself. Charlie beams at this promising sign, as Jean takes the vacant seat next to him.

'Have you forgiven me?' Charlie whispers in her ear, one arm sliding over her shoulder.

'Never,' Jean says, but with a playful curve to her lips. She can feel her resolve slipping away.

Sarah shines with joy as she strides up the aisle on her father's arm. The gown is a cream lace Dior, more girlish and less princess than Jean thought she would choose. The coiffure disaster has been solved by the garlanding of almost her entire head in daisies. From a distance, it is impossible not to get the impression Sarah sports a 1950s bathing cap, but the idiosyncrasy of it somehow makes her even more charming.

Her bridesmaids follow in wispy pink frocks at a mincing, less eager pace. The fact that Sarah is practically charging towards her future husband draws a titter from the older guests. Jean wipes a tear from her eye as Sarah takes her place beside Toby and the ceremony begins.

'Dearly beloved, we are gathered here today . . .'

A beam of sunlight pierces the expanse of grey sky as the couple exchange rings, as if the Holy Spirit itself graces them in celestial blessing.

The couple say their 'I dos', then laugh and nuzzle each other.

Toby dips Sarah in a swift ballroom move, before kissing her full on the lips. The pianist starts playing 'Your Song' as the guests stand up and cheer.

'I knew you'd come round,' Charlie says to Jean with a grin, as they watch the couple walk back down the aisle together, ducking confetti, hand in hand.

At this, Jean's smile slips. She opens her mouth to protest, but they are drawn into a crowd of well-wishers before she can set him straight.

After the bridal party are photographed beneath the garland, in front of the steps and in picturesque spots in the surrounding woods, the guests make their way towards the alfresco banquet. Platters strewn with rustic delicacies are laid out under a blue marquee in front of the Victorian manor house. Jean and Charlie heap their plates with smoked salmon, beef Wellington and roast vegetables, arguing under their breath about the necessity of The Talk, while also avoiding The Talk.

'I don't understand,' Charlie says, as he spears a bouquet of asparagus. 'Am I to await my execution all evening, making idiot small talk with the parents of people you went to primary school with?'

'Execution is a strong term,' Jean hisses. 'And I don't see how hard it is to speak to the father of the bride without saying his daughter looks like she should be wearing a bathing costume in a 1950s musical.'

'It's not my fault she appears to have scalped a synchronised swimmer!'

Jean shudders to remember Sarah's father's face at the not-so-veiled insult. He had terrified Jean as a child, all stiff, performative kindness over a steely core. Although he insisted she call him John, he will forever be Mr Marsh to her. She had wanted to impress him today. Mr Marsh has friends in advertising PR and she had hoped to follow up the wedding with a friendly email and investigate a change in career path.

Now that idea was shot to hell.

'Can you please contain yourself for the course of *one* evening,' Jean tries to say firmly, though her voice shakes. 'This is not the time nor the place to discuss your problems.'

'*Contain* myself?' Charlie says in a tone of sheer horror.

Luckily, two seats at Sophia's table are still free by the time they have filled their plates. Probably because it is more akin to a crèche.

'I do hope you will behave in front of the children,' Jean whispers like a schoolmarm in Charlie's ear as they sit down.

'Behave,' Charlie repeats. He has had at least six glasses of champagne and his boisterous high spirits have turned combative.

'We'll talk later,' Jean smiles. 'Sophia, are you still living in that charming gated house with the thatched roof?'

'What is there to talk about? I won't do it again!' Charlie interrupts in a stage-whisper. Jean kicks him under the table.

'Talk about what?' Sophia asks, in between feeding her youngest tiny shreds of beef.

'Jean is pretending she may break up with me, so that I will be suspended in an agony of uncertainty for as long I can endure it. Vengeful tactic, don't you agree?' Charlie says, pouring himself a large glass of red and grinning dangerously.

'Oh my! Really?' Sophia says, blinking rapidly, her fork suspended in mid-air.

'I'm not pretending or punishing you! You were the one who turned up here against my orders!' Jean finds herself actually wagging her finger at him in time with the words.

'Orders! Ah, *there* we are. Jean's true colours revealed,' Charlie pushes around the gigantic pile of food on his plate. He rarely eats much of late, but he still has hungry eyes. 'The Governess General.'

'Oh do fuck off,' Jean says before she can stop herself, then claps her hand over her own mouth. Three adorable blond boys giggle back at her, shouting 'Fuck off!' over each other like a tiny, profane Greek chorus.

'Jean, language!' Sophia says, clapping her hands over her youngest's ears.

'If she were a superhero, her name would be Killjoy Supreme,' Jean thinks she hears Charlie share conspiratorially with Sophia's eldest son.

'What did you say?' Jean sputters.

'I said the truth is she is my superhero, my joy supreme,' Charlie says with soulful sincerity as he stares into her eyes.

Jean genuinely does not know if this is an act of gaslighting, or a paranoid aural hallucination on her part.

'I never know these days, when unmarried people are having a laugh!' Sophia giggles nervously, casting around for her AWOL husband out of the corner of her eye. He is standing above a table across the room, chatting to a spinster aunt. When he looks in her direction, she mouths: 'Roger! H.E.L.P.'

'I can spell, Sophia,' Jean says tiredly. 'I'm sorry, we'll leave.'

'No, no, no. Stay, do!'

Sophia's mouth says no, but her eyes say yes.

Clink! Clink!

The best man Sean stands up at the large family table to face the other guests, grinning sheepishly. Toby laughs at something Sarah has whispered in his ear. She claps her hands with glee, as far from demure and blushing as a bride can be.

'Ladies and gentleman, may I have your attention please. Before we eat this wonderful food, painstakingly selected by my best friend's wife, who has now made an enemy of nearly every caterer in the county,' Sean pauses for the guests to chuckle as anticipated. 'I would like to make a short speech in honour of the love and support I have witnessed Sarah give Toby over the past five years. Who would have thought that when she crashed her bicycle into his Range Rover in the Waitrose car park . . .'

The guests laugh uproariously.

'That Toby would be so easily taken in by her ruse, as to believe it an accident. How many months had you been trying to catch his eye, Sarah?' Sean asks cheekily.

Sarah giggles into her husband's shoulder, before shouting back.

'Two and a half!'

Jean joins in the laughter, studiously avoiding looking at Charlie. She can feel him simmering with hurt beside her.

'And this very clever woman was far too modest to realise that Toby had been obsessed with her for months,' Sean continues. 'Poor me! Incessant conversations about this "marvellous creature" Toby kept seeing all over town, whom he didn't have the balls to speak to. Sarah, if you had known how whipped he already was, you would have saved yourself the trouble!'

More laughter. Sean shoots Sarah a mock-flirtatious glance.

'Perhaps you would have cycled into my car?'

Charlie stands abruptly. Jean looks up in confusion as he mounts his chair.

'Never give all the heart! For love will hardly seem worth thinking of to passionate women if it seem certain.' Charlie recites Yeats for the second time that afternoon, his voice sonorous with booming mischief. He pauses to sip deeply from his wine glass.

Sean coughs, affronted. Toby and Sarah exchange bemused glances, unsure if this was planned. Jean desperately tugs at Charlie's trouser leg under the table, as she mutters 'Shuttupppp!' under her breath.

'And they never dream, that it fades out from kiss to kiss; for everything that's lovely is but a brief, dreamy, kind delight,' Charlie says, as the other guests look at each other in bafflement. 'O never give the heart outright!'

'Is this the latest thing? A nuptial poetry reading?' an old man shouts at his companion on the next table.

Sean adjusts his necktie, glancing at the bride and groom, unsure what to do. Sarah and Toby whisper something to each other. Her father's expression darkens thunderously. Across the table, Sophia's mouth hangs agape.

'Good advice, mate. Should have saved it for the stag!' Sean interjects, trying to get back on track. The guests laugh again, nervously this time.

Charlie quaffs his wine, still standing.

'Charlie. Sit. Down!' Jean says through gritted teeth.

'For they, for all smooth lips can say, have given their hearts up to the play. And who could play it well enough,' Charlie continues unabated, almost talking to himself, 'if deaf and dumb and blind with love?'

Sarah and Toby's jaws slowly unhinge. Jean covers her face with her hands, peeping through the cracks of her fingers, unwilling to continue watching, yet unable to look away.

'When will this end?' Sophia's husband asks Jean bluntly.

'He that made this knows all the cost, for he gave all his heart and lost,' Charlie finishes softly, his big eyes gazing down at Jean with a deranged mixture of adoration, spite and drink.

A maelstrom of shame consumes her.

'Thank you, Charlie! I'll . . . be in touch should we divorce.' Toby forces a laugh and slow claps, trying to pass it off as a good-humoured bad joke between friends.

Bless Toby. He and Charlie have only met twice, years ago.

'That poem is a beautiful reminder, isn't it, for those of us not as fortunate as Sarah and Toby,' Sean says, recovering his composure quickly. 'That true, enduring love is difficult and rare and precious. It is a gamble, but the risks of playing it safe outweigh the risks of seizing love and fighting for it. To Sarah and Toby. May they spend the rest of their lives giving all their hearts, without loss! There is no other couple I would feel safer betting on.'

'To Sarah and Toby!'

The wedding party stand and raise their glasses to toast the happy couple, the jubilant mood of the afternoon restored.

Jean wobbles to her feet, mouthing the words through the tears clogging her throat.

Chapter Two

'Stop apologising! It's not your fault. I mean, yes, Charlie did ruin the speeches with "love is doomed" poetry and I'll never forgive him. But! I've had a few dabs of MDMA and that's taken the edge off of *that*,' Sarah whispers into Jean's ear with a conspiratorial air.

'That's so kind of you, Sarah,' Jean says, smoothing her dress down nervously with her hands. In the sticky humid evening, the fabric has started to rise as if it were a soufflé. 'I'm sorry if he lowered the tone. It was such a beautiful ceremony and you look stunning!'

'As stunning as a synchronised swimmer?' Sarah asks archly, patting the daisies on her head.

'N-not at all! Did Charlie . . .?' Heat rushes to Jean's cheeks.

'My father loves nothing more than to be outraged by the rudeness of strangers,' Sarah says with a low laugh. 'Which means he can't help but relay every insult!'

Jean winces and puts her head in her hands, trying to convey her regret without using the words 'I'm sorry' for the tenth time. Her sister Danielle always admonishes Jean for being too conciliatory and not owning her shit. Or, in her actual words: 'You are cringing and spineless'. But how can Jean learn to be unapologetically herself when her personality is, well, apologetic?

'I'll have a stern word with him later,' Jean says instead.

'You haven't already?' Sarah says, shocked.

Aside from a clipped 'That was completely inappropriate' after the speeches, Jean has been ignoring Charlie since dinner.

'If I do, he won't remember it. I know his pattern. After belligerence comes the outrageous behaviour, followed by offended dignity – that's where we are now – and very soon he'll become melancholic and contrite. Then he'll pass out,' Jean says.

If she timed things correctly, Jean could have him plead for her forgiveness and be fast asleep by 10 p.m., leaving her free to enjoy the rest of the party in peace.

'Is that all you want from life?' Sarah asks, her expression torn between pity and confusion. Jean sips her gin and tonic in stiff silence, lost in morbid contemplation of her future as a babysitter-maid.

'Hello sex on a stick,' Sarah murmurs in Jean's ear, distracted by the arrival of the pianist in the lilac suit. He sweeps his wavy strawberry blond locks to the side and congratulates her on his way to the bar.

Sarah blushes beneath her blusher.

'He looks like the Beast when he turns human,' Sarah says, mock-swooning at his back after he passes them. Although the pianist is definitely dishy, Jean remains unmoved. She is half-convinced she has become dead from the waist down.

'No one prefers the Beast human,' Jean scoffs.

'Oh my god, look at Cheryl,' Sarah says, gesturing at her bridesmaid, who is draped all over the best man. 'Her left tit has fully popped out. Should I warn her, or do you think that was intentional?'

Although Jean only sees Sarah every few years (the journey from Peckham to Kent feeling equivalent to Hobbiton and Mordor after a long week), they always fall into an easy camaraderie, as if no time at all had passed.

'Let's not shame her for doing a Janet,' Jean says, as Sean sticks his tongue down Cheryl's throat. 'Especially when it's working so well. Where did you get the MDMA?'

Jean turns her head away from the dancefloor, where Charlie is jerking around to ABBA. She used to find the shamelessness of his dancing endearing. He looked like a puppet whose master had been Tasered. Now, the sight of him only stirs a familiar bloom of embarrassment in her chest.

'Sophia had some left over from pre-pregnancy,' Sarah giggles, as she accepts a champagne top-up from a waiter.

Jean is startled into her first true laugh of the day.

'She was micro-dosing for post-natal depression. A bit experimental, but it seems to work for her. She always has loads of energy for her kids. She's, like, the best mum *ever*.'

'Is she on it now?' Jean asks incredulously, watching Sophia dance wildly with her husband under a spinning disco ball. Perhaps that was why she had said she loved Jean's dress. She had been off her fucking tits.

'No . . .' Sarah says doubtfully, her leg tapping to the music. 'Listen darling, I must go and circulate. But so good of you to come. I'll see you on the dancefloor!'

The playlist changes to The Bee Gee's 'Nights On Broadway'. A song Jean had always enjoyed, until Charlie insisted it was a disco ode to rape. She sighs, watching her boyfriend stumble to a chair by the entrance to the tent and slump over. His head lolls back at an angle suggestive of recent orgasm or fatal gunshot wound, as he fumbles for something in his suit pocket.

Jean checks her watch. 9.25 p.m. Right on schedule.

She sways to the music on her way to the bar. Soon she will be free.

'Hello, could I have two espressos please? One decaffeinated with lots of sugar, and one caffeinated with cream.

Thank you,' Jean orders, touching up her makeup in a small hand-mirror. It's all smudged and melted, but in that sultry way that accidentally occurs once every five to ten years. Her chignon has regained buoyancy from the salt of nervous sweats. The effect is sensuous and tragic, like Lana Del Ray after a night crying on the town.

'I very much enjoyed your husband's contribution to the speeches,' A rich baritone voice says at her shoulder. Jean looks up into the long-lashed, greenish eyes of the pianist. Or were they blue? Whichever, they glimmered with a teasing amusement. 'Long day?'

'A very long three years,' Jean finds herself laughing lightly.

As the espresso with milk arrives, Jean takes it in one shot. Emboldened by the incipient demise of her relationship, Jean catches the pianist's eyes and holds his gaze.

'And he's not my husband.'

'Good,' the pianist says simply, a wry twist to one corner of his mouth, as he sips a martini and his eyes narrow minutely. Covetously.

A shiver runs down Jean's spine.

'Not dead yet!' her nether-regions seem to say, in the manner of a *Monty Python* plague victim prematurely loaded onto a corpse-wagon. Jean suppresses a silly grin as she turns away from the pianist to take the decaf brew to her boyfriend. She will saunter away and not look back, like some mysterious film noir siren.

A scream pierces her reverie.

Jean whips around to see the fabric of the polyester tent, as well as her plans for a studied-cool exit, go up in flames behind Charlie's head. Sarah and Toby pause from their dancing in the middle of the room, as still as the miniature effigies on their wedding cake. It creates a ripple effect where one by one, the other guests stop and turn to look at the source of the interruption.

'Christ!' The pianist arms himself with a water jug and dashes to where Charlie's body floppily extends, silhouetted by fire. He chucks the liquid over the tent, but the flames shoot higher. Jean grabs an open bottle of San Pellegrino and lifts up her skirt, pushing past appalled bystanders to join him.

As Jean attempts to add her contribution, struggling with the narrow spout, a waiter with an expression of one who has seen it all before sprays down the marquee with an extinguisher. Crisis averted, Jean stares down at her water bottle, trembling with rage.

She upends it over Charlie's blissfully unaware head.

He sputters awake.

'What the devil – Jeannie!' Charlie says, shaking the fizzy water from his hair and attempting to stand. He wobbles on his feet. The pianist, concerned, stabilises him. Charlie brushes him off, before tripping over his own shoelaces and careening headfirst into a bowl of punch.

'Someone get that lout OUT of here!'

The shout comes from Sarah's father, his glowering face flushed with a rage so potent he is almost purple. Charlie wipes the punch off his face and into his hair, attempting a charming grin from where he is sprawled, arms akimbo, on the floor.

Jean's lips tremble. A soothing hand rubs between her shoulders.

'Deep breath!' the pianist says in Jean's ear. She takes a shaky inhalation and blinks back tears. 'I'll help you get him to bed. Where are you staying?'

'The Railway Hotel,' Jean says, as she helps Charlie to his feet for the last time. Though tall, the pianist is slender, but he slides his drunken charge over his shoulders with ease. Jean casts a look back at Sarah and Toby, whose patience has clearly reached breaking point. She turns on her phone to book a taxi.

Seven missed calls, all from Jez. This is not her night.

'You've been so helpful. And I don't even know your name,' Jean says miserably as she takes Charlie's other arm and helps to drag him away from the tent.

'Gabriel,' the pianist says with a surprisingly shy grin from underneath his hair. He looks, for a moment, exactly like Princess Diana.

'Well, you're certainly living up to your namesake,' Jean says with a watery smile. 'A car should arrive in a few minutes.'

'I'll take him from here,' Gabriel says as they reach the front lawn. 'You've had a rough night. Go back, enjoy the party.'

'Are you sure?' Jean says.

'It's the unspoken law of weddings that musicians deal with brawls and accidents,' Gabriel grins. 'It's my pleasure.'

'Thank you,' Jean whispers, although what she really wants to ask is if he is returning.

She stops herself. It is too pathetic. The poor man is carting home her paralytic boyfriend out of the goodness of his heart, and here she is hoping to take advantage of his pity with a flirtation. She turns and walks away.

Unable to face bright lights and laughter, Jean plods over the lawn to the Mount Ephraim Gardens stately home. In the marble washrooms, Jean sits down on a couch and has her first official panic attack of the summer. Ranging in severity from 'Is-This-A-Heart-Attack?' to 'Just-Shy-Of-A-Nervous-Breakdown', she has suffered them on a semi-regular basis since her early twenties, when she first entered the workforce. Surprisingly, this is only the third one to have been Charlie-induced.

'Was that your husband causing a ruckus?'

Jean looks up from hyperventilating with her head between her knees, into the judgemental face of a maiden aunt. The term is rather sexist. Are we to be defined by whether or not we have been claimed by a man into our golden years? But there are some women who have 'confirmed spinster' written all over them.

'I beg your pardon?' Jean wheezes, unable to hear through the ringing in her ears.

'Was that your husband who caused the ruckus!' the woman shouts.

Jean wipes streaks of mascara from her face. Somehow, she hadn't realised she is crying.

'My boyfriend. Things have been bad for a while, but never so publicly. I'm preparing myself to dump him. Obviously,' Jean confides, uncharacteristically. Staring at the running water coming from the tap as the woman washes her hands, careful not to wet the fabric of her Chanel knock-off tweed, Jean has an epiphany.

What had started as a whisper of delusion, a cover up here and there, excuses, minimisations, rationalisations, had somehow mushroomed into a full-blown Stepford Wife performance of normalcy. All her energy went into the façade, a role that felt more real to her than realities she tried so hard to ignore. Maybe because she was scared of being alone, or maybe because despite it all, she still loved him. She wasn't quite sure why, but she did.

Maybe because it was all she knew.

'Don't be too picky dear. You're not all that and a bag of chips,' the old lady says, her dentures un-popping slightly in a wide cruel grin.

'This is a very unflattering dress,' Jean says defensively, feeling less guilty about her withered-virgin prejudices. The old woman dries her hand on a fluffy towel and leaves the toilets imperiously.

Jean desperately wants to call Tess, but that would mean further unravelling the string of lies that has kept her world turning. That Charlie was pretty well, on the whole. That their problems were the problems of any young couple. Admitting to having told so many untruths might undermine their friendship. What had at first seemed a harmless smoothing over of the jagged edges, had become too careful to be anything but deception.

Jean stands up and splashes her face with water, feeling very alone. It occurs to her that there is someone she might talk to, whose voice she hadn't heard in months. She could hear it any time, of course, or at least on weekends after 9 p.m.

Her sister, Maude Stevenson, has for some time now been going by 'Danielle Sauvage' on her radio show, doling out harsh advice to lovelorn sops like herself. The programme's called 'Have Your Cake And Eat His Heart, Too' or something equally hostile. Imagine if Jeremy Kyle wore a strap-on and advised his guests to solve their marital woes with pansexual orgies.

Subtle, she is not, but sometimes one needs an objective perspective. And given that Maude – sorry, 'Danielle' – had bailed on their family years ago, she is the one person in Jean's life to care about her well-being without being swayed by the influence of Charming Charlie. Because he hadn't always been this bad. Jean's friends loved him. Sometimes she worried they actually preferred his company to her own. Her father has openly said so.

But her father is famously a bit of a tit.

Jean enters a toilet stall, sits on the bog, and tunes into the show. Danielle's voice comes through the airwaves, crackly. Whether this is from poor transmission from her houseboat broadcasting setup or a whisky-fuelled sex-capade is anyone's guess. Danielle would certainly prefer that her audience assume the latter, frequently wondering why she hasn't yet expanded from her niche and been picked up by the BBC.

'Maybe if you stop calling people "shitcunts" so often . . .?' Jean had once suggested, only to be met with scorn.

'. . . Classic example of Jean C. Delis's "The Passion Paradox",' Danielle is saying in her throaty growl. 'You're smothering. Do you want to be true to yourself, or do you want to *win*? Because let's be clear, being "true to yourself" usually means following every insane impulse and always ends in tears.'

Jean smiles to herself at the familiar advice as she pees. Next would probably come the Grace Jones refrain.

'Love is a drug!' Danielle shouts.

Bingo!

'What you think of as "love" is actually your lizard brain on sex-meth, hijacking your capacity to reason. Would you send an iguana on crack into battle?' Danielle continues.

The crack-lizard is a new analogy.

'. . . What?' the caller says in utter confusion.

'Ignore that. The point is. Love is war.'

'Surely love is the opposite of war?' says the caller, uncertainly.

Danielle ignores this.

'You need to strategise. Like Napoleon.'

'I just want my boyfriend to be honest with me, not to invade Prussia,' the caller responds, her sarcastic eye-roll audible. Jean flushes the toilet and returns to the sink, where she places her phone on loudspeaker on the counter and touches up her makeup.

Seven years older than Jean, Danielle was cast as the black sheep of the family when she emerged shrieking from the birth canal born with a full set of teeth (the sign of the devil). Her first act of rebellion was to gnaw off one of their mother's nipples. Their parents had kept Jean (the sweetest, most toothless baby) as cloistered from the malevolent influence of her sister as they could throughout their childhood. Danielle ran away aged fifteen, and lived with a commune of warlocks in Spain for several years. She would only return when exceptionally broke, or if she had found a particularly preposterous lover to enrage their father with over supper.

'Life is a game of cat and mouse, my friend. Come-hither, go away. If someone knows they have you hook, line and sinker,' Danielle says omnisciently, 'love dies.'

'But I don't want to play games,' the caller says miserably. 'I mean, the whole point of being in a long-term relationship is that you can relax and stop the chase! We've been living together for five years now. He's my best friend. Or, he was my best friend.'

'"Domestic bliss is erotic hell",' Danielle quotes. 'That's from the divine Ms Esther Perel, therapist and love-guru. Without tension, there can be no desire. Why do you think Eastern European women are so successful with men?'

'They have high quality . . . hair extensions?' The caller hazards a guess.

'No! Well, that too. But what they have is *mystery*. They understand the importance of continuous seduction. They are elusive and cruel. Like Siamese cats.'

Danielle's first, and as far as Jean is aware, only real heartbreak had been in her mid-twenties, when a Latvian contortionist had thrown her over for an oligarch. The enigmatic ways of Eastern European women had since become a creepily frequent touchstone in her life's philosophy.

Danielle is usually rigorously PC, but as she doesn't consider elusive cruelty to be a negative character trait, she doesn't see this as sweeping xenophobia.

'It all sounds like such hard work,' the caller sighs.

'Preach,' Jean says into the mirror.

'Look, did you call me to hold your hand and tell you that he does love you deep down, underneath the late nights at the office and phone calls at odd hours and cold shoulder in bed and irritable conversations? Or to have a woman who's been around the goddamn block tell you that, yes, that shitcunt *is* having an affair, yes, he *is* planning his exit, and if you want to keep him, you should start having *fun*, look after yourself, and take a hot lover sharpish?'

Jean can vividly picture Danielle saying this, with her feet up on the charred mahogany wood of her desk, strewn with cigarette butts and yesterday's knickers. Wearing nothing but the paisley men's smoking jacket that was made in the sixties but is so threadbare it could be Jacobean, leaning sideways into her microphone, blowing a perfect smoke ring. The all-knowing mistress of her sex-ship, in total control of her mind and heart.

'He's going to leave me, isn't he,' the caller sobs.

'Not if you leave him first, my dear. Take your fucking power back. Godspeed and good luck to you, sweetheart.'

Danielle hangs up on the crying woman. People call her for the brutal truth. The aftermath she leaves for their friends and psychologists.

On impulse, Jean grabs her phone and dials her sister nervously.

'Jeannie?' Danielle answers, her voice echoing oddly through the phone. 'My baby sister! How the devil are you?'

'Not good,' Jean says, taking in her reflection as she speaks. She looks harder than she used to. Exhausted. Careworn. 'I actually . . . called for your advice.'

'Do you mind if I put you on speakerphone and broadcast your secrets to the nation? Because I already am.'

'It's about Charlie,' Jean says through the lump in her throat.

'Charlie? You're always saying things are great with Charlie. I thought it would be about your shitcunt boss,' Danielle says, sounding put out. 'AKA Mephistopheles' microphone. Listeners, can you believe my sister does PR for politicians?'

Jean's job has long been a bone of contention.

'We can't all be anarcha-femmunists who don't believe in currency and think that indoor plumbing is a luxury of the bourgeois,' Jean says, annoyance taking the edge off her grief. 'And Jez isn't a shitcunt. He's a very stressed-out man with very important clients.'

'Keep telling yourself that, Doctor Faustus.'

Jean rolls her eyes.

'This isn't about politics. I'm at Sarah and Toby's wedding,' Jean says, her face scrunching up with suppressed tears. 'Charlie heckled the speeches with Yeats.'

Danielle bursts out laughing.

'Sorry, sorry. That's terrible. But also hilarious. And not at all surprising. Isn't he a massive child-lush?'

'He also set fire to a marquee,' Jean sniffs, slightly put out that her drama had met with such an underwhelming response. 'Passing out with a lit cigarette.'

'Of course he did. Charlie is basically Lord Byron with wet brain. Although he'll end up looking like Shane MacGowan.'

Jean winces, before starting to giggle hysterically.

'And then he fell headfirst into a punch bowl!'

Danielle barks a laugh from the depths of her tarred lungs.

'Well, it sounds like you know exactly what to do. Do you really need a second opinion? Because if so, I'm concerned for you.'

Jean considers this. She loves Charlie stupidly, in a way that is beyond her control. They are bonded by drunken escapades and hurt feelings and dizzying makeups and the sweetest of apologies, imbuing the see-sawing unpredictability of his behaviour and her resentment with a sort of poignant longing.

It is a stupidity she is determined to end, if not for this crushing guilt.

'I think it's partly my fault things have got this bad. Have I been too much of a, I don't know, a "Cool Girl"? Always letting him off the hook?' Jean feels a lump rising in her throat.

'Jeannie, the man pisses in your shoes. That is not Cool Girl.'

Jean knew when she texted Danielle a picture of her stained stilettos that she would come to regret it. Any other fabric she could have saved, but urine on velvet is irretrievable. They had become symbolic. Of her relationship with herself. Like Dorothy's ruby slippers.

'N-not Cool Girl?' Jean whimpers through a hiccup.

'You have never been a Cool Girl. You are a swot and a doormat. Like mum. And by the way, taking on the emotional burden of a man's choices as if they are your own is, like, totally mental enslavement to The Patriarchy.'

Jean intakes a sharp breath, feeling as if she's taken a punch to the gut.

Doormat. Mum.

Jean's worst nightmare has come true. A woman whom the feminist cultural revolution has entirely bypassed, her mother Doreen is known by all as 'Door', short for doormat. Perhaps Jean was doomed from the start. She had after all been named after her father George's favourite sitcom character, the magical drudge from *I Dream Of Jeannie*.

The show had taken on a bizarrely significant pop cultural role in their household. Where other families watched *Friends* together, the Stevenson household would be forced to watch 'morally appropriate' reruns. This mainly became an opportunity to point out the many ways in which nervous mummy screwed things up in comparison to Jeannie, 'the perfect woman'. Danielle used to bite back, 'What, because she has the soul of Dobby the House Elf in the body of Hooker Barbie?' before she fled the family.

While Jean is closer in character to Dobby than she would like to admit, she hadn't got the Barbie bit. She could, in good lighting, pass for a brunette Skipper gone to seed. 'No Tits' had been a particularly shit university boyfriend's pet name for her, but at least she'd dumped him. Or had she? It is hard to say who ends a relationship when your erstwhile lover steals your coursework and then starts necking your arch-nemesis outside the halls of residence.

Mutual. It was mutual.

'Oh my god,' Jean finally replies. 'I AM a doormat.'

Jean can see clearly now that her whole life has been a performance of frantically smiling subservience. First for the approval of her father, followed by her professors, then her bosses and always for her boyfriends.

'Of course you are,' Danielle says. 'Why do you think you're so miserable?'

'I guess I thought life was supposed to be melancholic if you did the right thing. Like Lancelot and Guinevere in the King Arthur story. Or that I have a chemical imbalance,' Jean sighs wretchedly. Her GP had told her she fit all the criteria for depression at her last doctor's appointment, offering an array of pharmaceutical aids for her malaise.

'You don't have a chemical imbalance. You just don't have any balls!' Danielle crows. She has been waiting to say this for years, Jean can tell.

'Life isn't supposed to be all fun and games, you know,' she sulks.

'It can be,' Danielle trills, sounding smug as fuck.

Jean wants to kill her.

'All right for some! You've dodged every responsibility, birthday, dinner, funeral we've had. Never had a *real* relationship. Been fired from every dead-end job you've taken. Feckless, commitment-phobic, selfish—'

'God, you sound like Dad! You're nothing but a close-minded, serial monotonist,' Danielle says calmly. 'What would you do if you stopped living by other people's rules?'

'What?' Jean asks, dumbfounded.

The idea has never occurred to her.

'Do you want to go through life failing to live up to the unattainable standards of people like our parents? It's dishonest. Ignoble! And worse, it's *boring*. How fulfilled has this "Perfect Girlfriend", "Model Employee", "Good Daughter" bullshit made you? Do you even know who you are?'

Danielle's fisted hand, index finger sharply pointed, is undoubtedly striking the air with every point.

'No,' Jean admits, like a petulant child.

'Good. That's the first step to finding out. I'm proud of you.'

Jean can hear Danielle's interest waning, as it always does, on the other end of the line. A wave of desperation hits her.

'But – but what should I *do*? To find out?'

'Take what you can. Give nothing back,' Danielle says, with finality.

'Isn't that . . .' Jean trails off, trying to think where she has heard that phrase before.

Danielle hangs up.

Jean maximises her internet icon and presses play on the radio station.

'. . . A sad sack. Well, that's all we have time for tonight on "Have Your Cake And Eat His Heart, Too." Live long and prosper, maneaters! And remember, don't do anything I wouldn't do,' Danielle purrs in her radio voice.

Jean turns off her phone, frowning. Then it comes to her.

It is definitely a line from *Pirates of the Caribbean*.

Great. Her father is Bluebeard with an elf fetish, her mother is a shell of a ghost-serf, and her sister has advised her to implode her whole life based on the pirate code in a *Disney* film.

But maybe, just maybe, Danielle has a point. Maybe it *is* time to reinvent herself. To live life on her own terms. To take control, to take back her power, to take responsibility for her own pleasure and happiness. To live as a woman heels-over-head, and not head-over-heels, in love. To take what she could.

To give nothing back.

She applies a lick of dark purple lipstick, ready to return to the party and dance her goddamn heart out. When she saunters into the marquee, the lights on the dancefloor have dimmed further, suit jackets have been thrown off and skirts have been lifted. The wedding guests thrash to 'X Gon' Give It To Ya' with the unbridled enthusiasm of a mostly white middle class audience living a nineties hip hop urban fantasy. Jean goes straight to the bar.

'Three tequila shots please,' she says.

'Are those all for you?' a deep voice whispers in her ear.

'I'm toasting myself,' Jean smiles into greenish sparkling eyes. 'One for my past, one for my present and one for my future.'

'I'll join you. Make that six,' Gabriel says to the tired-looking barman. He has removed his lilac jacket and unbuttoned his white ruffled shirt to just below the neck, revealing an expanse of tan, freckled skin and a hint of golden chest hair.

'To the past!' Jean raises her shot glass and takes the contents in one, biting into a crisp, cold lime. Gabriel joins her.

'Your boyfriend is fast asleep, safe and sound in your room.'

'He's not my boyfriend,' Jean says, not breaking eye contact.

'To your present!' Gabriel grins, lifting the second.

They down them swiftly. Jean sputters as the tequila caresses her throat with an unmistakeable liquid burn. Jean leans into him, her movements melting, relaxed for the first time in oh so long. She has held herself rigidly all day, all year, her body stiff in anticipation of the worst.

Gabriel's hand lightly catches her own, running over the knuckles where she'd brushed salt over her skin. His fingers are long and elegant. Jean finds herself becoming tongue-tied.

'Did you become a pianist because you have beautiful hands?' she says lamely, trying to ignore the heat rising in her cheeks. It has been a long time since she's flirted with a stranger. 'Or do you have beautiful hands because you're a pianist?'

Gabriel, mercifully, ignores this.

'You don't have to be beautiful . . .' Jean sings along as the music turns over to Prince. Gabriel leans against the bar and lightly brushes a tendril of hair off of Jean's hot neck.

'Would you like to dance?' he asks her, handing her the third shot of tequila.

36

They toast each other, smiling, silent, the space between them buzzing with a mysterious power, of enchantment or life force or pheromones, a heady tension that makes her forehead buzz and skin vibrate with the anticipation of touch. They set down the glasses. Jean takes his hand and leads him into the throng of bodies, close to her, his heat a whisper away. They are already in tune with each other's steps.

Chapter Three

Jean awakens half-naked in her Spanx with a pounding headache, her mouth a thick layer of fuzz, her head stuffed with cotton wool and her throat burning with thirst. She opens her eyes to find herself staring directly into the whites of Charlie's, rolled up under half-closed lids, his body lying diagonally over the bed. She shoots upright with a start.

From this new angle, he appears to be sleeping peacefully, resting with the serenity of the dead. Jean flops back with a groan, burying her head in the pillow. A wave of angst and last night's tequila hits her. She was usually a three glasses of white wine spritzer or two ciders in the sunshine kind of gal. Dancing on tables and necking shots was always Charlie's scene, but heartbreak, anger and lust could drive any woman over the edge. She surveys the room as if viewing it for the first time, trying to reconstruct the end of the night.

It has the usual English countryside boutique hotel look. Old frayed shaggy carpet, weird lamps, oddly orange lighting, hideous curtains the colour of pea soup. Her suitcase lies open on the floor, contents spewing everywhere. A drunken rummage comes back to her in a Polaroid picture flash.

Oh my god. Gabriel.

Jean smacks her hand over her mouth with a whimper. She hadn't kissed him. She thinks. Just pressed up against him on the dancefloor, slut-dropped like *Dirrty*-era Christina

Aguilera and invited him back to the hotel for a nightcap. He had waited in the bar downstairs while she came up to look for ancient condoms she had been convinced were stuffed into the luggage lining, along with a disposable camera she still hadn't developed from the last time she took a holiday with Tess, about oh, five years ago now.

From the looks of things, she had groped through her suitcase, forgotten the condom mission, stripped off her dress and passed out cold next to Charlie. It was for the best. She shudders to imagine herself stumbling down the stairs, bulging out of her latex girdle with a Trojan between her teeth, mouthing around the wrapper: 'I've slipped into something more comfortable . . .'

At least, Jean assures herself, she hadn't ever mentioned the plan to arm herself with prophylactics to Gabriel. That ridiculous determination to seduce him was wrought out of frustration that despite her best efforts, he had been such a goddamn gentleman. Jean half-remembers making a lame excuse about needing to brush her teeth.

No, wait. That part was more than an excuse. She had puked in a hedge outside the hotel after a carsick taxi home. Running her tongue over her incisors, Jean gags at the vom-fur coating her mouth.

'Whhhyyy . . .' she moans aloud. Next to her, Charlie stirs.

Jean tiptoes out of bed to the loo, where she closes the door softly behind her and runs a bath. Glugging water from the tap, she catches sight of the SRD (slutty red dress) she had brought, hanging on the door hooks. She had apparently intended upon a costume change. A desperate act, but at least not certifiable.

Jean submerges herself underwater, resigned to the fact that Gabriel must have left this morning, and she would never see him again.

Helping herself to the hotel shampoo, Jean scrubs her scalp slowly, numb from hangover and unsure what to feel. It isn't so much that she doubts her decision to break up with Charlie, as accepting his terrible behaviour has become reflexive, forgiving him second nature. In her own way, Jean has been as badly behaved. Resentful, dishonest about her true feelings, and completely off her nut. Not to mention intending upon infidelity (albeit too incapacitated to successfully execute an affair).

Jean gets out of the bath, pulling on a white fluffy robe over her sopping wet body. She creaks open the door and gets on her hands and knees to rifle through her suitcase. Her eyes narrow as she notices a stain all over her ugly lilac dress. Was that . . .?

Jean picks it up and sniffs it.

'Charlie,' Jean says, getting to her feet and grabbing his duffle bag, unopened and untouched on a chintzy chair. He grunts. 'Charlie!'

Jean throws the bag against his chest.

'You have urinated on my clothing for the last time,' Jean says, with the finality of the 'Our Love Is A Bad Meme, Bye Felipe' variety.

Charlie struggles upwards in bed, rubbing the sleep from his eyes.

'But Jeannie,' Charlie has the temerity to smile in a wheedling fashion, his gaping fly mocking her pain. 'You hate that dress.'

'I hate it when you call me Jeannie!' Jean explodes, kicking the bedframe, ripping the duvet off the bed, grabbing a pillow to punch, hurling it at his head, then throwing her hands in the air and rending her hair. She has really lost her shit for perhaps the first time in her life, and it is invigorating.

Charlie's mouth hangs open, dumbfounded.

'And that is absolutely not the point,' she continues with regal dignity, gathering the bathrobe around her neck and lifting her chin in an impression of Princess Margaret. 'I want you out of this room and *out* of my life.'

Jean swans back into the bathroom and slams the door behind her. She turns on her phone, putting on some soothing Chopin. She has twelve missed calls, but whatever fresh hell work has delivered will have to wait. Jean listens to Charlie stumbling off the bed. The rustle of the duffle bag against his trouser leg.

The click of the latch behind him.

Jean shimmies into the SRD, a silk slip that luckily requires no bra, as she will have to burn the contents of her suitcase. She is having one of those oddly flattering hangovers, that give you an orgasmic afterglow. Or maybe she is still drunk. In any case, a slick of tinted moisturiser, a blast of the hairdryer, a touch of mascara and she's ready to face the day. Slipping on her heels and a pair of gigantic shades, she blows herself a kiss in the mirror.

She strides out the door, feeling in sync with the universe and ready to take on the post-nuptial brunch in style. Jean decides to create a mood board in whatever housing situation she finds next, covered in palm trees and vintage cars, to manifest an idyllic future doing luxury hotel PR in post-commie Cuba. She suppresses the fear that she will return to Charlie's flat, to discover all her things stuffed into bin bags in the front garden.

Waiting for her Uber downstairs, Jean smiles disarmingly at the man at reception as she takes a pink peony from the vase in front of him to slip into her hair. He does not protest this flagrant act of theft, but smiles conspiratorially. Jean is amazed at the difference in the way she is received, compared to her usual excessively polite reserve. All these years she has armoured herself in restraint to disguise her crippling social anxiety, when a cheeky grin and free-range tits were all one needed to sail through life effortlessly.

The sun beams bright outside the red brick building. A light breeze ruffles her bouncy hair. It is the perfect English summer weather, the kind that promises Pimms O'Clock and shirtless construction workers. Her driver pulls up in front of the hotel and gets out of the car to open the passenger door. Jean flashes her best Audrey Hepburn gracious smile.

'Lovely morning!' the driver says cheerfully.

'The best,' Jean says. Linkin Park ft. Jay Z comes on the radio. Jean rolls down the window and grins into the breeze. 'And this is my tune!'

The driver turns it up and they sing along together. At the second chorus, Jean's phone starts to buzz. She puts it on silent, wondering if it is Charlie begging her forgiveness, wondering if she should throw it out of the window. Although, maybe Charlie was locked out of his car? She should pick up. He might have forgotten his keys. Charlie was always forgetting things. Like he forgot to fight for her, even a little, even at all. She didn't want him to, but still. That was a lie. Of course she wanted him to. Three years of sharing her life and heart and his final words were: 'But you hate that dress?' It beggared belief.

The phone buzzes incessantly against Jean's leg. She caves in to her treacherous anxiety for his wellbeing.

Not Charlie, but Jez. Jean rolls her eyes, pushing her sunglasses up on her forehead. She should probably take this. But only to lay down the law. Like the new, no-holds-barred, don't-take-any-shit queen she is. Jean breathes deeply, trying to channel the Cardi B. meets Samuel L. Jackson badass motherfucker she knows lives somewhere, deep down, very far inside of her.

'Jez! So nice to hear from you,' Jean starts, exactly how Cardi B. would not answer the phone to a record label interrupting her iced-out champagne bath, or whatever she was likely to do on Sunday mornings. 'I got in touch with *The Times*, *Guardian* and *Spectator* yesterday and they were all receptive to the mugging ruse. In fact what with the latest Trump/Kim Jong-Un love in, I doubt it will even make the third page—'

'I've been ringing you nonstop! What the hell have you been doing? Lord Kinder is a close personal friend and he is aghast that in his hour of need, the representative I have assigned to him has gone fucking AWOL!' Jez shouts, his voice breaking.

Jean worries that Jez's two-pack a day habit is turning into the first stages of emphysema. His lung capacity isn't what it used to be. When Jean first started working for him, he could yell for five minutes without interruption.

She inhales deeply and imagines herself lying on a sun lounger at the Chateau Marmont, in a tiny gold chain bikini with wraparound shades, sipping on a cocktail straw through a metal grill. The sort of woman who keeps a gun in her Gucci handbag and knows how to use it.

'I told you months ago that I would block off this entire weekend for my dear friend's wedding, I gave all relevant details and contacts to Cynthia who agreed to cover me, and I have, out of the goodness of my heart, gone the extra mile for you and Lord Kinder knowing what a valued friend and client he has been all these years,' Jean expels in one long breath, looking out the window at the passing highway, the phone trembling in her hand.

She had been aiming for 'nightclub owner moonlighting as a mercenary' vibes à la Pamela Anderson in *Barb Wire*, and sounded like Theresa May. Still, it was an improvement on her usual cap-doffing servitude.

'This is a *special* case,' Jez screams, his voice reaching a gravelly pitch of anger usually reserved for interns who had fucked up for the first and last time. Jean imagines levelling a .45 Magnum at his head and demanding a bonus.

'It's always a special case! And I have always picked up the slack! Christmas, New Years, my grandmother's funeral, my own birthday! Just because I'm the only one without a "real family,"' Jean pauses, biting her tongue in fury, reminding herself to keep it professional. 'If you want me to be on call 24/7, get me a goddamn assistant. I am taking a personal day tomorrow as I have split up with my boyfriend and need to not be homeless. Goodbye.'

Jean cancels the call and turns off her phone.

The driver whistles as the car turns off the road, driving towards the stately home.

'Nightmare boss?'

'He's charming really. In his own tyrannical fashion,' Jean sighs, the excuse sounding flat and unbelievable. 'I've spent so much time trying to lean the fuck in that I tumbled face-forward and let everyone walk over me.'

'This is why I work for myself. No more bullshit and nothing but bangers,' her driver grins, turning up the radio again. They share a moment wailing along to 'Encore' as he pulls up in front of the house.

'Oh!' Jean exclaims as the door opens for her. A familiar strawberry-blond head peers around the frame of the car. 'Gabriel. I didn't know you were still here.'

Her surprise coming off as a lack of enthusiasm, Gabriel's smile shifts from a grin to a nervous laugh. He puts out his hand to help her out and Jean grasps it lightly, firmly, more composed than she would have thought possible.

'Yes – I, well, Sarah invited me to come last night. Don't you remember? When we were all dancing, she banned Charlie and said I could have his place.' Gabriel looks awkward, as if he might have overstepped the mark. Feeling the easy familiarity of the night before withering like a vampire in sunlight, Jean beams up at him.

'Oh yes, of course,' Jean says, recollecting nothing of the sort. The evening was a collection of photographic stills. Shots. Disco ball. Dancing very close. Cab. Puke. Like any other wedding. She takes Gabriel's arm with the disarming flirtatiousness of an entirely different person, as her heels dig delicately into the gravel-lined path.

'I'm very glad you stayed. I wondered if I would ever see you again,' Jean says, the boldness of her words lightened by her playful tone. 'Especially as I appear to have stood you up at the bar.'

'I had a feeling that . . .' Gabriel looks as if he wants to say something. He stops himself. 'I hope I didn't cause any trouble with your boyfriend.'

'He's not my boyfriend,' Jean says. 'Remember?'

Gabriel opens the front door. Jean takes a deep breath and sashays through, casting back an inviting look as if it comes naturally to her.

'Then I'm glad I stayed for brunch,' he says, taking her hand as they walk through marble halls to the dining room. The immediate comfort of his tactility gives Jean a small thrill. Could it be that everything might work out, from toxic to true love, just like that?

No. Jean makes a conscious effort to stop herself from falling down the rabbit hole of fantasy projections, yet again. The new Jean will be the master of her mind, not a slave to her emotions. Bold, free and unencumbered by idiotic attachments that end in disaster, betrayal and urine.

The dining room is high-ceilinged and bright, with creamy wallpaper and sparkling white table cloths with a thread count so high they could be used as bedsheets. The guests are almost invisible behind the enormous bouquets decorating every table. Sarah wears a neon pink cocktail dress, while Toby sports a Hawaiian shirt over jean shorts and boat shoes, ready for their late afternoon flight to Athens to island-hop on honeymoon.

As Jean and Gabriel enter the dining room hand in hand, Sarah and Toby's eyebrows shoot up at the hook-up their body language suggests.

'Such a beautiful ceremony,' Gabriel congratulates them again, before a flower girl in the throes of her first crush grabs his pant leg and draws him out of earshot.

'How was your wedding night?' Jean teases, as Sarah kisses her on the cheeks.

'No surprises, but I can't complain!' Sarah laughs.

'She fell fast asleep in her gown,' Toby says, rolling his eyes. 'And spent all morning yakking in the toilet.'

'And it seems *you* had an unexpected evening?' Sarah asks, with a nod of the chin towards Gabriel before lowering her voice. 'Of which I am painfully jealous.'

'Nothing happened,' Jean whispers. 'To my eternal regret.'

'There's still opportunity! In any case, I'm *so* glad you've ditched Charlie,' Sarah says, exchanging a look with Toby. 'High time, I never liked him.'

'Really? I thought you loved him!' Jean says in surprise. 'You said he was hilarious.'

'He could be hilarious,' Sarah says diplomatically. 'As a person. But I didn't like the way he took you for granted as a boyfriend.'

'Best not to comment on other people's private lives, I always say,' Toby chimes in. 'But Charlie is a prick.'

'I told him to get out of my room and my life this morning,' Jean says with a deep breath. She was still processing it. She wouldn't mention the lilac dress; her final straw was too humiliating. 'So . . . now I just need to find a flat!'

'Oh gosh, that's so tough on such short notice. Champagne?' Sarah offers.

'My friend Richard has a spare room I'm sure I could crash in,' Jean says, accepting the flute gratefully. 'While I'm looking, at least.'

'Is this the Richard your mum always says you should marry?' Sarah laughs.

'Yes, but we are far too similar. You can't have two push-overs in a relationship, nothing would ever get decided!'

Richard had been in Jean's halls in first year, and they'd become fast friends and study buddies after being painfully dumped around the same time. He was the only man she knew who did not mock her for preferring white wine spritzers and in return, Jean had not once suggested he was closeted, despite his deep and abiding love of Barbra Streisand.

'You both like the chase, that's the problem,' Toby says, with all the worldly-wisdom of the recently hitched.

'I hate the chase!' Jean protests.

'I always say, you're either the watering can, or the flower. You, Jean, are a watering can. You just need to choose less shit flowers,' Sarah says, explaining Jean's life to her in thirty seconds. She leans her head on her husband's shoulder. 'I'm obviously a flower.'

'I'll see what I can do. Wow, the food looks amazing!' Jean changes the subject as Gabriel returns, too close for comfort. 'I'm famished. I'll let you get on with greeting everyone!'

Jean and Gabriel take their seats across from the little flower girl, who glares at her balefully from around the corner of the giant bouquet. When Gabriel is distracted by the arrival of the first course of watermelon gazpacho, Jean slips the square card with Charlie's name on it under the vase. It is a small gesture imbued with symbolism. Jean smiles to herself and the flower girl, with blinding smug-as-fuck-ness.

As Gabriel waves away the offer of a coffee, Jean catches sight of something for the first time. Something she is shocked she hadn't noticed previously.

A glinting gold ring on the third finger of his left hand.

'Umm . . . Ahh . . . Errr . . .' Jean starts incoherently, unsure how to address the decked-out Indian Wedding elephant in the room. Had the outrageous flirtation she thought was mutual actually been one-sided? Had she been out of the game for so long she misread the signs? Was *this* why he had been such a gentleman?

A terrible thought occurs to her, that he had been acting out of a misplaced sense of duty, squiring her like a walker for rich women.

'Were you wearing that last night?' She points at his finger as if it has offended her.

'Oh, you mean my ring? No, I don't wear it when I'm working. I get more job recommendations that way,' Gabriel says with a wink. 'Terrible as that sounds! I think it's something similar to single bartenders getting better tips.'

'I see. So . . . you're married,' Jean says, shocked at her own naivety. The sexual tension she imagined was between them explodes into farting nothingness.

'Yes, happily. For about ten years now,' Gabriel says casually, sipping a glass of sparkling water, as if they hadn't been dancing as close as thrashing eels in a very small plastic bag last night. Of course, dancing wasn't cheating.

Bastard! 'We've been together since we were nineteen. Did everything young.'

Jean nods, staring into her gazpacho with manic intensity. Was she crazy? Did she make up the seductive tone, the eyefuckery? He hadn't actually *said* anything that was overtly sexual. Apart from 'good' when she said Charlie wasn't her husband, it was all an implication of tone. But that might have been the normal reaction of anyone who had witnessed his behaviour.

'I'm sorry, I thought . . .' Jean stammers, more grateful than ever for the champagne, although she will need more than one glass to quell her lunatic fantasist shame. 'I don't know what I thought. I'm sorry, I have to ask. Why were you holding my hand?'

'We're very liberated in terms of rules and restrictions,' Gabriel smiles, his hand covering hers again over the table, his manner as open as apparently is his marriage. 'For a few years now. My wife Poppy works in the States six months out of the year, and it made more sense for us to explore all that life has to offer. We don't believe that love is possession.'

'I see,' Jean says, digesting this along with a spoonful of soup. 'Then what is it?'

'What?'

'Marriage? If not possession.'

Gabriel looks temporarily stumped.

'Sorry. Is that a stupid question?' Jean asks.

'No, not at all. We're great friends, and lovers, who recognise that over a lifetime together there might be other attractions, other loves, that come along the way. And that doesn't need to diminish our love for each other,' Gabriel says smoothly, with the well-practiced charm of one who has explained this before. 'Polyamory keeps us faithful.'

49

'You're polyamorous?' Jean asks, biting her lip. 'But you're so . . .'

The word conjures images of Danielle's friends whom she had met at squat parties, before Jean finally admitted that squats made her uncomfortable and she didn't 100 per cent believe that crack *could* be used casually. Men nude but for gimp masks, mime-begging their dominatrix girl-friends to unzip their mouths in order to partake in a joint. Women who dressed like Anime characters in daily life, loudly rejecting every oppressive social convention except for whalebone corsets, pigtails and hobble-heels. Boys in their late teens raised by Tumblr, convinced that they had the soul of a dragon. 'Call me Smaug,' one had said before licking the inside of her ear in greeting, Jean shudderingly remembers.

'So normal?' Gabriel says with raised eyebrows.

'Yeah,' Jean laughs, relieved he has not taken offence.

'What could be more normal than following one's heart in a spirit of total honesty?'

'Monogamy and lies?' Jean offers.

Gabriel laughs, a deep rich chuckle she is getting alarmingly used to.

'We communicate wonderfully, and we trust each other implicitly,' Gabriel says.

'Why haven't you joined her in the States?' Jean asks, waving to the waiter and tapping sharply on her empty champagne glass with her nail. A rude, but necessary act.

'My parents died in a car accident when I was twelve and my nan raised me. She's in a care home near where I live in Greenwich, I like to visit at least once a week,' Gabriel explains. 'She's still in good nick, but she is ninety!'

Jean nods sympathetically, her hand reaching out to squeeze his forearm, sorry for his loss and ecstatic to hear he lives in London.

'Are you waiting to join her in the States . . . eventually?' Jean asks.

'Maybe. Maybe not. I like New York to visit, but I don't really want to live there. We have the rest of our lives with each other, so we don't see long distance as an issue. We believe that to truly love is to be free, to take joy in your spouse's happiness, wherever that may be, whomever that arises with.'

'How romantic,' Jean says, considering. It wasn't as if her relationships had been improved for being exclusive, or their love made more valid. There had still been jealousy, pain and suffering. Just with less compensatory sex.

'Not to be bound in a trap of exclusivity until death,' Gabriel continues earnestly.

'You should do wedding speeches!' Jean laughs, as the waiter tops her up.

'What I'd like to do,' Gabriel says, his knuckles brushing softly against her hand before threading through under her palm, 'is take you out.'

'Out?' Jean parrots, her mouth hanging open comically.

'Do you enjoy opera?' Gabriel asks.

'Opera?' Jean repeats after him stupidly, again.

She had never before considered dating a married man, given the whole troth-pledging-to-another thing. However, Jean has to admit she finds the unapologetic freedom of Gabriel's lifestyle intriguing. The unabashed generosity in pleasure, their clear trust in one another, a perfect balance of excitement and security. It is all so delightfully bohemian.

And Gabriel's hair does glint so very golden in the sunlight.

'We have season tickets at the Royal Opera House,' Gabriel says. 'Would you care to join me next week?'

51

Jean wonders who this Poppy is, a woman so cool and self-assured that she doesn't mind her husband taking strange women on dates to the ultimate romantic comedy stage. Had she never seen *Pretty Woman* or *Moonstruck*? Didn't she know that to weep culturally in front of a man was to win his heart forever?

'Yes, I love the opera.'

Jean accepts before she can further over-analyse, become consumed by doubt and say 'No!' to life, as has been her habit since childhood. After all, it's just an evening out. And she hasn't been to the opera in, well, ever. If Danielle could live the fun, frivolous side of the sexual revolution, then so would she!

'Good,' Gabriel says, his gaze sparkling beneath his eyelashes, imbuing the word with many-layered meaning. Jean swigs nervously from her glass as a flock of butterflies go apeshit in her stomach.

Chapter Four

As Jean's post-brunch taxi back to London shoots by the Three Horseshoes, she is shocked to see Charlie, still in Kent and thoroughly occupied being barrelled down the lawn by the flirtatious barman. So, Charlie has gotten his wheelie-bin races after all, and Jean has at least an hour's head start to pack up her life with him on her own. Of course, she has nowhere to live afterwards. The thought of ending up at her parent's place in Clapham for a month fills her with dread. She dials Richard's number.

He picks up on the first ring.

'Jean! Just the person I want to speak to,' Richard mumbles through the sound of a tissue being blown. 'Anne's gone.'

'What?' Jean asks in confusion. 'But she just moved in last month!'

'I don't know what I've been doing wrong! I send flowers to her work, wake her up with breakfast in bed, she *says* I'm the most attentive and thorough giver of cunnilingus—'

'Have to stop you there, Richard!' Jean shudders.

Though she hates to doubt her friend, 'attentive and thorough giver of cunnilingus' is such a horribly unlyrical turn of phrase. It invites visions of the most creepily persistent of Nice Guys, the kind who start out merely pathetic and later morph into violent incels.

'Maybe I wasn't trying hard enough?' Richard asks pleadingly.

'Maybe you were trying too hard? I think flowers are best reserved for special occasions.'

'We met on a Friday, it was our weekly special occasion!' Richard defends himself, before gasping in horror. 'Oh my god. Waves of desperation must have been coming off me like cheap perfume!'

Being a divorce lawyer, one would think that Richard would be a whizz at taking preventative action when all signs point towards relationship doom. Unfortunately, his profession has driven him into such a state of romantic anxiety that his last three girlfriends have followed the same whirlwind pattern. First, the initial ecstasy of finding a man unafraid of commitment! Followed by increasing irritation at his clinginess after they've moved in with him. Then one day, they mysteriously disappear, leaving only a note. Usually within the space of three months.

'I'm afraid so,' Jean says. 'Anyway, I dumped Charlie.'

'Hurrah!'

'I thought you loved Charlie?' Jean asks for the second time that day.

'He can be funny, but he treats you like a—'

'Prick?' Jean says.

'Yep.'

'Right. Well, thanks for letting me know that zero times over the last three years. Listen, I have nowhere to stay, is there any way I could crash at yours for a bit while I look for a room?' Jean stares out of the taxi window at the concrete highway.

'Crash? Stay! I have my spare room. It's only me and Yentl, now. It's terribly lonely.'

Yentl is the name of Richard's cat, a foul-tempered Sphynx whose moniker exemplifies both why Jean loves Richard and why Jean could never *love* Richard. 'She just

54

wants to learn!' Richard had wept in Jean's arms as Barbra chose the Talmud over Mandy Patinkin, the first of many times he forced her to watch *Yentl* the film. 'She's a true feminist,' Jean had agreed, handing him a tissue.

'Thanks, my love! Lifesaver,' Jean says, breathing a sigh of relief. 'Can I come around early this evening? I'm going to pack ASAP, so Charlie and I don't have a run-in.'

'You don't want to have one last wailing row with him, for old times' sake?' Richard says through a throat thick with tears, clearly wishing he could have another toxic encounter with Anne.

'I never want to see him again,' Jean says, before her phone buzzes with another call. 'Hang on, Mum is on the other line.'

'Tonight, we can watch all four versions of *A Star Is Born*!' Richard says hopefully.

'Yes, we will,' Jean agrees, giving herself a pat on the back for this act of true friendship. 'Wait, I thought there were only three?'

'There's a Bollywood version from 2013,' Richard explains.

'Oh god. I mean good! See you in a few hours,' Jean switches calls. 'Mum?'

'Jeannie?' Door whispers in greeting. She always sounds surprised her call has been accepted. 'Are you still at the wedding?'

'No, I'm in a taxi home. I mean, to Charlie's flat. Actually, I wanted to ask, can I stop by the house and borrow George's van? Charlie and I broke up and I need it to move all my things into Richard's place. Thanks!' Jean rushes through the words, unwilling to explain the series of indignities that have led to this point.

'Oh no, Jeannie, not Charlie. Oh no. Such a sweet boy. Your father loves him like a son,' Door says haltingly. Jean knows her mother is wracked with fear at her daughter's uncertain future without a man at her side. After a pause, the inevitable comes. 'Do you think he might be willing to take you back?'

'Why are you assuming he dumped me?' Jean says, losing her temper. She can feel her mother cringing on the other end of the phone and restrains herself. 'Look, can we not talk about this now? I just need the van.'

'Your father took you off the insurance . . .' Door says hesitantly. 'He could help you pack? He hasn't seen you in so long? It could be nice for you both . . .'

Jean expels a long, miserable moan of reluctance from the very pit of her lungs, that sounds like the last gasp of an exorcised demon.

'Can he be there in an hour?'

'Yes, dear. I'm sure? I'll ask. I'll get right back to you,' Door says, before hanging up the phone. The arrival of a footprint emoji five minutes later confirms his acceptance.

Jean's father pulls up in his camper van in front of Charlie's once shiny, now dilapidated front door in Peckham. The tiny garden is swamped by weeds and a broken-down bicycle Charlie promised to fix but never did.

Her possessions are even more meagre than she thought, only two suitcases of clothes, a bin bag full of hair and makeup tools, one beat-up leather armchair from a flea market and a vintage side table. She owns DVDs but no player, an old boom-box but no CDs. When it came to entertaining, Charlie's record collection was much more impressive than her own Top 40 tastes.

'That's it?' her father says gruffly as he grabs the bin bag from her hand and lets her struggle behind him with the luggage. He is one hour late, timed with military precision for when she has actually finished packing.

She stuffs the suitcases into the RV, her father's splashy sixtieth birthday present to himself. It has become his private haven during the WWII re-enactment weekends away he is obsessed with, as he dislikes interacting with the other anoraks when out of uniform.

'Could you help me with this chair?' Jean says, pushing it in front of her along the pavement.

Her father lifts it with ease, his barrel-chest still powerful, though he has not played rugby in decades. Jean occupies herself with the table, and within in a few minutes Jean's life with Charlie has been squirreled away into a trailer, as if it had never happened.

'What did you do this time?' her father asks as Jean straps in her seatbelt.

This is George trying to be sympathetic, Jean tells herself.

'I stood up for myself,' Jean explains, staring at her feet. Her father's gaze is so full of penetrating judgement, she can barely ever meet it head on. 'I deserve better than to play nursemaid to a drunk.'

'What you are is a thirty-year-old woman, playing as if you still have options,' her father says, shaking his head as he pulls out of Charlie's road. 'Handsome chap, clever, from a good family. He likes his drink, as do most men.'

Jean notices that 'he loves you' is not one of the qualities her father cared to mention, although it was the only reason she had stayed for so long. She types Richard's Kentish Town address into CityMapper. Fifty minutes with traffic. She tries very hard not to cry at the thought of nearly an hour with her father in his van of mental torture.

'You really think you can do any better?' he continues.

Jean always used to ignore his barbs rather than be shouted down, but today she stands her ground.

'Yes, definitely. I know I can.'

'Being headstrong and independent and going it on your own is a feminist *lie* sold to young women by the government so they can tax more workers,' George starts the old familiar rant. 'It will never bring you the happiness of a family, your own home and husband and children. What have you been doing all these years, Jean? Apart from wasting your youth. What was the point of going into political PR, if not to marry an MP?'

Jean turns on the radio, blasting MAGIC 105.4 to tune him out. Her father moves to turn it off, but his hand stiffens and falls when he recognises the Barry Manilow tune. Full-blown misogynists, Jean has noted, are often the most mawkishly sentimental of men.

'Learning the importance of not being a doormat,' Jean finally answers him, her voice shaking.

'Fine wine and curdled milk, Jeannie,' her father contents himself with muttering. 'Fine wine and curdled milk.'

She bites her tongue and thinks about what Tess said after she met George for the first time, that he was nothing more than 'a cowardly shit threatened by the force of your power'. By the time the RV pulls up in front of Richard's mint green terraced house, Jean's mouth is full of blood. She is almost ready to follow Danielle's lead and disown her father completely. She stumbles out of the car to the back, flings open the doors and hurls her affairs onto the road with the fury of Maleficent in dragon-mode.

'I would rather be a lonely old hag than spend a nano-second married to a man like you!' Jean shrieks as she slams the trunk shut behind her and kicks her armchair over the curb onto the pavement.

Richard opens his front door a crack, his black springy curls peeking out of the two-inch space, behind which one eye spies on their domestic. Her father, outraged, glares at

Jean as he rolls up the driver's window and takes off into the dusk.

'Good chat?' Richard asks, opening the door fully when her father is safely out of view. He is wearing a unicorn-print frilled ladies dressing gown that Jean suspects Anne left behind.

'Boarding school and the army ruined a generation of men,' Jean huffs as she pulls her suitcases up the front path. 'Thank god ours isn't so . . . so . . .'

'Dastardly?' Richard suggests, as he takes the suitcases from her grasp.

'Masculine!' Jean says, lifting the chair into the air with a strength born of rage.

'I'm not masculine?' Richard asks in mock offence, drawing the robe close around his throat like Blanche DuBois.

And so began Jean's new single life with the most emo straight man in London. Whatever concerns she had of Richard being an overly attentive, needy or demanding flatmate were misplaced. By the following week, Jean found to her delight that living with Richard was like living with a hyper-considerate robot. Imagine C-3PO singing Broadway tunes whilst doing the washing up. It was perfect. The fact that Charlie hadn't contacted her at all bothered her not one whit. Not when she had a text flirtation with Gabriel to distract her.

Richard swings open the door, saying 'Honey, I'm hoooome!' and gives Jean a theatrical peck on the cheeks as he tosses his briefcase on the sofa.

'Darling! I've missed you!' Jean says, clasping her hands like Snow White in full-pining mode, surrounded by wittering love birds.

'What smells amazing?' Richard asks, as Jean follows him into the kitchen.

'Nigella brownies,' Jean says, as Richard places three bottles of Chablis on the counter. 'And you bought the wine without my asking! Tell me, why have we never lived together before?'

'Because we were both cohabitating with a series of lunatic sociopaths who rinsed us dry for affection and then left us with naught but cynicism and heartbreak to cling to,' Richard grabs two glasses from the cupboard and takes a breath to uncork a bottle, before continuing unabated. 'As desperately as Rose upon her plank of driftwood, as Jack froze and drowned!'

'And here I thought you were moving on,' Jean says, untying the Cath Kidston pinny she had borrowed from him and hanging it up.

'It's week one. I'm allowed to hate-love her still,' Richard sulks. 'Besides, what sort of she-demon breaks up with you by writing "I Feel Trapped" on the bathroom mirror, so the next time you shower the traces are left behind in the condensation?'

Jean smothers her laughter. It was an awful thing to do. But awfully funny.

'She's got Narcissistic Personality Disorder!' Richard continues, outraged.

'I pathologised all my exes' cruel behaviour in my early twenties,' Jean says, as she checks on the rising brownies in the oven. 'But unfortunately, with the passage of time and a degree of maturity, I've had to accept that maybe they just didn't love me back.'

'TOO SOON JEAN! Too goddamn soon,' Richard says, ignoring the glasses and glugging straight from the bottle. 'Anne is a coldblooded succubus who ensorcelled me before disposing of my lifeless corpse.'

'You're right. She is evil personified. I hate her,' Jean says supportively, pouring herself a glass of Chablis and adding a splash of soda water to the top.

'Thank you. When's Tess coming over?'

'She said 8 p.m., but you know how it is with Zhang,' Jean sighs. 'It could be ten.'

Tess has lived with her mother Zhang ever since her baby-daddy suddenly split to find himself in Goa. Without much success, it appears, as he hasn't been heard from in more than three years. Tess describes her mother as a Chinese Mrs Bennet, gone psychotic. A night out always begins with a row about the desperate necessity for Tess to find a rich stepfather for her son, just as she is preparing to leave the house.

'I want to get her opinion on my Tinder profile,' Richard says, putting on the pinny and getting out some onions and tomatoes to chop for bruschetta.

'You don't want my opinion on your Tinder profile?' Jean asks archly. 'I *am* PR guru extraordinaire for sex-addict politicians and the Prime Minister's uncle.'

'Maybe I don't want to attract the sort of woman who responds favourably to politicians and perverts,' Richard says, but slides over his phone.

Jean swipes through his profile photos. In a floral suit with a glitter beard at a wedding, holding up a glass of champagne and baring his goofiest grin. In fancy dress at a Halloween party, the year Jean had convinced him to be *Scarface* Michelle Pfeiffer to her Al Pacino. He was trying to look coy but appeared scared. Being bitten by a stranger's Doberman in the park, screaming. Below them, it states simply: Richard, 31, Lawyer. Available. Keen. Kind.

'Well, you definitely won't attract the type of woman who likes politicians or perverts,' Jean says slowly.

'Why do you make that sound like a bad thing?'

'Why have you included a photo of yourself being bitten by a dog?'

'It's more original than cuddling a puppy. And shows that I'm nurturing and I don't fight back,' Richard says proudly.

Jean's eyebrows knot over her nose.

'I think this is too available, too keen and too kind,' Jean says, her mouth twisting in a grimace as she flips through the photos again. 'Forgive me Richard, but there is no other way to say this . . .'

'What?'

Richard pauses his chopping to look up, full of all the vulnerability that accompanies having a friend give you their true opinion of your sex appeal.

'You look like Liberace consumed by self-doubt.'

'Liberace was an icon,' Richard says, snatching his phone from her grasp.

'Because he believed himself iconic!' Jean points out. 'You make yourself sound like an unwanted stray at Battersea Dogs Home.'

'I asked my ex-girlfriends to describe me in three words and those were the most common adjectives they chose,' Richard says, throwing up his hands in frustration.

'Surely you see the problem in using the opinion of EX-girlfriends on a dating site?' Jean asks. 'We need to give this a makeover.'

'Goddamn it. You're right.'

'I'm always right,' Jean sighs, draping herself over the counter. 'It's a curse.'

The doorbell goes.

'Tess! You're on time,' Jean says, swinging open the door and giving her best mate a bear hug. It has been two weeks since they've seen each other. Two weeks that have involved so much emotional upheaval they feel like two months. Tess pats Jean's shoulders around the giant package she's carrying under one arm.

'I've started telling mum my plans are an hour earlier, so she wraps up the "You're the only single mother in Dulwich!" lecture on my schedule,' Tess says dryly, pushing up a pair of mirrored aviator sunglasses and rubbing tired eyes.

'Is she still going on about that? It can't be true,' Jean says, taking her friend's present in her arms and shaking it gingerly.

'Housewarming present,' Tess says. Her short hair is sticking up in messy tufts and her usually proud shoulders are slumped in exhaustion. 'She associates exclusively with Chinese people whose daughters got hitched by twenty-three. In her eyes, I'm an old slut maid. The other day she begged me to pretend to be widowed.'

'She can't judge you by those standards,' Jean says, leading Tess through to the kitchen, where Richard is sautéing slices of baguette. 'You're English!'

'She says when she looks at my choices, she regrets ever moving here,' Tess says through a pained half-smile. 'But she is great with Fynn, of course. The golden grandson . . .'

'Hello darling,' Richard says as they kiss each other on both cheeks. 'You look ravishing.'

'Really? Mum's taken to calling me a "rotten banana". White on the inside, yellow on the outside and developing age spots.' Tess laughs with surprisingly good humour. Jean hands her a large glass of wine. Tess drinks deep and narrows her eyes in a thousand-yard stare. 'The only reason I've stopped talking about wanting to kill her is that I'm afraid I might actually do it.'

'If push comes to murder, I'll help you dispose of the body,' Jean offers.

'Thank you, Jean,' Tess says, hand on chest. 'I'm truly touched.'

'Crimes of passion serve less time,' Richard advises. 'You don't want any obvious planning involved. An open window is better than arsenic, for example.'

'I'll keep that in mind,' Tess says, manspreading on a kitchen stool. 'What a pathetic intro! Same old shit with me, but you two have had a way worse time of it I gather.'

'I've been surprisingly OK!' Jean says.

She struggles to open the perfectly bow-tied, professionally wrapped parcel with her nails. Whatever combination of patience and hand-eye coordination genes separate Asian presentation from the rest of the world, Tess has inherited them.

'I, on the other hand, have been terrible,' Richard says. 'So, Anne, who shall henceforth be known as The Narc-Witch . . .'

As Richard fills Tess in on the merciless manner of his dumping, Jean tires of trying to save the wrapping paper and shreds it in half, only to reveal the best thing ever.

'Labyrinth: The Board Game!!' Jean exclaims in glee.

'Oh my god. Shotgun Sarah,' Richard says, clapping his hands.

'I thought Games Night deserved an update. If I have to play *Yahtzee* one more time I'll stab myself in the eye,' Tess says. 'And *Cards Against Humanity* has started to give me dangerous ideas. "Eternal Damnation / In a wood chipper / Sweet Matricide . . ."'

'That's quite poetic,' Jean says.

'What happened with Charlie? You gave me the bare bones on the thread, but I was working flat out and didn't really follow. He heckled the ceremony?' Tess asks.

Their group thread evolved from IM-ing on Myspace back in the day, to Facebook and now it has moved on to WhatsApp. The 'Thread: Revolution!' mostly consists of work-woe, pictures of Fynn, romantic obsessions, Netflix recommendations and intermittent panic that we may be barrelling towards WWIII and or the climate change apocalypse.

'Not the ceremony. Only the speeches,' Jean says. 'Then he set fire to the marquee.'

'And then he pissed on your dress,' Tess shakes her head. 'Was that revenge?'

'I don't know or care. Maybe I'm deluding myself, but I think I got over him while I was still with him,' Jean muses, topping up her wine glass. 'I don't feel sad. I feel liberated!'

'Sounds to me like the words of someone who's already met someone else,' Richard says, in the voice of someone who knows very well she's already met someone else. 'For those of us without a rebound, recovery is not so simple.'

'Oh ho hoo . . .' Tess says, the 'e' implied by her tone. She pushes up the sleeves of her white T-shirt, to reveal a writhing dragon tattoo she has somehow managed to hide from Zhang for over five years. Jean grins.

'I spoke to Danielle at the wedding and she was really helpful and supportive! Well, in her way. She said Charlie is like Lord Byron with wet brain and I should have seen all this coming and called me a sad sack live on air afterwards. But she forced me to take more responsibility for my own happiness. Now that I'm single, I'm going to free myself from the shackles of how society expects me to behave,' Jean says archly. 'And become an erotic adventuress!'

'I like this rebranding of the more traditional term: slag,' Tess says, topping up her glass and finishing off the bottle. 'You know what, you should do PR!'

Tess chucks the empty bottle through the air. It somersaults in perfect arcs and sails directly into the bin.

'Tell me there's more,' Tess says. 'I need a vat of wine tonight.'

Richard opens the fridge and presents it like a gameshow hostess. Aside from milk, tomatoes and cheese, it is filled entirely with IPA, white wine and Prosecco.

'I treated myself to a heartbreak Ocado delivery,' Richard says, 'to prepare for my weekend of oblivion.'

'I swear you didn't even like Anne that much!' Tess says.

'Yeah, after your first date you said she was a bitchy snoozefest. And that she has the head of a llama,' Jean reminds him.

'Teeth of a llama,' Richard corrects her with a lovelorn quality. 'I took her to see *Jersey Boys* and she made us leave at intermission. She doesn't like music predating 2001.'

'There's an obvious incompatibility,' Tess points out. 'Didn't you say she complained about everything?'

'She was impossible to please and hated fun, it's true.' In typical Richard fashion, these qualities had made him try even harder to win her approval. 'But she was *my* long-toothed misery.'

'This is why I like spending time with you guys,' Tess says, serving herself a scalding wedge of dessert. 'You make me feel good about being loveless forever.'

'My love life is going very well, thank you,' Jean smiles smugly.

'Fine, fine. Tell me more about this erotic adventuress shit!' Tess says.

'Well, after the bed death caused by Charlie's alcoholism—'

'What?' Tess asks, her eyebrows knitting. 'You said the sex was great! And that he had got more of a handle on his drinking lately.'

Jean ignores this.

'The point is, I've had a string of long-term relationships under the assumption that's what you *do* to be happy. And they were all emotionally exhausting, crap shaggers! Everyone around me seems to be getting it left right and centre, and I haven't *ever*.' Jean sighs in frustration. 'I always thought maybe I'm not that sexual of a person. Or that it's the natural progression of a relationship, for love to become neutering. But what if I'm wrong?'

Tess stares at Jean, aghast.

'True love definitely doesn't neuter you,' Richard says, personally affronted. 'I may never have experienced it, but I'm also 100 per cent sure that *The Notebook*, *Dirty Dancing* and *Splash* tell no lies.'

'I'm not going to comment on *Splash*,' Jean says, 'But I agree that Patrick Swayze had too much integrity to mislead whole generations about the nature of passion.'

'Jean, this supposed shagathon is a media conspiracy to keep us buying unnecessary lady-products in horror at the failure of our sex lives,' Tess says, with a huff of annoyance at having to explain the self-evident. 'I mean, where is the market in crotchless thongs for straight men?'

'What?' Jean and Richard ask simultaneously.

'Exactly,' Tess says, biting savagely into her brownie.

'The point is. Danielle is always involved in some orgy or other. Why not me?' Jean asks rhetorically. Jean wasn't a prude at heart, not really. She simply feared being judged more than anything else in the world.

'The most experimental you've got is when Freddie bought a strap-on for Valentine's Day,' Tess says with an eye roll. 'For you to use on him.'

'Which one's Freddie again?' Richard asks.

'Post-uni boyfriend I met travelling,' Jean says around a handful of candied nuts.

'He was awful. Don't take them home when you've met abroad!' Tess says. 'It's like buying souvenirs from beach venders. Never works on native soil.'

'What did you say when you opened the strap-on?' Richard asks.

'From the packaging, I thought it would be the handheld Cuisinart blender I had requested. Needless to say, I burst into tears.'

'So, you didn't even try it,' Richard says judgementally. 'Wasn't he the one who ditched you on holiday a month later?'

'For an Italian dominatrix named Asia,' Jean confirms, her eyes narrowing into slits, still bitter after seven years. 'With very prominent nipples.'

Tess gets out her phone and types something into her search engine.

'We should all try Rio's Naturist Spa, it's your local now!' Tess jokes, before reading further. 'It has a 4.1 rating on Google. Along with the helpful tip: "I particularly enjoyed the biscuit selection."'

'You do love biscuits,' Richard agrees.

'My fantasies run more to the glam-cult *Eyes Wide Shut* variety,' Jean says.

The thought of liberation and sexual freedom was not quite so appealing when she thought of the men she'd seen going into Rio's, the notorious Kentish Town swinger's spot with the island paradise marketing. They were more akin to Phil from *EastEnders* than Tom Cruise circa 1999.

'Nicole is so beautiful in that film,' Richard sighs.

'What about lesbianism?' Tess asks. 'After all, maybe the reason you've had shit sex is because you've unwittingly been gay all this time.'

'Could you give me a Sapphic education before I attempt it and embarrass myself?' Jean asks. Although Tess hasn't dated women since 2011 when she got with her ex, and hasn't dated anyone since he left, she swings both ways.

'Do. Or do not. There is no educate,' Tess says, putting her fingers in a V and wagging her tongue between them suggestively.

'Fine! I'll have a threesome,' Jean smiles.

'I had a threesome once. It was so stressful!' Richard confesses. 'I was obsessed with each woman getting the same attentions. And I was overwhelmed by all the breasts.'

'Trust you to be too neurotic to enjoy the ultimate male fantasy.'

'You should join my Sexual Reinvention Tour! We can learn techniques from pickup artists. And magicians. I want to be like if Darren Brown used his powers for evil and left a trail of broken hearts in his wake,' Jean says.

'I will become an out-and-out bounder,' Richard agrees.

'Wait, who is this person you've already met? Seemingly a nanosecond after you broke up with Charlie?' Tess asks.

'The pianist from the wedding.' Jean grins sheepishly. 'He's married but open. Or polyamorous. I'm not sure what the difference is, but it all feels very light and free! He's invited me to the opera.'

The more she thought about it, the more Gabriel struck her as the perfect heartbreak rebound. Handsome, talented and excitingly unavailable, yet a not amoral choice. No-strings summer sex would be just the ticket!

'The opera,' Tess says with raised brows. 'Let me guess, *Carmen*?'

Jean doesn't know enough about opera to understand what Tess is implying, but doesn't like her tone.

'The greediness of modern love astounds me,' Richard says wonderingly. 'How does anyone cope with the anxiety of multiple lovers? More people on the brink of leaving you!'

'I can't believe you've fallen for that bollocks at our age,' Tess says, rolling her eyes. 'Open marriages are for cheaters without the decency to lie.'

'It's not like that,' Jean says defensively. 'And what is fidelity really, but a chastity belt for the heart?'

She couldn't remember Gabriel's turn of phrase, but it had been much more elegant.

'A giver of security and comfort, a life free from crippling paranoia?' Richard suggests hopefully. 'I see it more as a huge, winged maxi-pad for the heart.'

Jean ignores this.

'Well, be careful not to get too attached,' Tess warns her. 'There's a reason people don't like their lover sleeping with other people.'

'But why is that really, apart from patriarchal social conditioning to control women's chaotic sexual desires and reproductive capacity?' Jean asks combatively. Danielle had rubbed off on her more than she'd thought.

'Passion is possession!' Tess shouts, stabbing one finger in the air. 'If you learn one thing at the opera, let it be that. Where's his wife in all this?'

'She lives in New York six months of the year,' Jean explains. 'His nan is elderly and he doesn't like to leave her. He said they have their whole lives to be together. It's all very bohemian. I don't really get it, but it clearly works for them.'

'Can't dislike a man who looks after his nan,' Richard says sweetly.

'Whatever. I guess if you keep your eyes open and heart closed, it might not be a complete disaster. Promise?' Tess says, the fight going out of her. 'I don't have the energy to deal with my best mate having a nervous breakdown on top of everything else.'

'I swear it,' Jean says, offering up her pinky finger for Tess to shake. 'I will be a wise, dutty, man-eating hoe with no emo attachments.'

'What about you, Tess? Any emo attachments on the horizon?' Richard asks.

'How can I, when board games have replaced bar-hopping in our Saturday evening repertoire?' Tess complains. 'My one night off. Anyway, what with trying to get Pussy Willows ready for the launch party, I don't even have time for bad sex, let alone go on a journey of sexual discovery.'

Pussy Willows is Tess's long-standing ambition: her very own feminist cat-café meets flower shop. She's spent years sourcing furniture, picture frames and books from flea markets, scavenged from skips and found on street corners. Her handyman skills have reached a professional level from watching YouTube DIY videos.

Jean had welled up a bit when Tess had proudly showed her the finished hand-painted Pussy Willows sign, a beautifully rendered portrait of Simone de Beauvoir stroking a cat in Warhol block-print style. Ironically, Tess had saved up to rent and re-do the Dulwich Village shopfront by working as a receptionist for a plastic surgeon over the past four years. She justifies this by reframing plastic surgery not as a feminist issue, but one of capitalism and self-loathing that, while not a net positive for women, is technically genderless.

'I'm working round the clock,' Tess continues. 'My life at the moment is: make Fynn breakfast, take him to nursery, go to work, secretly take care of my paperwork, go home, feed Fynn, go to the shop, build the fucking shop, paint the walls, sand shit, work until 2 a.m., lie on my pillow for an hour before I can shut my brain up. Then I wake up at 6 a.m. having slept badly for less than four hours, rinse, repeat. All the while with my mum screaming at me that I'm a bad mother because I haven't actually put my son to bed in a month.'

Tess gives a deep sigh that almost turns into a sob, before collecting herself. Jean pats her on the back comfortingly.

'It's nearly there, though! In two weeks' time you'll have the grand opening and make your passion your career!' Jean says with all the enthusiasm she can muster. 'And when the money comes rolling in, as it will . . .'

'You can fire your mother,' Richard says, handing Tess a glass of vodka and ice. 'Move out and treat yourself to an amazing nanny!'

'And then you can join our Sexual Reinvention!' Jean says, flapping her arms and waggling her hips in the least alluring belly dance ever. 'Like sex-phoenixes from the ashes!'

Tess does not look amused.

'Too much levity, too soon,' Tess says, downing the vodka.

'To the Dynamos of Amatory Resurrection!' Richard says, lifting his glass in a toast.

'Res-*Erection* . . .' Jean giggles, waggling her eyebrows suggestively.

'You're sure *you* aren't the ones who are bad in bed?' Tess asks, with a cynical cruelty only forgivable because her life sounds like an unending nightmare.

'Yes,' Jean and Richard say at the same time, deadly serious.

'Right. What about we shake things up with a bit of impromptu karaoke?' Tess asks pleadingly. 'I need to be out amongst people in the world. People who don't depend on me for their survival or belittle me at every turn.'

'Lucky Voice?' Richard suggests.

'I'm down,' Jean agrees.

'Thank god. Belting Donna Summer may be the only thing that stands between me and murder-suicide,' Tess laughs with the sort of brink of despair mania that makes Jean concerned she may be serious. At Jean's wary look, Tess flaps her hands reassuringly. 'Just give me disco.'

Chapter Five

Jean fiddles with the thin strap on her borrowed silver cocktail dress nervously, hoping it reminiscent of Bianca Jagger riding a white stallion into Studio 54, and not a minimalist Miss Havisham. Waiting in the magnificent glass and iron bar of the Floral Hall for Gabriel, gazing through the bright fan-shaped window into the early evening outside, Jean eavesdrops on the conversation next to her and tries not to feel intimidated.

A stunning American woman in her forties, rail-thin and the picture of poise, chats about renovating her chateau in Aix-en-Provence to a man whose protruding belly may be entirely composed of *foie gras*. The woman wears stacked diamond Cartier bracelets from wrist to elbow, as casually as if they were wooden bangles bought in a souk. They look as if they shot out of the womb in fur coats and heirloom jewellery, silk bow ties and Italian brogues. The sort of people whom if cut, bleed champagne.

You would think that hobnobbing with politicians and their wonks would have made Jean more accustomed to people for whom sophistication was not an affectation, but a birth right. Except an after-hours in Parliament was rowdier than a Margate McDonalds queue at 1 a.m. Saturday morning. And even when the riotous high spirits reached a post-apocalyptic level, Jean was never quite allowed to forget where she stood in the pecking order.

Jean feels a soft touch on her lower back, before Gabriel's voice whispers in her ear, his mouth so close to the nape of her neck he tickles a tendril of hair. She shivers.

'Beautiful,' he says simply, as Jean spins around towards his tall frame, slips on her heel and careens directly into his armpit. Despite the oppressive July heat, his open white linen shirt is sweat-free and fragrant. Gabriel steadies her, his hand as cool as marble.

Jean wipes away droplets of perspiration from her upper lip, styling it out as if she were fanning rouged cheeks, wondering if she has stumbled upon some sort of statue given life by Aphrodite. Or alternatively, a biorobotic android from the future. Gabriel's other hand moves from behind his back with an almost mechanical grace, to present Jean with a small bouquet of lily of the valley.

'Thank you for joining me,' he says, as Jean takes the bouquet in silent surprise. She stares down at it. Charlie had never brought her flowers before. On special occasions he would buy her books, explaining that he refused to be conned by the capitalism of transience and that she should feed her mind. Is this something human men do? Jean thinks suspiciously, smelling the delicate white bells dripping from thin stems. Or is he some sort of replicant?

'What are you thinking?' Gabriel says, as he tilts his chin towards the bartender, who clearly recognises him and slides a menu over.

'That the line between machine and man is both vast and profoundly thin,' Jean blurts out, paraprasing the film *A.I.* At least she didn't say that he reminds her of Jude Law's nihilistic pleasure unit, Gigolo Joe. Gabriel's eyebrows shoot up in surprise and he laughs.

'It is indeed,' Gabriel says, as he opens a menu under his nose. 'Do you care for a glass of champagne? Or do you prefer wine?'

'A glass of bubbly would be marvellous, thank you,' Jean says in a stilted accent, as she carefully nestles the flowers in her bag.

Getting ready at Danielle's place earlier that evening, her sister had thrust the dress in Jean's face and told her to calm her fucking tits.

'Here is some advice for you,' Danielle had said, speaking out of the corner of her mouth as she smoked, her hands twitching the dress into slinky perfection. 'You must embody the deep yet playful, open yet mysterious, exotic but familiar, fundamentally unknowable essence of the Divine Feminine.'

'What the hell is the Divine Feminine?' Jean had asked, baffled by how her sister could be simultaneously so harsh and so new age.

'A long and paradoxical list of qualities, which most women are incapable of performing at the same time,' Danielle had explained. 'It's just another way to fail, really.'

'Fabulous,' Jean muttered sarcastically. 'Divine Feminine sounds like a pheromone perfume concocted with smegma and patchouli.'

'I have some of that, if you like?' Danielle had grinned, nodding her head towards the broken door of her filthy houseboat toilet. 'This looks much better on you than its original owner. Her breasts were too bountiful. It's more elegant with a tiny B.'

'Great pep talk,' Jean had said. 'I will never do this again.'

'We'll take two glasses of the Ruinart *blanc de blancs*, Joseph,' Gabriel says to the bartender, in his element and on a first name basis with the staff. Jean shakes herself back to the present moment.

'So, tell me . . .' Jean says, her mouth hanging open, not having fully completed her thought process. The combination of the heat and Gabriel's steady gaze seem to have fried her brain. '*Cendrillon*. What's it about?'

'Are you familiar with Cinderella?' Gabriel asks in amusement, brushing his strawberry blond hair out of his eyes. With his bronzed, lightly freckled face, delicate bone structure and broad shoulders, Gabriel looks like a parody of Prince Charming himself.

'Yes. I meant, tell me about Massenet's version. The music is Wagner-esque, is it not?' Jean says, as she accepts the chilled glass Gabriel passes to her.

'Why, yes!' Gabriel says, pleased.

As the bell sounds to usher the audience inside, Jean breathes a sigh of relief she won't have to expand on the fragment of Wikipedia information she remembers.

'You're familiar with Wagner?' Gabriel asks, as he takes her arm and leads her up a gilded stairwell towards the Upper Circle. They emerge into an opulent expanse of gold fixtures and burgundy velvet seats, with a grandeur befitting its royal name. Jean wonders if the swish lifestyle he feels so comfortable within is due to his wife's money, or inherited.

'Familiar is a strong term,' Jean says under her breath, smiling with a vagueness appropriate for someone who until recently was convinced that Beethoven was Mozart's surname.

'What?' Gabriel asks, leaning in close. She can feel his breathe exhale against her jaw, the most erotic thing to be expelled out of a nostril, she believes, ever.

'Magnificent,' Jean says, as she pauses in the entryway to admire the stunning interiors of the Opera House. The tumbling waterfall of scarlet curtains in front of the stage speak of the lavishness of a bygone age, the pomp of kings and queens, a fairy tale alternate universe. If one knows where to look it is still present, a rich seam of ore running through the dirty mine of the capital. A middle-aged gentleman behind her coughs impatiently.

'Isn't it? I do prefer the Met, but only by a hair. And there is nothing quite like a Roman amphitheatre on a starlit night. Have you ever been to Verona?' Gabriel asks with sweet, boyish enthusiasm as he steers her to their seats.

He had apparently taken her at her word at the wedding that she loved opera. Jean had thought the lie transparent, if only because of her drunken admission mid-slutdrop that 'Stripped' was her favourite album, ever. He probably thought her musical taste multi-faceted. This would only be true if a vast difference could be detected between the opuses (or was it opii?) of Justin Bieber and Shawn Mendes.

'I have a confession to make,' Jean whispers. The strain of pretending she is familiar with one of the most exclusive and complex of cultural realms is too much for her nerves to handle. 'I've never been to the opera.'

'Oh?' Gabriel says, his eyebrows shooting up.

'I've never even listened to opera. Up until recently, I thought Amadeus was a small county. Like the ones wedged between Montenegro and Serbia,' Jean confesses as they sit down upon on plush red cushions.

'There aren't any countries wedged between Montenegro and Serbia,' Gabriel tells her, crossing his legs and leaning back to look at her, his eyes narrowed in amusement.

Jean, with a tinge of annoyance, begins to wonder if Gabriel enjoys her company because she is what her mother would describe as 'a dizzy so and so'. She certainly isn't coming across as mysterious or exotic, unless the borderline witless were so atypical in his circles as to be strangely fascinating.

'That was a joke!' Jean says defensively.

'I'm sorry, I didn't mean to make you feel small,' Gabriel replies, with such a pure, doe-eyed innocence that Jean immediately feels contrite. Gabriel smiles shyly, looking as if he is trying to find exactly the right words. 'I find you very . . . beguiling.'

'Oh,' Jean says, stunned into silence. Usually the adjectives used to describe her were much less enticing. She was sensible, dependable, highly prepared, or the dreaded colloquialism: a good egg, which Jean hopes will one day be excised from the English language. No one should have to suffer the suggestion that they have the personality of a chicken period.

'And I'm honoured to be the one to introduce you to it,' Gabriel says, taking her hand and stroking the knuckles as the curtain rises. He always knows the right thing to say. He is almost too perfect. Jean forgets this line of thought as the set reveals itself, a grand white living room inset with many doors. The hushes, in audible waves of appreciative silence. The orchestra starts. She smiles.

As the sumptuous music lulls her into a trance, the extravagant French baroque costumes expand before her like a dream. Initially, Jean finds the age of the singer playing Cendrillon disconcerting. The girlish lyrics are voiced by a soprano of at least forty-five, wearing a startlingly pigtailed wig. But as the actors dance and whirl through the familiar tale, she finds herself transported by the story of a servant elevated to the realms of a princess, if only for one night.

The audience claps wildly as the curtain sweeps down for the intermission, in front of Cendrillon placing one foot into her delicate glass slipper. Jean thinks of her own abused pumps used as a toilet, and nearly sheds a tear. She feels a sharp stab of rage against Charlie, for everything she put up with. Jean is not over him at all. In fact, she hates him, with all the passion of real love gone truly sour.

'Are you crying?' Gabriel asks, as Jean sniffles indelicately beside him.

'No,' Jean says, a tear rolling down one cheek. She wipes it away, horrified. 'Must be a dust mote.'

'I would have expected that for *Madama Butterfly*, but I didn't think you would be so moved by Cinderella,' Gabriel teases, taking her hand as they stand and slowly walk down the aisle towards the exit.

'I was thinking about my favourite shoes,' Jean laughs, as if she is not admitting the reality of her sad, sad life. It is embarrassing how hard she relates to a scullery maid who needs a coterie of magic mice and fantastical vegetables to lift her out of a life of exploitation.

'Same again?' Jean asks as they approach the bar. 'Thank you for the tickets.'

'My pleasure,' Gabriel says, stroking her face lightly. A jolt of electricity runs down her spine. Gabriel leans in, as if to kiss her. Before he is able to, his phone buzzes loudly.

'Oh! That must be Poppy,' Gabriel says casually, as he removes it from his back trouser pocket.

'Poppy?' Jean says stupidly, swaying on her feet, drunk with desire.

'My wife,' Gabriel reminds her. She had forgotten. Poppy. She repeats the word mentally, familiarising herself with the idea of her. Wife. Mustn't forget that detail.

'Do you want to FaceTime with us?' Gabriel asks, as Jean moves away to queue up.

'Why don't I get these drinks and then if you guys are still talking, I'll say hi!' Jean says, the sentence trailing off into an awkward squeak.

As Jean orders the *coups de champagne*, she reminds herself that this may be an old-fashioned date, but it is with a very modern man. In their world, nothing could be more normal than the wife and prospective lover having a friendly chat. She should be reassured that Gabriel offered; it lends credibility to the whole total honesty thing.

Jean decides to follow Gabriel's lead and say 'yes' in these matters. And to possibly do more research. There must be an XOJane.com article on how to make pleasant small talk with your date's spouse somewhere on the interwebs. Jean pays for the drinks, takes a deep breath, and searches out Gabriel armed with the flutes and beaming fake smile.

He is leaning against a far pillar, staring into his phone and laughing. Gabriel looks so natural and at ease, in a way he hasn't with Jean, or at least not yet. He catches her staring and waves her over, nodding his head at the screen.

'Poppy! This is Jean, the girl I told you about. We met at that Kent wedding gig,' Gabriel says, tilting his phone rather too close to Jean's face for comfort.

A silken blonde head in front of what must be the Hudson River and a view of Manhattan skyscrapers stares back at her, at what must be a close-up of Jean's chins and protruding nose. Jean leans away from the phone and waves with palpable fear.

Gabriel had told Jean that his wife works for Oscar de la Renta, but if Poppy were a brand, she would be Isabel Marant. Natural, luxe, bohemian. If Jean were a brand, she suspects she would be Clarks. Practical, inexpensive, durable. The sort of shoe you could run over with a van and would spring right back into shape.

'Hiiiii,' Poppy says cheerfully through a bright white smile. She has sparkling blue eyes, a deep tan, hair the colour of wheat and a gluten-free body. The sort of woman so confident of her husband's eternal love, she lets him have free reign across the ocean.

'So weird to meet you,' Jean blurts out in Freudian slip, before slapping her hand over her mouth.

'You're right, she's funny,' Poppy laughs, flicking a lock of her hair back. Jean's stomach flip-flops oddly at the thought of them discussing her as a couple. Poppy turns her phone to pan over the shining water and then back around to a hipster dock bar in front of a series of warehouses. 'Here I am by the river in Greenpoint! Isn't it beautiful?'

'Stunning!' Jean says, in a voice as sunny and bright as Poppy's view, impersonating someone for whom this situation is the most normal thing in the world. 'What beautiful weather.'

'Are you enjoying *Cendrillon*?' Poppy asks once back in focus, squinting into the sun, her little nose wrinkling like a bunny.

'It's beautiful!' Jean says, trying desperately to think of something apart from boring platitudes to say. 'It's my first time.'

In the back of Jean's mind, one thought whirrs incessantly. Into how much detail will Gabriel's total honesty go, when they wind up in bed?

'It's everyone's first time once,' Poppy says with an odd smile.

Gabriel muffles a chuckle, as Jean's face flushes fuchsia.

Poppy and Gabriel have similar features and colouring, similar mannerisms, Jean observes as she watches them interact. They could play siblings. On *Baywatch*. In comparison to their lean Nordic beauty, Jean feels as squat and sexy as a Hobbit.

'So lovely chatting to you. I'm dying for a wee, just going to dash to the toilet while there's still time,' Jean says, nodding her head frantically at a follow-up question that is not forthcoming. To Gabriel she says, 'I'll meet you inside!'

'Sure,' he replies, caught off guard.

Jean power walks towards the sign for the ladies' loo. In the queue of the plush toilets, Jean turns on her phone. Twenty-four WhatsApp messages, three texts, ten missed calls from Jez and one million emails, all from work in the last hour.

Two of the texts are from her mum, asking: 'When will we see you?' and 'When will you visit again?' The last thing Jean wants is to feel Door's unspoken disappointment in the failure of yet another LTR, or massage the truth about her current dating situation. Door is not so much conservative as she is a convent-educated Edwardian prude, unhappily trapped in the twenty-first century. As for her father, well, Jean has flatly refused to see him again until he apologises.

The other is from Danielle, asking: 'How's life on the wild(ish) side?'

So patronising. It's not like it takes a special skillset to get invited to sex parties as a single lady. From Jean's research, you only need to turn up.

The emails and missed calls from work, Jean leaves for tomorrow morning. She has not bent under Jez's daily power struggle over her set working hours, and he seems to begrudgingly respect her for it. Jean scrolls through the Thread: Revolution! messages sent by Richard (saved lovingly in Jean's phone as: Dickface) and Tess (who saved herself under the alter ego: MeiQween).

MeiQween:

have you shagged him yet

🦅 🍆 🐿

Dickface:

She's at the opera.

MeiQween:
there are toilets everywhere

Dickface:
Opera-toilet shagging is tenth anniversary material.

For millionaires.

MeiQween:
pleb-exclusionary, richard

Dickface:
Do you feel more like Cher, or Julia? Is he wearing a suit?

MeiQween:
is he wearing a rubber

Dickface:
Must you always lower the tone

MeiQween:
yes

slag

Dickface:
She's an erotic adventuress.

MeiQween:
😶

how adorbs is Fynn

[photo of her son almost entirely covered by a cardboard box]

Dickface:
Why's he hiding. Do you beat him?

MeiQween:
dunno my mum took it

i just convinced charlotte crosby she doesn't need a 3rd nose job

god i hate my life

Dickface:
Don't worry, you'll be fired soon.

MeiQween:

omg guys

ive actually just been fired

Jean gasps as she finally enters the toilet cubicle and locks it behind her. Tess had poured all her savings into the shop and intended to keep working reception on weekdays, while her mum manned Pussy Willows. Without the extra cash to fall back on, Tess will have to make an immediate killing to stay open.

Jean types a response with one hand as she pushes her knickers down with the other and sits on the loo.

Jean:
are you ok???

84

MeiQween:

im ok

cant tell if im in shock or pleased

maybe this is 👍

ill have to make Pussy Willows WERK

werk werk

Dickface:

Where are you?

MeiQween:

gone home to kill myself

Jean:

anxious toilet selfie

Not shagging

I met his wife by FaceTime

Dickface:

???

MeiQween:

wot 4 y

Jean:

gtg deets laters

By the time Jean returns to her seat, she has regained her composure. Rome wasn't built in a day, and nor could her subconscious be freed of ideas like 'cheating' and 'marital fidelity' in the space of one evening. The betrayed and vengeful spouse is an archetype as old as agriculture, when nomadic man became stationary, woman became chattel, and ideas of love as ownership first arose. According to Danielle anyway, who had pressed a copy of *Sex at Dawn* into Jean's hands when she came round earlier with the words, 'Set yourself free.'

Jean hadn't started reading it, but from the blurb on the back it was an evolutionary biology argument for boundless, sharing, tribal love being the natural order of things throughout pre-history. Which sounded very reasonable, although Jean had to confess that in any random selection of 150 people (the average size of nomadic bands), she would probably find 0–3 individuals in any way sexually enticing. Perhaps monogamy wasn't so much an institution of patriarchy, as a sensible pair division based on the age-old question: 'Who here do I *actually* want to bone?' in a time before vodka.

The lights go down and the curtain rises by the time Gabriel finally walks down the aisle and into his chair. Unlike the first half, Jean finds it increasingly difficult to shut off her mind. It takes all her attention to focus on the whirling Baroque dervish of the ball scene. She is distracted by a vague unsettled feeling, not guilt or anxiety but something adjacent to them. The second half passes in a blur and before she knows it, the curtain falls. Rise. Wild applause. The performers take their bows. Once, twice. A third time. The clapping escalates. The curtain falls again.

'Shall we go for a walk?' Gabriel asks with a shy smile as the curtain rises. Jean nods, gathering her bag and wits, as he leads her down the winding staircase towards the exit. As they spill out onto the street, a crisp breeze blows through the dark violet night, strung up with stars. A hotwire runs through her, desire and something else, electric.

Jean inhales deeply, wondering why it is that Gabriel's more introverted nature has tipped her emotions into the hyper-reactive. With Charlie, she realises, she was always so swept along by his unpredictable current that she never really experienced how she felt, moment to moment. She had spun within his realm of distractions. With Gabriel, she felt very present, dizzy within the stillness of herself. It is a not entirely comfortable sensation.

As they follow the Georgian buildings towards Shaftsbury Avenue, Gabriel whistles a tune from the performance under his breath. Jean fights the urge to blurt out something, anything, to fill the silence. Until she can't resist, saying the first thing that comes to mind.

'Do you miss her a lot?'

Gabriel purses his lips in consideration.

'Of course. But we're used to it. We've been friends and lovers for so long that whether together or apart, our lives blend together seamlessly,' Gabriel responds.

Jean usually gags when men, or anyone really, uses the word 'lovers'. Apart from those rare occasions when they are simultaneously channelling the high camp of Jim Carrey in *The Mask*, or doing a spot-on Bette Davis impersonation. Yet Gabriel somehow manages to make it sound unaffected.

'Do you miss Charlie?'

Jean bites her lip. She would miss Charlie if she allowed herself to think about Charlie. In the way that suddenly unfollowing someone on social media means not that you want them out of your life, but that you can't bear to be reminded of their continued existence without you. She has cut him out of her heart with the swiftness and dexterity of Danny Trejo in *Machete* and refuses to look down to assess the wound.

Of course, she'll have to think of something rather more pleasant to say to Gabriel, to disguise her mounting bitterness and the occasional revenge fantasy that pops into her mind with the power of a flash flood.

'It's all too fresh to really miss him, you know?' Jean says after a pause. 'Maybe I will when everything . . .'

'Settles?' Gabriel asks politely. It is funny how quickly it becomes normal, talking about other loves, past and present.

The lingering anxiety Jean felt over his marriage dissipates. If she is going to do this, she will have to take him at his word. She will also need to find a second love interest herself, sharpish. Having fallen hard before for men who were charmless, mean or unremarkable in every way, Jean knows that if she isn't going to get hurt, she will need to add multiples to her rotation.

'Rotation' is a new word, gleaned from Danielle, for her dating harem.

'I'm happy though. I feel liberated!' Jean says, lifting her arms up and doing a twirl. Gabriel catches her elbows in his arms as she stops, drawing her closer to him.

Jean smiles and ducks her head as they pause in front of an overspill of flowers, on the shadowy pavement in front of The Cross Keys pub.

'I'm glad,' Gabriel says, leaning towards her. They had been meandering directionless. As his gaze caresses her lips, Jean's hands start to shake.

'Shall we get a pint?' Jean says breathlessly, nodding her head towards the pub. 'I'm parched.'

'Sure,' Gabriel says, dropping her elbows and taking a step back uncertainly. He gets a pack of cigarettes out of his back pocket, offering her one.

Jean declines.

'You take me to the opera, I take you to Wetherspoons,' Jean says. 'I'll get these, what do you want?'

'Whatever you're having.' Gabriel shrugs as he lights up. Her nervousness has accidentally lead Jean to play it cool, dipping out of his touch, talking about his wife, running away to the toilet, running away to the bar.

'I hope you like cider,' Jean calls over her shoulder as she walks away. It is packed with a Thursday night scrum starting their weekend of sun and fun early.

Whether it is because she is too quiet or she has some mutant ability to disappear into a crowd, Jean is habitually ignored whenever she tries to order a drink. Determined to be served in a timely fashion, she leans heavily onto the burnished wood and follows the barman's every move with the intensity of a serial killer on the prowl.

'Yes?' He asks her, after less than one minute, clearly unnerved. Result!

'I'll have two pints of Aspalls please,' she says.

As he pours their drinks, a man and two women's conversation next to her catches Jean's attention.

'Worse than that "Boy George rent-boy chained to the radiator" thing!'

'What is a fungeon anyway? It sounds like a fish.'

'A fun dungeon.'

'It's kink for pussies. Like merry waterboarding. Or a tranquil rack.'

Jean accepts the first pint of cider and sips, stifling a laugh.

'A tranquil rack is what I pay my chiropractor three hundred pound an hour for.'

'Apparently he has a collection of ball-stretchers and vibrating testicle stimulators to rival Ann Summers.'

'Is Ann Summers still a thing? Surely everyone buys toys online.'

'There's one on my high street. But it has a very Marks and Spencer vibe.'

'I wonder if Whole Foods do edible knickers.'

'Where did he keep this stuff? Some sort of sex bunker on his wife's estate?'

'According to the *Sun* he has a private party place in London, apart from his main residence.'

'If he's got a fur-handcuff flat, why on earth did he bother cruising on the Heath? What's the point of being rich if you can't order in?' one of the women asks in bafflement.

At this Jean chokes on her cider, her eyes goggling out of her skull, remembering the millions of emails she'd ignored, the missed phone calls from the office.

'To my knowledge, Deliveroo don't do escorts. I'm sure he could afford a dirty sex takeaway, but there's something to be said for the hunt. Fresh air. Uncertainty,' the man is saying to the women, who look annoyed. 'The sting of a rejection, the thrill of a smile.'

He is clearly a fan of catcalling.

'Excuse me,' Jean says, turning towards them. 'I couldn't help but overhear . . . who are you talking about?'

'Lord Kinder,' all three answer in unison.

'It just broke on Twitter,' the man adds. 'Hashtag MaleToo.'

'Thank you,' Jean squeaks, her throat closing like a vice.

While she had been flirting at the opera, her client's balls were on the line. Which evidently he enjoyed, but not in so public a fashion. Jean closes her eyes and wonders if both she and Tess will both be sacked on the same day. They did often have significant life events that were weirdly in sync. Like the time they sent each other photographs of their gigantic Christmas dinner log poos within nanoseconds.

But there were other explanations than cosmic unity for that, such as a shared love of *South Park*.

Shit! Shit shit shit. Jean takes a huge gulp of her pint and shimmies through the crowd to join Gabriel. She'll have to run to the office for crisis control.

'Are you alright?' Gabriel asks solicitously. 'You look a bit pale.'

'I'm fine,' Jean says, taking another glug of her cider before setting it down on a window ledge, distracted. 'Listen, I—'

'Before you say anything, I have something to tell you,' Gabriel says.

He takes a sip of his pint and sets it beside hers on the ledge. He takes her hands in his, before running his fingers up her arms until they are lightly resting on her neck. Jean can feel that magnetic pull again between them, drawing her close to him. Her mind goes blank, the oddest feeling brewing in the pit of her stomach, like she'd been sharply punched and enjoyed it.

'Yes?' Jean says, as Gabriel trails off, his face coming closer towards hers.

His lips meet hers softly at first, lightly pressing against her with the delicacy of a flower being brushed against her skin. His hand runs up the back of her skull, massaging her neck, as Jean goes as limp as a ragdoll cat. Her knees are weak, her body slack yet bound tight with desire, her nerves sparking with electricity. His mouth tastes sharp and sweet, the hint of nicotine setting off a long-dormant addictive power.

Her hands rise to capture his face, feeling the beginnings of a five o'clock shadow on his smooth skin, up into his hair, as soft and silken as a girl's. As he deepens the kiss, the hips of his jeans press into the softness of her stomach beneath the thin fabric of her dress, and Jean lets out a moan.

She pulls away, takes a moment to breath, unnerved by the energy coursing through her. She feels like Frankenstein, moments after reanimation by lightning.

'Is that all you have to say?' Jean asks through a dazed laugh.

'Yes,' Gabriel says through a half smile, before kissing her again, pressing her back towards the wall of the pub. Jean hears bystanders laughing, probably staring. They are making a spectacle of themselves. She is lulled into a trance again, by his tongue, his skin, his scent. Her senses fade away, retract to the prism of their bodies melding.

'What were you saying?' Gabriel asks, as he pulls back to look deeply into her eyes, kissing the edge of her jaw, up to that sensitive bit below her ear. He breaths on it, nibbles her earlobe.

'I have to go,' Jean says breathlessly, pushing him back with her hands.

Gabriel stares at her blankly, blinking over and over, like one of the women in the *My Dad Wrote A Porno* podcast.

'Where?' he asks, as if nothing could possibly take precedence over this perfect moment. Which would be true, in a parallel universe in which her employment wasn't about to be terminated due to a sado-masochistic fungeon escapade gone awry.

'The office,' Jean says, straightening her dress, all bunched up around the tops of her thighs and hips. Her hair has been massaged into a bird's nest. She reaches into her purse for her phone and orders an Uber with one hand as she babbles an explanation to Gabriel. 'I overheard at the bar, one of my clients has been accused of sexual harassment. Again. It's just broken. I haven't been checking my emails after hours, but if I don't sort this I'll be fired.'

'I see,' Gabriel says, his disappointment adorably undisguised. 'Well, I had an amazing night—'

'Me too!' Jean says, kissing him quickly on the cheek and grasping his hand in a hurried goodbye. 'My car's here! Let's do it again sometime.'

Jean runs into the taxi checking her Twitter feed, the magic of their evening at the opera dissipating in a puff of pervert smoke, as she descends into the quagmire of Lord Kinder's formerly secret sex life.

Chapter Six

The Uber pulls up round the back of Liverpool Street Station and Jean dashes into the glass office block she had exited just hours before, waving to the receptionist as she runs to the lift. It is 11.30 p.m. As she opens the heavy wooden door beneath a gold plaque with Addington Media Agency embossed upon it, she sees Cynthia, still at her desk. Ten years older, with two kids under five, Cynthia is technically her subordinate but only really answers to Jez. She types fretfully in the empty dark office, lit only by the blue light of her computer.

Jean flips on the main lights, illuminating what looks like a miniature set from *Mad Men*. It is all angular 1950s wooden furniture, long brown couches, posters of Chet Baker and Miles Davis (like many middle-aged borderline psychopaths, Jez is a fan of soothing jazz), red velvet armchairs, and gigantic glass ashtrays he and his favourite clients continue to use despite the smoking ban. Jean breathes a sigh of relief. She got there first.

'Cynthia! Thank god. Have you seen Jez? I've rang him five times, but my calls keep going to voicemail,' Jean says, flinging her bag on a sofa and turning on her computer.

'He's on his way,' Cynthia says, as she continues to type. 'He's *very* upset with you.'

'Is he with Lord Kinder?' Jean asks, wondering how the hell she will pay the rent if she is fired. She has no savings.

More credit card debt than she would like to admit to. Student loans. She always seems to live five per cent above her means, but for the life of her she can't work out what she spends it on, apart from food, wine and taxis.

'Yes,' Cynthia explains helpfully.

Although Cynthia bears the distinction of being even more submissive than Jean, she is leagues preferable to their former co-worker, Charlize. Charlize had the crafty eyes of a fox on the make and Jean had learned never to trust her with any funny stories, lest they be warped into the pathetic or strange and broadcast to all.

Jean checks her reflection in the light of her computer screen. Her lipstick is smudged below her lips, her mascara flaking on her cheeks, a reminder of the heat from her perfect, abandoned date. She licks her finger and rubs away the residue.

'I'll take it from here. Why don't you go home and put Sid and Nancy to bed?' Jean suggests, walking to Cynthia's station and squeezing her shoulder.

Cynthia is so sheltered that she has unintentionally named her children after the most destructive love affair of the punk scene, and no one has had the heart to tell her.

'They'll already be asleep,' Cynthia sighs. 'Thank god for my Paul.'

'Then go home to Paul,' Jean says. 'Don't worry, I can handle him.'

'Oh, I'd better not without Jez's say-so,' Cynthia says, looking up at Jean with big, sweet, brown cow-eyes. Jean stares back as if into a mirror of her future. Overworked, exhausted, rarely seeing her family, yet bizarrely loyal to the enterprise.

Her phone beeps. She looks down in dread. It is from the last person she expected.

A moment of pointless triumph. He loves her still. Ha! Jean blocks his number.

Both women stiffen in fear as the door swings open to reveal their boss, followed by Lord Kinder. When Jean had started Jez looked rather like Gabriel Byrne, but after years of bad habits and shaving his goatee, he looks more like Gérard Depardieu.

'Jean,' Jez says through narrowed eyes, his lips drawn into a thin, unrelenting line. 'I was saying to Lord Kinder not two moments ago that if you weren't here before our arrival, your head would be upon the chopping block. Cynthia, you're still here.'

Jean laughs nervously, the mention of torture devices reminding her of Lord Kinder's indiscretions. According to the media, the cage fighter moonlighting as a male escort had refused to use a spiked truncheon upon Lord Kinder's back, fearing he'd kill the older man. Enraged, Lord Kinder had tricked the young man into a cupboard where he locked him for five hours. Upon his eventual release, Lord Kinder refused to pay for his services, citing false advertising.

'I wouldn't miss an emergency PR pow-wow for the world!' Cynthia exclaims.

'You're a star, Cynthia,' Jez says, staring solemnly into her eyes as he sits on her desk. 'I don't know how I would ever get on without you.'

And there it was. The magic crumb that kept his female employees psychologically bound to him in a Stockholm Syndrome whirlpool of daddy issues.

'But I simply won't have you stay a moment longer. You get home to your family now, pet,' Jez murmurs, before glaring up at Jean. 'Jean will stay as long as it takes.'

'This is more than an emergency. It's a travesty!' Lord Kinder booms, in a voice used to ordering around servants, his wife, members of parliament and imprisoned rent boys. 'My name must be cleared of all charges!'

'Of course, Lord Kinder. Come this way,' Jean says in her best nanny-voice, as she leads them into Jez's private office.

She turns on the lamp, opens the shutters, fetches the box of Cuban cigars and pours two large whiskies with calming efficiency. The men sit on giant leather armchairs, staring into a disused fireplace with the tragic gravitas of Churchill contemplating his 'We shall fight on the beaches' speech.

'Mendacity! Embezzlement! Exploitation! Blackmail!' Lord Kinder says into his whisky. The swivelling whites of his eyes and the trembling of his fat fingers belie his fighting words. 'Who could believe such an *abominable* tale?'

'No one with any sense,' Jez says, with the hard-bitten stare of a man whose only professional requirement is to be a liar as convincing as he is compulsive. 'Your longstanding reputation as a man of honour and family values will stand you in good stead in the press.'

'It certainly will,' Jean nods sycophantically.

'A despicable tale spun by my enemies, who must have put the boy up to it . . . my nemeses at Parliament . . . dark machinations . . . out to ruin me and my reputation . . .'

Lord Kinder continues to mutter about plots of ruination, clearly hoping the word of an honourable lord against that of a sex worker will win in the court of public opinion. It is moments like this that Jean wonders if Danielle is right, and she is indeed a stooge for Lucifer. Maybe it's not too late to do something meaningful with her life. She could retrain as a nurse. Or a primary school teacher.

'So, I should inform the press of your categorical denial of events?' Jean asks with hesitation. It will make their job that much harder if he refuses to tell them the truth. 'There were many intimate details of the flat, as well as intimate details of your . . . figure . . . that the young man attested to, which correlate to pictures online.'

'If you were able to find out that information at such short notice, then so would the boy in his plot to frame Lord Kinder,' Jez points out with a glare.

'Of course, forgive me,' Jean says, with the docile servitude of Igor.

With one sentence, Jez had made her purpose at this meeting clear. She is to act as moral support, feminine comfort, Matron-meets-maid for the wounded ego of a man watching his life go up in flames. She will gather and file away information in silence, to strategise at a later date.

'Now, my P.I. has dug up prior criminal offenses by your accuser . . .' Jez continues.

Jean pulls up a chair next to them and makes soothing noises at the right moments, injecting short phrases of praise on autopilot, as the men talk. She tries desperately hard not to think about how Charlie might have continued the conversation, had she not deleted him from her phone and therefore life. After an hour of this, the conversation going around in circles, bored out of her skull and in need of a distraction, Jean downloads Thrinder. She creates a profile, while pretending to take notes on her phone.

The men rant about the evils of the free press, the regretful impossibility of a super-injunction, of his inability to sue and the likelihood of divorce, evading any and all questions about his culpability. Meanwhile, Jean instigates a flirtation with a pansexual yoga-teacher couple under the table.

JeanGenie DM:
omg!! SO beaut. Where is that?

Their photos show them in a series of impossibly bendy positions on beaches in far-flung island destinations across the globe. Places Jean would love to visit, once she gets out of this prison of misogyny she has somehow made her life's work, for a reliable pay-check and random ego-affirming lashings of praise. She hopes her messages are not dripping in desperation, her self-loathing apparent in her excessive use of emojis and demented enthusiasm.

'Deny, deny, deny,' Jez says to Lord Kinder as he walks him to the lift hours later, Jean trailing behind them. Jez presses the button and waits for the door to open. 'Your name will be cleared of the muck, I promise you.'

'Thank you, old sport,' Lord Kinder says, one eye shining with a tiny tear of gratitude. They had done such a convincing impersonation of believing the marvellous tale he'd concocted, he is deluded the rest of the world will also buy it. 'Excellent work. I'll call you tomorrow.'

'Do, do,' Jez says, patting him on the back as he spirits him into the lift.

The doors close.

'Deny?' Jean repeats, as the old man disappears into the mechanical ether.

'He's fucked,' Jez says, lighting a cigarette and rubbing his forehead in exhaustion. 'We're all fucked.'

'How long do you think it will take him to come around to admitting sex addiction, childhood abuse and/or alcoholism?' Jean asks, the questions so rote that she only belatedly realises how awful it is to have to ask.

'I'd give it till Monday. He's stubborn, but there's more to this story yet to come,' Jez says with the fatalism of a man who has defended the dregs of humanity for decades. Then, he claps her on the shoulder and flashes her one of his most rare and charming of smiles. 'Well done tonight, Jean. You have almost redeemed yourself.'

And quite against her will, Jean's pulse gives a little leap of pleasure.

Chapter Seven

'There's *more* to the story to come? How much worse can it get!' Danielle asks in outrage, as Jean finishes telling her about Lord Kinder's ludicrous denials. They step out of North Dulwich train station into a crisp Saturday evening. Although Pussy Willow's first official day will be on Monday, Tess is hosting a soft opening for friends, family and locals to enjoy complimentary libations and a 10 per cent discount on bouquets.

'It can always get worse!' Jean sighs, taking her sister's arm as they cross the road and march towards Dulwich Village.

'Explain to me again why you haven't found another job?'

'I've had so much emotional upheaval, I can't cope with more change right now,' Jean says defensively. 'Charlie's dramas completely took over my life the past three years, I'm only just finding myself again. It's well-paid work that I'm good at, even if for the worser-ment of humanity. And as much as Jez can be a dick, he can also be very kind and generous at unexpected moments!'

'Sometimes when I hear you speak, all I hear is "I'm a coward", over and over,' Danielle says.

'Fine! I'm a coward. I concede that,' Jean huffs.

Although flower shops aren't Danielle's usual scene, Jean has felt closer to her of late. She had invited her hoping they could continue to reconnect over that quintessential form of female bonding: bad men and cheap liquor. It is not quite going to plan.

'I read a study on rats recently and thought of you,' Danielle says.

'I would say go on, but I know you will.'

'It's a variable-ratio reinforcement study done by Skinner. When rats press a lever and are consistently rewarded with food, at first they press it over and over. Then they lose interest. Certainty kills the reward drive. However!' Danielle stabs one grubby fingernail in the air. 'If the food is given at random intervals, inconsistently, even if the reward is not given for days and days on end. The rats *never*. Stop pressing. The lever.'

Danielle stops in her tracks, looking at Jean significantly.

'So?' Jean asks, annoyed. 'I'm not a fucking rat.'

'I have just handed you the key to unlocking your broken brain,' Danielle says, shaking her head in disbelief. 'And you are too blind to see it.'

'I told you I'm going to look for a new job! What more do you want from me?' Jean shouts in exasperation.

'Are you sure about that?' Danielle asks, checking her phone distractedly.

'Yes! After summer, when I've paid off some bills and employers don't immediately associate Addington Media with Lord Kinder and fungeons.'

'If you say so,' Danielle says.

Jean tries to bury the familiar whoosh of resentment. While Danielle had gallivanted off living her ridiculous nomad life, Jean had been the one forced to stay and soothe Door's nervous breakdowns and her father's temper. Jean had blamed Danielle for leaving, for not staying to suffer alongside her, as if the only noble option was martyrdom in the name of family. However, she is starting to suspect that the only way off the carousel of doom is to jump, to run, to never look back.

'Doesn't it look beautiful!' Jean gushes to Danielle, changing the subject as they near a chic young crowd milling around the Pussy Willows entrance.

The neon lilac storefront is covered in lush foliage and fairy lights. Simone's cat portrait hangs from brass knobs above large glass window panes, behind which lie colourful kitten playground emporiums Tess had constructed by hand. With a flower shop in the back where clients can browse for plants and bouquets, and little wicker chairs in the interior to play with the kittens and flip through *The Second Sex*, Pussy Willows is a gloriously camp, feminist haven.

'Stunning,' Danielle says, shaking her long fringe out of her piercing blue eyes. She is wearing her uniform of flares, Converse, a thin T-shirt and no bra, but tonight her usually cucumber-cool presence is replaced by the twitchy, agitated air of a squirrel.

As they enter the shop, Jean admires the bookshelves devoted entirely to women writers, the cat-rainbow-sky muralled ceiling, and walls papered with posters of iconic singers from Billie Holiday to Blondie. Glorious bunches of peonies and chrysanthemums spill over the till, behind which buckets of pre-arranged blooms beg to be bought. Patti Smith blares out of pink retro speakers. From the excited chatter of the crowd, almost entirely composed of women and gay men, the opening is already a smash hit.

'I've joined Thrinder . . .' Jean says, as Danielle picks up a long-stemmed rose and sniffs it, without expression.

'Why limit yourself to two?' Danielle says, putting down the flower to check the messages on her phone. The mobile is a recent and unexpected addition. Danielle has always contested that her ultimate dream is to be contactable only by carrier pigeon.

'I'm not limiting myself, I'm experimenting! I figure if I'm going to keep seeing Gabriel, I need to find other love interests as well.'

Although Jean had been too consumed with the clusterfuck at work to maintain any sort of bantz, Gabriel had been in touch with comforting regularity.

'Smart cookie,' Danielle says automatically. 'Never give more than what you take.'

'I've been talking to a couple who teach yoga all over the world, they want to meet up when they get back from Brazil in two weeks,' Jean says, waiting for her sister to pipe up with loud instruction on how to make a woman scream with ecstasy.

But tonight, Danielle is strangely subdued.

'Frederickkk', Tess belts out, strumming an air guitar, wearing ripped black jeans and her favourite Prince shirt. After she finishes headbanging, she spies Jean and Danielle and rushes over with two glasses of cava.

'Congratulations my love!' Jean squeals as she hands Tess a card and kisses her on both cheeks. 'I knew it would look wonderful, but this surpasses everything. It's like if Gertrude Stein gate-crashed Frida Kahlo's surrealist Dolly Parton wet dream. Plus cats!'

'That's exactly the vibe I was going for!' Tess laughs, before clocking Jean's sister. 'Danielle! Oh my god, it's been years. You look fantastic!'

'Not like Jane Birkin if she spent the last decade smoking crack?' Danielle says with an aggressive lift to her eyebrow and a flip of her, yes, very Jane-Birkin-by-way-of-the-crackhouse hair. Tess looks from Danielle to Jean, bewildered.

'Tess never said that. That was Charlie,' Jean reminds Danielle, mortified. She had forgotten her sister's complete disregard for the social graces. Danielle relaxes instantly.

'Oh sorry. Gorgeous shop!' Danielle coos, kissing Tess on both cheeks. 'I'd buy a kitten, but I don't believe in enslaving animals for my own amusement.'

'I wouldn't call them . . . enslaved . . .' Tess says with an odd smile, doubtless thinking of the hours it took her to construct what amounts to a feline Alton Towers in the windows.

'Tess is doing an amazing thing by helping a local animal adoption charity to display their newest arrivals for them!' Jean says, elbowing Danielle in her skinny ribs. Danielle smiles on cue and starts rolling a cigarette with one hand.

'Animal charities are all the same. Imprisoned or executed, but where are the roaming bands of wild dogs and free felines?' Danielle says under her breath as she licks the rolling paper, her eyes flickering back and forth suspiciously.

She places the cigarette behind her ear for later consumption and stalks off.

'She's in a weird mood tonight,' Jean explains to Tess.

'You've said that every time I've met her,' Tess says. 'Which is, like, four times in fifteen years.'

'That infrequent?' Jean says in surprise. She watches her sister browse the store, picking up and then abandoning items as soon as they are in her grasp, sweeping flowers against her cheek, checking her phone again, and again. 'She's usually weird, but not weird in *this way*.'

'Tell that bitch that if she talks about exploiting the animal kingdom to any of my clients, I'll kick her out,' Tess says through her teeth as she smiles hugely and waves to a new guest. 'Oh, Charlotte came! And she doesn't look like she's melting. I must say hi.'

As Tess bounces to meet and greet, Jean continues to watch Danielle mope, puzzled. Danielle sticks her head in a vase full of anemones, before her phone buzzes against her hip pocket and she startles into a skittish leap. She checks her messages again, reads them with a grin, grimaces with a spasm of embarrassment and responds as quickly as her ham-fisted phone poking will allow. She returns to Jean's side with a beatific smile on her face, as if given a gift, or granted a reprieve.

'What is *wrong* with you?' Jean asks, deeply unnerved by her sister's behaviour.

'Jean,' Danielle says, seizing her hand and drawing her away into a corner. She lowers her voice, looking shiftily from side to side. 'I have something to confess.'

'For fuck's sake, I told you not to take any drugs tonight,' Jean says, annoyed. She points and swirls her index finger at Danielle's head, her expression taut with conflicting terror and happiness. 'Is this the face of meth?'

'Far worse!' Danielle winces, peeking through her fingers as if covered in disfiguring smallpox. 'I think . . . I'm . . . in . . . love?'

After a moment of stunned silence, the words sink in.

Jean bursts into hysterical laughter.

'No need to mock my wretchedness,' Danielle hisses, plucking the petals from a daisy before biting the beheaded stem. 'I've never felt so pathetic.'

'Sorry, this is too good. I am free as an emotionally liberated bird and here you are, an idiot pining over some stupid romance. What a delightful reversal in fortune!' Jean grins, before becoming concerned as her sister stress-eats the flower. 'You'll have to pay for that, you know.'

Danielle spits the half-masticated daisy on the floor.

'It's *horrible!*'

'Flowers aren't for eating, Danielle. So, who's the lucky girl? Or fellow . . .s . . . or neutral gender pronoun?' Jean asks, sipping on her lukewarm cava. She grimaces. Tess is clearly too skint to give out anything but the most poisonous of Tesco's Finest.

'His name. Is Harry,' Danielle says, taking breathy pauses as if she is about to have a panic attack. 'He's thirty-four. He treats me like a queen. And I'm crazy.'

'About . . . him?' Jean asks, unsettled by her sister's intensity. Danielle grips Jean's arm with zombie-like fierceness.

'*Crazy!*'

'Hookaayy Danielle I get it, you have a boyfriend—'

'He's not my boyfriend!' Danielle practically shrieks.

'Are you sleeping with anyone else?' Jean asks in amusement.

'No,' Danielle glares back defiantly.

'Right. Exclusive non-labelling,' Jean says, rolling her eyes. When would this fear of commitment end? She imagines Danielle in her mid-seventies, telling a younger lover of fifty-five that she doesn't believe in being boxed in by mere words.

'And he's a,' Danielle whispers in a tiny voice that Jean has to press her eardrum into her sister's chin to hear, 'property developer.'

'Moneybags! That's off-brand.' Usually the men in Danielle's life were couch-surfing transients, professional skip-divers with no bank account.

'You don't understand. He's a suit-wearing former rugger-bugger, country casual on weekends,' Danielle says, seeming as if she's about to weep.

Jean grins. After a lifetime of ménage-à-trois, orgies and lesbian flings, at the grand old age of thirty-seven, Danielle has finally found herself out of her comfort zone. Madly in love with the type of man their parents would adore. Given that Jean has been continuously derided for her safe choices for decades, the irony is delicious.

'Buenas noches bitches!' Richard says as he arrives, kissing Jean on both cheeks. When he catches sight of Danielle, still clutching her face in full emotional cripple mode, he pulls back with alarm. 'What happened to you?'

'She's in love,' Jean says, as Danielle shushes her.

'My condolences,' Richard says with total sincerity. 'May your heartbreak be, if not insubstantial, then swift.'

'She's not heartbroken. They're still together!'

'Traitress! Everyone has functioning relationships but me,' Richard complains with a flounce, as he picks up a scented candle and sniffs it. 'Never fear, I have a diabolical plan.'

'He's a property developer named Harry, who owns and wears a suit,' Jean explains to Richard, who immediately understands the source of Danielle's distress.

'A human with their shit together. Beware of those. They draw you in with pretty phrases like, "Yes, I'd love to live with you, Richard!" and then disappear after you tell them you had a divine vision of all your past lives together,' Richard says with a bitterness that is excruciating to hear. 'But my worm will turn . . .'

'What does that mean?' Jean asks Richard in confusion.

'The problem with Harry is, he has a heart of gold,' Danielle interrupts, eager to continue talking about him now that she's got going. 'And a perfectly absurd sense of humour. His wealth does disgust my principals, but he is an excellent tipper. For now, the sex might be fantastic, but what does this mean for my future? Domestic entrapment will ruin my reputation, my career!'

Danielle has worked herself into a frenzy of fear, envisioning her sex show being derided as emotionally fraudulent in a think piece on some obscure AnarchaFem corner of the internet, read by at most five hundred people.

'Take heart, the property market is due for an implosion. No need to catastrophise an infatuation with a kind, rich man,' Jean says comfortingly, stroking Danielle's arm. 'With any luck, he'll be impoverished within the year.'

'Do you think so?' Danielle says, perking up.

'My worm will turn!' Richard repeats dramatically, attention-seeking after his blatant conversational bypass.

'If "worm" is what you call your penis, I'm not surprised Anne bolted,' Jean says.

'It's an expression used to convey that even the most docile of creatures will retaliate or seek revenge if pushed too far,' Richard says superciliously, having clearly been at the Wikipedia. 'It was first recorded in a 1546 collection of proverbs by John Heywood, phrased: "Treade a worme on the tayle, and it must turne agayne."'

'Promise me you're not going to stalk her,' Jean pleads.

'Anne is dead to me,' Richard sniffs. 'As living well is the best revenge, I'm going to become the most thoroughly debauched, lascivious lout since Casanova.'

Jean and Danielle burst out laughing. Tess, intrigued, joins them.

'What are you talking about?'

'Richard is becoming a sexual degenerate.'

Tess laughs uproariously for a full sixty seconds, until her left eye runs with tears.

'Sorry. That's the best thing I've heard all month.'

'You'll see!' Richard says, storming off into the crowd.

'Is Zhang here?' Jean asks Tess, accepting a top up of cava. 'This drink is truly terrible, by the way.'

'I stole it from behind a shitty Turkish restaurant, I think it might be off,' Tess says, drinking it regardless. 'Mum's looking after Fynn at home, so I'm free to partaaaayyy!'

'Everyone's having an amazing time! Business will be popping,' Jean says, spitting her yellow cava back into the glass. 'Would you be offended if I ran to the shop to gin up? I'm too old for piss vinegar, sorry.'

'This does taste more like crisps than champagne,' Danielle agrees, swishing around a mouthful and spitting into a plant pot, with the practiced air of someone who once spent a summer squatting a chateau in the Loire.

'Not if you share it with your bezzer,' Tess says through a wide grin and a finger gun.

'A bottle of Bombay Sapphire for the lady,' Jean bows, before edging through the customers in the rammed shop.

Forty-five later, Tess, Danielle and Jean sit on the Pussy Willows till, singing along to Pat Benatar's 'Love Is A Battlefield', doing shots of gin and giggling as if they are getting away with a crime. From their perch, they have been watching Richard slink about like a Bond villain approaching every woman under fifty.

'Richard, I was half-convinced you'd start twiddling an imaginary moustache and invite that girl to meet you at the railroad tracks at midnight,' Jean teases him as he returns, his chest puffed up beneath his floral shirt.

'What was that strange pastiche of masculine stereotypes?' Tess says, taking another shot of gin.

'I was a roaring success, thank you very much,' Richard says with smug self-satisfaction. 'In less than one hour, I've got five phone numbers, two Instagram monikers and one Twitter handle. It's like shooting fish in a barrel!'

'Hey,' Tess says, pointing at him and glaring through drink-blurred eyes. 'Don't call my clients fish.'

'Was that some Neuro Linguistic Programming shit?' Danielle asks, clearly more *au fait* with pickup artist techniques than Tess and Jean.

'Maybe,' Richard admits, before stage whispering: 'I've started sleep hypnosis sessions telling me I am as virile as Tom Hardy.'

'Richard, that is by far the least virile thing I have ever heard a man say,' Tess laughs.

'I am as virile as Tom Hardy!' Richard repeats, irate.

'No one is as virile as Tom Hardy,' Danielle says, with surprising sympathy. 'But you don't need to Bane-up to be masculine.'

'Why Tom Hardy?' Jean asks, struggling to think of an occasion when Richard had suggested watching anything but a rom-com. 'I could see you being hypnotised to be as virile as say, Hugh Grant in *Four Weddings* . . .'

'I had to beg him to watch *Legend* with me. And he left halfway through due to the gratuitous violence!' Tess says accusingly. Richard pouts and glares.

All of their jaws drop.

'Actually,' Jean says. 'You do look a bit like Tom Hardy.'

'Like Tom's flamboyant, malnourished cousin . . .' Tess admits with an eye roll.

'Um, Jean,' Danielle says, poking her sister in the shoulder. 'Isn't that Charlie?'

'Oh my god,' Jean says, shrinking back to half-hide behind Danielle and peek out at him from behind her sister's sheath of long brown hair. 'He texted me last week saying he missed me. But I blocked him.'

Her heart thumps in her chest like a caged rabbit. She feels sick and sad and thrilled, all at the same time.

'Nothing like blocking a man to get him to rock up uninvited where you are,' Danielle observes.

On the plus side, Charlie looks bad. His face is more bloated than ever, his hair slicked back with grease. He is as pale as a haddock, and generally appears as if he could be a two-day-old corpse pulled out of the Thames. On the minus side, judging from the yearning pangs she suffers watching the way he moves across the room, laughs uproariously with a guest he recognises, with that old sparkle in his eye, she still has feelings for him.

Confused feelings.

'What is he doing here?' Jean asks, looking at Tess.

'No idea mate.'

'Do you think he's here to win me back?' Jean winces, hating and loving the thought at the same time.

Rationally speaking, she never wanted to see, talk or hear about Charlie ever again, let alone get back together with him. Emotionally speaking, he had made such frustratingly little effort to keep her, that she felt she was owed at least one fucking public serenade in cosmic comeuppance. If he fell to one knee and whipped out a tiny mandolin, then she could kindly reject him before skipping merrily into her future, unencumbered by rage.

'I suppose I should be the bigger person and go say hi,' Jean says, sliding off the table and wobbling as she puts on her heels.

'Don't do it!' Danielle shouts after her. 'You're giving him back the power!'

Jean ignores this as she runs her hand through her hair and strides through the crowd with as much confidence as she can muster. She intends to be sweetly imperious, accepting his pitiful apologies and attempts to renew their relationship with gracious indifference. Then, she will cut the conversation short and leave him choking on thwarted desire and eternal regret.

'Charlie! How *are* you,' Jean says breathlessly instead, her hand involuntarily shooting out to stroke his clammy arm. Her betraying eyes film up with a layer of tears.

What the fuck?

Charlie pulls away from her and smirks, looking through the winding down party for Tess. He waves at her best friend over Jean's head, as if she doesn't exist. *I've missed you.* The words almost tumble across Jean's tongue, bubbling up from some disloyal wave in her subconscious mind. Oh, gin shots. You are always a mistake.

Horrified, Jean forces her thoughts to swing in the opposite direction, only to find herself speaking as if possessed by the demonic spirit of scorned ex-girlfriends.

'If you think turning up at my best friend's shop and ignoring me will win back my favour, you're sadly mistaken,' Jean says, in a voice dripping with false pity. She is shocked by how quickly she has lost her shit. And yet, she continues. 'I really have no interest in ever seeing you again, so you might as well give up now.'

'Jean,' Charlie is startled into a patronising laugh. 'I'm not here for you. I'm not even really here for Tess.'

'Then what are you *doing* here?' Jean yells, losing the last fragment of her cool.

'Charlize invited me,' Charlie says with a sadistic glint in his eye, as he is joined by a small giggling blonde. Jean's stomach drops and she goes bright red with mortification, as her former co-worker and sometime frenemy hangs off his arm.

'Charlie and Charlize! Of course,' Jean says, before giving a weirdly theatrical laugh, her head thrown back and mouth full of spray. 'How perfectly charming!'

Jean had invited Charlize over for dinner once, exactly one year ago, before her intentions revealed themselves as undeniable designs upon Jean's boyfriend. Over supper Charlie and Charlize had flirted audaciously across the table, as Jean cooked and presented courses and pretended for as long as possible that it was all in her head.

Only when Charlize had used a pepper shaker in manner so suggestive that Jean was reminded of Kinga and the wine bottle in *Big Brother 6*, had she called her out on it. Charlie had defended Charlize and publicly dressed down Jean as being both 'profoundly paranoid and unforgivably rude'. Jean now wonders if kitchen appliances feature regularly in Charlize's sexual repertoire, and if a wine-corker butt plug has finally enabled Charlie to maintain an erection.

'Hi Jean. How *are* you,' Charlize says through a smile as fake as her perfect eyelashes, as she paws Charlie familiarly.

The most unjust part of all this, Jean thinks as she watches her nuzzle Charlie's chest, is that she does in fact bear a passing resemblance to Charlize Theron.

'Never better!' Jean exclaims brightly through clenched teeth. She grabs a bottle of the week-old cow's piss masquerading as sparkling wine and leans towards their glasses in revenge. 'Would you care for some champagne?'

'No thanks, Jeannie. Given up the sauce,' Charlie says through a thin smile, ostentatiously sipping on a bottle of Perrier through a straw. His eyes are flat and cold.

Jean feels whatever love she had left for him curdle.

'I made it a condition for him to be my boyfriend,' Charlize smiles. 'It wouldn't be right to stand idly by while he was clearly hurting himself. We're both sober!'

Sober. Boyfriend. Jean's jaw drops for a full thirty seconds, her tongue lying floppy and thick on her slack palate, eyes bulging out of her skull, the lids blinking over and over. She hadn't been deluded enough to think Charlie would change for her, although obviously Jean hoped he would change for himself while she was with him. But to have gone dry for Charlize of all people . . .

The humiliation is unendurable.

'That face. You look like a raped fish,' Charlie says with icy amusement, as Charlize titters into the back of her hand.

Jean's mouth snaps shut.

'Isn't it wonderful you are both so healthy and well-suited,' Jean says robotically, as she gets out her mobile and flips through her contacts list to dial Gabriel's number for an out-of-the-blue booty call. Was this weird? It was weird. Jean didn't care. She needed a dignified exit with a beautiful man at the end of it, pronto. 'So good you've found each other at the same time as Gabriel and I.'

'Gabriel?' Charlie asks, startled into a wounded expression, his first real emotion of the evening. Jean notes his pain with satisfaction.

'The pianist from the wedding, do you recall? He helped you into a taxi and then into bed when you were falling over drunk. Very handsome, such a gentleman.' Jean smiles so broadly she shows every last molar, as finally Gabriel picks up.

'Hello?' His voice mumbles into the phone, with the raspy air of one suddenly awoken from deep slumber.

'Hi baby,' Jean coos as if they are lovers in the full heat of the honeymoon period and not near-strangers who have shared one kiss. 'I'm sorry I had to leave like that the other night, you know how busy work gets. I *so* loved the Royal Opera House and the performance was just stunning. Thank you for taking me.'

'Of course, it was my pleasure,' Gabriel says, surprised but pleased at her adoring enthusiasm. 'I hope I can see you again soon?'

Jean sees a vein in Charlie's neck go crimson and start throbbing all the way down to the base of his throat. His hand tightens around the Perrier glass, the knuckles whitening.

'What are you doing now?' Jean purrs, as she watches Charlize watch Charlie's face.

'I'm in bed,' Gabriel says, a teasing note to his voice.

'Can I join you?' Jean says, her voice lowered, seductive and American in a flat-out Sharon Stone impersonation.

'Y-yes,' Gabriel almost stutters on the other end of the line. 'I mean, if you want. We could always, you know, watch Netflix.'

'I don't want to watch Netflix,' Jean says, pursing her lips into a babyish pout.

Charlie's face turns from ash to white and the Perrier glass trembles with such force it might shatter. Jean enjoys this new dark power over his jealousy.

'I'll call you an Uber,' Gabriel says, his voice lowering in tandem with her own. 'What's your address?'

As Jean gives him the Pussy Willows postcode over the phone, Charlie turns away from her abruptly. He marches across the room to gaze furiously into a potted Monstera, as if he could sustain life in the dark, smoke-filled apartment he used primarily to pass out in. Charlize follows him and rubs his back, casting a baleful look in Jean's direction. Jean waves in vicious cheer, before heading back to her friends to collect her bag.

'I am going to Gabriel's house for much boning,' Jean says, half-giddy and half-fuming, as she grabs her things and hands Tess what remains of the bottle of Bombay Sapphire. 'You can keep this.'

'Um,' Tess says, looking over at her guests. 'Are Charlie and Charlize a thing?'

'They are a couple,' Jean says, her jaw hinging together in repression. She fears that at any moment it will snap open like a rattlesnake, to spray bystanders in venom. 'A sober couple.'

Tess and Danielle exchange an astonished look.

'Why did you invite her?' Jean continues. 'You know she's my backstabbing sexy evil dwarf nemesis!'

'Her Instagram feed is so cool and she has loads of trendy followers and she likes flowers,' Tess says with a grimace of guilt. 'I'm sorry.'

'She does actually look like Charlize Theron in miniature,' Richard says tapping his lips, before yelping when Danielle kicks him in the shin.

'Only in *Monster*,' Tess says supportively, although Jean knows this to be a lie.

'It's OK,' Jean says, taking a deep breath and adjusting her breasts to Full Cleave. 'They go low, I shag Gabriel.'

'Revenge sex is petty,' Richard warns her, unimpressed. 'And always ends in tears.'

'Revenge is never petty,' Danielle says encouragingly, squeezing Jean's upper arm. 'Fuck like the wind.'

'This has nothing to do with revenge,' Jean replies, putting on a fresh layer of crimson lipstick. 'And unlike Richard, I am not a weeper.'

'That was one time!' Richard defends himself.

'That you admit to,' Tess says sceptically.

'Right. I am off to have mind-blowing sex with a handsome man who is nice to me,' Jean says too brightly, as she waves goodbye. 'Ciao ciao! Great party.'

Jean makes a big show of practically skipping through Pussy Willows on the way to her Uber, glowing with delight. Once inside, she puts on her headphones, plays Justin Beiber's *All That Matters* (written during a happy time during him and Selena's relationship, Jean had once read), and breaks down into hot salty tears for the first time since she broke up with Charlie.

Chapter Eight

Gabriel opens the door to his brick terraced house in Greenwich shirtless, in low-slung Adidas tracksuit bottoms. His hair is loose, falling in waves to his shoulders, and he wears horn-rimmed glasses. He looks like a mash-up of seventies Robert Plant and a chavtastic professor. Jean steadies herself against the railing, trying not to swoon too hard.

'Hi. It's nice to see you,' Gabriel says, his eyes cast down, sweeping back a lock of hair bashfully. Jean still hasn't worked out what he has to be timid about. Perhaps he is embarrassed by the sheer bounty of his good fortune. Looks, talent, money, or so it seemed, as well as a beautiful libertine wife. What more could any man want?

Jean has never been with a man who suffers from self-doubt or modesty. Her type has always been the kind to charge through life with the brash confidence of a bull which thinks itself a matador. Gabriel's moments of deer-like shyness have the effect not of making Jean withdrawn, but far bolder.

'You too,' Jean says, walking up the top steps slowly before launching herself into Gabriel's arms. She kisses him passionately, with all the force of someone anxious to forget another.

The tactic works.

Gabriel's soft lips press against her own, his warm mouth opening slightly as he clasps her against his slim hips and

Charlie dissipates into the murky, painful waters of her subconscious. For the first time, Jean grasps the wisdom of Danielle's advice, imparted over post break-up drinks: '*Always* have a jump-off! It's the difference between falling onto a trampoline and hurling yourself into a pit of spikes!'

Gabriel wordlessly draws her into his home and pushes her against the wall, his hands moving lightly over her arms, across her clavicle to cup her breasts. He shuts the door behind him with a kick from his back foot. As his fingers expertly play with one nipple, Jean gasps into his mouth, her body melting into a puddle. He pulls away from her, looking into her eyes, his own dark with lust, as his hand moves up underneath her skirt and around the softness of her inner thigh. Jean breathes heavily as his fingers move across the silk edges of her knickers.

Chemistry, that ineffable quality, shimmers between them. It is as if no time has passed since she was last clasped in his arms one week ago. His skin burns with heat, his touch, undirected, exactly right from the first moment his hands lie upon her body.

As Gabriel lowers the straps of her dress and takes her breast into his mouth, he slides a finger inside of her and Jean cries out, muffling her voice by biting into the back of her hand. Jean feels a familiar but long-lost sensation building up, so quickly and surely that she doubts it is real, could even be possible.

Before her pants are off, before Gabriel's tongue has entered her, before she has even seen the living room, Jean comes hard against his hand, shuddering against the hallway wall.

Gabriel covers Jean's neck with a feather-light dusting of kisses as she trembles and shakes herself back to some semblance of normality, of reality.

'I-I'm sorry,' Jean finds herself apologising, catching her ragged breath, having literally cum in her pants like an over-eager schoolboy. 'That doesn't usually happen so quickly.'

'Isn't that my line?' Gabriel grins, the hard rock of his erection pressing through the fabric of his tracksuit. Jean moves her hand across his thigh towards his cock to recip-rocate, but Gabriel grabs her hand and places it behind her back, continuing to kiss her neck. 'Let me get you a glass of wine.'

'Why?' Jean breathes, quite happy to fuck all night in the hallway before getting a taxi home. How had she put up with it for so long, all these years without the craving of desperate want, without this white-hot heat already curling up inside her again?

Gabriel pulls her dress down and straightens it, readjusts her straps over Jean's shoulders, before kissing her lightly on the mouth.

'I'll show you the house,' he says, taking her hand and leading her through to the living room.

It is airy and high ceilinged, with large creamy sofas surrounding a working fireplace and a grand piano in one corner. The walls are mirrored in art deco frames and covered in empty champagne boxes stacked together to create book-shelves, brimming with literature. Jean flops weakly on a plush sofa, as Gabriel walks ahead of her and turns on the light of a bright, feminine kitchen. William Morris floral wallpaper, in a faded yellow. An expensive, jade-coloured kettle.

'White or red?' Gabriel calls as he opens the matching Smeg fridge. No single man would ever spend so much on a glorified icebox. It is so clearly a couple's home that Jean can't help but feel perturbed she has just orgasmed in the hallway.

Jean gulps as she turns her head towards him and is confronted with a large, silver-framed wedding portrait. Gabriel and Poppy walk down the steps of a church, kissing tenderly beneath a hail of rice, looking like a Hollywood rendition of love's young dream. Next to it is a black and white headshot of Poppy, her face more mature, eyes meeting the photographer's lens with the direct confidence of Carolyn Bessette. Jean turns away from the picture, determined to block it from her mind.

'White please, with a splash of spritzer if you have it,' Jean requests.

Say what you will about Charlie's flaws, and there were many, but one thing she had been certain of was his sexual devotion. However outrageous his flirtations with other women, men and occasionally animals, she had always known her only real competition was with the bottle's siren song. Until Charlize . . .

Jean grits her teeth as she thinks of the triumphant sparkle in the other woman's eyes, as smug as a gluttonous cat in a bowl of Cheshire cream. She had always known there was a spark between them, and that Charlize was as aggressive as Charlie could be vengeful. She shouldn't have been surprised they turned up at Pussy Willows, really the only shocking thing is how unimaginative their *coup* was. If Charlize thought she could tame Charlie's drinking, good luck to her.

Good luck to them both.

'Are you OK?' Gabriel asks as he pads over with two glasses of wine and takes a seat next to her on the sofa. 'You look a bit . . .'

'Pensive?' Jean suggests as a suitable alternative to enraged, as she takes the wine from his hand and sips. He'd gotten just the right balance of vino to soda, cool and crisp and not too sweet.

'Sad,' Gabriel says, with a comforting tilt to his head.

It is true, underlying her fury is an oozing vulnerable wound-pond of seething hurt. Jean looks at Gabriel with fresh eyes, surprised that he is even more perceptive of her moods than she is. His gaze flickers from her face to the portrait of his wedding day.

'I can move that if you like?' he continues.

'What? Oh. No, it's not that,' Jean says, annoyed. However sensitive compared to Charlie, Gabriel is still human, and thus fated to see everything through the prism of his own narcissism. 'It's ongoing work stuff, playing on my mind.'

'So, you get what you want from me and then immediately start thinking about work?' Gabriel asks with a playful smile, as he tucks a lock of hair behind her ear and rubs her shoulder.

'Sorry baby,' Jean says, in her best Don Draper impersonation. She sets her glass on the table next to his wife's portrait and pulls his face close, kissing him deeply. 'Next time I'll leave business at the office.'

As their tongues entwine, Jean presses her hands against his smooth golden chest, thinking about Charlie opening the door of his (formerly their) flat, now tidied of the empty bottles that had lined the entrance hall, dumped in plastic bags for the recycling. She closes her eyes and runs her hand under Gabriel's tracksuit, thinking of Charlie picking up Charlize and carrying her over the entranceway, like he used to with Jean.

As she strokes Gabriel's hard velvet cock, she thinks of Charlie again, depositing his new girlfriend on their – no – his couch in the dirty living room that Jean had tried to spruce up with flea market finds. It had only made it look grubbier. Charlize has probably fumigated the apartment and filled it with Habitat furniture. Shots of Charlie kissing

Charlize, like Jean is kissing Gabriel, urgently, carnivorously, as he had not done with her for years, flicker through her mind like stills from a blue movie.

As Jean's lips move down Gabriel's chest to lick his nipples, the gin and wine and pain and passion combine into whirling rage of lust. As Gabriel interrupts their foreplay to get a condom from a drawer underneath his wedding portrait, Jean tries not to wonder how many other women he has slept with beneath his wife's watchful eyes. Jean closes her own to block it all out, making love to Gabriel with her body and rage-fucking Charlie in her mind.

Afterwards, lying naked with her head against Charlie's – wait no, Gabriel's – chest, his long fingers playing with her undone hair, Jean casually asks the question that had been bothering her of late.

'So, who's your wife's side dick?'

Gabriel startles beneath her head, and Jean raises her face to watch his expression more carefully. Perhaps the question was inelegantly phrased.

'I mean, neither of us would say . . . side chick or side dick . . .' Gabriel answers evasively. 'I don't see our liaisons in such crude terms.'

Jean resists the urge to roll her eyes.

'All right, your wife's lover, or lovers?' Jean forces herself to laugh, to keep the mood light. 'Her human bouquet.'

'She's more naturally monogamous than I am,' Gabriel says carefully, sitting up so that Jean rolls off of his chest onto the couch. *I see.* No, wait, she didn't at all.

'What?' Jean asks baldly, feeling as if she's been slapped in the face or dowsed with cold water, her eyebrows hovering in the vicinity of her hairline. 'How is that fair!'

'She is less sexual than I am,' Gabriel says, with an edge to his voice that is trying very hard not to be defensive. He sits up and puts on his glasses, as Jean pulls herself up onto her elbows. She arranges her hair so it covers her breasts. What a moment ago felt like a natural and effortless intimacy, now feels like exposure, confusion. Guilt.

Taking Jean's silence as acceptance, Gabriel continues more calmly.

'She always has been. We were faithful for a long time, but eventually . . . life on the road, touring in your twenties. You know how it is.'

Jean did not know how it was, her twenties having been spent trailing after a string of personally disastrous but otherwise completely unremarkable men, expecting that somehow the act of having been chosen by them would be, in and of itself, fulfilling.

'I can imagine,' she says instead.

'So, it was maybe inevitable that eventually I did, yes, have an affair. It didn't last long before I told Poppy. Obviously, she was upset about the lies. After sitting with it for a while though, she realised she wasn't actually jealous per se. It was the dishonesty that was the betrayal, not the fact that I was attracted to someone else and acted upon it,' Gabriel says earnestly, pushing his glasses up the bridge of his nose.

'She wasn't jealous at all?' Jean presses him in disbelief.

Maybe it had been naive of her to assume Poppy was also taking advantage of their open marriage. To trust that a man would be fair, and not conveniently oblivious. Jean's gaze flickers to his wife's portrait, to the bold stare, the self-possession emitting like a halo from the angular planes of her face. She looks for hidden cracks beneath the public façade. The image is too perfect to reveal a chink, frailty or flaw.

'I mean, there may have been some of that, but not enough to destabilise us. She worked through it. Not that

124

we haven't had our issues, of course we have. But we are both reasonable people who recognise that one person can't fulfil every role in your partner's life,' Gabriel finishes, taking his abandoned glass of wine from the table top and drinking deep. 'I mean, who can live up to that pressure?'

'She sounds very reasonable indeed,' Jean says quietly, digesting this information.

Jean had always thought of the 'one person can't be your everything' philosophy as indicating you should maintain your own friendships, have a stimulating work life, and if possible, hire a cleaner. And yet, if every man, every woman and every marriage has a fatal flaw, it makes sense to choose the one that bothers you least. Apparently, for Poppy, that is sexual fidelity. Who is Jean to judge?

Gabriel's hand tentatively brushes over her own, again. Squeezes. Jean's stirs, then squeezes back. He draws her towards him for a kiss. Jean reciprocates but cannot relax.

'It's late,' Jean mutters into Gabriel's lips, pulling away from him. 'I'd best go home.'

'You don't want to stay?' he asks. 'I have a more comfortable bed upstairs that we could share.'

'No, that's OK, I have a lot of . . . paperwork to do,' Jean says, scrabbling for an excuse. She isn't ready to hop into his marital bed, it is too strange.

'OK,' Gabriel says, looking boyish and vulnerable with his glasses and long limbs and clean-shaven face. 'I'll book you a cab.'

'Thanks,' Jean says, pulling back on her knickers, grabbing her bra stuffed into the cavity of the couch. She feels very tired, and very sober.

'I want to see you again,' Gabriel says simply when her Uber arrives, and he walks Jean to his front door. She still hasn't seen the second floor of the house. He leans down to kiss her. The whirling punch-drunk butterflies of her foolish desire stir crazily, and Jean knows that she will go to him, that she can't help but not to.

Sunset Icon DM:
Dinner would be 🔥

But we like to keep things playful

at first.

What about crazy golf

?! lol

Monday morning back at the office, Jean smiles to herself secretly as she checks her messages and makes another pot of coffee for Jez and Lord Kinder. The yoga threesome couple chat has evolved from its beginnings on Thrinder to following each other on Insta, suggesting an advancing commitment to their non-relationship. Now a real date appears to be on the cards, Jean reflects that she should probably start referring to them by their actual names (Sinbad and Stacey), rather than objectifying them via their super-flexi sexual licentiousness.

If only his name wasn't Sinbad.

JeanGenie DM:
crazy golf = 👏😂

She makes a mental resolution to work on her DM seduction skills.

Sunset Icon DM:
When?

'He's being impossible. You get him to open up,' Jez's acrid breath whispers in Jean's ear. She hides her phone in her pocket and presses down on the coffee filter.

Jez is on Jean's case to crack Lord Kinder's annoying insistence upon total innocence. As if her being a woman means she possesses skills of tact and emotional manipulation which automatically create a confessional atmosphere.

What they really need is an indiscrete priest.

'Excuse me, Lord Kinder, I have to make a conference call. I'll leave you in our Jean's very capable hands,' Jez says as he abandons her to the disgraced peer.

Jean pours the coffee, adding a splash of whisky for Lord Kinder and milk for herself, mentally going over the latest stories that have come out in the papers and blogs. The boyfriend he had hidden from his rich wife when he was courting her, decades ago (*Daily Mirror*). The dog walker he had propositioned at 4 a.m. only a few months prior (*London Evening Standard*). Escorts, escorts, escorts (*Every Broadsheet in The Land*). His policy, unbelievably, is still to deny, deny, deny. As if all the public relations advice he needs to weather the shitstorm is Shaggy's 'It Wasn't Me'.

Jean has wasted enough time pacifying him, soothing his wounded ego, saying she believes his recollection of events, and gently attempting to get him to open up. In her darker moments, she wonders if she would still perform this role were he Harvey Weinstein. If she didn't do the job, someone else would. That was the old excuse.

Jean hands him the Irish coffee, in the leather armchair in which he sits slumped and brooding, staring at a blank corner of the wall.

'Lord Kinder,' Jean says firmly. It is time to turn bad cop. 'If you aren't honest with us about your double life, it is impossible for us to do our job, let alone to do it well.

At this point, the only thing you have going for you is that these relationships were consensual, with men of age. This is a scandal of your ideological hypocrisy, but not a crime.'

Jez had finally convinced Lord Kinder to pay off the rent boy he locked in a closet, and the charges had been dropped. Technically speaking, the kidnapping case had gone away.

'If you own up to it and admit your internalised homophobia, it will make our lives much easier. We can anticipate and mitigate the damage,' Jean continues sympathetically.

'You said you believed me,' Lord Kinder pouts with fleshy lips, slinking further into the chair. He looks simultaneously very old and very young, a querulous old man on the brink of a tantrum.

'I did,' Jean lies smoothly, sitting down next to him and patting his hand. 'But the other stories that have come out this weekend make your claims of conspiracy hard to believe, you must understand that.'

'Moles, grassing me up,' Lord Kinder mutters. 'This is all Lord Drummund's doing. I didn't support his housing bill and he has exacted his price. But two can play that game. I will not be the only one ruined in this moral charade!'

Jean's ears prick up. This is the closest he has come to a confession.

'Lord Drummund,' Jean muses. She had heard whispers that he is the organiser of the 'Night of The Hunter' masked sex parties held in stately homes around the capital. The event's name had quickly morphed into 'Night of The Punter' amongst the political cognoscenti, and they were said to be attended by the best and the brightest MPs, along with D-list celebrities and models looking to make an extra buck on the gift circuit.

'If I unmasked their deceits, the corridors of Parliament would be emptied within the week!' Lord Kinder continues, as indignant as Edmund in *King Lear*. Jean half expects him to rise up and rail, 'Now, Gods, stand up for bastards!'

Feeling jaded by the usual smoke-and-mirrors PR strategies and wishing to forestall any more virtue signalling from a sexual predator, Jean suggests something audacious.

'Would you consider . . . espionage?'

'How do you mean,' Lord Kinder asks through narrowed eyes, showing interest in the workings of her mind for the very first time.

'I've heard of Lord Drummund's parties,' Jean says. 'What if I went as a voyeur, to gather counter-blackmail information?'

'Excellent notion,' Jez says as he re-enters the room and closes his office door firmly behind him. 'A strategy of derring-do in the old style, before modern life became so damned litigious.'

'Quite right!' Lord Kinder agrees, smiling for the first time since the scandal broke.

'I didn't think you had it in you, Jean,' Jez admires. 'The balls, I mean.'

'Thank you, Jez,' Jean says graciously, as if it didn't take cojones and a spine of steel to withstand his tirades without crying in the toilets.

'This may be the making of your career,' Jez says as he sits behind his wooden desk, leaning back in his leather armchair with his hands behind his head. Lord Kinder nods in agreement.

Although Jean is largely motivated by a combination of professional boredom and sexual curiosity, a thrill of inclusiveness goes straight up her spine. Finally, she is part of the boys' club, or at least promised a seat at the table, not treated as some godforsaken cross between Jeeves and Jiminy Cricket.

'I'm so glad you approve,' Jean says, looking at her watch. 'Half past twelve! It's time for lunch. I'll return in an hour.'

Jean swans out of Jez's office, grabbing her handbag from her desk without looking behind her.

'Where are you going?' Cynthia asks worriedly, her head swinging from Jean, to Jez's closed door, and back again. 'I didn't see Lord Kinder leave?'

The unspoken rule at Addington Media is that no staff member can take a break while a client remains in the building.

'He hasn't left,' Jean smiles brightly, pulling her colleague up by the hand. 'Come, Cynthia, let's go for a slap-up meal. Do you like modern European?'

'Oh, I'm on a budget,' Cynthia mutters in terror, planting her buttocks ever more firmly in her chair.

'I'll expense it,' Jean says, before shouting at Jez's door, 'I'm taking Cynthia with me for an expensed PR pow-wow at the Hawksmoor!'

'Fine!' Jez shouts back, annoyed to be bothered.

Maybe Jean does like her job. Maybe she just hasn't been *exploiting* her job.

'Oh,' Cynthia says, torn between slavish loyalty and a free meal. Jean takes her arm and practically drags her out of her chair. 'No, no, I'm sorry. I simply can't.'

'As you wish,' Jean gives up, sliding on sunglasses and clicking out of the office on her new red vinyl fuck-me heels. She checks her messages, diving into the thread.

Jean:
Mata Hari eat your heart out!
What a time to be alive.

Dickface:
What have you done?

Jean:
I've taken my lunch break with a client still in the building.

MeiQween:
👀

Jean:
And let's just say

I'll soon be ticking off 'Kubrick-style orgy' on my bucket list of sexcapades.

MeiQween:
only you can make an orgy sound nerdy af.

Jean:
Am not nerd. Am brazen hussy and spy.

Dickface:
I'm scared to ask.

MeiQween:
one hallway orgasm and she thinks she's jack nicholson

Jean:
One hallway orgasm plus couch sex,

Plus yoga threesome date,

131

And yes I do feel like Jack
Nicholson.

Her Insta DM pings, again. Sinbad and Stacey are down for crazy golf at 4 p.m. next Sunday. Another ping. It is a text from Gabriel. He had been messaging all last night, but she had barely replied. The power is on her side and she is afraid to relinquish it. Jean hopes Gabriel is all twisted up inside, with lust and an unexamined longing, just as she is.

Jean ignores her messages and puts on her headphones. Today is an 'I Woke Up In A New Bugatti' kind of day. For once in her life she is a player ruling, not played by, the game.

Chapter Nine

'Stop it! I've got to go,' Jean squeals, as Gabriel pulls her back onto his bed the following Sunday afternoon. 'I need to get home and change.'

'Why would you change,' Gabriel says, rolling her underneath him and teasingly nibbling at her ear. 'You're perfect as you are.'

'I can't rock up to crazy golf in the nude.' Jean's laugh trails off into a sigh as Gabriel's hands slip under her arse and he draws her closer to him. She wriggles away. 'Seriously! I'll be late.'

'Wear what you arrived in on Friday,' Gabriel says, pulling her back towards him and burying his head between her thighs. 'That was very nice.'

So nice he had stripped her naked but for her heels the moment she entered his house and proceeded to give her the best head of her life against the doorframe. Jean looks at her phone on the dresser, considering cancelling the whole thing to linger in Gabriel's bed for one more night. But Danielle's voice, warning her to keep her rotation stacked, rings like an alarm bell in the back of her mind. Jean reluctantly pushes Gabriel's head away, untangles her legs from his arms and stands up.

'Stilettos and a minidress are not very sporting either,' Jean says, running her hands through his hair and leaning down to kiss him. As Gabriel makes another grab to pull her back onto the bed, she runs away from his clutches into the bathroom to inspect herself in the mirror. 'Good lord, what have you done to my hair!'

'You look the height of fashion,' Gabriel says coming up naked behind her, sweeping it over one shoulder and kissing her neck. 'Very Kate Bush.'

'Kate Bush electrocuted by a stage lamp,' Jean says, grabbing his hairbrush and attempting to detangle the ends. They had spent the entire, lazy weekend in bed, only ever rising to put on silk robes and collect the takeaway delivery, or to smoke a cigarette with a glass of wine on his terrace overlooking the neighbour's rose garden.

It was perfect.

'What sort of person plays crazy golf anyway,' Gabriel mutters, turning Jean to face him and kissing her deeply. 'Are you going with Richard?'

'Nooo . . .' Jean says, weighing up whether or not to tell him about her forthcoming Thrinder experimentation. This is the third time Gabriel has asked about Richard, in an oddly possessive manner. Not having met her flatmate, he clearly harbours doubts about the truly platonic state of their friendship. Given that Gabriel is the married one, Jean is somewhat baffled that he cares. Surely a lack of sexual boundaries is the whole point of an open relationship?

'Tess then?' Gabriel asks.

Jean smiles vaguely, running the brush through her hair.

Gabriel takes it from her hand and softly helps her pull it through to the ends.

'Not Danielle, I hope. I get the feeling she wouldn't trust me.'

Jean had made the mistake of letting Gabriel listen to an episode of Danielle's show last night. Danielle must have had an argument about exclusivity with the non-boyf, as the entire program she was railing hard against men who only pay lip service to the liberation of women, who like the *idea* of an 'enlightened activist unshackled by hetero-normative cultural norms', but ultimately only want to have it all without extending the same freedoms to their partners.

The 'enlightened activist' was clearly a thinly veiled represen-tation of the one and only Danielle Sauvage, as it had nothing to do with the caller's phone-in question about how to have casual sex as a freshly sober alcoholic. When the poor man said as much, Danielle had blithely suggested he take Class As instead. Which some people might think insensitive, but then, Danielle did not consider cocaine to be a drug.

'Actually, I'm going on a date. Ouch!' Jean yelps as Gabriel's hand jerks through one heavy brush stroke. Their eyes meet in the mirror, Jean's startled, Gabriel's surprised and hurt. Jean's heart beats heavy in her chest, the only sound she hears in the prolonged silence that follows.

'A date,' Gabriel repeats, recommencing brushing her hair, more carefully this time. He tries to smile with casual approval, but Jean can tell it is forced. 'Who with?'

'A couple I met on Thrinder,' Jean blurts out. 'They teach yoga.'

'Sounds . . .' Whatever Gabriel had intended to say gargles in his throat. He clears it, and hands her the brush. 'I'll let you finish. Do you want a cup of tea?'

'Sure,' Jean says warily, as she finishes brushing her hair. He shuts the bathroom door quietly behind him. After Jean hears his feet pad downstairs to the kitchen, she grabs her phone from the bedside table to text Tess, who responds immediately.

Jean:

Um, I think G is annoyed I'm going on a date with another couple.

MeiQween:

LOL

of course he is, this whole situation is based on lies

Jean considers this through knitted brows as she turns on the shower. It wasn't based on lies. Everything they'd shared had been based on complete honesty, more so than any other relationship she had been in. Jean runs her hand under the spray of water. Too hot. She turns back to her phone.

MeiQween:

if not to you than to himself

Jean:

Should I bail on the date?

MeiQween:

NON!

yes. cancel on all them mofos

entertain yo bestest

am bored af so empty today

Jean steps into the shower, worried for Pussy Willows' future. Only a week in, and Tess has already sprung for a nanny, the first step in getting out from under her mother's thumb. If business doesn't go well, however, the whole thing will explode like a glitter bomb, a brief but brilliant paroxysm of kittens and pizazz.

The bathroom door opens. She hears Gabriel set down two mugs.

He opens the plastic curtain and steps inside to join her, pushing Jean against the wall, dripping honey-scented shower gel into his palms and soaping up her body. He kisses her hard, his teeth biting into the flesh of her lower lip, his hands squeezing her hips and breasts almost until they hurt. Jean moans into his mouth as he lifts her up and her legs wrap around his waist as he takes her, roughly, only a shade of his previous tenderness remaining. Afterwards, sunk on the floor together, Jean straddling him, the water still pouring over their faces, he looks deep into her eyes and cradles her face possessively.

'What do you think,' Gabriel asks, the first words he's spoken since he left the bathroom. 'about being London exclusive?'

Jean's breath catches in alarm.

'What do you mean?' Jean asks through a wrinkle of confusion in her nose. She tries to distract him by kissing him full on the mouth.

'I mean you and me, in London. Exclusively,' Gabriel says, pulling away, his eyes soft and vulnerable as he puts his hands through her own.

Jean rests her chin on his shoulder and looks away from his face, unsure what to think, unsure what to feel. What could exclusivity mean with a married man? She may be naïve, but she is not so foolish as to think this is a proposal to leave his wife.

'What time is it,' Jean asks without expecting an answer, as she buries her face against his chest. 'I'm going to be so late. I'd better let them know. Maybe I should cancel.'

Somehow, although she cannot see his face, she can feel Gabriel's triumphant flash of a smile. She will rearrange with Sinbad and Stacey. But she can't allow this to continue to happen, whatever it is. To allow a man who isn't committed to her dictate her actions.

It appears she had better keep some things to herself. The 'Night of the Punter', for instance, she does not imagine going down well. She still has every intention of going, if only to take advantage of the work-comped Brazilian, La Perla lingerie and expensive wig she had convinced Jez were absolutely necessary to remain incognito. It is for work, after all, and none of his business. So why does she feel guilty?

'Yes, stay here,' Gabriel growls with satisfaction, rubbing his thumbs over her ribs and down her spine to the small of her back. Biting her shoulder. Pressing her against him.

'I'm going to meet Tess instead,' Jean says distantly, pulling away from his grasp and slipping out of the shower into a towel. How quickly their spirit of total honesty had been broken.

Feelings, and the need to protect them, could ruin everything.

'I miss sex,' Tess says in a tragic tone later that evening, as she stares into her empty wine glass. Pussy Willows has shut up shop for the night, the kittens rounded up and put to bed.

It's just Tess and Jean and a bottle of wine, like the good old days when they would sit and drink and talk about their future plans. When Tess had still been going to law school, before she dropped out to have Fynn. When Jean still thought Addington Media was a pit stop to better things, before it became a cyclical routine that consumed all her time. Their lives had both narrowed and expanded, were enriched and deepened. But painfully, and not in the ways they had hoped.

'It's been so long that I'm pretty sure I'm all sealed up,' Tess continues with a sigh, trying to put a humorous spin on things, but unquestionably maudlin.

'That's 100 per cent anatomically impossible,' Jean says as she goes to the record player, flipping through the albums stacked next to it in a wire basket. She holds up Nick Cave's *Let Love in*.

Tess shudders in response.

'No! Not that,' Tess says, refilling her wine glass. 'Far too triggering.'

'Because of . . .'

Jean hesitates to say Xavier's name.

They never speak of him. After a year of heart-wrenching tears, in which Tess had gone through the five stages of grief while raising a baby on her own, eventually she had stopped mentioning Xavier and Jean had followed suit. They pretended as if he hadn't been Tess's constant companion for years, the perfect relationship that everyone else aspired to, until one day he left. Out of the blue. To Goa. God knows where he was now. In all this time he hadn't even sent a postcard; they had no way of knowing if he were alive or dead. Always on the paranoid side, Xavier had become increasingly wary of the internet. He never replied to emails and despite their scouring, there was no sign of him on social media.

The closest Tess had come to acknowledging how it had nearly broken her, was when she admitted she had obsessed so long over him, convinced herself so thoroughly that one day he would return, out of the blue as was his wont, that the fantasy had become imprinted upon her brain. A rewired, false reality that never came. That she could feel the ache of his lack as a physical part of her, like a phantom limb.

Jean selects Pink Floyd's 'Wish You Were Here'. As the opening notes start, Tess throws her hand over her eyes.

'Are you trying to kill me!'

'Do you own any non-triggering albums?' Jean asks, stopping the spinning record abruptly and turning back to today's played pile. The other options were equally lovesick. Dinah Washington, Tom Waits, Nico.

'You know this is our anniversary?' Tess says glumly.

'Of your first date?'

'Of when he left.'

Jean sits down next to Tess on the counter and squeezes her shoulder.

'Do you still miss him?'

'Oh god. I can barely remember what his face looks like any more,' Tess laughs through a throat thickening with unshed tears.

They both know this is her way of saying: all the time.

Tess had burned most of their photos together, in an atypically mystical white witch ceremony, in an attempt to forget him. She had saved only a few favourites that she kept locked up in a trunk for Fynn to have one day. 'Sometimes I think my heart is buried in that chest', she had once said.

'It's lucky Fynn takes after you,' Jean says, rubbing Tess's back.

'They have the same expressions,' Tess says, looking into the distance, her face indecipherable. 'Especially when he doesn't get what he wants.'

Jean squeezes Tess's hand. There is no advice she can give, no way to make it better. She can't even imagine it, has never felt an equivalent pain. Some aspects of life are gut-punches that can only be endured.

'Sorry, boring,' Tess says, wiping away the hint of a tear and slapping her face. 'It's been four years! I really am over it, it's only today that's been hard. Distract me with your love life, I've had enough of moping around after a ghost.'

'So you can yell at me about how it's all going to end in disaster?'

'Exactly,' Tess says through a crooked grin. 'Call me fucking Cassandra.'

'Well, I told Sinbad and Stacey—' Jean pauses to allow Tess to sputter through a mouthful of wine.

'Sinbad! Sorry, carry on,' Tess says when she's recovered herself. 'I'm feeling better already.'

'In Sinbad's defence, his mother is Persian, so it's not like a white boy has dubbed himself this in his mid-twenties,' Jean says defensively. 'Anyway. I told them something came up with work and they were very understanding. We've taken a crazy golf rain check.'

'Are you going to follow through?'

'I'm not sure,' Jean says, thinking about how simple it was with Gabriel, how at ease they were together already. Crazy physical connection aside, they make each other laugh. He listens to her. He is thoughtful, kind-hearted, always looking out for her in small ways. Throwing new people in the mix would mean anxiety, awkwardness, bad attempts at flirtation. How does one even have a threesome? It's the ultimate third-wheel date. 'I'm not that bothered about sleeping with anyone else at the moment. I've mainly been pursuing it because I don't want to get too attached.'

'Smart.'

'Gabriel said something weird before I left, about wanting to be London exclusive . . .' Jean mumbles into her wine glass, her eyes cast to the floor.

'What does that even mean? You can only shag other people abroad?' Tess says, reaching under the counter to grab a packet of corner shop biscuits and offering Jean the tray. 'I hope you didn't agree to that.'

'Obviously not. It's just annoying. Here I am, finally getting a taste of sexual freedom, and my married fling wants to tie me down.' Jean grumbles, taking a stale chocolate chip cookie. 'You know Charlie sent me a greeting card of a puppy at work after that night at Pussy Willows? The interior was blank. I think it was his broken way of saying sorry.'

'No stirrings?' Tess asks, proffering a flower at Jean's heart.

'Only rage. All this time I've been so eager and available and *good*, when it turns out, men love to get competitive with each other.'

'Preach,' Tess says.

'The problem is, with Poppy out of the country, it hardly feels like polyamory at all.'

'I knew it!' Tess says through a mouthful of food. 'This can only end badly. Are you jealous?'

'No,' Jean says, considering. And it's true. 'He talks about her, but it doesn't bother me. I haven't even internet stalked her. It's like she's in a parallel universe. And in this one, it's as if she doesn't exist.'

'She does, though,' Tess says in alarm.

'I just don't get it. What does he want from me?' Jean asks.

'Exactly what he said! He wants you all for himself. He's a married man offering to sleep only with his wife and mistress. It's a tale as old as time!' Tess says, jabbing her finger in the air. 'In my humble opinion, you are being wilfully naïve to the damage this could cause you, Gabriel and his wife. And if by some miracle it's all gravy and you fall in free love, he's blatantly going to move to New York when his nan dies. It's doomed!'

'Doomed is a bit much. They've been open for years and seem to be cool with it,' Jean counters, deciding not to mention the whole Poppy-not-dating-outside-the-relationship thing. It's not as if she *couldn't* have others. She chose not to. 'And he doesn't seem keen on New York.'

'Well, even if *they* are cool, remember the damage this could cause you,' Tess says, her voice raising. 'And maybe you should stalk her. If only to remind yourself that this woman definitely does exist!'

'I knew you'd make this way less fun,' Jean says, rolling her eyes.

A knock on the front door interrupts what is turning into an argument.

'That must be Bjorn,' Tess says, for the first time that evening perking up into a semblance of her old self.

'Bjorn?' Jean asks in confusion.

'My manny,' Tess replies as she slides off the counter to walk towards the dead-bolted shopfront, the night dark behind it.

'Manny?' Jean repeats stupidly. Tess had left out that detail.

As Bjorn enters the shop, Fynn sleeping peacefully on his shoulder, Jean's jaw drops. Tess had left out more than his sex. She had also left out that he is a strapping hunk of man-boy, with the gentle eyes of an angel and the gigantic hands of a welder, with guns that appeared to be hewn out of stone.

'Good evening,' Bjorn greets them in a Swedish accent, as Jean makes a weird high-pitched cheep sound and Tess throws her a look that says: 'Contain yo'self'.

'How was he?' Tess says, as Bjorn slides her sleeping son down his rippling chest and into her arms.

'Our day was very enjoyable. We played football in the park with his little mates, and later that afternoon I made him spaghetti ragu, and then we start to play Monopoly. However, it was far too long a game, and in the middle he fell sleeping,' Bjorn says sweetly, in the halting yet excessively precise English of someone using as many words in their vocabulary as possible.

Jean realises who he reminds her of. *Vikings* Season 5: Bjorn.

As Tess walks to the counter to collect her purse, Fynn stirs in her arms and calls out to him, adorably. After Tess sets him down, Bjorn comes over and throws him quickly in the air, then chases after him as the little boy runs around the shop, in a last gasp of energy before bedtime. Jean's heart melts. She looks at Tess, who is staring at Bjorn with an expression of tender lust on her face.

When she catches Jean's eye, she quickly wipes it from her face.

'Thanks so much for today. See you tomorrow morning!' Tess says as she hands him some cash, her hand trembling slightly. Bjorn grins as he takes it, waving as he exits the front door.

'Sweet dreams!' he says in parting.

'Sweet dreams!' Tess repeats after him, her voice wobbling like a pubescent boy.

'Well, well, well,' Jean says simply, as Tess sets Fynn on a couch and covers him with a blanket. He falls immediately to sleep.

'Shush,' Tess says quietly, before tiptoeing back over to her and topping off their glasses with the last of the wine. She responds to the unspoken query shouted from Jean's rapid-waggling eyebrows. '*Obviously*. I haven't had sex in four years and have hired a Nordic Manny-Adonis. Fynn loves him. He cooks. His arms are like gentle logs of shapely wood. I am batshit crazy obsessed with him.'

Jean nods along to all this and sips her wine.

'You're a dark horse, Tess.'

'He's only nineteen,' Tess says guiltily, knocking back her wine. 'I could never.'

'A *very* dark horse.'

'Even thinking it feels exploitative,' Tess says, lowering her voice. 'Does this make me a quasi-predator?'

'All's fair in love and war,' Jean says, thinking about the width of Bjorn's neck. She had felt safer when he was in the room, as if he were a bomb shelter of masculinity that could protect them from all the world's unpleasant things.

'That is a common philosophical take,' Tess agrees.

'And as a Viking, Bjorn would understand that,' Jean adds.

'Yes,' Tess says, a demented glint in her eye. 'No. I can't. I'm a terrible person!'

'When vaginas develop their own consciousness, they will dream of Bjorn,' Jean whispers confidingly, as Tess makes a grimace of horror. 'You can't help it. None of us can.'

'That is fucking weird but also true.'

'At any rate, it's a harmless fantasy. Not some romantic delusion, right?' Jean asks, finishing off the last of her wine.

'True love and wedding bells between an aging single mother and her nineteen-year-old Scandi dreamboat employee?' Tess shakes her head and laughs at the ridiculousness of the idea, but her eyes are shifty. 'Madness.'

Chapter Ten

Jean fiddles with the strap of her thigh-high stockings in the taxi barrelling through the empty dark streets of Belsize Park. Her mother's voice rings in her ear. 'You're all fur coat and no knickers,' she said, whenever Jean did something that disappointed her. If only Door could see her now, all dolled up in a fake fur coat and crotchless knickers, on her way to the infamous 'The Night Of The Punter' party.

Jean giggles to herself, sipping from the miniature bottle of Veuve Clicquot that Richard had handed her as he wished her luck in her new life of sex and crime. Jean had accepted it graciously, before flashing him in the hallway as she opened the front door. He had thrown his arms over his eyes and shouted, 'Don't do anything I wouldn't do! Which is *everything*.'

As the taxi pulls up in front of an enormous mansion overlooking the Heath, the street crammed with blackout window SUVs, Jean adjusts her long, blonde, fringed wig in the rear-view mirror and adds an extra lick of scarlet lippy. She struggles to breathe in her tight leather La Perla corset, but she enjoys the feeling of constriction. Her posture has never been so swan-like, nor her breasts so flatteringly squashed, a pair of S&M peaches.

The corset serves dual purposes: to look amazing, firstly, but also to hide the miniature camera and recording device Jez had sourced from his safe when they discussed the espionage plan in more detail. If nothing else was to be gained from this experience, Jean had learned never to speak freely in his office again.

Danielle had found her get-up ridiculous, after Jean WhatsApped her a photo of what she called her *50 Shades of Almost Famous* ensemble. 'You can't enjoy an orgy if you're playing a part!' her sister had replied. But not everyone has the confidence to rock up nude but for a yeti-bush and underarm hair the length of a yogi's beard in front of complete strangers. Jean is convinced this will be an evening of debauchery in which she will be more at ease than Danielle. After all, she has performed in a disguise of one form or another her entire life.

Jean takes a black velvet mask out of her handbag and slips it over her eyes with a dangerous smile. This time, playing a part is part of the fun. Tonight, she could leave all her insecurities and romantic neuroses behind. She could be anyone, desire anything, without consequence to her heart or reputation.

She wonders what she should call herself as she opens the car door and steps out into the cool night air, wobbling in her knock-off Gucci platforms. She steps carefully up the gravel path to the intimidating front door, her hips swinging boldly from side to side. In her coat pocket, her blood-coloured manicure strokes the edge of the invitation Lord Kinder had procured for her.

Poppy.

The name is the first to spring to mind.

Jean stumbles on the path, unnerved by the *Single White Female*-ing that has apparently been brewing underneath her *sangfroid*. She will not take on the name of Gabriel's wife.

She thinks of other flower names. Tulip? No. Delilah? Meh. Lily. Yes. Lily is unpretentious, but sophisticated.

Not so obscure it is unbelievable. Lily is a woman she can play with confidence.

Jean strides towards the handsome bouncer standing like a statue in a suit behind red velvet ropes. If he is any indication of the sex appeal of the other guests, this will be a night to remember. The mansion boasts imposing white pillars and a shiny black door affixed with golden lion knockers the size of her head. Jean's knees tremble with nerves and anticipation as she hands him the invitation, gazing heatedly into his long-lashed brown eyes. She ignores the disturbing question of why exactly she bought a wig in the same shade and style as Poppy's hair.

'Enjoy your evening, mademoiselle. The cloakroom is to your left, and you will be required to sign a non-disclosure agreement,' the bouncer says as he opens the door to an expanse of marble flooring.

Jean steps through, holding her breath, the true illegality of what she has proposed to do striking her for the first time. Is she really going to risk prison for Lord Kinder of all people? There is no point in worrying about it. She has come for the dirt on one man only: Lord Drummund. If he is not present, it is hardly her fault. And even if he is, she can always pretend he has been a no show. Jean decides to think of this not as an espionage mission, but the sort of sexual work-perk enjoyed by men in banking and finance the world over.

The cloakroom girl in a pink lace slip looks as if she could have stepped out of the pages of *Seventeen* magazine. She wordlessly rifles through Jean's handbag and removes her phone, sliding over a contract for Jean to sign. Jean scribbles her signature at the bottom. The girl places her mobile in a velvet pouch on the same numbered hanger as Jean's coat, before handing it back over the counter. It contains only the essentials: cigarettes, lipstick, condoms.

Jean shivers as she turns around to face the other guests, fully exposed in her lingerie for the first time this evening. The clock on a mantelpiece is about to strike 10 p.m. and the sparse crowd suggests she is an eager beaver. She catches a glimpse of herself in the mirrored foyer and double takes. She feels not at all herself, in the best possible way. In the candle-lit dimness, she can almost pass for a pre-boob job Iggy Azalea. Jean flicks back a lock of her poker-straight plastic hair and steps through the hallway into a ballroom.

Guests in masks and various states of undress ranging from the magnificent to the obscene sip champagne from long-stemmed bottomless flutes offered by highly symmetrical waiters. They're held upright through holes in bronze sculptured trays made with interlocking abstract forms, that Jean realises are genitalia upon closer inspection.

Jean takes a glass and sips it, her stomach buzzing with nervous excitement.

'You like the champagne tray sculptures?' an elderly gentleman asks as he walks straight towards her.

He is naked but for an extravagant cravat and a Venetian mask with a long drooping nose. Jean fears it is a foreshadowing of his penis.

He lightly brushes the back of her shoulder, all the way down to her elbow. From what she understood, he was supposed to ask before he tried to touch her in any way, but the movement was so subtle it might be accidental. Jean struggles to keep her gaze strictly above his Versace-print neckerchief.

'They're magnificent,' Jean replies in the soft deep whisper of Lily's voice.

The man's hand moves from her elbow down her back to cup her arse, in a feather-light molestation she has definitely not agreed to.

'Privately commissioned from Jake Chapman, but they pale next to your radiance,' the old man grins, baring a row of crooked yellow teeth. They put Jean in mind of collapsing tombstones, jammed every which way in an ancient cemetery. He squeezes. 'May I lick your pussy, my darling.'

Jean almost spits out her champagne. Her body jerks away from the looming, copious, naked belly pressing against her thigh. In an ultra-posh apologetic accent, she demurs.

'I am terribly sorry, but I'm afraid I'm waiting for my husband. We've come as voyeurs, you see. Wedding anniversary surprise. Role-play, don't you know. Otherwise I would, of course, be delighted.'

The excuse rolls easily off of her tongue, as if she is rejecting an unwanted canapé and not the offer of cunnilingus from a man old enough to be her grandfather. Disgust mixes with an odd sensation of guilt. She is at a sex party after all, is her revulsion not based on ageism and, for lack of a better word, uglism? Were libertines with one foot in the grave not also deserving of human contact? But if her vagina had vocal chords, right now it would be screaming: 'Run, Bitch, RUUUUNN!!'

Jean turns on her heel and stomps as fast as her platforms can carry her towards a moonlit terrace, wondering for the first time what the devil she has got herself into.

On the terrace, Jean breathes as deeply as she can, calmed by the night air. It smells sweetly of youth and promise. She reaches into her bag with trembling fingers for the pack of cigarettes. She gave up years ago, but as Gabriel smokes, she now enjoys the odd post-coital puff that is threatening to turn into a full-blown habit. Gentle Gabriel, with his skin so fresh and lovely, his balls so perky and uplifted. What had she been thinking? People would pay good money *not* to see Parliament in the nude.

As Jean takes a drag, her ears attune to a high-pitched moaning coming from her left. She warily turns her head only to lock gazes with a short man naked but for a cape, flung dramatically to the side like Batman. A woman in a string of silver chains shivers in the breeze and makes gagging sounds as she kneels on the hard ground giving him a blowjob.

The high-pitched noises are emerging from his throat in a hideously feminine whimper unbecoming of a man of at least forty-five. He bares his teeth and thrusts more deeply into the woman's mouth as he continues to stare at Jean. She has accidentally become a part of their sex game, not the watcher but the watched. He jerkily finishes in the woman's mouth and she spits unenthusiastically into a plant pot.

There is no sight so demoralising as a jaded blowjob. Jean stubs out her cigarette under her heel and backs away from the terrace. Spying a dimly lit bar at the far end of the ballroom, Jean orders a Moscow Mule and tries to get into the rhythm of Eurotrash techno. She sits on a stool and sips through a metal straw as she checks out the male patrons, half-heartedly looking for Lord Drummund's distinctive, boulder-shaped head.

The one thing she could not have anticipated, was that 'The Night Of The Punter' would be . . . boring. Like any other party mostly composed of middle-aged businessmen, if they could bring beautiful escorts decades their junior to public functions without ridicule. Jean tries to strike up conversations with a few women, but no one seems interested in chatting. Only threesomes. Which Jean might have been up for, if their male partners hadn't resembled the ungodly spawn of John Prescott and Gordon Brown.

Jean casts her eyes over the barman longingly. If only she were allowed to proposition the staff . . .

Jean wanders up a broad winding staircase to explore the rest of the house, finding herself less and less titillated with every room. She has finally cracked open the door to the old ball's club, and thirty years of naivety are stripped from her in less than an hour. Images she will never be able to unsee dance across the back of her eyelids. The girl wearing a horse mask being pounded by a corpulent man, sweating like a pig and in a fittingly porcine disguise. The dominatrix in a horned mask breathing heavily as she whips a slender elder, whose withered testes are bound to the bedposts.

'Would you like some guidance?' A friendly member of the wait staff asks, proffering a tray of salmon-erection blinis decorated with caviar pubes. 'You look lost.'

Jean pops the canape in her mouth and chews, her mouth twisted in an ironic smile. In all of her childhood birthday photos she looked confused at the party, and now as an adult, she looks bewildered at the orgy.

She shakes off this defeatist line of thinking. It isn't that Jean has lost faith in finding emotional empowerment via sexual freedom. It simply isn't arousing to be adrift in a house full of mating politicians.

Her stomach rumbles loudly.

'Is there somewhere I could find something a little more . . . substantial?' she asks after swallowing, the only penis of the evening thus far. The waiter raises her eyebrows, eyes flickering from the room in which geriatric men are being pegged by a three-foot dildo, back to a bored-looking Jean.

'If the dominatrix isn't intense enough for you, there's a fungeon in the basement . . .'

'I meant the food!' Jean shares a laugh with the young woman, whose eyes twinkle in amusement beneath her mask.

It is one of those instant connections where Jean is sure that in other circumstances, they would be fast friends. As things stand, should they ever meet in public again, they would implement the power of the blank. That delightful force field where you can pretend to live in a universe where whatever it is you want to forget, has never occurred.

'There's a kitchen with cheese platters and veggies on the ground floor, behind the grand staircase,' the girl says, flicking back a tendril of red hair.

Jean thanks her before picking her way down the staircase towards the marble-topped open plan kitchen, empty but for a tall man in intense fetish gear. The skin-tight black rubber catsuit over his grasshopper-long legs makes him look like a pond insect caught by a transmogrifying machine. It is all very *Honey, I Magnified The Sex Beetle*. At Jean's startled look, he apologetically unzips the gimp mask. It unpeels to reveal a pale fleshy face, cheeks squashed inwards by the zipper, with melancholic hooded eyes and an aristocratic nose.

'Excuse me. Very cumbersome. For eating and chit-chat,' the man says in a thick Russian accent. He takes a china plate and wields the knife over a platter filled with room-temperature cheeses and stale-looking biscuits. 'Stilton?'

'That would be lovely, thank you,' Jean says, relaxing for the first time this evening. There is nothing like nibbles to reinstate a sense of normalcy, even when one is completely alone in a room with a man wearing a chain-link codpiece. 'Everything but the brie.'

'You don't like brie?' He asks aggressively.

'Not when it's all melted. I prefer it firm.'

The man smiles bleakly, as if he has thought of a biting double-entendre but can't be bothered to voice it. The laconic nihilism of the Slavs runs deep. Jean is simply relieved to have found a companion who also appears to be having a shit time at the orgy. She comes closer to his side of the free-standing island and dips her hand into a bowl of almonds.

The man portions out hefty hunks of cheese for her, and then serves himself. They both slice a sliver of Stilton on a cracker and chew in a contemplative silence. It is horrible, both gooey and hard, mouldy in exactly the wrong way. Jean grimaces.

'The cheese tastes of caviar and the caviar tastes of cheese,' the man says grimly, spitting it back out into a napkin. 'Is not at all what I expected of English hospitality.'

'It is rather subpar,' Jean agrees, also one to be intensely disappointed by a poor catering effort. 'And there are *so* many good cheesemongers in this area. Did you come from the fungeon?'

'Yes. It was very light-hearted,' he says, visibly depressed.

'Oh,' Jean says, unsure what to say.

'It made me sad,' he says, looking into his wine glass with a thousand-yard stare.

'I'm sorry to hear that,' Jean says, leaning over to pat his arm. She wobbles, slips on a fallen grape, trips over, falls on her knees and bashes her forehead against his cod-piece. The man lets out a gruff near-chuckle as he helps her to her feet, pressing her up against his rubber-clad belly.

'Is lucky I am not wearing the pointy studs,' he says with an attempt at a leer. Jean can tell his heart is not in it.

Click.

They look up at the noise. A man with a paper bag over his head has opened the kitchen door and stands shiftily in a black leather trench-coat, evidently living out some wino-flasher fantasy. He approaches them. Jean pushes herself off of the Russian man's chest. He re-zips his mask.

'I'm going to investigate the fungeon. I hope your night improves!' Jean says to his be-rubbered face.

The man nods. Jean can tell his disenchantment is too potent for the evening to recover. He's having one of those occasions where it's all downhill post dressing-up in your room, dancing in front of the mirror, fantasising about all the things that end up definitely not happening. She is, too.

Jean shakes out her wig and fluffs up her tits, deciding to give 'The Night Of The Punter' one last chance to excite her as she walks into the basement to investigate. Perhaps she'll find Lord Drummund hanging from a rack, conveniently spot-lit in an otherwise dark room, where she could photograph him from the shadows and then make a speedy exit.

She steps down a darkened staircase into an antechamber where a naked man with his face painted like a tiger is chained up to a door. He squeals as a striking woman in an elf costume applies ball-clamps and uses the end of a pink feather duster to penetrate him from behind. Jean immediately recognises the MP. It is not Lord Drummund, but another one of her clients. She turns on her heel and walks back up the stairs.

Jean thinks of Gabriel's gloriously youthful visage and sweet disposition as she steps into her taxi. It is fifteen minutes past midnight. The night's promise could still be retrieved. She texts him simply 'I'm coming over' and changes the Uber driver's destination address. She hopes this is sexy and not psychotic. She hopes he is, in fact, home. She throws the blonde wig out of the open window as they sail away from the Heath, not wanting to be reminded of Poppy. She wonders why she picked out a false name, when no one had even bothered to ask it.

'Weird night?' the taxi driver asks her.

'The weirdest,' Jean says, shaking her hair out of the tight bun plastered to her head. Her phone pings. Gabriel. No, not Gabriel. Richard. Jean opens the thread and catches up on their messages.

Dickface:

How's the sexfest? Is Lord D there?

MeiQween:

get that vitamin d

or you end up like me

Dickface:

You've made a rap.

MeiQween:

i have sex rickets

Dickface:

You should write for Drake.

Jean

Jean

Are you alive?

Jean bursts out laughing. She thinks about how best to describe the party in one sentence. She types furiously.

Jean:

So there's a reason Kubrick cast Tom Cruise and not John Belushi.

MeiQween:

Belushi died in 1982?

Dickface:

I knew it.

As the taxi nears Greenwich and with no reply from Gabriel, Jean starts to worry she has made a terrible mistake. Finally, when she is about to shamefacedly update her destination for a second time, he replies. 'I'm glad. I have something important I need to tell you', the text reads. Jean smiles, thinking dangerous thoughts. She half-fears, half-hopes . . . whatever it is he might say. Maybe his marriage is on the rocks. Maybe he has realised that he and his wife are great friends, but the passion is dead. Maybe he is in love with her.

She reapplies her smoky black eye and texts him a sexy photo with the message: 'I dressed up for you'. This is the beauty of dating someone new, someone with no idea how primly repressed Jean has been for the last ten years. For all Gabriel knows, Jean has always been a wanton hussy, an erotic carpet bomb, an absolute firecracker in the sack. By the time Jean rocks up on his doorstep, lighting a cigarette and leaning on his buzzer with her elbow, she has finally come to embody the character she has wanted to be all her life.

Herself, but way more interesting.

Gabriel swings open the door to Jean flashing her leg back and forth under her open coat as she pushes her hair out of her eyes. As for whatever important thing he needs to talk to her about, all conversation goes out the window. He drags her into his house by the fake fur lapels and pushes her against the door, kissing her urgently as it slams shut behind them. The coat falls to the floor as he rips open the front of her corset.

They have wild sex all over the living room and kitchen, slowly making their way to the bed via a pitstop shagging on the stairs. And just before they doze off on the bedroom floor, wrapped in each other's arms and a fallen duvet, Gabriel strokes the hair off her face to look deeply into her drowsy, post-orgasmic eyes.

'We could really have something special if . . .' Gabriel whispers, kissing her lightly on the forehead, seeming unsure that she heard him.

Jean's eyes close fully, and she pretends to have been asleep. She is lulled into dreaming with a smile on her face, wondering what this 'If . . .' could possibly signify, scared to let herself hope.

Chapter Eleven

'What was it you wanted to tell me?' Jean asks as she nuzzles into Gabriel's neck the next morning, smelling his soft fragrant hair, running her hands down his back. He had woken her up by going down on her and then they had had sleepy sex twice. She can't quite believe she had thought 'The Night Of The Punter' party would be better than this. Whatever it is they have, she is aglow with it. Passion, intimacy, tenderness. Love?

Gabriel pulls away from her embrace, smooths back his hair, puts on his glasses, looks at her with his full, sombre attention. Jean giggles and runs her finger down his nose.

'Why so serious?' she asks. Gabriel's brows knit and he bites his lip, casting his eyes down to the floor.

'Recently . . . Poppy took a lover in New York,' Gabriel says, as if he can't quite believe the unfamiliar words tumbling from his mouth. Jean's eyes widen in surprise, before she shrugs.

'Oh. Good for her, right?' she asks, naively. 'I mean, isn't that the point of the whole love beyond possession thing?'

'Yes . . . I mean, yes. I was pleased she had found someone, and all we have ever wanted in this situation is each other's full happiness. But in light of that,' Gabriel rushes through the last words, 'and what we ultimately think will make us *most* happy long-term, we've decided to try monogamy for a while. I'm flying into JFK this afternoon to reconnect with her and to experiment with fidelity.'

'. . . what,' Jean asks, blindsided.

'We're closing our marriage.'

Gabriel has the grace to look embarrassed. Jean thinks of them kissing heatedly against the door, rolling around on the living room floor, having sex on the kitchen counter, boning on the stairwell, and finally the last two sessions this morning half-asleep in each other's arms. And not once had he found a moment to tell her it was for the last time.

'I see.'

Her astonishment transforms swiftly into cynical acceptance. How could she have been so stupid? She had thought him so different, evolved beyond the common human responses of jealousy, possession and ownership. She knew it was never his intention to hurt her, but she can't help but feel caught up in the same old rigged game, royally played.

She looks anywhere but at his face, blinking back tears. An open suitcase lies on the bench underneath the window, half-filled with clothes. In her drunken sex haze, she hadn't noticed it. There were a lot of things she hadn't noticed, it seemed.

'When are you leaving?' Jean asks, clearing her throat and shaking her hair out of her face.

Gabriel looks at his watch.

'In a few hours,' Gabriel says, stroking her back tentatively as she stares away from him at the floor. Jean sits up and reaches for a discarded stocking.

'I'd better go,' she says, arms blindly searching for her other meagre articles of abandoned clothing. The corset had taken thirty minutes with Richard's help and a bucket of talcum powder to get into. How humiliating it will be to struggle back into it alone, sticky with sex and sweat.

'There's no rush,' Gabriel says sadly, his hand falling away from her.

She wants to feel his touch again, for the last time. She also wants to slap him across the face. She wants so many things. And here she is, left yearning again.

'You can stay here and sleep if you want. Help me pack?'

Help you pack? Jean thinks furiously, as she heads into the bathroom to splash water on her face. Choose which shirt best brings out the green in your eyes, for Poppy to admire when she meets you at the airport? Which jacket might suit a night on the town as you hit up a jazz café or the theatre, before a rooftop bar where you will kiss her dizzyingly beneath the glimmering Manhattan skyline and re-pledge your troth, or whatever the fuck it is experimental monogamists do?

And she had thought him so sensitive.

'I think it's best if I head home,' Jean says to her reflection. Her hair is a crazy bird's nest, her lips are bruised, there are hickeys on her neck and her ribcage is scratched from steel boning indentations. She wipes at her panda eyes and smears a trail of black over her cheekbones.

'I understand,' Gabriel says quietly, staring at the floor. He has the nerve to look hurt. Jean leans against the doorframe and watches him.

'Do you have an old T-shirt you wouldn't mind not seeing again?' she asks, gesturing down at her bruised semi-nudity. 'Won't you mind not seeing me again?' is what she really means by the request. Gabriel stands up and rummages through a pyjama drawer. He takes out a faded, baggy white shirt and hands it to her. She slips it over her head, before gathering her things.

'I'll call you a cab,' Gabriel says.

'Thanks,' Jean says, searching desperately for her phone and biting the inside of her mouth so she won't cry.

Downstairs, with her platform shoes dangling in one hand and her corset stuffed in a plastic bag in the other, fake fur coat thrown over his white T-shirt and her black stockings, Jean struggles into her Uber of Shame. She feels betrayed and seedy and sad. The weight of her melancholy has pulled apart her rage. All that is left is a tattered remnant of what she thought they had, and her own dissipating, foolish delusions.

Gabriel watches the car pull away, one hand raised in farewell.

'Have a nice life,' Jean says to him from behind the window, her fingertips on the glass, more bitter than sweet. As the car pulls away and he falls out of view, she tugs up the neckline of his shirt to her nose and inhales his scent, more sweet than bitter. She closes her eyes and rests her head against the cool leather seat and tries to go about the business of forgetting him utterly.

Flashbacks flicker across her mind's eye, in a reel of pornographic heartbreak.

At home, she staggers through the front door, strips off all her clothes in the hallway and locks herself immediately in the bathroom. She sits on the edge of the tub and turns the faucets until hot water gushes through the pipes.

'Jean?' she hears Richard call out from behind the door. 'Tell me everything!'

'Later!' she says, choking on the word.

'Are you OK?' Richard asks, tapping, concerned.

Jean swallows, hard.

'Great!' Jean lies, dumping Imperial Leather into the tub until it is as frothy as a cappuccino. She slides underneath the bubbles. She opens her phone and Instastalks his perfect wife and their perfect life, falling down a rabbit hole of insane jealousy.

Poppy on the deck of a yacht, looking impossibly glamorous in a white mesh dress over a gold string bikini.

Poppy and Gabriel in a throwback snap in Peru, tanned and wearing matching straw hats and aviator sunglasses. Poppy at an awards ceremony with a group of fashionable friends, looking like the only one who had rocked up effortlessly. Poppy holding a friend's Chihuahua, laughing as it licks her face. Gabriel asleep on her mattress, his arse half covered by a sheet, a sunbeam shining on his golden hair. Poppy's reflection in a mirror behind his naked body, a black Polaroid camera covering her face.

Poppy, Poppy, Poppy.

Chapter Twelve

'I'm grrrrreeeeat!' Jean exclaims like an inebriated Tony the Tiger, swigging from a vodka bottle and clapping Danielle heartily on the back with false cheer. 'So great. Excellent!'

'She's well,' Richard adds dryly, as he checks out the sparkly, spangled and scantily clad talent in the queue behind them. A drag queen in a hot pink bikini and stunning feathered headdress winks with one sequinned eye. Richard casts back a flirtatious glance in response, smoothing the line of his ruffled flower-print blouse.

'I never thought you'd be this enthused by an erotic poetry reading,' Danielle says with raised eyebrows, stiffening under Jean's overzealous hug. The Languorous Lick is a monthly night Danielle hosts in her friend's warehouse in East London. It has a cult following as an event where art is made and displayed and you are almost guaranteed to get laid. 'I've invited you like ten times and you've never come!'

'That was when I was a relationship-spinster who faked orgasms her entire adult life and thought mothering a man was the only way to make him love you.' Jean laughs crazily. She stops abruptly as Danielle and Richard exchange a look of concern. 'What?'

'Is she really OK?' Danielle asks Richard. His face compresses like a scrunchie and he shakes his head violently from side to side. Jean rolls her eyes.

'I'm allowed to bitch and grieve my abrupt post-shag dumping,' she defends herself as they walk through the graffiti covered door and up a dingy concrete stairwell. 'It's only been a week!'

'It's been ten days,' Richard corrects her.

'Is grief really the word? You've only known him two months,' Danielle says as she leads them through a crusty burgundy velvet curtain into a dark cavernous room.

'Is dumping really the word? He *is* married to someone else,' Richard points out, grabbing the vodka bottle from her hand and taking a swig. He gags delicately.

Jean represses her annoyance and takes in the scenery. Chairs surround a spotlit stage in the shape of ginormous breasts, underneath a spinning disco ball where a young woman in a tiny plastic miniskirt and no top is reciting into the phallic microphone. A sheet of paper is held in one hand, a chain leading to a naked man kneeling with a red ball in his mouth in the other. After her sex party downer, Jean finds herself bitterly resenting the literal nature of the décor. Must everything be a tit? Couldn't the stage be, quite simply, a fucking circle.

'There was more to it than just shagging,' Jean mutters sulkily.

It is too pathetic to voice the 'But he wanted to be London exclusive!' thing, her one shred of proof that he cares about her as more than a plaything.

'Shagging is the best part! It's when you catch feelings that it goes to hell,' Danielle says as she rage-types something into her phone.

'Preach, sistah,' Richard chimes in.

'I've done a lot of drugs in my time, but love is the only one that scares the shit out of me,' her sister adds, staring into the distance wretchedly.

Jean watches the young woman on stage tug on the man's collar and kick him in the buttocks as she enacts a line from her poem. The audience roars with laughter. Jean sympathises with the submissive man. She feels the same: exposed, vulnerable, raw. Only without the resulting erection.

'But you don't think he was . . .' Jean struggles to find the right words to express her indignity. Gabriel had been honest from the beginning; the circumstances of his marriage had changed. She couldn't really blame him for that. Which somehow made it worse. The right to feel betrayed had been taken from her.

'A prick? Yes! So what? You've moved from love triangle to line segment,' Danielle shouts, waving her hands in the air. 'Get over it!'

The woman speaking casts her a dirty look, but as host of the night, Danielle does what she wants. She always has.

'Is she a line segment? Or a full stop,' Richard laughs.

'Too soon, Richard!'

Jean snatches the vodka out of his clutches and drinks, considering this horrible new self-image. *A line segment.*

'This is why quadrangles are better,' Danielle explains. 'Safety in numbers.'

'I'm at the centre of a pentagon, myself,' Richard says smugly, as he flirts under his lashes with a beautiful woman in a neon yellow leotard and a striking afro.

'You're the bloody Warlock of Eastwick,' Jean says, with no small irritation.

Richard's multi-dating Tom Hardy hypnosis has been both shockingly successful, and gone straight to his head. Jean has lost count of the girls he had brought home over the past few weeks who cheerfully tried to impress her over breakfast. She eventually took to calling everyone 'babe'.

Not outing Richard as a man-ho has become a strange and unwelcome reversal in their fortunes.

It wouldn't bother her so much, had he not also stopped doing the dishes and started to blast Eminem at all hours.

'I'm caught in an existential malaise, sister,' Danielle confesses, swigging from a beer left on a table that Jean knows is definitely not hers. 'I'm a fraud.'

'Get over it,' Jean parrots back her sister's helpful advice.

'Not only am I in love,' Danielle whispers, as secretive as a tinfoil hat conspiracy theorist afraid his conversation is being bugged by the government. 'I'm broody as hell!'

'Really?' Jean asks, gobsmacked.

Danielle has always claimed she never wants children, for the usual reasons. Firstly, because she hates to feel trapped more than anything else in the world, and secondly, because she doesn't want to ruin her life.

'It's all the fucking oxytocin,' Danielle says helplessly, finishing off the beer. 'An aging uterus and staying the night have unhinged my goddamn senses.'

'It is hard to imagine you with a baby as queen of this realm . . .' Richard agrees. Behind them, the young woman steps off the tittie-stage, dragging her sex-pet behind her.

'I *know*. Who wants to listen to a sex show by a cis, heterosexual, monogamist breeder?' Danielle says, swiping the vodka from Jean's hand and finishing it off in two greedy glugs. She throws it in the air behind her where it lands, miraculously, in a bin. The implication that this might not be the ideal environment to raise a small child has similarly flown right over her head. 'Right, this is me.'

Danielle steps onto the stage, flipping her hair back under the spotlight.

'Queers of all nations!' she shouts throatily into the microphone. Upon closer inspection, Jean sees that someone hollowed out a two-foot sparkly dildo and fit it over the stand, so the mike serves as a fuzzy bell-end. 'A round of lascivious applause for the luscious Lady Matilda and her devoted slave, Steve.'

The audience clap and shout. To the side of the stage, nervously waiting to go on, is a skinny youth in an Adidas tracksuit and Burberry cap. He is a chav of the old school, rarely observed since people of all social classes came to aspire to look like reality stars. He stares at his shoes as Danielle claps him on. Jean braces herself for an erotic ditty reflective of the German gonzo gangbang porn boys of his generation are exposed to, where endearments like 'Little fist-pig, ja?' fall as fast and hard as the thrusting.

Instead, the boy raises vulnerable eyes and says softly, 'This is a poem called *Latex Love*,' before, in a sing-song, heartfelt voice, describing the pain and social isolation of a Tinder culture in which everyone is reduced to an image. That we have allowed ourselves to become sexed and disposed of, discarded like used tissues, at a time when emotions are viewed as a fate worse than gonorrhoea, and preserving our dignity by not giving a damn is more vital than gambling with our hearts.

It speaks to Jean's fucking soul.

'That was beautiful,' Jean whispers in the boy's ear as he steps off the stage, squeezing him lightly on the shoulder. 'Forgive me, I didn't think you'd be so . . . sensitive . . .'

'Don't patronise me bruv,' the boy says, shaking her off. 'Don't touch me neither. I know my rights.'

'I'm *so* sorry,' Jean apologises desperately. She hopes she is not giving off predatory vibes. The boy must be all of seventeen; to him, her thirty-year-old face must be ancient, her red pleather miniskirt a deceptively girlish ploy to entrap him into elder sex. Guilt mixes with admiration that he possesses a bodily autonomy she never had at his, or any, age.

'Do you think I'm complicit?' she asks Richard as they walk towards the bar at the far end of the warehouse. A couple are slow dancing, French kissing, with the sort of blissed-out exhibitionist passion Jean had expected from the sex party.

'In becoming a line segment?' Richard asks in confusion after he orders two cans of Red Stripe. 'Or in thinking you're entitled to love, when all you agreed to was sex?'

'Wow that's . . . harsh . . .' Jean stammers. 'I don't think I like Tom Hardy. In fact, I think Tom Hardy is a real dick.'

'Real talk, babe,' Richard shrugs, popping open his beer and letting his eyes rove over the female guests in a way he never would done one month prior. 'I read Lord Kinder's *Sunday Times* spread. Did he really donate last year's salary to a charity for sex workers?'

'Yes,' Jean says, raising her beer to toast herself. At least some good could come from working within the annals of corruption. 'I finally convinced him!'

'Did you also convince him to come out as gay and express the hardship for a man of his generation and social position to come to terms with his sexuality?' Richard asks with judgemental eyebrows.

'Of course. I mean, I had no counter-blackmail information. It was our only hope,' Jean says. The social media reaction had been a mixture of sympathy and outrage, but it was an improvement on just outrage. 'It's my job! I'm like a defence attorney in the court of public opinion. Don't you believe that everyone has the right to a fair trial?'

'It isn't really fair, is it though?' Richard says. 'An escort against a lord.'

Jean doesn't answer. For some reason (which Danielle insists is Mercury Rising) they are all prickly tonight. There is bad juju fermenting that she cannot handle exploding on this particular week. Jean cracks open her beer and sips, watching the stage lights dim as Danielle announces a thirty-minute intermission. In the corner, a D.J. starts to blast trap rap.

Jean decides not to mention the fact that Jez, impressed by her powers of persuasion and willingness to go to any length for her clients, has given her a fat bonus. What should elate her weighs on her conscience, and she fears her willingness to go that extra criminal mile will come back to bite her in the arse.

'What are you talking about?' Danielle asks as she approaches them. She takes the beer from Jean's hands and swigs deeply.

Jean turns to the bar and orders a second can.

'How do I get over Gabriel?' Jean says, to change the subject.

'This whole heartbreak fandango could have been avoided if you actually followed my advice and put more people in your rotation,' Danielle points out.

'The rotation,' Jean says. 'How could I forget. Well, Charlie keeps emailing me and texting from different numbers since I've blocked him.'

'Charlie isn't a rotation, Charlie is a mistake that went on for years,' Richard points out, as if he hadn't sung Charlie's praises the entire time they'd been together.

'This is entirely your own fault,' Danielle continues.

'Totally,' Richard smiles dreamily. 'I've met a woman I could fall in love with. I would be head over heels, if I didn't have six others on the go!'

'Which one is this?' Jean asks.

Thus far, there had been a thick blonde, a skinny redhead, a tattooed mixed-race girl, a zaftig Italian, a deep-voiced Russian, an adorable Argentine and one of the cast of TOWIE.

'Valentina. It's so delicious to be in control of my emotions! I haven't once felt the need to ring her ten times in one day,' Richard continues, lost in the mists of infatuation. 'For the first time in my life, I'm falling in love, but not like I'm about to lose my shit at any moment. I feel calmer, less mental.'

'Yes, well, power does that, doesn't it,' Jean says with frustration.

'What happened to your threesome date?' Danielle asks.

'I caught feelings and lost the will to bone strangers,' Jean sighs in defeat.

'Get back on that horse,' Danielle chastises her. 'Sex with people you don't want to have sex with is literally the only potion to make you forget about sex with the person you want to have sex with.'

'That is so fucking depressing,' Jean says by way of agreement, whipping out her phone and reactivating Thrinder for the first time in weeks. She hopes Sinbad and Stacey will still be up for it. She has accidentally played very hard to get, which may work in her favour. She decides to flirt like every man she knew was messing her around, but that she was unable to resist.

JeanGenie DM:

hey sexys

soz been AWOL life got busy

♂ next wkend?

love to c u 2

Stacey responds almost immediately. After less than one minute of text flirtation, they have rescheduled their date for six o'clock the following Saturday.

'Done and done,' Jean says with false triumph as she shoves her phone in her bag. Determined as she is to put her whirlwind romance with Gabriel behind her, Jean is also not feeling it at all. 'Crazy golf shagging ahoy!'

'Just go for it,' Danielle says, patting her shoulder. 'You're lucky you got out when you did. If you stick to no contact, you'll struggle to remember his face in a few months.'

Jean smiles and sips her beer in silence, while ignoring the little voice piping up from the deep, dark pit of her bruised heart, a voice that says she doesn't ever want to forget his face.

Chapter Thirteen

Jean walks beneath the Gherkin, wondering why the aptly named Swingers would choose the office block and corporate restaurant end of Liverpool Street to host its madcap events, and if this is Sinbad and Stacey's extremely literal first-date venue for all their prospective paramours. The first and last time Jean had played miniature golf she had been about thirteen, on a miserable holiday with her parents in Florida. Her mother had shown a beginner's knack for it, while her father had spent the entire time shouting at windmills, an unhinged Don Quixote suffering from a fit of slighted masculinity. His ego was somewhat soothed when her mother intentionally lost the last rounds, and he contented himself with decapitating a decorative pink flamingo on the way out.

Jean had forgotten all about it, until she opens the door to the blue-lit, trendy golf course and the scent of plastic AstroTurf hits her like a breathy scream. Shaking off her trepidation, Jean asks for directions to the bar. All dark wood, bronze fixtures and dive bar lamps, it is as far as can be from the sweltering poverty, swastika tattoos, mullets and male rage that were her lasting impressions of Crazy Larry's Crazy Golf, Orlando.

Sinbad and Stacey, unmistakable in their matching floaty silk harem trousers, topped by a Hole T-shirt for him and a tight white vest for her, nuzzle each other as they sip cocktails at the bar. Stacey's undercut, nose ring and impressive guns give her an ambisextrous vibe, while Sinbad's long locks tied up in a sequinned scrunchie speak highly of his masculine security. They share a moment of laughter, unaware they are being observed. Jean likes them immediately.

'Hello!' Jean says with a shy grin as she approaches them. She hopes that her outfit, skinny jeans paired with a Fred Perry shirt and combat boots, suggests that she is indeed the single bi-girl Unicorn spoken of with longing on poly message boards. She worries her choice of Dolce & Gabbana *Light Blue* perfume, the most basic bitch of basic bitch scents, will out her as a straight. 'So lovely to finally meet you.'

'I'm glad the timing finally worked out!' Stacey says, embracing Jean in a warm hug. Sinbad kisses her on both cheeks and raises his glass from the bar. Butterflies stir in Jean's stomach while her nerves simultaneously calm. The couple emit a tranquil aura, the kind that only people who spend weeks meditating in jungles seem to.

'Mojito? We've taken the liberty of ordering a dozen fried oysters,' Sinbad says with a wink, as he takes the liberty of grasping her shoulder blade and massaging it.

'Perfect!' Jean chirps, setting her handbag on the floor.

His forthright touching does not bother her at all, in contrast to the sex party groping. Perhaps it is the flirtatious text preamble, or the fact that they are all here for one thing. Mostly, it is because Sinbad is one sexy motherfucker, with the piercing amber eyes of a hawk. His deeply tanned, lithe yet powerful tattooed forearms remind her of *Aquaman*. Desire is a fickle creature, and it must be enticed. Jean is enticed.

'Excuse me, sir? A mojito for the lady,' Sinbad says to the bartender.

'How was Peru?' Jean asks.

'Amazing, as always. We do a retreat there twice a year, one month of community yoga in return for free lodging and Ayahuasca ceremonies with one of our shamans,' Stacey says, her eyes dazzling with the clear brilliance of the spiritually initiated.

'Wow, that sounds fantastic,' Jean says, not knowing anything about Ayahuasca beyond the brew being so stomach churning that shit-buckets are provided, in case of mid-trip explosions. 'How many shamans do you have?'

'I have five,' Sinbad says, smoothing back an escaped lock of curly black hair. 'Stacey has three.'

'You can never have too many shamans,' Stacey says with a laugh, staring deeply into Jean's eyes. 'My journey into Source only started two years ago, so I have some catching up to do.'

Usually a phrase like 'journey into Source' would make Jean break out in rational materialist hives, but Stacey says it in a playful tone free of piousness or sanctimony.

'Crikey! I haven't even journeyed into crazy golf,' Jean jokes lamely, deciding to opt for the blank slate excuse for her terrible swing. As the fried oysters arrive, Jean adds her own painfully obvious double entendre. 'Tell me, how long have you two been Swinging?'

'Three or four times,' Sinbad says, referring to the venue.

'From the beginning,' Stacey purrs, taking Jean's hand in her own. Jean smiles and takes a deep sip of her cocktail. Stacey's forwardness alleviates any lingering doubts Jean has about her ability to sleep with a woman, which were mostly based on sheer laziness and the fear of throwing her back out while using a strap-on. A hand is a hand is a hand, surely, and a mouth is a mouth?

They polish off the oysters and finish their cocktails, before heading to a stand where they arm themselves with clubs.

On the flower strewn faux-woodland greenery strung up with fairy lights, laughing as they badly attempt to putt into impossible holes, the last of her nerves uncoil and dissipate. Jean and Stacey sit on a stationary golf cart covered in roses watching Sinbad take a swing. Stacey leans into her cosily, slinging her arm over Jean's shoulders and playing with the rings on her fingers.

Jean hears Sinbad curse as he misses his shot, but she doesn't notice, captivated as she is by Stacey's rich brown eyes. As their lips lightly touch, she feels Sinbad approach them from the other side. Jean turns her head towards him and is about to engage in her first ever three-way kiss – in public no less! – when her gaze is arrested by a slack-jawed blonde in tennis whites, stopped in mid-swing on the course directly across from her. It is the last person in the world she wants to see at this moment. Her only true nemesis.

Charlize.

Jean scrambles up from the golf cart between the two lovers, who collide in a dazed and messy kiss behind her, before looking up in confusion.

'Jean,' Charlize says, a twisted grin on her face. As she approaches them, her eyes narrow in gleeful derision. 'How *are* you?'

Never has the word 'are' been so loaded with evil intent. Jean resists the urge to beat Charlize's perfect teeth in with her golf club and beams back freely.

'I'm great! Never better,' Jean says, her stomach churning sickly. 'And how is Charlie? Still on the wagon?'

Apart from the messages she sporadically receives and deletes without reading, Jean mostly pretends that Charlie has been wiped off the surface of the earth in a freak brewery explosion. Petty and unfeeling, yes, but oh so satisfying.

Charlize's face flickers in a micro-expression of fury that tells Jean everything she needs to know about the true state of his sobriety.

'Never better,' Charlize parrots her back with a malicious smile.

'I believe you,' Jean says, in a patronising triumph of sick burns.

'And who are your new . . . . friends?' Charlize eyes up Sinbad and Stacey, who have stood up behind Jean and look her over curiously.

Jean takes Stacey's hand in hers, Sinbad's in the other and draws them towards her.

'These are my yogini lovers, Sinbad and Stacey,' Jean says defiantly, kissing Stacey's hand even as she feels Charlize's brain whirring with mocking judgement.

'Yogini is feminine, not a plural term,' Stacey whispers into Jean's ear.

Sinbad's eyebrows raise in a silent query of her gun-jumping use of the term 'lovers'.

'Wow! Jean, I always thought of you as so rigid and straight-laced, not boring exactly but,' Charlize wrinkles her nose to suggest that boring is exactly what she means. 'Who knew you'd become so *wild* in your old age?'

'I'm six months older than you, Charlize,' Jean says through gritted teeth.

Charlize is to gossip what bedbugs are to hostels; this will spread like blood-sucking insects. Except in the story version, Jean will be painted as a desperate faux-dyke failing to be more sexually adventurous than is natural, while Sinbad and Stacey will be transformed into crusty, creepy hippies.

Jean starts to doubt herself. Perhaps that is exactly what they all are.

A small, betraying part of her wonders what Charlie will think. If he will view her with disgust, if this will be the final lurid nail in the slut-coffin his love gets buried in. It isn't that Jean is still in love with Charlie, herself. She just wants him to rue what he was not careful with, forever lost in woeful pining.

'How does this all . . . work?' Charlize asks, using one manicured fingernail to draw a disgusted circle in the air.

Jean feels shame rising within her, her stomach knotting and quaking unpleasantly. She wants nothing more than to flee Swingers, flee swinging, retreat back to her old life of cyclical stress and boredom punctured by the odd Games Night and meditation sessions that were really a fucking nap.

The only way out of anxiety is through it, and Jean is sick of retreating back to the unhappy known. She threads Sinbad and Stacey's arms around her waist and leans her head against his shoulder. She is a free agent with two liberated, fun, attractive, mad-flexi humans on her arms. Why stay small and staid when there is so much adventure to be had?

'Like this,' Jean says, owning it. She embraces first Sinbad then Stacey lingeringly, encircling them in a multifaceted kiss in front of Charlize's shocked face. Pulling back, she murmurs, 'Shall we go back to my place?'

Sinbad looks questioningly at Stacey, who grins in response.

'Let's bounce,' Stacey says, taking Jean's hand and drawing her towards the exit. Sinbad and Jean wave a cheerful goodbye to Charlize, a spring in their synchronised steps.

'Was that your ex-girlfriend?' Stacey asks, as Jean fumbles with the keys on the lock of her front door thirty minutes later.

The taxi ride home had been a jumble of legs, arms, clothing, kisses, tongues, teeth. The driver had gotten an eyeful, and Jean is in a daze. She is simultaneously very turned on and very queasy. She hopes it is first date jitters and not the oysters.

'Charlize?' Jean asks in surprise as the door finally opens. She supposed she was, in a way. They had shared the usual trajectory of love gone sour. An intense closeness followed by betrayal, regret, recrimination, jealousy, bitterness, and one-upmanship. 'Sort of.'

'I could tell she was jealous of you,' Stacey says, kissing the back of Jean's neck.

Of what, Jean can't possibly imagine. Charlize's career had taken off when she left Addington Media for music PR, she now had Jean's (bastard dipsomaniac sloppy-seconds) man, she owned her own flat, and enjoyed petite, girlish, physical near-perfection.

'Let's not talk about Charlize,' Jean says evasively.

She flips on the lights and leads them through the corridor towards her room. She tidied up earlier, the bed made as perfectly as in a hotel, with flattering pink fairy lights wound through the frame, and fresh flowers in a vase on her dresser. As if she is one of those people whose private life is always Insta-ready. Jean taps her open computer and brings up Spotify. She clicks on her sex playlist (almost entirely composed of D'Angelo) and dims the lights. She can hear Sinbad and Stacey kissing behind her. Her nerves reignite and her stomach churns. Is she really about to do this? Her anger towards Charlize had distracted her from the mechanics of what is actually happening.

'I'll just go get some Prosecco from the fridge,' Jean says, hurrying out of the room and gripped by the sudden paranoid conviction she is going to pass gas.

'Richard?' Jean calls out into the kitchen, to be met with silence.

Since he'd turned into the Don Juan of Kentish Town, they barely hang out at home any more. He was off tom catting, slinking in and out at all hours of the day and night, his life a revolving door of work and assignations. She didn't like it.

Opening the refrigerator door, Jean rubs her cramping lower belly and lets out a testing toot, before being overtaken by the power of her flatulence. It is one of those farts with a life of its own: a slow, moaning, trumpet echo, exactly like whale-song. Jean pops the Prosecco bottle open and prays the noise of the cork and beeping of the fridge and the seductive opening notes of 'How Does It Feel' in the other room have covered for her. Jean grabs three glasses while running over the odds of a recurrence in her mind.

Yentl jumps out from on top of the cupboard where Jean had startled her, hissing dementedly, before running away to hide in her litter tray. It is a bad omen.

'Here we are,' Jean says, returning with her kegels and anus clenched tight.

Jean refuses to be farty threesome girl. She will exert pelvic self-control and be crazy-tight pussy girl. Sinbad sits on the bed shirtless, while Stacey straddles him and nibbles his ear, disrobed down to her bra and pants. Jean hands them the flutes of Prosecco and they clink and drink. Sinbad draws her into a kiss, probing her mouth with his tongue deeply. A little too deeply, but in a way suggesting oral skills that will make her current gag-reflex worth it. Jean sets her glass on the bedside table. Stacey lifts up Jean's shirt and pulls it over her head, undoes the top button of her trousers.

As D'Angelo croons about wanting to make whatever lucky lady inspired this song wet, Jean tries to struggle out of her jeans in a seductive fashion. They cling to her legs with the force of a Velcro banana peel.

'Relax,' Stacey says, helping Jean to wrench them off her ankles, bound together on the floor. Jean kicks them off of herself in embarrassment, as Sinbad strokes the back of Stacey's neck and watches with a small smile on his face.

'I'm relaxed!' Jean laughs in high-pitch, tightly clenching her buttocks, her belly rumbling oddly. She is very aware that her seized-up rump will have made her cellulite extra apparent.

She grabs her glass and takes a swift glug.

'Breathe,' Stacey says, as Jean rises and flings off her bra, determined to get this sex party started.

'I'm breathing,' Jean says forcefully, before pushing Stacey against the bed and kissing her with passion. Sinbad drops his trousers with the elegance of a Chippendale genie and gets involved. Finally, the threesome regains the hot and heavy, easy lust of the taxi ride over. Their yoga-honed bodies are bendy and limber, silky and strong, like snakes or spider monkeys. Sinbad's dick has a mind of its own, behaving like a prehensile tail. Jean kisses the length of Stacey's torso and removes her pants. She licks the inside of her thigh. Stacey moans. Another stomach twinge. More severe this time. Jean winces.

'First, there is . . . desire!'

Jean's head jerks up from where her finger has started to stroke Stacey. The opening notes are unmistakable. *Moulin Rouge*. This could only mean one thing.

Richard had gotten to her sex playlist.

RRrriiiiip! The fart shoots out from her intensely compacted sphincter like machine gun fire. Perfectly aligned with the shouted lyrics: 'Then, passion!' Jean desperately hopes they will think it part of the musical. She looks up guiltily to see Sinbad sniffing the air.

'Then, suspicion . . .' the music continues.

'I'm so sorry, I-I think I have to,' Jean chokes out, mortified.

'Jealousy! Anger! Betrayal!' the singer shouts.

Jean staggers to her feet towards the blessedly en suite bathroom, engaged in a repellent *Ministry Of Silly Walks* waddle-dash. It is clear that she is about to shit her pants. Slamming the door behind her, she hears smothered laughter coming from the other room. She flings her burning arse towards the toilet, making it just in time to prevent a gruesome spray of faecal devastation across the tiles to the tune of 'El Tango De Roxanne'.

'When love is for the highest bidder, there can be no trust!'

'Jean? Are you OK?' Stacey asks, tapping on the door.

Jean feels bile rising in her throat.

'Without trust, there is no love!'

'B-bad oyster!' Jean manages to say before projectile vomiting with a throaty roar into the bath, not unlike Regan from *The Exorcist*.

'Jealousy, yes, jealousy. Will drive you . . . MAAAAAD!!'

'We're going to let ourselves out, OK?' Stacey shouts through the door as Sinbad fails to disguise his laughter. 'I hope you feel better!'

Jean retches thunderously in response. She leans her putrid, jaundiced face against the porcelain sink. She wonders if the accidental aversion therapy of total humiliation to the tune of the *Moulin Rouge* will have ruined a perfect film, forever. She curses Richard's name before another wave of gut-clenching shellfish spew sputters up to strike.

Chapter Fourteen

The next morning finds Jean half-asleep in the bathtub for easy access to the toilet. Every time she thinks the food poisoning has well and truly passed, that there is nothing left inside her, that she is as hollowed out as a didgeridoo, her innards find some last corner to squeeze of life force. She has never felt so depleted, but at least sheer physical weakness means there is no room for shame. Shame takes energy, and it is all Jean can do to turn on the hot water tap with one toe, before her body melts back in exhaustion and she wonders if this is the end.

'Jean? Are you OK?' Richard knocks against her bedroom door. 'I haven't heard a peep from you all morning!'

Jim Broadbent's powdered and rouged face looms in front of Jean's watery eyes in a dehydration hallucination and tells it to her straight: 'You're dying, Satine'.

'I'm dying,' Jean whispers into the air.

Richard does not hear. More knocking.

'Jean? Your music is still on and I know you had a hot date, so I'd appreciate it if you'd let me know you're still alive,' Richard says waspishly.

Jean's tampered sex playlist has been running on a loop all night, in an erotic R&B/musical theatre hellscape. The misery mix peaked with Jean retching to Aladdin's 'Friend Like Me', re-mourning the death of Robin Williams with hot salty tears, before berating herself minutes later for continuing to stream R. Kelly's year 2000 hit, 'Feelin' On Yo Booty'.

'I'm coming in . . .' Richard says, an alarmed edge to his voice. Jean hears him shuffle into her bedroom. Fling open her closet. A tentative knock against the bathroom door. She knows Richard too well; he's never trusted hippies. He will be envisioning opening it to a brutal murder scene, the ending of *Fatal Attraction* performed by two cast members from *The Beach*. 'Jean? I'm coming in!'

Richard flings the door wide dramatically, shrieking to see her floating in the tub naked in the foetal position, her eyes open but immobile. As Jean shows signs of life via a solitary blink, Richard wrinkles his nose.

'Good god, it reeks! What on earth happened?'

'Bring me . . . my phone . . .' Jean says, her hand shakily lifting out of the bath. Richard rolls his eyes and turns away to search her room for her mobile. 'Turn off the . . . music . . .'

Her Spotify torture comes to a merciful end.

'You look like reanimated undead Golem,' Richard says, handing her the iPhone as he holds his nose with one hand and looks in the other direction. 'Are you hanging?'

'I've been felled . . . by an oyster,' Jean croaks through her bile-rasped throat, shivering in the bath as she flops over the side of the tub and checks her messages with one slow fingernail. 'Tell my parents . . . they failed me . . . and Danielle . . . her advice . . . blows . . .'

'Christ. I'll go to the shop and get you some electrolytes and Imodium. And bleach. And air freshener,' Richard says, throwing a towel in her direction. 'Can you stand a banana and oatmeal?'

Jean shudders in response. She sees an email from Charlie. The subject line is: 'R U a gay now'. She deletes it immediately.

'And tell Charlie . . . I hate him,' Jean says to Richard's retreating back.

'I thought you didn't care about Charlie!' Richard calls out in a singsong-y voice before she hears the front door slam shut behind him.

'I don't,' Jean mutters to herself sulkily, as she scrolls through her news feed. Her eyebrows knit together as she clicks on a viral Buzzfeed link entitled *Animal Abuse At Floral Shop*. 'What the hell . . .'

Jean recoils as a phone camera zooms in on a pack of tiny kittens retching, the hands of a sobbing woman rubbing their contorted little spines in an attempt to soothe them.

Wait.

She recognises that chipped black nail varnish, those bitten square cuticles.

'Dear god, no,' Jean whispers as she clicks out of the link and minimises her internet, trying to pretend this isn't happening.

A coil of anxiety blooms in her stomach, unstoppable as the expelling oysters. She has to know more. Heart leaden with dread, she is about to click into Google when her phone pings with a Twitter notification. It is a breaking news live feed: 'Pussy Willows Kitten Poisoning'.

A reporter stands in front of the beautiful storefront with the epic cat playground in the windows. They are filled with puking animals, mewling and crawling around blindly, in a piteous display not unlike a trench warfare mustard gas scene.

'Disaster struck a flower shop and cat café this morning, when Pussy Willows owner Tess Li's four-year-old son fed the kittens orchid feed. While undoubtedly a tragic accident, the viral video of vomiting bands of cats has called into question what, if any, animal rights protection measures Ms Li has been taking,' a reporter who looks and sounds exactly like Alan Partridge says in a deadly serious tone. 'And indeed, the broader issue of whether cross-businesses of this kind are in fact dangerous and exploitative to prospective pets.'

The camera pans back to the shopfront, where Tess sits with her head in her hands on the stoop, sobbing. Bjorn, with a screaming Fynn slung over one arm, is speaking to someone Jean hopes is a veterinarian and rubbing one of Tess's shoulders.

'Animal rights protesters are gathering outside the quaint Dulwich Village shop, which opened one month ago to great success. It is a small business with a noble mission. To spark joy in female-identifying individuals with that trifecta of lady-comfort: cats, flowers and feminist literature. Sadly, Pussy Willows is now doomed to closure, before it could ever really take off. Tess Li has fallen victim to the Achilles heel of working women everywhere. How to follow rules properly,' the reporter concludes patronisingly.

Jean clicks out of the link in disgust.

When Richard bursts through the front door screaming 'OmigadOmigad!', Jean surmises that he has found out, too.

'Have you seen the news?' Richard shouts as he storms into the bathroom, his arms loaded down with white carrier bags, Lucozade tops and cleaning spray ends poking out of them. 'Pussy Willows is in peril!'

'I know, it's terrible . . .' Jean says, stretching out one trembling arm towards the bags. Richard drops them and throws a pack of Imodium in her face. 'Do we both have to go?'

'Pull yourself together woman,' Richard says as he hits the shower nozzle tap, spraying Jean with cold water. She sits up, sputtering. Richard shoves a juice under her nose. 'Our best friend is in need. We must go and comfort her!'

Jean groans, stepping out of the bathtub on rubbery legs as Richard dashes into her room to rifle through her closet. She wraps herself in the towel and sinks to the floor in despair. It is one of those days when everything feels completely pointless, attempts at happiness or self-actualisation or even walking as ill-fated an act of hubris as Icarus's wax wings.

'I've soared too close to the sun,' Jean whimpers piteously.

'Wear these,' Richard ignores her, flinging a pair of track-suit bottoms and a grey jumper in her direction, before pelting her head with a pair of flip-flops. 'I'll call a cab.'

The taxi pulls up in front of a throng of protesters, bearing signs with sad cat faces under slogans like 'Flora and Fauna: The Only Apartheid I Support' and 'Me-OW: A Voice For The Voiceless'. It is at least ten feet deep, with news outlets recording them throughout.

'Have people nothing better to do?' Richard asks in shock as he swings open the door and drags Jean behind him through the crowd.

'Feline Fascism! Feline Fascism!' a middle-aged woman yells, as she throws a stuffed toy cat at the shopfront and tries to get the other protesters to join her chant. When that doesn't catch on, she goes for the old classic: 'Murderess!'

'She's an overworked single mum!' Jean screams in the woman's face. 'Trying to live her best life under the steel boot of patriarchy!'

'Tess!' Richard shouts as he bangs on the locked front door. 'Let us in!'

'She can't hear you,' Jean says as she rummages through her bag and gets out a key. 'Shield me from the mob! I have her emergency set.'

They slam the door shut behind them and walk into the darkened flower shop. An acrid smell lingers below the floral blooms with mulchy undertones. The floor is sticky.

'Tess?' Jean calls out. 'It's us, where are you?'

'H-here,' Tess moans from the back room.

They rush over, to find her huddled, distraught and sobbing into a dirty mop in the storage closet, her body slumped over the killer sack of orchid feed.

'Everything's ruined . . .' she moans, taking a swig from a nearly-empty bottle of cheap white wine and wiping her snotty nose on her shoulder. 'I'm all washed up.'

'That's not true! You can bounce back from this,' Jean says, crouching down to sit next to her as Richard closes the door behind them to drown out the gathering shouts of 'Murderess!'

'I'm a social pariah. An animal abuser!' Tess sobs. 'No one can recover from killing kittens.'

'That's actually the name of a famous masked sex party,' Jean starts before Richard shoots her a 'Really? Now?' look. 'I'm just saying there's always room to rebrand!'

'Did you bring any booze?' Tess whimpers as she holds the wine bottle upside-down and shakes the last droplets onto her tongue.

'Are the kittens definitely dead?' Richard asks with a wince, getting a large bottle of Tesco Imperial vodka out of his coat pocket and handing it to Tess.

'I don't know. Bjorn took them to the vet,' Tess says, taking a shaky breath and unscrewing the cap with trembling fingers. 'Fynn is devastated.'

'What about rebranding as Pussy Poltergeist?' Richard muses, before it's Jean's turn to shoot him The Look.

'That sounds like a heavy metal bar I went to in my misspent youth,' Tess says with an attempt at a smile. 'The only scene that would have me now.'

'Metalheads can be very aggressive vegans, I've found,' Richard says doubtfully.

'You'll always have us! We can make our own scene,' Jean says, elbowing his ribs.

'You guys aren't a scene. You're just two prudes on the rebound! If Gabriel ditched his wife, you'd be exclusive in a heartbeat. And the only reason Richard has a "harem" – which by the way, ew – is he's terrified that Valentina will see through him and leave like all the others,' Tess says bitterly, before guzzling from the bottle and burping.

'That's not true! I haven't even said his name in seventeen days,' Jean defends herself, sitting on the floor and snatching the vodka. 'I've been using meditation tapes to train my brain to wither all Gabriel-synapses from disuse. I am the master of my mind, not a slave to my emotions! Just as the Buddha advised.'

It is almost working.

'All using meditation tapes to never think about someone means, is that you really fucking want to think about them,' Tess points out. 'Also, can you both wake the fuck up! YouTube tutorials aren't going to *transform* your lifelong personality traits!'

'Jeez Louise, no need to be such a spoilsport,' Richard says, slumping to the floor.

'I'm going to let this slide on the basis that there's a baying mob outside and you've had a very bad, no-good, terrible day,' Jean says, squeezing Tess's thigh.

'My business is in tatters and it had barely begun,' Tess says shakily, staring dully between her knees at the floor. 'All my savings . . . Fuck, why did I allow Fynn to be involved in the cat care, that was so *stupid* of me!'

Jean can't help but nod her agreement.

'Things never do work out as we hope,' Richard muses. 'Look at Jean! She intended to become an erotic goddess, and has thus far only been pumped-and-dumped by a married man after a sexless sex party. Then last night she chunder-shat all through her yogic tryst.'

'Really?' Tess burbles a laugh and wipes the tears from her face.

'It wasn't "all through" my yogic tryst,' Jean says, before grinning. 'I did shart with my face in my first vagina.'

'Vulva,' Richard corrects her.

'What did they do?' Tess smiles wetly.

'They fled.'

'So, shit got scatological. There are worse things,' Tess says, her face crumpling up again. 'Like feeding weed killer to baby cats.'

'We don't know for sure that they are dead,' Jean points out.

'They could be half-dead!' Richard agrees. 'And if you've seen *The Princess Bride*, you'll know that means true love may yet prevail.'

'I haven't seen *The Princess Bride*.'

'You haven't seen *The Princess Bride*?' Richard gasps in horror.

Jean is struck by a brilliant idea.

'Hey, why don't we go on holiday? It will be just like old times!'

'What part of "I am impoverished and socially reviled" do you not understand?' Tess asks with incredulity.

'It'll be my treat! I got a fat bonus for persuading Lord Kinder to come out and salvage the last shreds of his reputation,' Jean explains. 'I was going to buy a course of ten colonics, but hells bells, I prioritise your wellbeing above the cleanliness of my rectum.'

'It sounds like the oysters already did the job,' Richard adds.

'Maybe *I* should come out as gay,' Tess says, her mind whirring with PR strategy.

'Sleeping with five women ten years ago and having one dragon tattoo, does not make you gay,' Richard says, rolling his eyes. 'And has nothing to do with cat murder.'

'Just because I was with he-who-will-not-be-named for years and had my heart smashed to smithereens so I can't bear the thought of being intimate with *anyone*,' Tess shouts, irate, 'doesn't mean I'm not still a goddamn queer!'

'Guys. We are probably all gender-fluid and that's why we get on so well. I'm offering a free jaunt abroad and you're not even paying attention to me?' Jean interjects.

'*You* gender-fluid? You're a walking stereotype of feminine neurosis,' Richard laughs. 'Like if Woody Allen had tits.'

'*And* a handmaiden for the patriarchy,' Tess slurs from the floor.

'Also, let's not forget, a generous patron to social outcasts?' Jean adds, annoyed. 'And I swear to god, I'm either going to find a way to improve my job so that it benefits mankind, or hand in my notice by the end of the month.'

'Benefits mankind? That's lofty . . .' Richard says with obvious doubt.

'Oh shut up, breaker-upper of families!'

From the floor, Tess sighs deeply, staring into space.

'Stop fighting, children. Sorry for being such a bitch. You're right, I need to get away,' Tess says, lips twitching with a sliver of her old self. 'From the village, from being a mother, from my goddamn life. What about we go to an orgasmic meditation retreat in Ibiza?'

'I didn't think you were into swinging,' Jean says cautiously. After last night's performance, she has started to doubt if she is either. Jean had been thinking more along the lines of a secluded monastery in the Spanish hillsides, with slow yoga and raw juices to repair her intestinal tract.

'I'm not, really. But I've tried so hard to do everything right and it's blown up in my fucking face. D'you know my mum insisted I read *The Rules* recently?' Tess mumbles into her vodka.

'I did not,' Jean says, wondering where this is going.

'I've read *The Rules*!' Richard chimes in. 'I'm defo a *Rules* Boy.'

Jean shushes him, annoyed at an interruption when Tess is in the midst of confessing something she finds truly embarrassing. Jean is usually the one who is the punchline of sad-true jokes. This is a rare event she will secretly cherish.

'I mean, it's retrograde anti-feminism that drips with self-denial and misogyny, *but* . . . it does work,' Tess sighs. 'I've become so desperate for love and stability of late. I've even considered saving myself for marriage with a Swiss banker, to please my mum and give Fynn a rich step-dad. But I can't bring myself to actually do it, as men in finance make me want to vom boredom. So, I'm kind of . . . stuck. But I want to love again, you know?'

'Awww, Tess,' Jean gives her best mate a bear hug. 'You've emotionally evolved!'

'Has she?' Richard asks, confused.

'She's become open to the idea of cracking the withered husk around her heart that protects her from pain, but which has come to prevent her from truly living life,' Jean explains. She learnt all about behaviours that no longer serve you last week, while watching YouTube tutorials on surviving narcissistic abuse. 'If you cut off the place that has given you agony, you also cut off the place that brings you ecstasy.'

'That's exactly right, Jean,' Tess says in surprise.

'She just wants love!' Jean laughs in relief, taking the vodka bottle from her friend and toasting her. 'And all this time I thought you were dead inside.'

'I mean, that too,' Tess grins.

'I'm confused, are you a Rules Girl or a swinger or a husk?' Richard asks. 'You can't be all three!'

'She can be whomever she wants to be, Tom Hardy!' Jean says.

'I'm a husk toying with the rules, but really wanting to swing,' Tess explains.

'Duh,' Jean says, still annoyed with him for throwing flip-flops at her head.

'Anyway, back to Ibiza. One of my clients raved about a sex meditation villa there. It's called OHMIGADHHH or something. She was glowing, completely transformed,' Tess says, looking like someone in dire need of transformative glow. 'The past four years have been so fucking hard. Heartbreak, financial insecurity, stress, being a mum, trying to start a business. Failing at all these things . . .'

'You haven't failed . . .' Jean says weakly.

'The point is, I can't interact with anyone without real life whirring in the back of my mind. And there's no libido-killer like raising a child on your own,' Tess huffs. 'Apart from my embarrassing fixation on my babysitter, I'm, like, sexually paralysed.'

'You don't have to convince me,' Jean says, after a moment of consideration. It is her bezzer's hour of need. If Jean needs to pay for her to fly to Spain and multigasm in the hands of strangers, so be it. 'I'm down!'

'I also need to learn to reset in a way that doesn't involve drinking myself to death,' Tess says, slurping up the last drops of the spirits. 'I'm too old for Tesco vodka hangovers.'

'As amazing as all that does sound, I don't believe in watching my mates cum,' Richard says, picking at his perfectly buffed nails. 'So, I'm going to give this one a hard pass.'

'Oh, come on, when was the last time we were all on holiday together?' Jean asks.

'Never. You two haven't invited me! Anyway, I'm too busy with my harem and real person job,' Richard says with a sigh. 'A divorce lawyer's work never ends.'

'Neither does a political PR's, but *I* am going to book off next week,' Jean says, Googling 'SEX RETREAT SPAIN' and dashing off an email as she speaks. 'Assuming they still have available places.'

'To orgasmic meditation!' Tess says from the floor, raising the empty bottle of booze in a sad salute. 'Slash the funeral for my dreams.'

Chapter Fifteen

'According to Trip Advisor, "The OhhhM retreat, though similar in many ways to the OneTaste cult, is a more spiritual spin-off. It has branded the meld of kundalini yoga, tantric practice and hallucinogenic trauma therapy as 'Responsible Hedonism'. Ohhhmers rave that it is transformative, healing both physical and psychological problems as varied as Nogasm, Daddy Issues and IBS,"' Jean reads aloud from her phone the following Thursday, as their taxi speeds across the highway of the island towards the sex-spiritual villa. 'Plus "the cuisine is gluten-free, sugar-free, non-processed raw vegan, with no vegetables sourced that kill the plant during harvesting." Which I guess means no potatoes, onions or carrots.'

'Great, we'll be shitting for England mid-orgy,' Tess says, her hungover head hanging out of the open window, tongue lolling like a dog. Since Pussy Willows closed its doors, she has been in a perpetual state of drunkover.

'I've basically done that, and it *is* survivable,' Jean says with good cheer. It is their first holiday together in five years, and she is not about to let a little thing like Tess's ruined life bring them down.

'What's the OneTaste cult?' Tess asks, rather unenthusiastically for a lady being gifted a free erotic tourism package by her bestie, Jean thinks with resentment.

'They do orgasmic meditation with latex gloves and a timer. It's basically a fifteen minute lady hand-job, induced by rubbing in concentric circles on the upper left quadrant of the clitoris,' Jean explains, watching a group of foam-covered club goers in neon spandex climb down a verdant hill in the distance.

'Why the upper left?'

'No one knows. I listened to a Love + Radio podcast about it. It sounded quite mad,' Jean says. 'Allegedly in OneTaste, they shun women for not accepting their O's from any man who offers. Even if they find him repellent. This one seems less cult-y, more spiritually legit. More drugs, clear consent.'

'Since when are you into drugs?' Tess laughs.

Although a youthful caner, Tess had mostly given up the class A's since Fynn's arrival. Jean had been too sensible to risk losing that much control. But her brief encounter with Sinbad and Stacey left her curious not only about opening up her sexual boundaries, but also her spiritual ones. She likes the sound of hallucinogens in a tropical setting sprinkled with woo and hopes this weekend will introduce her to the first of many shamans.

'Since my carnal awakening,' Jean reminds Tess, 'An ongoing process that is turning my guilt and repression into shameless self-pleasure, hellooo.'

'Ah yes. I forgot that going down the rabbit hole of my failed entrepreneurial venture,' Tess sighs, rubbing puffy eyes. 'And becoming the only executioner in the village.'

'Can you stop calling yourself that? They didn't die!'

'Yes, but hardly anyone knows. People love to watch a viral video about cat murder, but when they *survive*, it isn't newsworthy!' Tess says sullenly.

'Tess, I doubt you'll be able to find your clitoral bliss if you're whinging on about a business blip. Trust me, I do this for a living! People have short memories and they love an underdog,' Jean says with forced enthusiasm. 'Today you're a falsely accused cat murderer, tomorrow you're the single mum rising up from the ashes!'

'Of cremated kittens?' Tess asks hollowly.

'Turn Pussy Willows into a feminist flower shop, the cat café thing was always too complicated. I know it's hard to resist a pun, but we can all use this as a teachable moment. Just because something is a double-entendre, doesn't make it a wise life choice.'

'You *always* thought the cats were too much?' Tess asks, wounded.

As the driver pulls off onto a dirt road, the taxi jerking back and forth, Jean looks out the windows at the green and pink foliage sprouting out of rocky terrain, pops of colour catching the light of the setting sun.

'Truthfully, yes. I didn't think things would end this dramatically, but there's a reason we don't go to Homebase to buy puppies. Too many gardening shears, for one thing.'

'Why didn't you tell me?' Tess shouts, exasperated.

'I don't know! You seemed so determined. I thought you might work it out on your own,' Jean says, equally exasperated. 'I mean, we're both adults. I didn't think you'd appreciate criticism of your new business! What do I know about cats, or flowers?'

'Or feminism,' Tess says sarkily, biting her nails.

'Says the feminist who worked for a plastic surgeon for four years?' Jean asks.

'I dissuaded as many as I could!' Tess defends herself, before sighing as she looks out the window. 'I'm sorry, none of this is your fault. It's not like these are my first hopes to be dashed like a piñata donkey, showering me in a confetti of wretchedness.'

'True.'

'I have to let it go,' Tess says in a voice that says she really wants to bitch and moan all weekend. However, as the taxi turns onto a white-stone paved entrance to a creamy compound surrounded by palm fronds, Tess perks up for the first time in days.

'Hot damn. I can't wait for the infinity pool,' Jean says enthusiastically as she opens the door to the taxi and walks to the trunk to collect their duffel bags.

'I would like to extend a warm welcome to our new souls, on behalf of all of the Lightworkers residing at OhhhM!' A crinkly-eyed, deeply tanned Caucasian woman in flowing white robes, bare feet and a gold turban greets them as she steps through the gates. A yellow parakeet sitting on her shoulder lets out a squawk. 'I am Aadarshini Anand, the founder and guide for your stay. Although you can be assured, there are no leaders and followers, gurus and disciples, or teachers and students in this sacred space.'

Tess looks at Jean with raised eyebrows. Her eyelid had started twitching at the first mention of 'Lightworkers'. Jean bites the inside of her lip, fighting the giggles. Tess has a horror of what she calls 'White Lady Mystical Appropriation' and it appears this weekend will be inescapably WhiLMA.

'I'm Jean Stevenson, and this is my friend Tess Li,' Jean says as she dumps their luggage on the floor.

'Here, we are all energetic beings,' Aadarshini explains, grasping each of them by the hand and placing a tiny piece of paper in each palm. 'Equals, lifting each other vibrationally as One. My first gift to you: a portion of cosmic unity. Bless it.'

Tess looks down into her palm.

'Is this a shred of acid?'

'Yes. Have you micro-dosed before?' Aadarshini smiles widely.

'I've macro-dosed,' Tess says with a wry smile. 'This ain't my first trauma rodeo.'

Jean looks down at the miniscule paper in her hand with disappointment, certain it will have no effect on her whatsoever, as Aadarshini lifts a wooden tray with two tall glasses filled with murky brown water towards them.

'Can we have less of your nihilism and more of her LSD please?' she whispers into Tess's ear, who snickers.

'Now, place your portion of cosmic unity into the blessed holy water. I bring this back seasonally from the Ganges river,' Aadarshini says, as Jean takes the proffered cup and inspects what appears to be pond scum. 'We will let it absorb on the garden alter for twenty-four hours and in the morning your first session will begin. We store them in the refrigerator and when you leave, you may take this bottle home with you. The therapy is continued every three days.'

'Groovy!' Jean says. 'Why three days?'

'We want to elevate the subconscious and create a fluid brain state without hallucinations, with no need to increase your dosage for the same effect,' Aadarshini says.

'What's the point if we're not tripping balls?' Tess asks, put out.

'Micro-dosing augments flow states, empathy and self-reflection, creativity and productivity while diminishing undesirable states such as depression, anxiety, PTSD and addiction,' Aadarshini says kindly, taking Tess's hand in her own. 'It will greatly benefit you, especially. Your aura is absolutely covered in black leeches.'

'Are you sure they aren't black kittens?' Tess asks superstitiously.

Aadarshini gives her a strange look.

'Never mind,' Tess sighs, rubbing her face. 'That does sound like what I need. I've felt borderline mentally ill of late.'

'We prefer not to use the term "mentally ill" here, so as not to pathologise a state of being which can be an essential component in the process of self-actualisation,' Aadarshini says sagely, before giggling like the Mad Hatter. 'After all, who can say they are "sane" if they have not known what it is to be "crazy"?'

'Doctors?' Jean suggests, only to be ignored.

'The acid will help,' Aadarshini states with finality, clicking her fingers to call a tanned little boy in white linen trousers out from the shadows of the entrance. He dashes to their feet to collect their fallen duffle bags. 'Timon! Show our new souls to their chambers.'

'This is more bizarre than I could have possibly anticipated,' Tess says the next morning. They sit in an enclave dripping with plants, watching two naked French women meditate upon the sunlit tiled floor in front of the infinity pool. It is not the nudity that Tess finds odd, but the fact that thirty minutes earlier while Tess and Jean helped themselves to the raw vegan breakfast, the women had declined, citing Breatharianism. As in, they sustain their life force solely through prana absorbed by sunlight.

'Mmmm . . .' Jean hums, trying to keep her mind clear of Tess's negative vibes.

'What sort of deranged nu-anorexia is that?' Tess continues.

'I'm sure I read that Michelle Pfeiffer was a Breatharian in her youth,' Jean says, biting into a tomato and nectarine salad interspersed with mint leaves and drizzled with balsamic vinegar and olive oil. She tilts her head back in the morning sun and smiles, full of heat, health and wellbeing. 'Maybe there's something to it.'

'Your indefensible love of *Grease 2* doesn't mean that Michelle Pfeiffer wasn't also capable of being a complete idiot in the 1970s,' Tess says, rebelliously crunching on a contraband bag of carrots she had bought at the airport.

Timon the child-servant has already told her off twice for tacitly supporting field mice genocide.

'When do you think the micro-dosing will kick in for *you*?' Jean asks. They took the first droplets a few hours earlier, watching the sun rise in a kundalini dawn meditation, doing breathing exercises while clenching their yonis on the beach. 'I feel great!'

'I need something stronger,' Tess mutters. 'Maybe we should source some E.'

'Would you mind if we join you?'

Jean shields her eyes from the sun and looks up. Two English brunettes with tasteful highlights in swimming costumes and sarongs approach their table with plates heaped with vegetables. Jean heaves a sigh of relief.

'Of course!' Jean says, motioning to the empty chairs. 'I'm Jean and this is my friend Tess. Don't mind her black mood, she's mourning the overnight implosion of her business. What are your names?'

'Raziel,' the more shell-shocked looking of the two says.

'And I'm Noa,' the sprightlier one says, pushing Gucci sunglasses off of her face.

'So, what brought you to OhhhM?' Jean asks, observing the massive sparklers on both women's ring fingers. She wonders if their husbands are also here, and if she would accept or reject the touch of married men who may be portly middle-aged bankers.

'Divorce,' Raziel says, as she bites into a raw courgette and chews with achingly slow mindfulness.

'Post-natal depression,' Noa says with a self-deprecating smile, sipping a cup of hot water with lemon. 'My husband wasn't too keen on the idea of my going on a "sex retreat" without him, like, why couldn't I go on Prozac like all the other Hampstead mums?'

'He has a point,' Tess says.

'But I prefer natural health cures,' Noa continues. 'And when I explained that OhhhMers have reported skyrocketing well-being as well as libido, he soon came around.'

'You seem very sunny for a woman with depression,' Tess says accusingly.

'Yes. My GP calls it "smiling depression". A lot of women suffer from it, as we can't bear to have others feel bad for us. Yet, inside, we are empty shells,' Noa laughs gaily. 'I think it's generational. My mother was the most brilliant hostess, the life and soul of any party, an absolute charmer. Until we found her hanging from a Pucci scarf in the closet.'

'Oh my,' Jean says, her eyes involuntarily flickering down to the woman's Pucci-print sarong.

'I'm sorry, I judged you harshly as yummy mummies with beautiful diamond rings and supportive husbands and nannies and gardens and no jobs,' Tess says, her eyes suddenly filled with tears. 'I forget sometimes, that everyone has their shit.'

The micro-dose has finally kicked in.

'I mean, the husband, nanny, garden and no job help,' Noa admits with a dry half-smile. 'But there's a special kind of awfulness about having everything you ever thought you'd want, and still wanting to hurl yourself into traffic.'

'Are there any men here?' Raziel asks, staring with disappointment at the perfectly slender, golden sunbathing Frenchwomen, who look like they've been transported straight out of an erotic film.

'Until we are rebirthed at noon, the men are staying in a separate compound,' Jean says, leafing through her itinerary. 'I guess it's a sort of re-baptism in the infinity pool, after which "our auras will be cleansed, we will relearn sexual interaction divested from the toxic masculine and reclaim ownership of our inner goddesses."'

'My husband said I'm not feminine enough,' Raziel interjects suddenly, her big hazel eyes two endless pools of hurt. 'He would tell me to dress more sexy. But then when I asked what was sexy to him, he wouldn't tell me! Always pointing out when I looked wrong, never when I looked right. I tried so hard to please him, but he was never pleased. And then, I caught him with his intern.'

'So cliché,' Noa says, patting Raziel's hand. 'And, I think, illegal.'

'You're very feminine,' Tess says sympathetically, stroking Raziel's shoulder.

'Thanks,' Raziel says with a sweet, shy smile. 'That means something, coming from a real lesbian.'

'*Thank* you,' Tess laughs for the first time in days, before muttering to Jean. 'See? She knows I'm queer.'

'I never said you weren't!' Jean reminds her.

'My souls! Bonding already,' Aadarshini says as she sashays into the enclave, pushing aside the strands of a pearl succulent so luscious it resembles a willow tree. She clasps Tess and Raziel's heads to her bosom and smiles beatifically at her eager congregation of utterly desperate women. 'Touch, that which is tactile, sensual, comforting, is the greatest healing tool at our disposal in this third dimensional reality.'

The Frenchwomen stand and walk towards the breakfast table, smiling and eager. Jean notices with surprise that they are both extremely hairy and begins to question her assumption that national stereotypes aren't true.

'It connects us to the fifth dimension,' Aadarshini continues, waving one hand in the air and looking around as if she can see it shimmering before her very eyes. To be fair, it is much easier to believe in cosmic love energy in a villa in Ibiza than in, say, a bedsit in Kentish Town. 'We have incarnated for a purpose. To experience the flesh, in love, as the divine!'

'Hear, hear!' Tess cheers, raising her vintage china mug filled with green tea, no longer disappointed she is not allowed to spike it with gin.

'The tantric practice you will learn is not about pleasure, although it is pleasurable. It is not about lust, although it will stimulate lust. It is not about understanding, for there are more things on heaven and earth than are dreamt of in any philosophy,' she paraphrases Hamlet. 'It is about the spiritual bond, using your body as a conduit between your God and your earth. You will feel the scent and taste of the soil; you will touch the very sky. You will tremble from your root chakra, until that trembling becomes an earthquake!'

The women look at each other with raised eyebrows and grin.

'And by the end of this retreat, I promise, you will weep tears of joy for the unconditional love you will carry forevermore, for your most sacred yoni.'

'Them's fighting words,' Jean grins at Tess, who for the first time has not visibly winced at the term and whispered 'Vulva!' under her breath.

As nearby church bells start to ring, Aadarshini leads them to the sparkling infinity pool, which seems to meld into the gently swaying ocean of the beach below. She instructs them to shout out all the things that have caused negativity, anxiety, lack, sadness, scarcity mentality, depression, fear and pain in their lives.

The women yell about their period shame, diets, coerced sexual encounters, forced sexual encounters, oppressive beauty ideals, eating disorders, expensive haircuts, cosmetic enhancements, waxing, plucking, shaving, lasering, useless creams, stabbing their faces with tiny needles to stimulate collagen, minimising comments, mansplaining, disproportionate housework, burden of childcare, emotional caretaking, emotional abuse, insults, physical abuse, self-abuse, degradation, abandonment, self-abandonment. They scream all the fears and expectations and criticisms that have been instilled within them and continue to be enforced by them, since the day they drew fucking breath! It is a cacophony of cultural mendacity against which they hurl a final Amazonian battle cry, ripping off any remaining clothes and diving into the infinity pool. They emerge, beaming and naked, flopping in an ecstasy of false-paradigm release on the hot cement.

Having been re-baptised with holy water and declared pure expressions of the creator's love, the entire group listen rapt to Aadarshini explain Tantric yoga later that afternoon.

'Tantra is not just sacred sex. It is about the sacredness of all life's experiences, of which sex is one of many,' she says in a deep, soft, sensual tone. 'Mastering your own sexual energy and elevating it, so this powerful force flows through all aspects of your practice. Your practice is your *life*. Sacred rituals lift and empower your emotional and spiritual state. Conscious attention with an open heart, the mindful sharing of your soul, is true intimacy. Once you master your fear of sex, which is really the fear of cosmic *love*, you will blossom, liberated into the divine feminine or the divine masculine.'

However beautiful the sentiment, Jean is finding it very difficult to master fear of sex and love and enact inner goddess self-and-other-worship as she sits stark naked, sucking in her stomach on a strange man's lap. She tries very hard not to laugh or fart or look down to see if he has a boner, and instead focus completely on keeping her spine in perfect alignment. They stare into each other's eyes for a full twenty seconds.

'Bliss breath! As I taught you! Together now! Again!' Aadarshini says, referencing the deep, long, slow nasal breath that when done correctly, sounds exactly like an asthmatic sexual predator lurking in a bush and beating himself off.

Jean clears her throat nervously and begins the raspy throat gargle as she adjusts her legs around his torso, crossing her feet behind his back.

Time passes with aching slowness.

His eyes are the deep brown of a muddy river, the Ganges maybe, his eyelashes short but thick and silky, perhaps like his penis, which she has studiously avoided looking at but can't help thinking about. The purpose of the tantric yoga pose 'Yab Yum' is to clear the mind and create soul-to-soul intimacy unencumbered by old paradigms of bodily sexual expectation.

Jean is not very successful at it.

She sneaks a glance in Tess's direction. Her bezzer is having no problem whatsoever sticking to the regulation deep stare, partnered as she is with a startlingly handsome international playboy and former professional polo player named Santiago. Jean vaguely recognises him from dentist copies of *Hello!* magazine; for a very hot minute he had dated Charlotte Casiraghi. Had they had babies, they would have been the most perfectly formed infants this world has ever seen.

'My souls,' Aadarshini says. Jean snaps out of her reverie and flicks her gaze back to her partner Alain. She can see from the expression in his globular eyeballs two inches from her own, that he is hurt by her wandering attention. 'Now that you have exchanged spirit-to-spirit energy, close your eyes and bring your foreheads gently touching together.'

Jean and Alain's heads touch, lightly, their throats gargling out of sync like the death throes of Darth Vader.

She closes her eyes, trying to concentrate and relax and be natural and clench her yoni and embrace goddess-hood.

'Inhale deeply. Yes! Once more! Longer this time. Yeeees. Good. Breathe in harmony. One! Two! Three! Exhale. Two. Three. Inhale!'

The OhhhMer men had been introduced earlier at the beachside picnic table lunch, where for the first time the whole group had mingled to talk about life on the outside. Three French men had joined the French women, explaining that they are all actors doing research for their feminist softcore porn reimagining of *Madame Bovary*. Tess had tried to bond with them over erotica by expressing her love for BDSM classic *The Story Of O*, only to be met with disgust that she enjoyed a film that glorifies the abuse of women. Tess insisted O's subjection was consensual, then they then got into a sticky and heated debate about submission and power.

Jean had extricated herself by running away to dive into the sea.

'In Tibetan Tantra, we see sex as a healing art that integrates "pleasure as medicine",' Aadarshini is saying, as her bare feet pad lightly over to Jean. 'It releases unhealthy emotions and heals trauma, in order to shed yourself of taboos and shame. To worship yourself and your lover, as an empowered goddess!'

Jean concentrates on Alain's breath. She holds hers until she is in time with his next exhale. She tries to mimic him precisely. Although she is far from feeling like Aphrodite, the force of her nasal attention allows her, for the first time since she sat on him, to relax.

'Excellent, Jean. Light shoulders, straight spine, soft tummy. Your fat is not the enemy!' Aadarshini says as she claps Jean's belly flab from behind and wiggles it in a very self-conscious-making form of massage.

Jean's eyes snap open and she swivels her eyeballs to glare at their sensei, catching Tess's amused little smirk in the process. Her friend takes her hand off Santiago's shoulder for a moment to finger gun his cartoon-beautiful face with an expression of deranged lust.

'Now, we move into Boat Pose . . .' Aadarshini says, lifting Jean off of Alain and pulling her backwards. 'Move your feet together so they are pressing against one another. Feel the sensation in your yoni . . . Clench . . . feel the energy travel up your spine! This is where we incorporate the kundalini breathwork we learned this morning. It will activate the pineal gland and bring you to braingasm . . .'

'Ahhh . . . Ahhhhhh . . . ARRRGHH!!' On the other side of the pool, Raziel is in the throes of a no-touch orgasm, an ecstasy so extreme she sounds possessed by a fleet of demons, her whole body spasming over and over, her spine twisting up and down like a tasered cobra. Jean is torn between jealousy and fear. It is an equally amazing and shocking sight to behold; she is not sure if she is capable, or even wants, to let herself go so completely.

'Yes, Raziel! Feel the power course through you! Let the serpent uncoil!' Aadarshini shouts, transported by joy for her disciple's mad orgasm. 'You are the divine feminine!'

Jean is quite convinced she will never, can never, so release herself as to publicly fit-cum on a stranger's lap in the midday sun in front of ten new acquaintances. She thinks, actually, that she wants to escape.

All of a sudden, with an intensity that takes her aback and a sharp, sad stab of pain right in her gut, she misses Gabriel. His smell, the heat of his gaze, his voice, his laugh, his touch. She hopes this is misplaced nostalgia and not an acid-revelation. Whatever it is, she wants to be rid of it. To crack open like Raziel into the sensual vista of an unknown land, where men and women are free from attachments, where all is physicality and endless pleasure and non-specific united love for humanity.

A place where she won't be afflicted by this terrible pull towards him, ever again.

Mushrooms. Mushrooms are the key to it all, Jean thinks as she waves her hand in front of her face and giggles hysterically at the colourful after-images. Beams of shimmering light emit from the tips of her fingers, like a Disney transformation scene. Why had she spent so much of her life in the third dimension, when all this time Psilocybin tea was widely if illegally available, to lift her out of the muddy muck of quotidian illusion that poor souls who know no better call reality?

'Magic!' she manages to say aloud to Tess, as she waves her hands in front of her friend's laughing face. 'Life is magic. My hands are magic. *You* are magic.'

'Yes, we are magic,' Tess says as she holds Jean's hand in her own. She is much more *au fait* with hallucinogenic experimentation, and far more with it than Jean. 'Now, remember what we promised. No matter what happens, no matter what sort of crazy orgy evolves, we are not shagging each other. It would be too weird.'

'Weeeird,' Jean agrees, flopping onto her back and staring up at the darkening sky, which now is melding and transforming in thick swirls like Van Gogh's 'Starry Starry Night'. She turns her head to look at Tess, who is staring at Santiago and Raziel making out on a deck chair with a transfixed expression.

'The whole world looks like an episode of *Rick and Morty*,' Tess murmurs. 'Either Dan Harmon and I have had the same trip . . . or . . . *Rick and Morty* . . . is real . . .'

Noa sits next to Santiago and strokes his hair. He lifts up his face and draws her towards him. Raziel, eyes dazed with lust, turns her kiss-swollen face towards Tess. She reaches out a hand towards her. Tess stands unsteadily and walks towards the yummy mummies and the playboy. As Raziel bares her massive breasts, Tess and Santiago's heads lower in tandem to suck her nipples.

'Romulus and Remus,' Jean mutters, the men and women's thrashing hair and writhing bodies casting half-human, half-animal shadows to her warped mind. 'She-wolf, mother of Rome . . .'

'Bonsoir,' Alain says to Jean as he joins her on the sand, naked but for Noa's Pucci sarong wrapped around his head.

Jean rests her chin on his shoulder and strokes his face.

'I'm sorry I couldn't look you in the eyes,' Jean says, as her hand falls down to rest upon his heart. Now, she cannot look away. She stares entranced as his big eyes expand even bigger, like FKA Twigs's in the 'Water Me' video. 'I wanted to, but I was so afraid.'

'We were all afraid once,' one of the French women says, holding hands with another porn star as they emerge from a trip-dip in the sea. 'That which you fear most is the thing you must do. Follow the fear. Ride it like a wave. With your yoni.'

'What?' Jean asks, too mashed for philosophy.

'Your boobs are like round fruit on your chest and your nipples . . . are like grapes . . .' Alain says, his gaze flickering down to stare at her body. Jean takes his hand and places it on her chest. He lightly brushes her breast with the expertise of years of pleasuring women in lady-directed feminist erotica. Jean moans, throwing her head back.

'She is a cornucopia of fruit,' the other French woman says as she joins them, appearing as if from nowhere behind

Alain and kneeling in the sand. She runs her hands through Jean's long hair, before massaging the scalp. 'May I?'

Jean nods, too transported by whatever Alain is doing to her neck for speech.

'There is a beach bed,' the other French woman says, motioning to the mattress underneath a tree that earlier today Jean had seen a tramp using as a summer home. With her new spirit-vision, it has all the glamour of a club bed under a cotton canopy in one of the chicest of the island's resorts.

'Yes,' Jean repeats, feeling the serpent uncoiling from the bottom of her spine. The woman grabs the small of Jean's back and gently lifts her up in her arms, embracing her softly. Jean will meet God tonight, through cocks and tits and vulva and bushes that would make an old man blush, through intertwining limbs and sensitive feet and glorious hair, tumbling like the waves crashing at their feet. 'The cobra is stirring!'

Chapter Sixteen

'Well, I certainly feel freed from the false paradigm of romantic expectation and social consequence,' Jean says to Tess the following afternoon on the Easyjet flight home. 'I can't believe I had an orgy on a homeless man's house with the cast of a French porno.'

A middle-aged woman across the aisle gasps loudly in disgust.

'It's a feminist reimagining of *Madame Bovary*, very *highbrow* softcore,' Jean finds herself explaining. Her freedom from social consequence did not last for very long. She finishes by whispering in Tess's ear, 'We didn't use condoms. Porn stars are, like, checked on the super reg, yes?'

'Statistically speaking, you're more likely to catch something from a rando than a pro,' Tess yawns beneath the maxi pad she has stuck to her sunglasses, in rebellion for the fact they are now charging for inflight eye-masks. 'God, I feel great! You would think it would be weird to sleep with two women who are friends, but they were so in tune with each other. And Santiago has already been with so many women, it felt like we were being choreographed by a maestro.'

The man seated next to the older woman shares a look with her and stares over at them, aghast.

'It was a privilege to experience not only the breakdown of our sexual boundaries, but the very fabric of reality with you,' Jean says defiantly, taking Tess's hand beneath the towel she is using as a blanket. 'I totally braingasmed, like, three times.'

'Me too! Thanks for this,' Tess says, squeezing back and pushing the maxi-sunglasses back on top of her hair. 'I feel so much better about life. I think I am even at peace with the fact that I am a known cat-murderer.'

The middle-aged woman is shocked into a coughing fit. Tess lifts her middle finger.

'We are now beginning our descent into London, Stansted,' the flight attendant's voice says through the intercom. 'Please fasten your seatbelts . . .'

'I wonder how our new mentalities will translate to our old lives in Kentish Town and Dulwich,' Tess continues. 'Our yonis have tasted liberty. They may never let us live dishonest lives again.'

'I'm not sure my yoni has such grand plans,' Jean says, staring out the window as the plane tips down towards the grey, dreary concrete of the airport. Had she met the Frenchies in a Camden pub, she would have found them pretentious. Noa and Raziel would be with their posh married crowd, and they would never have interacted so intimately. Santiago could usually be found banging supermodels. Whatever sexual enchantment had been cast seems to be withering the closer they are drawn back home. 'Perhaps true sexual freedom is only possible abroad?'

As they walk through the gates towards security, Jean turns her phone back on for the first time in three days. Being without technology and not even thinking about it was, in and of itself, healing. No missed calls from people she wanted to avoid, no missing calls from people she wanted to hear from, no care in the world for stupid validation apps and stories designed to keep you helplessly hooked on those whom you would otherwise forget and photo upon photo of the much more glamorous lives of others . . .

'OMG,' Jean says, stopping in her tracks, her eyes running over and over a text message from the last person she thought she would ever hear from again. A wave of heat hits her root chakra, rising up towards her chest. Three perfect sentences, saying everything she hoped he'd say.

Gabriel:

I miss you. I can't stop thinking about you. Can we please talk?

'What?' Tess asks, garnering curious glances from fellow travellers looking at the sanitary towel still stuck to the sunglasses pushed up on her head.

'Gabriel wants to meet!'

'Of course he does,' Tess says, rolling her eyes. 'His "She's Moving On!" mantenna is buzzing after your Gallic sexcapade. He can't bear the thought that you're not sad-wanking alone to his memory.'

'Why do you have to make everything into a seedy game? Maybe he actually just really likes me. Maybe he really does just miss me,' Jean says, rereading the message, her heart fluttering wildly and waves of electricity running up and down her spine. 'Look at this! He's practically begging to see me.'

'I don't think you can call three sentences begging, whatever the content,' Tess says with a cursory glance at the screen.

'You didn't even read it!' Jean pouts.

'I don't have to! It's what every man has ever said when he's still unavailable, but still wants it. In three sentences.'

This is impossible to argue with. But Jean decides not to tell Tess to rip off the damn maxi pad already and will let her ride that weird wave all the way back to Dulwich.

'I'm not sure I believe in mantenna. Is it supposed to be an instinct they are born with, like homing pigeons?' Jean says, annoyed that her hard-won emotional freedom has evaporated with one text now she's back on home soil. 'Or psychic powers passed down from father to son, like Aboriginals on walkabout.'

'Can we leave Aboriginals out of this,' Tess says, with thinning patience. 'All that matters is: he is trouble. Let it go.'

'Not even for closure?' Jean asks, staring at her phone mournfully.

'He's closed his marriage. How much more closure do you need?' Tess asks with incredulity.

Tess's words ring in Jean's ear the very next evening as her feet inexorably lead her towards a bijoux café in Primrose Hill, where a slice of cake is seven pounds and the waiters look like movie stars. She is eager beaver early, so she stopped at a Costa on the way to have a coffee and bum a cigarette and take a nervous poo.

Gabriel is already waiting for her, sitting outside, backlit against the lilac early September sky. He is wearing a slightly too cool for him leather jacket, that Poppy must have bought for him in New York. His strawberry blond hair is pulled back high in a man-bun, also a look likely styled by his wife. It has only been three weeks since they last saw each other, and she feels like she's meeting a different person.

The risks one takes for heartbreakingly amazing goodbye forever sex.

'Hi,' Gabriel says, standing nervously. His thighs knock the table and shake his glass of tap water. He is the kind of man who wouldn't dream of ordering until his date arrived and he could offer her a hot bev at the same time. Why was his gentlemanly code so delightfully old-fashioned when it came to restaurant etiquette, and so annoyingly modern when it came to love?

'How are you,' Jean says casually, leaning over to kiss him on both cheeks.

'Good. How are you?' he asks, staring wide-eyed and unsure into her face, trying to work out her inscrutable expression.

She is breezy, so fucking breezy.

'Great!' Jean beams. 'I'm just back from holiday.'

'You look great. Sun-kissed,' Gabriel says. 'Can I get you something to drink?'

'Just a green tea for me, thanks,' Jean says. She takes a seat and inspects her hair quickly in the reflection in the window, as he walks inside to order at the counter. She watches his long fingers strum against the table top as he orders. Her heart clenches in a poignant mini-seizure of lust.

She loves his hands, his beautiful hands.

Jean reminds herself that she is a liberated, free woman capable of orgiastic braingasming with strangers. She can live in the day and enjoy what life has to offer without heteronormative boundaries and regulations and restrictions and rules. She has learned about pleasure for pleasure's sake, people for people's sake, the unknowable known, the transience of everything worth having. Her tantric yoni practices Buddhist non-attachment.

She wonders how to explain all that.

'They're bringing them out for us,' Gabriel explains as he returns empty-handed. 'How are you?'

'You already asked me that,' Jean smiles.

'Yes. Er . . .' Gabriel says, stumbling over his words again as he sits down. 'I guess I don't know how to, whether I should just launch into it, or . . .'

'Launch into what?' Jean asks, her eyebrows raised in innocence, as if she hasn't been twisted up inside all day wondering what the hell he is going to propose.

'I guess I want to apologise, firstly,' Gabriel says, looking down at his hands on the table. 'I don't think I've been very fair to you.'

'I don't know about that,' Jean shrugs, non-committal, as if she doesn't remember her post-shag dumping and humiliating taxi ride home.

'I feel like I've actually treated you, kind of terribly,' Gabriel says slowly.

He looks up at her from beneath long lashes with melt-ingly blue-green eyes. It's that Princess Diana expression she had first fallen under the spell of at Sarah's wedding. So much and so little had happened, in all of three hot months.

'Oh?' Jean responds blandly.

'I should have told you that Poppy and I were trying the marital monogamous thing before we slept together. I mean, at that point I really shouldn't have slept with you at all. But then you showed up on my doorstep looking so unbearably beautiful, in those stockings and shoes and that corset thing . . .'

'A latte and a green tea,' the waiter says, bringing their drinks and laying them on the table. 'For the gentleman and the . . .'

The tramp, his eavesdropping mouth twitch implies to Jean's paranoid mind.

'Thanks so much!' Jean says, shooing him away.

'Not that that should matter . . . I feel like I've behaved like a bit of a heel, so I can understand if you don't want to see me again,' Gabriel says, pausing to sip on his coffee and looking up to inspect her face for signs of emotion. She is careful to show none. 'The truth is, I was scared. By how deeply I had come to care for you, in such a short period of time.'

She had been scared, too. But it is all so scripted, so cliché.

'Sorry, Gabriel, I don't quite understand,' Jean says, sipping her green tea with the serenity of a Zen master. 'To be perfectly honest, I thought you closed your marriage because Poppy was seeing someone else and you weren't comfortable with that.'

'No, no, that had nothing to do with it,' Gabriel shakes his head. Jean believes he believes what he is saying, but she does not think he is willing to look at his true motivations. It is so very convenient, not to. 'We hadn't seen each other in months, we were both feeling that . . . distance . . . which is dangerous in a marriage. But after spending the last few weeks together, we've bonded again, as friends and lovers. We really want each other to have a whole kind of happiness. I've met him, her boyfriend, and we've worked through our issues. With the help of a poly-fidelity therapist.'

'A therapist specialising in how to keep your marriage open?'

'Yeah. These are common, tricky situations for couples in our kind of arrangement. A momentary confusion doesn't mean we're not ultimately committed to being together forever, while also loving other people.'

'Sounds complicated,' Jean says, her eyes glancing at his packet of cigarettes on the table. 'May I . . .?'

'Of course,' Gabriel says, placing one between her lips and lighting it for her.

'Thanks.'

'So, in short . . . or in long . . . I guess what I'm saying, Jean, is that . . . Well. I fancy the shit out of you,' Gabriel says all in a rush, expelling a puff of withheld air and a bashful laugh. 'I want to try again. But more clearly this time. With you as my girlfriend.'

Jean puffs on her cigarette. She can't help a small half-grin from forming at the indelicacy of the phrase, so out of character for the Gabriel she thought she knew.

'You fancy the shit out of me?' Jean repeats with amusement, already knowing that with those words, she is his.

'And care about you deeply, of course,' Gabriel grins, his hand reaching out to cover hers. 'I haven't felt this way since . . .'

He trails off.

'Poppy would also like to meet you in person,' he continues. It is not the way Jean had hoped the sentence would end. 'Next time she's in town.'

Poppy. Poppy, Poppy, Poppy.

'Oh,' Jean says, processing this. She takes another deep drag on the cigarette, staring at the sliver of moon beginning to appear in the still-bright sky. 'Look, Gabriel, you have to understand how confusing this is for me. Your marriage is open, then it's closed, then open again. How do I know this won't go on endlessly? I mean, of course I'd meet Poppy at some point if we're still seeing each other. But becoming your girlfriend? I can't agree to that.'

'You'd still be free to see other people,' Gabriel says, his eyes hurt and hopeful. 'I can't say I'm overjoyed at the thought, but it's only fair.'

'I think we both know that if I carry on seeing you as we were, I won't want to,' Jean says simply, stubbing out her cigarette and leaning away from him.

Gabriel grins, gazing at her lovingly. There is no other word for it, she wasn't born yesterday or a delusional fantasist. Jean stares out for a long moment at the empty street, away from him, guarded and considering. His expression dims.

'Let's play it by ear,' she says finally.

'Really?' Gabriel says with disbelief, his boyish sparkle back.

'Maybe,' Jean smiles. 'I don't know. Let's not talk about it. Let's just . . . be.'

'Where was this holiday?' Gabriel asks with a curious smile. 'You seem different, somehow.'

'Ibiza,' Jean says, trying to pronounce it correctly without sounding like a knob. 'You seem different, too.'

Maybe he wasn't different at all. Maybe she had changed.

'Oh. Who were you with?' Gabriel asks, with studied nonchalance.

'I'll never tell,' Jean teases, flashing him a mysterious smile. Let him wonder. Let him stew. If she was going to do this, she would have to be careful with her heart. Careful and frugal. Like Danielle always warned her to be.

'I really think, Jez, that we need to expand our client list to incorporate the ethos of the younger generation, so Addington Media can continue to go from strength to strength in the decades to come. Not only to represent your . . .' Jean struggles to think of a word to replace cronies, '. . . Chums, but the rising tide of young MPs who are really striving to improve the landscape of government!'

Cynthia gives Jean a secret, encouraging smile, as she takes the meeting dictation next to her in Jez's office.

'MPs don't strive to improve a thing but their garden extensions!' Jez huffs. Seeing Cynthia's scrawling penmanship, he adds, 'Don't transcribe *that*, for God's sake.'

'Think how a young Sadiq or Jess Phillips could have benefitted from your stellar media contacts and unparalleled political *nous*,' Jean continues, laying it on thick. 'The tides are changing. People value authenticity and transparency. It's not just about mentoring rising stars before they become establishment, it's also damned good business!'

Jean leans back in her chair triumphantly.

'Phillips . . . Phillips . . . Isn't she the one who thinks schoolgirls should be taught how to orgasm?' Jez blusters, crossing his arms in front of his chest.

'Sex Ed in the U.K. is woefully behind other European countries in fostering healthy and non-stigmatised, consensual relationships of pleasure. With our own bodies and the bodies of others,' Jean points out reasonably. 'We could help foster sterling reputations for people who are genuinely trying to make the world a better place. Cynicism towards the government has never been higher, but it hurts everyone in the end. People need to trust MPs are looking out for them, or democracy ceases to function properly.'

'They could never afford me,' Jez says, lighting a cigar.

'We could do staggered rates,' Jean says. 'Means-tested, of a sort.'

'I'm not a blasted charity, Jean! Good God,' Jez says, but in a way that she knows he is mulling over her proposal. There have been one too many accusations of sleaze this year for comfort. If he didn't want to be known as a professional whitewasher for white male white collar crime, Jez Addington would have to fake a heart. 'I'll think about it.'

'Fantastic! I'm so pleased you're considering it. Thank you so much for being willing to take my concerns on board,' Jean grins, smoothing down the fabric of her pencil skirt as she stands up to shake his hand. 'I believe that the strategy I've outlined will benefit both Addington Media and the world.'

Jez waves her hand away.

'I said I'd think about it, Pollyanna,' Jez says, with a hint of a smile. Jean can tell he is pleased, despite himself. 'Now get back to work.'

Jean takes Cynthia's arm as they stride out the door.

'I propose a celebratory lunch on expenses!' Jean says. 'Thanks for your help with the data-pulling. I couldn't have done it without you.'

'You killed it,' Cynthia says admiringly, grabbing her cardigan from her desk. 'You've really risen in his estimation, you know. He's started to call you Pollyanna all the time.'

'I'm not sure that's a compliment,' Jean laughs, searching her bag for her mobile. 'In Jez's world, there is no worse thing a woman can be.'

'He used to call you The Mouse,' Cynthia says innocently.

'Oh really?' Jean's smile freezes on her face as the screen illuminates.

'He doesn't any more! Not for months!' Cynthia says, clapping her hand over her mouth. 'Oh my gosh, I've put my foot in it again.'

Jez still calls Cynthia 'Mouse Two', all the time. Jean had naively assumed Mouse One to have been her predecessor. She shakes off the insult. After nine years of keeping her head down and doing his bidding and unquestioning thankless toil, she *had* come to behave like a mouse.

'Don't worry about it. The important thing is, he doesn't any more,' Jean says. 'But I do suggest we get the most expensive bottle of red at The Hawksmoor in revenge.'

'How are things with Gabriel?' Cynthia asks as they call the lift.

'Perfect,' Jean says, for once in her life really meaning it. 'I mean, it's only been a month we've been trying this but . . . it's perfect.'

Since they'd reconnected, they were practically living together. They texted constantly, were laughing always, argued never and the shagging was completely divine.

'But you're still not official?' Cynthia asks for the fifth time that week. Having been with her husband since her late teens, she finds Jean's ambiguous situation hard to wrap her head around. 'And he's still married.'

'He is the perfect married non-boyfriend,' Jean says with finality.

'But it doesn't bother you?' Cynthia asks searchingly, unwilling to believe Jean is not secretly miserable and emotionally abused.

'No, not at all,' Jean replies in all honesty. 'I chose this. I know how deeply he cares for me, how much we care for each other. Labels have never felt so meaningless and unnecessary to me. If we wanted to, we could do a title. But what's the point?'

'If you say so,' Cynthia replies. 'I worry about you, Jean.'

'Well, thank you for your concern, Cynthia. We are very happy as is,' Jean says.

What she doesn't mention, what she refuses to think about, is that Brooklyn and Poppy have never felt so very far away . . .

Cuddling into Gabriel's arms the next morning, enjoying a five-minute snooze fest before she really must haul arse to the office, Jean's phone starts to blow up.

'Who's that?' Gabriel mutters into her hair, still half-asleep.

'Ugh, it's Richard,' Jean says as her mobile pings incessantly. 'Something's probably gone awry with Valentina. Hang on.'

Jean pries herself out of bed, grabs her phone and walks to the bathroom, where she sits on the toilet and rings her flatmate.

'Richard? What's wrong,' Jean yawns, rubbing her eyes and starting to piss.

'Have you seen the morning papers?' Richard squeals, a high-pitched noise that is caught between terrible fear and terrible excitement.

'No, why?' Jean asks, her wee stream coming to an anxious halt.

'Your fucking face is splashed all over it!' Richard says in a tone that suggests he is loving the drama. 'From "The Night Of The Punter"! Next to a Russian double-agent in a coma!'

'WHAT!' Jean shouts, before muffling the noise with her fist.

'Boris Petrov, he's called. They want to track you down as a key witness!'

'Jean?' Gabriel calls out curiously from the bedroom.

'Ohmygodomygod . . . This cannot be happening—'

'Don't worry, with the blonde wig you're not *that* recognisable,' Richard tries to reassure her, but sounds rather too gleeful for Jean's taste. It's as if he's preparing to give a statement to the BBC *News at Ten*. 'I mean, I recognised you immediately, but we are best friends and flatmates . . . I can say I knew the millennial Christine Keeler when . . .'

'Fuckfuckfuck!' Jean whispers into her fist.

And life was finally going so well. Gabriel treats her like gold, Jez finally respects her, she is transforming her work into something that is not equivalent to soul-sucking demon worship, has at long last found a purpose greater than paying the rent . . .

'Jean?' Gabriel knocks on the bathroom door in concern. 'Are you OK?'

'I'm fine!' Jean says, wondering how swiftly everything she cared about would go down the toilet.

'It says here, "The police are searching for the woman, who may have been acting as an accomplice, on the last known point of contact between the spy and his target. The murder suspect is currently unknown." OMG. You didn't kill Boris, did you?' Richard gasps over the line.

'No!' Jean hisses.

Murder suspect . . . accomplice . . . key witness . . . target . . . the words spin in her head like sickening ingredients in a cocktail blender.

'I don't know, you do look a bit like Keri Russell in *The Americans* . . .'

'I am not a spy, Richard,' Jean says, before holding the phone away from her face to see incoming messages from Tess. 'And telly isn't real. I've got to go!'

She cancels the call and opens her WhatsApp.

MeiQween:
mate.

[Screenshot of bewigged Jean in the *Guardian*]

did you poison this dude cuz if so

dope

i'm down to join the Russians FYI

Jean:
I'm not a spy!!

MeiQween:
i will visit you in prison

seriously r u ok tho?

'Jesus Christ,' Jean says, wiping and flushing and trying not to freak out.

'Are you sure you're OK?' Gabriel calls out again from the bedroom.

'Just had a really painful shit!' Jean shouts back in desperation. She puts her head between her legs and takes deep panting breaths, trying not to burst into tears.

'. . . OK!' Gabriel says, amused. 'I'll go downstairs and make us some tea.'

As she throws on her clothes and dashes out Gabriel's front door without saying goodbye, she wonders how he will react if he finds out. Will he excise her from his life forever? Will 'Just had a really painful shit!' be the last words she ever says to him. Jean looks down at her relentlessly buzzing phone.

MeiQween:

2 pariahs 2gether 4evah

so cool

Jean bursts through the doors of Addington Media, greeted by Jez seated in the high-backed throne-like armchair in the waiting room, reading a copy of *The Times*. Her face features prominently on the front page next to the tragically near-death Boris Petrov, underneath the headline 'Poisoned By Putin!'. The office is otherwise empty. Next to him is a cardboard box filled with the meagre possessions from her desk: notebooks, personal files, a spare makeup bag, ballet slippers, a pair of stilettos.

'Jez, what the fuck?' Jean stutters, staring at the box. 'You're going to fire me after almost ten years, for doing *your* dirty work?'

'My dirty work? I don't know what you possibly could mean,' Jez says, slowly lowering the paper and casting a gimlet eye over her dishevelled appearance. On the table before him is a tape-recorder, whirring visibly. At least he had done her the favour of showing her he was documenting their conversation. It is a small bone thrown in her direction, so that she might carefully choose her words. 'It seems your *personal* escapades on your own *private* time have gotten you into a spot of trouble, trouble which reflects very poorly on my company. Your gimp-man Ruskie friend has met a sticky end. If there is one thing I have learnt in my many years in politics, it is to *never* poke the Kremlin in the eye.'

'I hardly knew him! We mainly talked about cheese,' Jean says frantically, hot tears burning against the back of her eyeballs. All she can think about, oddly, is when she watched the Hillary vs Trump debate in a noisy bar, and the subtitles spelt Kremlin as Crème Lynn. What a great stripper name that would be. 'It was entirely innocent!'

Jez pauses the recorder before continuing.

'When a man is in a coma, allegedly poisoned by Putin's henchmen, and my right-hand woman is the mystery girl in a Profumo-style affair, there is only one step I can take,' Jez says, in a tired voice that is almost sympathetic. 'Jean, I'm doing you a huge favour by not going to the police. You can't expect any more.'

'But I did it for you! For your approval, for this agency!' Jean says, tears starting to run down her face. 'Look at that photo, I'm wearing a wig. You can hardly see me for fringe! If you hadn't known I was going to that party, you never would have known that was me. My identity isn't even public!'

Jez sighs, rubbing his temples. He folds up the paper and puts it in her box.

'It isn't public *yet*. Whatever has happened, whatever you know, be aware that it will come out,' Jez says, in a tone that suggests Jean might do well to pack her bags and fly to South America before her passport is confiscated by MI5.

'Addington Media Agency is all I've known. You've been a father figure to me,' Jean says pathetically, slumping onto the couch opposite him.

'And you've been a daughter figure to me,' Jez says, a small sad smile playing on his lips. Jean looks up hopefully, touched that the sentiment is reciprocated. 'But you do know, Jean, that I haven't seen or spoken to my own daughter for, oh, fifteen years?'

'I . . . didn't realise you . . . have a daughter,' Jean replies, shocked.

'Family. You can't choose them,' Jez shrugs, betraying no emotion whatsoever. 'But you can choose your staff, and you Jean Stevenson, are officially media-toxic. Three months severance pay will be in the post, but it is conditional on your absolute silence. You will not involve myself, Lord Kinder or my agency in this clusterfuck of your own making.'

Media-toxic. Jean's worst nightmare has come true.

All her hard work, all her plans, all her contacts, and her C.V. down the drain, in the service of an old boy's club which has completely disowned her. She had been a fool for expecting anything less. How many times had she heard Jez declare that it is 'politics, not personal' before ruining someone's life?

Jez stands, holding out his hand for Jean to shake. She clenches it weakly, her wrist moving limply up and down, her blurred vision stuck on the box of her affairs at his feet.

'Still with a weak wrist, Jean. Still with a weak wrist,' Jez says in a tone of unsurprised disappointment that is exactly like her own father's. Jean picks up the box, straightening her back and shoulders, and walks with what pride she can muster to the door.

'You're a real shit, Jez,' Jean says, her head held high and her voice clear as a bell.

'I know, Jean,' Jez says, with a strange smile. 'I know.'

Chapter Seventeen

'What I should have said was, "I'm grateful to be free of you, this bullshit agency and all the toxic masculinity you defend!"' Jean says miserably to Richard that night, in between alternating bites of Häagen-Dazs Pralines and Cream with a tub of the Belgian Chocolate and handfuls of Monster Munch. 'This is long overdue. I should have left years ago. I'm like that horrible Kellyanne Conway woman.'

'Is she the velociraptor in a straw hat?' Richard asks, filing his nails.

'I prefer lying harpy in pearls, but yes.'

Jean wonders how she'll break it to Richard that if Jez's severance pay does not arrive in the post as promised, she is totally buggered for rent.

'Then yeah,' Richard agrees, putting his feet up on the coffee table and stealing a spoonful of the chocolate. 'But at least she's sold her soul for wealth, power and influence. You were always a lowly jobsworth. A shat-upon nobody. A loser.'

'Thanks,' Jean says hollowly. 'Do you have any cyanide I could sprinkle over this?'

Tonight, their habit of turning every trauma into a joke is starting to wear thin.

She looks down at her phone buzzing on the coffee table. It is Gabriel, again. She doesn't pick up, again. She can't bear the thought of having to explain herself, to know what other consequences she might face, all for one stupid night of excitement and novelty. He must be worried. This is the first evening they haven't spent together, and these past twelve hours of agonised dread are by far the longest stretch of time they haven't spoken.

'Well, if nothing else, it's solved your daddy issues in one fell swoop,' Richard tries to comfort her, as Yentl leaps up on his lap and bats her head underneath his chin, purring madly. 'Some women pay thousands of pounds over many years of therapy for that!'

'Most women *date* their daddy issues, they don't work for him and ruin their careers when shit goes tits up. Jez will never want me to move to a competitor, I know too much. And other agencies wouldn't want me, not when I've been defending a string of perverts for months. And when word gets out that I've been *fired*, I'll be properly finished!' Jean moans, trying to stroke the cat. Yentl hisses and spits at her, before burrowing away into Richard's armpit to escape her touch. 'Even the cat hates me, now.'

'She's always hated you. But to return to the question of your self-sabotage, I'd say this is all linked to your pitiful self-esteem,' Richard says thoughtfully as he scratches Yentl's back. 'You've sought out situations where you were treated like shit, because you feel deep down, you *are* shit.'

'The only reason I'm not taking your eye out with this spoon is because you bought my favourite ice creams and crisps,' Jean says with disbelief, before shovelling another huge portion into her mouth.

'Don't forget, I also ran you a hot bath and bought face masks,' Richard says, as he rips a rose gold Space NK package open and lays it carefully on his face. 'And anyway, this can't be new information?'

Jean stares into her ice cream, her diaphragm a spasmodic balloon of panic on the brink of bursting, wishing she could disappear from the face of the planet.

'No. Yes. I guess it's my Eureka moment, but it feels like Chernobyl.'

'So, you're unemployed and might be wanted by the police as a murder suspect,' Richard says, trying to look for a silver lining to cheer her up. 'At least you're not in a coma.'

'You told me if I lay low the whole thing would blow over!' Jean shouts, waving her two-spooned arms in the air. 'Richard, this is my fucking life on the line. As my friend and lawyer, I'm counting on your advice!'

'Jean, I'm a divorce lawyer. All I can say is, it's not obvious it's you. Nose, eyes, mouth, your features are indistinguishable from most English women,' Richard says reassuringly. 'Don't make a peep and this will all go away.'

'At last, being completely unremarkable has come in handy.'

'You know that's not how I meant it,' Richard says in exasperation. 'Look, apart from me, Tess, Jez and Lord Kinder, no one knows you even attended! Tess and I are your ride-or-dies, the Russian fetishist is half-dead, and the last thing Jez and Lord Kinder will do is court more bad press. The police have nothing to go on! Who would rat you out?'

'Gabriel could,' Jean whispers. 'I saw him afterwards, that very night. But he would never betray me like that . . .'

'You never know how people will react until words like "perjury" and "attempted murder" are bandied about by men holding guns,' Richard warns. 'Would he recognise you?'

'If I hadn't snatched my own wig in the taxi, he would definitely put two and two together,' Jean says, biting her lip. 'I mean, usually I would *hope* he'd recognise my face . . .'

'Most men looking at that photo only see hair and tits,' Richard says reassuringly. 'But you need to speak to him. Feel out what he knows, without outing yourself.'

'You don't think I should tell him the truth? Or go to the police? After all, I am completely innocent!' Jean says, irate, before considering. 'Of this crime, anyway.'

'But your *reputation*, Jean,' Richard reminds her. It is hard to take him seriously when his face is covered in what looks like a split-open sparkly condom with eyeholes. 'Gabriel is a wild card. The safest thing to do is to say absolutely nothing. I always tell my clients: when in doubt, trust no one!'

Jean thinks Gabriel is someone she can trust, always. But with the stakes so high . . .

'You're right,' Jean says, swallowing the lump in her throat. 'I'll say nothing.'

'Just act normal,' Richard says, resting on the couch with the poise of Greta Garbo.

'How do I explain my behaviour this morning?' Jean asks, stress-stuffing handfuls of Monster Munch into her gullet. 'I legged it without saying goodbye.'

'Say you had the shits,' Richard says, closing his eyes. 'No one questions the shits.'

'Yes, the shits. I'll be normal,' Jean says, repeating the word like a mantra as she dips a monster into the praline ice cream and eats it on autopilot. 'Normal, yes. So normal.'

'Why are you acting so weird?' Gabriel teases her the next Friday, as Jean takes the *baba au rhum* out of the oven and frantically rummages around Gabriel's cupboards for a toothpick. 'They're old friends, not a SWAT team come to interrogate you and judge your cooking.'

Jean stiffens in fear and nearly drops the cake. Only Gabriel's lightning reflexes save it from upending all over the floor.

'Did I say something wrong?' Gabriel asks, brow knitted in concern.

'Not at all!' Jean trills, hating that the words 'SWAT' and 'interrogate' have become triggering. She stabs a toothpick violently into the perfectly browned, springy golden confection. It emerges clean, yet slightly moist. Nigella never fails her.

It's bizarre how you can half expect armed men to belay through the kitchen window and arrest you, yet still appreciate a cake perfectly baked. Jean carefully tips it out of the pan onto a blue and white china platter, rinsing a box of fresh raspberries to use for the decoration. She wonders if this is what life is like for El Chapo.

'That smells delicious,' Gabriel says, putting his hands on her hips as he kisses the back of her neck. Despite the poorly disguised panic she has been suffering from all week, Gabriel's touch still has the power to sooth her. Jean shivers with pleasure, turning around in his arms. She looks up into his eyes, framed by long dark lashes.

The yellow flecks around his pupils are only visible when caught in the light, like the dappling of sunshine on a mossy forest floor. You know you've got it bad when you wax rhapsodic about the shade of someone's iris, as if it were a secret unknowable to the rest of the world. She cannot even bring herself to meet his gaze when they're in bed, lest she lose her heart to him forever.

'I hope your friends like me!' Jean says nervously. 'I mean, it. The cake.'

What she really wants to know, is if it's possible to impress his friends so much they root for their relationship when she winds up in prison. That is, if Gabriel doesn't dump her for lying about the whys and wherefores of her firing, which she claimed was because she finally lost it at Jez and shit got personal. She obviously did not mention her presence at a sex party filled with old pervs, or the incriminating photo in which it looks like she's just finished blowing off a Russian mole in a gimp suit. Confessing all is the only thing she wants to do, but waves of fear keep her quiet.

Even with the stress of being mistook for a spy-murderess on the lam, Jean appreciates how amazing Gabriel has been, taking the whole week off work to support her. Given that Jean can only forget her future when they are fucking, they have spent the entire time naked and entwined. The bubble baths, back massages and home-cooked meals don't hurt, either. For a technical non-boyfriend, he acts like the best she's ever had.

If Jean had lost her job while she'd been with Charlie, he would have taken her on the lash for several days running, happy to have a drinking buddy with zero obligations. Soon, however, he would have worried about paying her portion of the rent and encouraged her to find work in his favourite pub, so that they could spend more time together.

Jean sighs with relief that they are not an item during this crisis. When the trickle of angry/pleading emails had turned into a barrage, she blocked him across all media. Today while jobhunting, she noticed he had looked at her LinkedIn profile the last three days running.

It is the ultimate bottom-feeder stalking move.

'Flour,' Gabriel smiles, wiping something off her cheekbone with the back of his thumb before kissing the tip of her nose. 'And they'll love you.'

'Do you want to come to my parent's house in Clapham next weekend for a Sunday roast?' Jean asks, all in a rush. 'Danielle and my dad are finally trying to bury the hatchet, so my mum's cooking for Danielle's first ever label-official boyfriend, Harry.'

'I'd love to,' Gabriel grins.

'You don't have to. Danielle was begging me to invite you, to take the pressure off, my dad can be a bit of a shit. You probably don't want to really. I mean, *I* don't want to.'

'Jean, I'd love to,' Gabriel says again, rubbing her shoulders in concern. This is one unexpected benefit of their coupled uncoupledom. Requests that would otherwise signify something, mean nothing. 'Are you sure you're OK?'

'I'm nervous,' she admits, fiddling with her hair. She rarely used to wear it down, finding it too unruly, but Gabriel adores what he calls her Pre-Raphaelite waves. 'My woodland nymph,' he said last night as she lay on top of him, stroking the wild ends. It is nice to be seen as a mystical creature. Jean always felt more akin to a farmer's daughter, hauling a cart in some late eighteenth century scene of grim pastoral realism.

'Don't be nervous. Bella and Ben are very relaxed people,' Gabriel says, going to the fridge to get mustard for the salad dressing. 'We've known each other since the conservatoire. Travelled the world together!'

'Yes, of course. You're right. It will be fun!' Jean plasters on a fake grin and takes long belly breathes. It is dinner with friends, not torture by overlords. 'Can't wait to meet them.'

She will be calm. She will be normal. She might even be charming. Hyper aware of subtleties of language and tone, she is usually good at this sort of thing. She will people-please to the max! She ignores the passing concern that when Bella and Ben were at the conservatoire with Gabriel, it was also with Poppy. That when they had travelled the world, it was all together. That they were best mates, as a couple.

The doorbell goes. Gabriel kisses Jean reassuringly on the mouth and strides towards the hallway. Jean runs to the living room mirror to check her face for stray food particles. Her eyes are bright, her winged eyeliner even, her long-sleeved pink silk dress just warm enough for dinner on the terrace in an unseasonably warm October.

'Darling! You look very well,' Jean can hear a woman's voice in a clipped transatlantic accent through the hall. 'Although rather thin. Are you wasting away without Poppy?'

'Bella, gorgeous as always,' Gabriel says with his easy charm. 'Ben! You're a beast!'

'Crossfit,' Jean hears a man's deep voice reply, with a tinge of self-mockery.

'He's turned into one of those people who buy bulk boxes of whey protein,' Bella says wryly as she enters the living room. 'Well. Your house looks just the same as when we were last here with Poppy! Completely unchanged.'

Bella looks Jean up and down with cold, frank assessment. Jean's stomach plummets and her flimsy self-confidence evaporates in an instant. She feels both overdressed and underwhelming, taken in and then dismissed.

Jean straightens her spine and shakes the woman's reluctantly proffered hand.

'You must be Gabriel's latest,' Bella says, wrinkling her nose above a smile that does not reach her eyes. They narrow in recognition. 'Have we met before? You look bizarrely familiar. Though I can't think where our circles could possibly have crossed.'

It is clear from her tone that Bella's circles are exalted, and that she takes Jean to be as parochial as a milk sow.

'How do you do,' Jean says lamely, her head in such a tailspin at the woman's open hostility that she can hardly process the sally.

'Her name is Jean Stevenson,' Gabriel says, putting his arm around Jean's shoulders. His eyebrows raise in warning surprise. 'And I don't think you would have met, no.'

Jean pleads to whatever deity may be listening that Bella of all people will not be the one to out her, first to Gabriel and then to the police.

'Jean, pleasure,' Ben, a gigantic bear of a man, says as he gives her a friendly hug.

'I thought you were both American, I don't know why,' Jean babbles, fumbling on the table for the bottle of chilled white wine. Her trembling fingers struggle to uncork it. 'Gabriel said you'd met at Conservatory, so it makes more sense that you're English!'

Could she have possibly come out with a more boring conversational gambit?

'We've been there for oh, ten years now,' Bella says disinterestedly, walking across the room to inspect a painting. 'Long before Poppy. She and Gabriel used to visit often, and she fell in love with New York. When his grandmother dies, of course, he will join her. It's hard to say where is home to me, any more. Perhaps my cello is my only true home.'

At this, Jean can't help but feel that she would dislike the woman whatever the circumstance. Their mutual antipathy is inevitable, primal. Like cats catching flies.

Unfortunately, Jean is pretty sure that in this metaphor she is the fly.

Pop!

Liquid courage finally freed, Jean pours four glasses practically to the hilt and hands them to the visiting couple. She can feel Gabriel's large, fine-boned hand rubbing her back. She resists the urge to ask him if he is actually planning a total move to New York, and what state of health his nan is in.

'If my piano were portable, I would say the same,' Gabriel laughs. 'But as things stand, I have to say born in Greenwich, live in Greenwich and may well die in Greenwich.'

'Isn't that so hard with Poppy in Brooklyn,' Bella says with sugary pity, sipping her wine and throwing a calculating glance at Jean from underneath her lashes. Jean takes a gulp of wine and reminds herself that Bella is protective of her friend. The fact that she has taken it upon herself to defend Poppy's husband against an interloper, however unnecessarily, does not make her a noxious bitch.

'They're both free people. Come and go as they please! And quite right. Takes all kinds,' Ben says gruffly, his eyes shifting away from Jean in embarrassment. Whether it is for her, because of her, or on her behalf, Jean can't quite tell.

A buzzer goes in the kitchen.

'I should put on the fish!' Jean says with relief bordering on euphoria, pushing past them to the safety of a room where she is a cook, not a whore. Gabriel follows her.

'Are you all right? I don't know what's gotten into her,' Gabriel says, turning Jean to face him. She looks at the floor. Gabriel tips her chin up towards him. 'Hey. If this is too much, I'll ask them to leave. Maybe this is too soon.'

Did he mean dinner with his friends, or the way they behave together, acting like the only two people in all the world? At least this social nightmare will pale in comparison to the shame she feels when he finds out Jean is a fugitive from justice.

She smiles brightly.

'Don't be silly! Why don't you all sit outside and catch up. I'll bring out the first course,' Jean says, busying herself stuffing the seabass. 'You must have lots to talk about.'

'OK . . .' Gabriel says, kissing her on the forehead. 'Let me know if you change your mind. You know you can always talk to me. Right?'

'Right!' Jean says around a robotic grin. When he has left the kitchen, she grabs her mobile from her purse and texts the thread.

Jean:

This is going HORRIBLY

Bella HATES ME

MeiQween:

who's bella

Jean:

Poppy's best friend.

MeiQween:

of course she hates you

i would hate you

Dickface:

That is how friendship works, Jean.

MeiQween:

poison her. she'll respect you more.

Jean turns off her mobile in frustration.

The first course of sliced tomatoes, burrata and baguette goes smoothly enough, if only because Jean enacts the role of a waitress to escape Bella's passive-aggressive comments. She has heard the word 'Poppy' more often in the past forty-five minutes, than in the entire five months she has been involved with Gabriel. It's not that she compartmentalised and forgot the woman existed, as Tess keeps accusing her of. How could she, when they have FaceTimed, when Gabriel speaks to Poppy twice a day like clockwork and offers to engage Jean on speaker-phone in three-way conversations?

It is a privilege she has always politely declined.

Selective blindness, however, yes. She has to admit it now, as she neatly places the fish on china plates accompanied by sautéed vegetables. Wedding china, probably. She looks around the kitchen with fresh eyes, at the flowered wallpaper, the faded wisteria-print tea towels, the smart copper pans. At all the things Poppy must have chosen. She noticed it in the very beginning. How could she have then filtered it out so completely?

Jean serves the main course and mentally prepares herself to sit down without pretending to have something to occupy her elsewhere. Gabriel takes her hand over the table and smiles, his eyes crinkling at the sides, relaxed and slightly tipsy. The terrace looks beautiful in the clear fall night, lit by candles and fairy lights weaving through the wrought-iron balcony fence. They are all talking music again, she doesn't really understand about what. Unlike Poppy, who works in fashion, but plays the violin beautifully.

'Such a shame she doesn't have the passion for it, she has such natural talent,' Bella is saying with a sigh. 'But I suppose music must be a vocation, and she's doing *so* well at La Renta. Gabriel said you were recently fired, Jean?'

Jean gulps her wine, smiles a big, false smile, and looks questioningly at Gabriel.

'I said you'd left recently, not that you were fired,' Gabriel says, squeezing her hand and mouthing 'What the fuck?' to Bella's husband.

'Yes, well, reading between the lines. "Left suddenly" always means fired,' Bella laughs a tinkle-y little laugh, light as a wind-chime and as cutting as a knife.

'Actually, I left. I decided I want to stop representing clients whom I don't believe have integrity. I'm actually thinking about starting my own media company, exclusively for and by women,' Jean lies smoothly, with her best trust-me-I-know-what's-best-for-you toothy PR grin. 'Circumventing the bullshit that comes with working for alpha males. And of course, some rare catty females who treat their sisters like shit.'

As Jean says it, she almost believes it. It is a retelling of events as they could have played out, if only she had the courage to stick to some sort of ethical code. And actually, now that she thinks about it, it is not a bad idea . . .

'How interesting,' Bella says, sounding bored. 'Tell me, have you done this before?'

'Done what before?' Jean asks, between delicate bites of the seabass.

At least the food wasn't a failure. That was one thing to cling to.

'Your ménage-à . . .' Bella lets the sentence trail off and makes a baffled face, implying the number of their other lovers might be two or two-hundred.

'No, she hasn't,' Gabriel answers for her, his expression closed. 'We're taking things as they come and discussing everything with the honesty and openness and *kindness* we try to bring to all aspects of our lives.'

'Still, must be *unusual*, playing house with another woman's husband,' Bella grins cruelly. She has come right out and said it. Laid out the stark reality. Jean blinks rapidly and stands up from the table.

'Bella!' Ben admonishes his wife as Gabriel pushes back his chair and starts to rise.

'Excuse me, I . . . excuse me,' Jean mumbles, rushing out of the room, up the stairs, towards the master bedroom.

She can hear Gabriel's long legs striding after her. She slams the door before he can enter the room, begins collecting her strewn clothes from all over the floor and stuffing them in her open suitcase. Her makeup and moisturisers and cleansers and pants and shampoo are scattered all over the bathroom. She has more products here than at her own house. She starts chucking them in a toiletry bag, tears blurring her vision.

'Jean! I'm *so* sorry. I had no idea she could be such a bitch!' Gabriel says, closing the door softly behind him.

'I'm your latest? How many are there!' Jean finds herself yelling. She is surprised by the force of her jealousy. She had known about Poppy from the beginning. She knew how to cope with that. But the thought of countless others, of being one of many, of being *interchangeable*, makes Jean's heart ache and rage.

'There aren't any! I mean, there have been others in the past. Flings! No one I've ever introduced to my wife or my friends, no one else I've ever . . .' Gabriel stops himself from whatever he was about to say, uncertainly.

'No one you've ever what?' Jean asks, as her lower lip trembles.

Gabriel steps closer to her, cups her cheeks with his beautiful hands. Stares into her eyes, in a way that makes her very afraid she has already lost herself to him, completely.

'No one I've ever fallen in love with,' Gabriel says softly, kissing her so angelically it makes Jean's head spin.

As the kiss deepens, the shampoo bottle that she had been holding falls to the floor. Gabriel steers her gently backwards, pushing her onto the bed. He starts kissing her neck. Jean's head flops to the side in an ecstasy of submission. She moans as his hands push up the silk fabric of her dress. Until she opens her eyes, to find herself staring directly at his wife's portrait by the lamp table. A portrait she had somehow, in an epic mind-blanking delusion, never noticed.

Now that she's seen it, she can't look away.

'Gabriel,' Jean says softly, pushing back against his chest. She buries her head in the duvet and mumbles a confession. 'I've started to think . . . dangerous thoughts.'

Dangerous thoughts like, *you married the wrong girl*. Jean can't bring herself to say it. It is obvious.

'I don't know if I can bear this,' she says instead, against the cool, soft fabric. Fabric Poppy chose, for her marital bed. Jean had enjoyed Poppy's beautiful taste, her beautiful husband, for too long without considering the price it would one day exact.

'We can work through this, Jean. Have faith in me. Have faith in us,' Gabriel pleads, brushing a lock of hair away from her face. 'This is the hardest part. The leap of faith.'

At any other time in her life, she would be unable to resist him. But there is so much already at risk.

'I need time to think,' Jean responds, her heart in her throat. 'And I can't think when I'm with you.'

Pathetic tears spring to her eyes. Too much has happened this last crazy month, far too much enforced self-reflection and unexpected consequence for her brittle mind to handle. Nine days ago she was on top of the world, in rhythm with the universe, her mind and body in perfect sync with her most heartfelt desires. How could everything have gone so wrong so quickly, and so *weirdly*? Her head is spinning, her life is a mess, she is afraid that her reputation will be blackened forever. Love, actually, is the last thing she needs.

Gabriel nods slowly, and gets up off the bed.

'I'll let you pack your things.'

Chapter Eighteen

'Oh my fucking God,' Jean says as she stumbles out of the taxi in front of her house, mascara streaming down her face, her half-zipped suitcase overflowing with clothes, only to see Charlie sitting on the doorstep holding a bunch of yellow carnations. She jerks her luggage onto the pavement and flings her head up to the sky, to shout at the cosmos. 'Are you having a laugh!'

'Jeannie!' Charlie says, rising unsteadily to his feet with an eager smile, poofing back into her life like a genie from a vodka bottle. 'I've been waiting for you for hours! Have you been on holiday?'

He looks well, much better than before. Even for being completely drunk, his dry-out period of however long has restored some of the bones to his face, de-bloated his bags, added colour to his formerly greying flesh. His face is smeared with the kind of devotion that might have won her back a few short months ago.

Now, it makes her want to kick his shins.

'On holiday from reality,' Jean says, bitter and cryptic as she drags her suitcase behind her and pushes him aside to open the door. 'What are you doing here, Charlie.'

'You aren't pleased to see me?' Charlie asks, all hurt and hangdog, offering the flowers to her pathetically. He tilts his head to the side and stares with a loving sincerity that infuriates her, for being so very fucking late.

'Not at all,' Jean says truthfully.

'I've missed you, so terribly much,' Charlie says, as if that will be enough.

Jean chucks her things into the hallway ahead of her and closes the door. She doesn't want him coming into her new home, sitting on the living room couch, asking for a beer, remembering old times, trying it on. She wants him to say his piece and to be out of her life, as soon as possible. But she also hates to be rude.

'Thank you, Charlie,' Jean relents with a sigh. She looks down at the carnations, her most hated bloom, and notices the still swinging Aldi price tag. Her eyes narrowing in suspicion, she asks, 'Did you *steal* these?'

'I would never,' Charlie starts, hand on heart. Before his face melts into a puppyish grin. 'This is why I can't bear to be without you, Jeannie. You understand me perfectly.'

'Do I get any say in this?' Jean asks incredulously, rummaging in her coat pocket for a packet of cigarettes.

'You've started again! Me too,' Charlie says, lighting her fag with one quick flick of a match against his elbow.

'As if you ever stopped,' Jean says, blowing smoke into his face and leaning back against her doorframe, arms crossed over her chest.

'Don't be such a bitch,' Charlie says teasingly with a fond half-grin, lighting his own and leaning towards her, one hand resting on the wall above her head. 'It makes it difficult to explain why I so adore you.'

There is a strange comfort to the immediate chemistry of their interaction, however hostile. Only two people who have known and loved and hated each other completely can behave with such an instant lack of decorum, have such a resentful complicity.

'Charlie, I have had just about the worst . . . and best . . . and worst . . . week of my life—'

'So have I!' Charlie says, as if misfortune can serve as a bridge between them.

'This is not a good time to chat,' Jean says impatiently, rubbing the tension headache appearing on the bridge of her nose. 'Please, just go away.'

'But I'm here now! And you know how delightful I find you angry,' Charlie smiles, gently lifting a tendril of hair off her face and tilting her chin up so she is forced to look him in the eye. There is still that old familiar, toxic pull towards him she had thought was dead forever. 'You look like shit, by the way.'

'For God's sake Charlie!' Jean says, jerking her head away from him. The pool of unwilling tenderness she felt evaporates with a sizzle, like cat piss in the sunshine. 'Fuck off!'

Charlie looks at her, smiling, feet edging ever more determinedly towards her.

'I've heard all about your exploits,' Charlie says, placing one finger against Jean's infuriated lips. 'And I forgive you. I know that whoever that person is you've been trying to become, it isn't true to you, or what you truly want.'

'How could you possibly know what I want!' Jean yells, slapping his hand away from her mouth. She is unable to process the insane presumption of forgiveness he has decided to bestow upon her. 'You never gave me what I want!!'

'And I feel truly guilty for having treated you in such a way,' Charlie continues his little speech unabated. 'That I pushed you into this kind of crazy, whore madness, which is so out of character for you. I want to apologise for failing you, as a man. I can see now that I never cherished you as I should have. Can't we be together again, like before? Or, even better than before . . .'

Charlie reaches behind her head to the rose bush Richard had attempted to grow last summer. He clumsily removes a piece of black gardening cord, nearly bashing Jean's eye with his elbow in the process. Charlie falls to his knees before her. Jean's mouth hangs open, flabbergasted, as he shapes the metal into the semblance of a ring.

'Jean Stevenson,' Charlie slurs solemnly, as he presents her with the engagement wire. 'Will you do me the great honour of becoming my bride?'

'What the fuuuck,' Jean whispers, hands on her face, jaw gaping like Munch's *Le Cri*. Charlie tugs on her left elbow until he pries her arm down, shoving the makeshift jewellery on her ring finger. She stares at it in horror, a misshapen twist of romantic charade.

'Will you do me the great honour of becoming my bride,' Charlie repeats with a sloppy smile.

'Why on earth would I *marry* you? Especially after you called me a whore!'

Inside, Jean can hear Yentl shriek and shred the couch in rare sympathy.

'That was a joke!' Charlie says, affronted, as he struggles to get to his feet.

'The proposal? Or the insult!' Jean shouts, years of frustration boiling over into tempestuous rage. 'And how *dare* you presume that what I wanted was marriage. All I ever wanted was for you to get a FUCKING GRIP!'

'Jean, you're the only one for me. I love you,' Charlie says, somehow shocked that she has refused him.

Jean drags Charlie upwards by the collar to help him to his feet, before punching his shoulder repeatedly.

'I can't believe that after all the shit you put me through, you think I'd come back for more! A lifetime's worth! Are you insane? I don't want this! I'm furious this is my first proposal! I don't even want to remember this! It taints the institution of marriage! Which incidentally I'm not sure I *fucking* believe in!' Jean rants, her matted hair flying around her face. A fleck of spittle lands on Charlie's nose.

'Jean . . . I can see . . . you are still angry,' Charlie says, his eyes wide with shock, blinking over and over. 'And I think I know why—'

'I'm in love with someone else,' Jean says, her hands falling to her sides.

'In love?' Charlie says, his face going pale. 'It's only been a few months . . .'

'And he is amazing. And I'm not the least bit in love with you,' Jean says, with a coldness that is all the more startling for the heat which preceded it. 'And I thank my lucky stars for that. Because you aren't looking for a girlfriend, and certainly not a fucking wife. You're looking for a saviour.'

Charlie starts to protest, but it is Jean's turn to cut him off.

'Only you can be that. Pull yourself together, Charlie,' Jean says, her throat choking with angry tears. She doesn't love him, not any more, but she had once. And so much. She places her hand against his cheek, stroking the stubble along his jaw with her thumb, like she used to. One last time. Then it burbles out of her, unstoppable. The curdled love. 'The sight of you . . . it makes me feel *sick*.'

Charlie slaps her hand from his cheek, his wild eyes stricken by fury and humiliation. He lurches away from her, reeling from words, the wire crushed in his fist.

'Charlie!' Jean calls after him, her stomach clenching with shame and guilt and regret. So much regret. She watches his silhouette as it is swallowed by the darkness of the street. She has done it now. Said a thing that cannot be unsaid. Crossed a line that she cannot return from.

This is a forever ending, the kind that can never be repaired.

Chapter Nineteen

'So, Gabriel said he loved you after his best mate's wife said you were playing house together . . . and then Charlie proposed on our front doorstep with a bit of metal?' Richard asks the next morning at the breakfast table, over coffee and croissants.

'Yep,' Jean says, dipping a ripped hunk of buttery bread into her latte and chewing on it disconsolately. Her appetite is gone, the bread sticking in her throat. Is her nausea from the extra bottle of wine she drank alone in bed as she cried herself to sleep, or the grief of yet another poisonous ending? She forces it down. 'My life is in fucking shambles.'

'Girl, at least you've finally got some game,' Richard says with reluctant admiration. 'Think of where you were six months ago, a mouse-y doormat dogsbody. Now you're a femme fatale and a wanted criminal to boot!'

Jean had awoken this morning from a dream in which she, Gabriel, Charlie and Tess were being inexorably sucked into a dimension that was somewhere between a whirlpool of despair and a black hole. This hardly felt like game or improvement.

'Will you please stop calling me a criminal,' Jean says. 'It's hurtful. And untrue.'

At least the downward spiral is of her own design. She has evolved into the creator of her own destruction, from the follower of someone else's.

'Sorry,' Richard says, slathering his croissant with jam and seeming not sorry at all. 'Any regrets about Charlie? I mean, not that I think you should go back there, but what you did was brutal. You've, like, killed his spirit.'

'No regrets,' Jean says, full of regrets.

'And as for Gabriel?' Richard asks curiously. 'You know she's right, that Bella woman. At best it's a doomed tryst and at worst, you could waste years of your life as second-best. It's quite dangerous, Jean. He holds all the cards.'

'Does he?' Jean asks, putting her head in her hands. She doesn't like the turn of phrase. It sounds like he is manipulating her and Poppy, their licentious puppet-master. It feels more like they are very confused people with genuine love for each other, in a big fucking mess. Taking the leap of faith is the question. It might get better, wonderful even.

It might also get a lot worse.

'You know this can't carry on endlessly in some uncon-ventional *ménage à trois*,' Richard says, as if this is a self-evident truth. 'You aren't French.'

'Look, it might not be conventional, it might not be sustainable, and it might be dangerous,' Jean says, getting defensive. 'But even with all of that, it's a damn sight more respectful than any of my previous relationships.'

'True,' Richard admits.

'I'm so tired of living this contained life, pandering to social convention. Yes, it's hard at the moment. It might not be in a few months. And as pathetic as this sounds, Gabriel is the only good thing I have in my life right now,' Jean says, her eyes welling up. 'Look at me. I'm in bits. Everything I touch turns to shit.'

'Not everything . . .' Richard says, trailing off weakly.

'Really? What part of my life have I not totally or partially fucked?' Jean asks, desperate for hope. 'Any goal I set out to achieve, that I have actually accomplished?'

Richard says nothing.

'Exactly.'

'You finally had a successful threesome,' Richard says. 'That's something!'

'Most people don't fail on their first attempt,' Jean grumbles. 'At any other point in my life I would say you're right. But he's the only tiny spark of light in this dismal cave I've dug for myself.'

'You still have me and Tess,' Richard says, sipping his tea, eyes narrowed in offence. 'You could get really hurt, Jean. I hope you aren't secretly thinking he'll choose you. Because I've seen that film, and he doesn't.'

'To live is to hurt. Isn't heart-expanding experience a valuable thing in and of itself, even if it doesn't end in a traditional happy ending?' Jean asks, getting out her phone to text Gabriel as she speaks. She would rather break her heart than force herself into the misery of safety. Gabriel is more than a love. He is a drug.

Jean's addiction is in full withdrawal and she needs another hit.

Jean:

I'm taking the leap . . .

She pauses before she hits send. If Tess were here, she would say that it's always a heart-expanding experience when you have hope! It's when hope dies that it turns soul-crushing. All Jean knows is, she misses him desperately.

She presses the touchpad before she can change her mind.

'I see your mind is already made up,' Richard says, clearing their empty plates. He puts on bright pink Marigolds and begins to do the dishes, scrubbing and drying with increasing annoyance.

'It wasn't. I just need him,' Jean says pathetically, already anxious for him to reply.

'I don't know why you bother to ask my advice when all you ever do is hurl yourself into another shit decision,' Richard says, lips pursed in disapproval. 'And when was the last time you asked me about *my* life, Jean? You and Tess are both the same. Drama-vampires. Careening from self-induced trauma to self-induced trauma, all the while complaining about how *terrible* your life is. Without ever for one moment asking after your other dear friends!'

'I'm sorry, Richard,' Jean says, blinking back tears. 'You're right, I've been so self-involved the past few months. I thought you were busy and you didn't really care!'

'I mean, it is very time-consuming being Tom Hardy,' Richard says, somewhat mollified. 'It would just be nice if we hung out when you weren't having some sort of crisis.'

'I know. I'm a terrible shit. I've missed you.'

'As entertaining as your escapades are, a normal brunch wouldn't go amiss from time to time.'

'We can totally do brunch!' Jean says, paying him her full attention. 'How *are* you?'

'Fabulous!' Richard grins, wiping a dishwater bubble off his cheek. 'Tired. I've spread myself so thin, trying to keep track of what conversation I've had with whom, who I've taken to what at the theatre, who has or hasn't seen the John Hughes opus, etc. I think I'm going to ditch the rest and ask Valentina to be exclusive.'

'You've been saying this for ages. Take the plunge!' Jean says. Her phone starts ringing on the table.

Gabriel.

She looks up guiltily at Richard.

'Answer it. I only want the odd crumb of interest in my comings and goings,' Richard says, humming an ABBA tune as he finishes the washing up. 'How's tomorrow?'

'For brunch? Good! I've been fired if you recall, my schedule is completely clear.' Jean laughs for the first time in days, her eye on the still ringing phone, heart swelling with treacherous yearnings.

'Pick it up already,' Richard says, rolling his eyes as Jean runs to her room.

'Hello?' Jean says, answering her mobile as she sits by the windowsill and nervously lights a cigarette. 'How are you?'

'I'm OK,' Gabriel says, sounding miserable. 'I didn't sleep very well.'

'Me neither.'

'I got used to having you around.'

'Me too,' Jean says, through a pained smile. 'I've been thinking . . .'

'I've been thinking . . .' Gabriel says at the same time. 'Oh. You go first.'

'No, no, you go,' Jean says, her chest constricting with doubt.

'I guess I wanted to say that I understand, whatever you decide,' Gabriel says sadly. 'And I'm not asking you to give me an answer now, of course. But I can see that it's not a very fair position to put you in, to ask you to . . . accept what I have to offer. Which is not, will never be, all of me. Not when I've made a promise to Poppy. She will always come first.'

He pauses. His words sink in. Jean says nothing. She stares at the carpet on the floor, at the threadbare and moth-eaten rug, which goes so well with her withered self-esteem.

'I don't know if it was right to ask you to have faith in . . . whatever this is,' Gabriel continues, clearing his throat. 'You're an amazing person Jean, and you deserve everything life has to offer. A full and complete kind of love. The kind of love that I can't give to you. I wish I could. But I can't.'

'Are you breaking up with me?' Jean asks in disbelief, her heart thudding against her ribcage. Now that the decision is no longer in her hands, she is definitely not ready to let him go. 'If you aren't . . . if you regret . . . if you're not actually, in love with me—'

'No, Jean. I'm trying to do the right thing,' Gabriel sighs. 'Because I'm in love with you. And I want you to live your happiest life possible. And I don't know if that is with me.'

'It is with you,' Jean whispers, suddenly certain of it and unbearably afraid.

She never does know how she really feels until the point of total loss. Is that the nature of love, or a cruel psychological trick of the brain?

'Really?' Gabriel laughs with relief.

'Yes,' Jean says, her face splitting in a grin, not knowing how she thought this conversation could possibly end otherwise.

She is head over heels, crazy about him, utterly smitten, smote.

'What are you doing tonight?' Gabriel asks hesitantly.

'Seeing you,' Jean says, very sure of herself.

'Good.'

'Could you please pass the salt?' Jean asks her father the following Sunday, in as mild mannered a tone as possible. Even on best behaviour in front of the men, George Stevenson is every inch the gruff, perpetually irritable, army-to-oil management prick Danielle always says is the spitting image of Sergeant Hartman in *Full Metal Jacket*. Personally, Jean doesn't find the resemblance to be so strong. The association has probably been made because he called them 'little maggots' as a term of endearment when they were children.

'Don't be too judgemental, darling,' her mother whisperingly defended him earlier that morning, as Jean helped her with the gravy and they heard George shout at the TV in the living room. 'It might not seem so, but he *is* trying.'

'I didn't say anything,' Jean had said. She had long since given up on pointing out her father's flaws to the woman who always took his part. Her mother took her wedding vows very seriously, in particular the vow to obey.

'His bark is worse than his bite, you know, and he is very sweet to me in private. He was *so* very badly beaten in boarding school as a boy,' Door had replied. 'He does love us.'

Jean hates the old familiar refrain. When Door looks at her husband, she sees a broken, bullied child. Everyone else sees the biggest tool in the shed. In some sad validation love quest, both Jean and her mother have always bent over backwards to appease his foul humours, to be occasionally rewarded a smile that roughly translated means: 'You have risen two per cent in my estimation'. After years of hard emotional labour, Jean reckons he rates her about a twenty out of one hundred.

Danielle calls him a shitcunt to his face.

'Under-salted,' George now says, in a long-suffering tone to Door.

He hands Jean the little teak box his wife has dispensed pink Himalayan salt into, grinding it by hand with a mallet so just the right amount of sprinkle could be added to their perfectly juicy beef. Jean doesn't think she has ever eaten a meal that hasn't been both Michelin star quality, and relentlessly nit-picked. Door always tries so very hard, and always falls short. A lifetime of tiny failures are etched on her once pretty, now basset-hound face, the flesh hanging like her hopes in swooping streaks.

'It's gorgeous, Door,' Danielle says around a mouthful of meat. She has been vegan for years but makes a point of eating whatever Door cooks to come to her defence. Jean sneaks a look at her father. He is slicing up his potatoes thinly with grim concentration.

'Perfectly salted,' Harry says in agreement, squeezing Danielle's hand on the table and smiling at her reassuringly. He has a broad, kind face, a flattened nose and raffish hair. His gaze is gentle but firm, his body boulder-like underneath a Thomas Pink shirt. He has an everyman quality where it is clear that he has sailed through life effortlessly, and no one even holds it against him.

'Thanks babe,' Danielle says, leaning her head against his thick shoulder. Harry kisses her on the forehead, and her sister doesn't flinch at the public display of affection.

Usually at home Danielle is jumping out of her skin with misery, but Harry has a calming effect on her. In the forty-five minutes since she entered the house, she hasn't screamed, slammed a door or kicked the upholstery once. For a man to whom everything comes easily, Jean imagines her unpredictable, unconventional sister presents the ultimate challenge.

'Dr Bart suggested lowering your intake, dear,' Door says meekly to her husband.

'Dr Bart is a charlatan,' George blusters. 'A man needs salt to live!'

Jean's chest tightens with the old familiar crushing anxiety of luncheons riddled with landmines.

'I am *so* sorry if it's not seasoned properly,' Door says to her guests, limpid eyes full of apology. 'There's always some detail I forget.'

'It's perfection, Mrs Stevenson,' Gabriel says, his polite façade unperturbed by the roiling family tension. Jean can't tell if he genuinely doesn't notice the resentment that simmers and hangs like a force field around the dinner table, or if he is a very good actor. She never should have invited him. 'Is that a hint of rosemary I detect?'

'Thyme and bay leave,' Door smiles timidly. 'Like they do at Claridge's. We ate there once, for one of George's friend's ruby anniversary, and I asked the chef what his secret was. Wasn't that a wonderful evening, dear?'

'Outrageous,' George responds. 'Expensive, stiff, mawkish, tripe.'

'Quite right,' Door agrees hurriedly. 'Such a lot of money for one occasion.'

'Serving tripe at a ruby wedding?' Gabriel tries to lighten the mood with a very bad joke. 'How odd.'

A fragile silence descends upon the table.

Jean smiles at Gabriel gratefully, trying to think of another topic of conversation. It is hard, given that her father disapproves of Danielle's job, is under the impression that Jean still has hers, doesn't know about Gabriel's wife situation and has twice called Harry an estate agent ('He's a property developer', Danielle had repeated, to no avail) before ranting that all estate agents are soulless conmen.

It isn't as if he has any cultural interests to provide a safe common ground. Art is 'bollocks', films are 'pornography', spirituality is 'hogwash' and ruby wedding anniversaries are 'tripe'. There are the WWII re-enactments, of course, but no one wants to open that Pandora's Box of bore. Jean had been an idiot for thinking that perhaps, in his old age, George had softened and this olive-branch was sincere.

'Some people enjoy celebrating their milestones, George,' Danielle says tightly, spearing a length of asparagus and biting the head off viciously. 'As a way of fostering wellbeing in their relationships. Though obviously that has never been your priority.'

'Providing for this family has always been my priority,' George says icily, leaning back in his chair and sipping his red wine through narrowed eyes. 'And if you had an ounce of appreciation for all I have done to give your mother and you girls the very best in life, you would respect me at my own damned table.'

'Yes, darling, only the very best,' Door interjects, stroking her cashmere cardigan to calm her nerves. 'Three holidays abroad a year, and my very own gardener.'

'*Controlling* this family has always been your priority,' Danielle retaliates over her mother's head.

'If that is how you like to interpret the past, be my guest,' George smiles, with an unnerving lack of visible rage.

In front of the men, men with normal jobs and decent appearances (even if their hair was on the longish side), he would not resort to the bizarre and venomous name calling of their adolescence. Jean had been dubbed 'Plank' for standing rigid as wood as he and Danielle screamed at each other, while her sister was usually dismissed as 'that Slut-Cow'. Their mother he never shouted at, to be fair. George treated Door like a delicate, china doll, albeit one that could never be trusted to get anything right.

'It's not a matter of *interpretation* . . .' Danielle says, one eye twitching dangerously.

'At least I have one daughter who understands the real world. Not a dole rat living on a filthy boat hosting a parade of lowlifes and junkies. Scraping by on a pittance and a prayer at the age of *forty*,' their father contents himself with saying. He sloppily tops up his red wine, splashing the Malbec on Door's pristine white tablecloth. 'Blast!'

'Oh no, darling!' Door says, fussing over him with paper towels.

'Throw it out. You should have replaced this years ago,' George says gruffly.

Jean notices her mother's twisted expression of conflict. She loves this tablecloth. It was a wedding gift. She always uses it on special occasions. If Door takes it off and enacts her cleaning wizardry now, she can save it.

'Leave it! I'll take you to Peter Jones. I'll buy you the most expensive tablecloth they have,' George says, his eyes unwavering from Danielle's stony face.

Jean sits perfectly still, retreating to that 'Plank' place of silent, safe inaction. Her shaking fingers against the steak knife are the only visible sign that she is upset. She can feel Gabriel looking at her in alarm, but avoids returning his gaze. She bites her lip and prays the catastrophe about to unfold will somehow be disrupted. When George and Danielle get a taste of blood, it is like watching some dreadful experiment gone awry, a tiger shark and a pit bull spliced together and attacking itself on *The Island Of Dr. Moreau*.

'I'm thirty fucking seven, and I don't look a day over twenty-five!' Danielle bites back furiously. 'And Jean's bullshit job was despicable! Now that she's been fired she finally realises it.'

Jean's eyes pop open wide in alarm and she kicks her older sister under the table. Danielle winces and mouths 'Sorry', as if she isn't acting like a teenager again, diverting attention from her own truancy by ratting out Jean for skipping a school trip.

'Danielle, he's not worth it,' Harry says, rubbing her arm and warily observing his girlfriend's righteous anger. 'Let's leave.'

Like her father, once something sets her off Danielle is unstoppable, volcanic. She throws Harry's hand off her arm, leaning into the insult she knows will be coming.

'A *diamond* hard twenty-five,' George scoffs, his eyes glittering with battle lust. 'And what's this Jean? You've been fired! Jez was like a father to you. What did you do? You always claimed to be so good at your job.'

George manages to suggest by his tone that Jean both eminently deserves her sacking, whatever the circumstance, and may in fact have been getting away with total incompetence for her near-decade tenure at Addington Media Agency.

'Oh! Fired. Oh! Jean,' her mother murmurs in tragic tutting tones, as she tries to blot the red wine stain around her husband's angrily waving elbow as unobtrusively as possible.

'*Stop* that, Ma,' Danielle says, rolling her eyes.

'We both decided it was time for me to move on,' Jean says evasively, chugging back her glass of wine and praying for a tiny tornado or wormhole to consume her father's side of the table and relieve them of his presence forever. Her voice has lost its uneasy tremor. The fear has gone past the point of being tenable and she has reached a Zen-like zombie state, a blank at the centre of the anxiety storm.

'Jean,' Gabriel says, his voice lowering in concern as he takes her hand and squeezes it under the table. 'I don't mean to judge. But your father is . . .'

'Awful?' Jean whispers. She didn't know why she had invited him. Maybe she had wanted a witness. So that she could finally prove to herself that she isn't crazy, that it is just as bad as she thought.

'It's never your fault—' George says, as Door tries to pacify him by rubbing his back.

'Jean's only fault is giving shitcunts like you the benefit of the doubt!' Danielle defends her, pointing an accusatory finger in her father's face. 'Misogynist scum!'

Feelings whoosh back. Bad feelings. Jean's ribcage feels like it has been sprayed with liquid nitrogen. Danielle has gone for the guttural, and George will retaliate unmercifully.

'If I have learned one thing as a father of daughters, it is that it is *never* the woman's fault. Always shifting the blame, never taking responsibility for errors. Even when she spends her life broadcasting her promiscuity to the world, as if it isn't something to be deeply ashamed of,' George glares at Danielle, before saying the words that he hopes will ruin her chances with Harry forever. 'I'm glad you've finally grown out of this disgustingly chequered sexual history. Sleeping with tramps and vagabonds and women and God knows what else. Finally grown up, found a normal man to take care of you.'

'That's quite enough!' Harry says, standing up suddenly. He slaps his hands down on the table with such force the wine glasses quiver and the knives leap like fish. 'How *dare* you speak to her like that!'

'As if you have any idea about my life or decisions,' Danielle spits out, pushing back her chair and standing to her feet. 'I am a grown woman and I will always prioritise my personal freedom over any type of heteronormative commitment!'

At this, Harry shoots her a glance loaded with hurt and confusion.

'And I thought my in-laws were bad,' Gabriel whispers, before raising his voice. Jean stays as quiet and perfectly still as Beyoncé in the elevator, staring at the red stain on the tablecloth. 'Enough! You're their father, don't you care for them at all?'

'In-laws?' George asks, his eyebrows hovering at his hairline, eyeballs making a beeline for Gabriel's ring finger. 'You're *married*?'

'Married-separated, darling,' Door says reassuringly, as she looks to Jean for reassurance. Jean shakes her head slowly from side to side. 'Married-married?'

A long silence fills the air, as suffocating as the raised voices that preceded it.

'We're polyamorous,' Gabriel stutters, as if for the first time the word sounded silly to his own ears in a household that holds alternative lifestyles in utter contempt.

'Are you *trying* to kill me?' George says to Jean in disgust.

'H-homewrecker!' Door yells at Jean, for the first time raising her voice.

The querulous sound of it is so unusual, the table quiets.

'She's not a homewrecker,' Gabriel says angrily, rising and putting his arm around Jean's stiff shoulder. 'What we are doing is completely open. It is a radical kind of love, a radical honesty—'

'Ha!' George laughs, his face splitting in the first real smile of the day.

'Whatever you think you are doing, it is not love. It is radical *selfishness*,' Door says. The words emerge tremulously, as if she is spitting out her own broken teeth one by one. 'What must your poor wife feel?'

Jean stares vacantly into her folded, shaking hands. Poppy has her own boyfriend now. She is happy, Gabriel says. Isn't she? Jean can't be sure any of them are truly happy with these portions of each other, doled out and shared like tapas. Under the gimlet gaze of her judgemental father, her choices have never felt so narcissistic, childish and inane.

'I thought I had one daughter with a shred of integrity,' George says in disgust. 'But you're as sordid as your sister.'

'Oh. My. God. How can you lecture us about fidelity, when you had a fucking affair with Door's best friend!' Danielle shouts, dropping a bombshell into the conversation.

'What?' Jean says slowly, the first words she has spoken in five minutes, as mushroom clouds of nuclear rage come out of her father's ears.

The only thing Jean ever thought truly good about her father, was the fierce and abiding loyalty he always claimed for his wife. But loyalty is not the same thing as fidelity, as she has been told by many men in the confessional realm of her work.

'For how long?' Jean asks, dumfounded. It makes sense. Puzzle pieces coming together. Door's best friend Shirley was their family shadow. Until one day she wasn't, disappearing from all their lives after a particularly tense holiday abroad, in her early teens.

'Five years, at least,' Danielle says, crossing her arms defiantly and glaring at her father. Door stares at the floor, silent tears running down her face. 'I saw them together, many times.'

'This is ancient history that serves nothing, but to hurt your mother,' George says unrepentantly. 'That's all you ever do, Danielle. Bring pain and strife into this family.'

'This is too much for me to handle,' Harry says to Danielle, his arm reaching out to grasp her hand and lead her away from this chamber of mundane tortures.

Danielle doesn't see the gesture.

Jean watches it happening in slow motion. In her sister's blinding rage, the old assumption that love can never be counted on, will only go bad, rears its ugly head. Her wild eyes misread him, tell her that Harry is abandoning her, when what he wants to do is leave their toxic household.

'If you can't accept me as a free agent,' Danielle says, the words tumbling over each other. Fear that he will accept them at face value and not read the underlying terror is written all over her face. 'Then this is *done*. Forever!'

Harry looks like he's been slapped. With an expression of aching tenderness, he kisses Danielle on the lips, one last time. Before politely fixing his napkin on the table, turning on his heel and walking out of the kitchen door. Out of their house.

Out of Danielle's life.

The sound of his Range Rover sputtering to life on the drive signals that she has well and truly pushed him away, for good this time. Danielle bursts into tears and runs up the stairs to her old bedroom, slamming the door behind her.

'Jesus Christ,' Gabriel says, stroking Jean's hair. 'This is *so* much worse than I could have possibly anticipated.'

The doorbell goes. Door gets up from her seat on autopilot and walks to the door to answer it. Jean can hear the unmistakable high-pitched noise of their busybody next door neighbour chattering away. She rests her head upon Gabriel's chest and breathes deeply.

'Jean? What is the meaning of this?' Door whispers, re-entering the kitchen armed with the *Mail On Sunday*.

The headline reads: 'Millennial Mata Hari!' An incriminating photo of Jean in the wig next to the Russian, leaning over his thigh as if emerging from a sexual act. Beneath it in a giant circle is her own real-life headshot. A photo taken by Charlie, in fact, on a sunny spring day Jean had remembered fondly, where they had read to each other in the park.

Jean turns to Gabriel and watches his jaw drop. Then to her father, apoplectic with rage. Her mother, still crying. Time moves in slow motion. Ten seconds feel like an hour.

'What is the meaning of this!' her father shouts.

Jean ignores him, turning instead to Gabriel.

'Is that you?' he asks, bewildered.

'I-I can explain . . .' Jean says in a tiny voice, barely able to breathe.

'Get out of my house!' her father shouts, his face redder by the second, spittle flying in the air. 'You are a *disgrace*!'

Jean stands up and retrieves her coat, numb with shock. She walks out the door, Gabriel lagging behind. She pulls out her phone as her footsteps follow the familiar path towards the Tube station, Googling her name and dying inside. She flips the hood of her coat up, puts on a pair of aviators left floating in her handbag from the summer, when life was still simple, sex held no consequence, and she wasn't disowned as a national disgrace.

'Jean!' Gabriel calls out behind her.

Jean ignores him.

Charlie. Fucking Charlie! Three years of cleaning up his messes, looking after him when he was sick, caring for him, lying for him, going sexless for him, pretending not having sex in your late twenties was normal for him, and this was how he repaid her. One long overdue screaming argument in the street and he rats her out to every newspaper in town, selling her down the river like garbage.

'Jean, I can't help you if you won't explain what's going on!' Gabriel calls out as he jogs to catch up with her. 'You can tell me anything. I hope you know that.'

'Gabriel, please go away,' Jean says through a voice clogged with tears, as she scrolls through *Daily Mail* articles and hit pieces in the *Sun* and a long article in *The Times* she can't read due to firewall. Infamy. Her worst nightmare has come true. 'Leave me alone!'

Her phone beeps.

MeiQween:

got my passport ready if you
want to jump 🚢

Havana or Cartagena?

Jean:

my world is fucking ending

MeiQween:

this is the self-immolation bit
before you rise like a phoenix
from the ashes 🔥

'Jean, for God's sake,' Gabriel says, pulling her towards him and turning her shoulders so she is forced to look him in the eye. 'Speak to me.'

'I'm begging you, Gabriel. Leave me in peace!' Jean shouts into the cold night air, before flinging her phone down into the gutter. She instantly regrets her melodramatics when the screen cracks, shattering into a million tiny fragments, not unlike her brittle heart. She can't explain. What would she say? How could he possibly want her in his life after this. She is an unending trainwreck, unemployed, unemployable, broke, derided, with a psychotically damaged family and nothing to offer him but drama.

'But—' Gabriel's wounded, soft, Princess Diana face is back.

Jean can't stand to look at him, for fear of what she might see. She can't allow herself to depend on him, not now, when an unquenchable need threatens to overwhelm her. To accept Gabriel's love at her most vulnerable hour, to rely on him only to have it inevitably snatched away, on the day he saw her for what she was. Worthless. A nothing.

The thought is unbearable.

She reaches into the gutter, where she belongs, to take back her iPhone. All the apps are jumping around, as shook as her soul. She can't stand to hurt him, but she does. It's all she is capable of. She sees a black cab barrelling down Clapham High Street and practically flings herself in front of it.

He pulls over.

'Drive!' she says as she jerks open the door and jumps in, slamming it in Gabriel's crushed face behind her. She turns away from him, burrowing her head into the far corner.

Chapter Twenty

By the time Jean reaches her flat, paparazzi swarm the door. Men and women armed with video recorders, flashing cameras. Curious neighbours she has never spoken to peek around the throng, holding up their iPhones. A police van is parked outside. She is very tempted to give the driver another address and run, far away from the clusterfuck shitstorm she has brought upon herself. But where would she go, who could help? Flying to Havana with Tess in fancy dress is a short-sighted option.

She will have to accept the consequences, however brutal.

'Right up here?' the taxi driver asks curiously as he stares out the window. Jean pulls her hood further over her head and grabs a twenty from her purse, passing it into the change slot wordlessly as she opens the door. 'Hey, aren't you—'

'Keep the change!' Jean says as she hurls open the door, keys in hand and pushes through the crowd before they recognise her. Halfway through, she has managed to remain incognito. As she stumbles at the entry gate, they turn on her, devouring piranhas on a piece of raw meat.

'Jean! Jean Stevenson! Slut! Spy! Double-agent! Whore!'

The cacophonous voices ring in her head as her trembling hands shove the key into her lock and she flings it open before running in and slamming it behind her. She is unsure what was said and what was the vicious projection of her subconscious mind. What a week. What a month. A life that took years to build crumbling around her ears in seconds.

'Jean,' Richard says, holding a mug of steaming tea between two police officers, a short middle-aged man and a tall young woman. His face is ashen, the blood pooling in a reddish splodge at the bottom of his throat. 'This is Officer Hartley and Sergeant Pepper. They would like to ask you some questions.'

'Sergeant Pepper! Is her lonely hearts club band in the back of their van?' Jean bursts into hysterical laughter as she eyes up the grim-faced woman with bright red hair. Her unhinged giggles fade into a mini-sob. 'Sorry. That was inappropriate.'

'As your lawyer, I would advise you to delay and employ someone specialising in criminal defence . . .' Richard says, handing her the tea and trying to send her a coded message by waggling his eyebrows and blinking like a lunatic.

Jean pushes the aviators back on her forehead and takes down her hood, before accepting the mug. Tea and sympathy are all she has left now. Her family life, her career, her reputation, all has been destroyed. Her hands flutter like a leaf in a gale. She tries to convince herself there is no way she will go to prison for a crime that she didn't, actually, commit. She was in the wrong place at the wrong time. Nothing more, nothing less.

And if they thought she were a spy or murderess, she'd already be in handcuffs. There would be more than two coppers. She would be thrown in a cell. Surely?

'I h-h-have nothing to h-hide,' Jean stutters pleadingly, leading the police officers through to the living room where she sinks onto the couch. 'I h-have no idea what's going on! Besides what's written in the p-papers.'

'And what have you read in the papers?' Officer Hartley asks, as he sets a recording device on the table in front of her and switches it on. The police pull up two chairs and sit facing her. Sergeant Pepper watches Jean's trembling body like a hawk.

Richard stands nervously in the entranceway, looking like he wants to scarper.

'Lies. That I'm a regular, involved in these sex parties with politicians, that I'm a spy for Russia, or a double-agent, or prostitute,' Jean tries to make her weak voice sound more outraged at this injustice. 'That I was, I don't know, in cahoots with this Boris Petrov! A man I'd never met before and haven't seen since. I mean, it's awful what's happened to him . . .'

'From this series of photographs it appears that you had been, or were about to, perform a sex act on him,' Sergeant Pepper says coldly, as she spreads a series of the incriminating pictures on the coffee table between them. 'You were never intimate?'

Jean's cheeks redden. She prays for a bolt from the blue to strike her down.

'No! I slipped and fell forward. He steadied me. He made a joke about his codpiece, not having spikes this time . . . then someone else came in. In hindsight, it must have been the reporter. There was a clicking noise, I thought it was the sound of the door opening. And then Boris zipped up his gimp mask and I went down to check out the fungeon. Just out of curiosity, I wasn't looking for anyone,' Jean stumbles over her words.

She had nothing to hide re: Boris, Putin and poison, true, but she wasn't about to implicate herself in a failed crime and make this situation even messier than it already was. For one thing, if Addington Media is also dragged through the mud, Jez will kill her.

'I had never been to "The Night Of The Punter" before,' Jean continues more steadily. '"Night Of The Hunter" is what it's really called, although I guess you know that. Punter is a pun. The whole thing was a mad lark that went wrong. I mean, it didn't go *wrong* it just wasn't . . . what I expected.'

'What did you expect?' Officer Hartley asks, looking up from his notepad where he has been scribbling some notes.

'I thought it would be sexier . . . It felt exploitative. I was naïve. No one wants to see Westminster in *flagrante delicto*. It was foolish of me,' Jean says, shaking her head at her words, which sound even to her own ears like a transparent lie. 'I had a bad breakup a few months before and I guess I wanted to explore my sexuality. I'm not a prostitute or a spy, I thought it would be like *Eyes Wide Shut* . . . obviously Kubrick couldn't have known how little . . . anyone in real life actually looks like Tom Cruise.'

'Tom Cruise,' Sergeant Pepper repeats her words with scathing suspicion. She is either playing the role of bad cop or has taken an instant dislike to Jean. 'How often do you attend events of this nature?'

'Not often! Not at all,' Jean says quickly, before she remembers her last holiday. 'I mean, apart from an orgasmic meditation retreat a few weeks ago, but I went to that with my best girl mate to cheer her up after she was accused of mur– . . . anyway that doesn't matter.'

'Accused of what?' Sergeant Pepper says, her narrowed eyes darting over Jean's face like a lizard's tongue.

'It wasn't so much a sex party as trauma therapy. With orgasms,' Jean babbles. 'Very different. Holistic. Woo!'

'The point is, that was the first and last time she attended "The Night Of The Punter",' Richard interjects helpfully. 'Her other activities, sexual or otherwise, are irrelevant to this case.'

'"The Night Of The Hunter" is celebrated within a closed circle of politicians. How did you hear of it?' Officer Hartley asks, his face carefully devoid of expression. Jean thinks she detects a small sparkle of amusement in his eyes. She decides to address only him henceforth.

'Oh, I don't know, secrets are never safe are they? People gossip, even with NDAs. Prior to this exposé—' Jean starts to explain.

'Defamatory exposé!' Richard pipes up from the corner.

'Defamatory exposé, yes. I don't think it was widely known outside political circles. I can't remember when I first heard about it, to be perfectly honest.'

'And where did you get the invitation?' Sergeant Pepper asks.

Jean's eyes swivel from side to side as she tries to think of a valid excuse.

'Accidental post,' Jean says finally. 'It was misdirected to my work; it didn't have a name on it. Just "Addington Media" and a blank space where the invitees name should be. I assumed they were trying to expand their, er, clientele. It isn't illegal, to take an unwanted, unnamed invitation from work, is it?'

'Presumably it was meant for your employer, Jez Addington. Offences interfering with the mail can merit either a fine, or up to six months' imprisonment,' Sergeant Pepper says, her face as hard as cement. Jean lets out a huge sigh.

If she winds up going to jail over the fucking *post* . . .

'Jez isn't into that sort of thing. He hates people, and parties. In fact, yes, I remember, I said, "Oh, there's an invite to a party that must be for you, but it isn't addressed." And he said, "You have it, I hate parties." He probably wouldn't even remember the conversation, it was such a little thing,' Jean says, the mug shaking in her hands.

'Right. Back to Boris. What was your relationship to this man? What exactly did you speak of that night?' Sergeant Pepper interrogates her.

'I'm telling you, there was no relationship! I went into the kitchen for some nibbles, he startled me, he unzipped his gimp mask, we talked about the disgusting Stilton. I tripped and it looked like I was going down on him in that photo, though I most definitely wasn't! Not that that's a crime. And then I said goodbye and went, very, *very* briefly, to the fungeon. Which I quickly realised is not my bag. And then I left!'

'What brand of Stilton?' Officer Hartley asks, his lip twitching slightly.

'I think it might have been *Lidl*,' Jean says with a wince. 'Not that there's anything wrong with Lidl cheese, but for an event like that? It's just not on.'

'There are so many good cheesemongers in that area,' Officer Hartley agrees.

'Exactly what I said!' Jean beams, for the first time that day feeling like someone got her, and everything would be all right in the end.

'Boris Petrov is a double-agent for MI5. He is ex-KGB, turned informer for Britain. There are very important people who are very concerned what information might come out,' Sergeant Pepper says with a distinct lack of empathy.

Jean's blood runs cold.

'We need to know *exactly* what you know. If you are more deeply involved in this than you claim, you are in grave danger,' Officer Hartley adds in a tone that is both kind and deadly serious. 'This interview is not only to investigate the attempt on his life, but also to protect you if need be. You have to trust us.'

Jean stares into her mug, taking a deep breath. Staring into the silty tea leaves at the bottom of the cup, she has an epiphany. Before she can second guess herself, make up a lie, obfuscate and dodge, she decides to tell the whole unvarnished truth.

'All I can tell you is this. I may not be a double-agent for Russia, or a spy of any description, but I have been living my own form of a double life,' Jean says slowly, as to her left Richard waves his hands in a ferocious 'STOP!' gesture. 'I always thought of myself as someone who is not interesting, or good enough, as myself. My ex, Charlie, while a total rat-bastard, was also right about one thing. I've been trying on a new persona for size. I was so unhappy with who I had become. My sexual adventuring was an escape route . . .'

'This is how you got caught up in the criminal under-world?' Sergeant Pepper asks.

Richard mime-slices his throat in an 'ABORT MISSION!!' signal. Or perhaps he means that she is committing legal suicide or even signing her own death warrant.

Jean has never been very good at charades.

'No! I'm not a prostitute. But even if the world thinks I am, I don't regret any of it. It may be that I was not so much trying to fit a square into a round hole, as *turn* a square into a round hole,' Jean muses, as Officer Hartley sputters a surprised laugh. 'I mean, I'm not actually boring in bed. But I'm not Danielle either!'

'Danielle Sauvage is her older sister. Host of the radio talk show, "Have Your Cake And Eat His Heart, Too,"' Richard says, giving up his warning smoke signals.

'I listen to that show,' Sergeant Pepper says, looking at Jean with fresh eyes.

'The thing is, what I should have done post-Charlie was to focus on my own wellbeing and career, without compromise. Not to allow myself to be defined by my boyfriends, my job, or my sex life! Whatever state of confusion they may be in. And certainly not to base my choices on anyone else's opinion of me!'

'This is a lot of irrelevant "me, my, myself" talk,' Sergeant Pepper says, what modicum of respect Jean had earned withering on the vine of her narcissistic self-discovery monologue. Jean continues undeterred.

'In my life the patriarchy has been embodied in hypercritical form by my true shitbag father. And now I know all his talk of moral accountability is based on lies!' Jean pauses for breath. 'Why did I devote so much time and energy to preserving power structures that protect men from the consequences of their actions? Still, I must take responsibility for my own choices.'

Officer Hartley and Sergeant Pepper look at each other in total confusion.

'Does this have *anything* to do with Boris Petrov?' Officer Hartley asks.

'No! I'm telling you, literally all I know about Boris is he didn't like the cheese and the fungeon made him sad. The point is,' Jean says, taking a deep breath and smiling. 'I have to start afresh. Action my feminism! With meaningful work this time, something I truly believe in. To own my *own* power! Great sex can come later. Or maybe a great dildo. Who knows.'

'Slightly TMI, Jean . . .' Richard says into the prolonged awkward silence that follows.

Officer Hartley wipes one lone tear of suppressed laughter from his cheek. Sergeant Pepper, although totally unimpressed by Jean's self-actualisation rant, also appears to be convinced of Jean's total ignorance regarding Boris. And everything, really.

'Is there anything else you would like to know?' Jean asks with a hopeful smile.

'I think that will be all for today,' Officer Hartley says, clearing his throat and pressing stop on the recorder. 'You may be called as a witness when the trial goes ahead, when we eventually get our man.'

'Or woman,' Sergeant Pepper interjects.

'Or woman,' Officer Hartley agrees. 'In the meantime, don't leave the country! Stay out of trouble. And stay true to yourself.'

The officer gives her a secret wink and Jean grins with relief.

'I will! I promise,' Jean says as she shows the police to the front door. 'Thank you so much for understanding.'

'We'll be in touch,' Sergeant Pepper says, before shutting the door behind them.

'I cannot believe that imbecile babbling has actually worked in your favour for once,' Richard says as he slumps against the wall. 'So, how was lunch with the fam?'

'It was a fucking catastrophe,' Jean says, sagging against the doorframe. 'Danielle and my dad had a massive fight, she outed me as having been fired, and then him as having cheated on my mum, and then she broke up with Harry. And then our neighbour brought the bloody paper with my bloody face on to the front door, and I was cast out of the house in disgrace. And then I ran away from Gabriel without explaining anything and told him to leave me alone. So. I think that's definitely dunzo!'

Jean expects a flood of tears to hit her with the words, but she is too depleted to feel any real emotion. In a way it is a relief. All her secrets are out in the open and the damage is done. It is time to take stock of her ruined life and rebuild. Things could be worse. She could be a comatose Russian spy.

There's always a silver lining, if you know where to look for it.

'And I thought my family were dysfunctional,' Richard laughs. His family aren't at all dysfunctional; he is the beloved only child of a librarian and a chemistry teacher. They are still married and live in connubial bliss in Wolverhampton, where his mum sings in the choir and the most outrageous thing his dad ever does is to go on solo bird-watching jaunts to the Lake District. 'Are you going to try and salvage things with Gabriel?'

'I don't know that I can,' Jean says, following Richard into the kitchen and getting a bottle of vodka from the freezer. She sits on the floor to drink it. 'Maybe this is my destiny. Single and alone with a bottle of spirits, in a state of permanent unemployment.'

Even as she says the words, Jean refuses to let the sliver of hope they will reunite die. Even though she has lied to Gabriel, pushed him away, and is the most famous non-prostitute in Great Britain, there is a twinge in her gut (love or premonition or gas) that says he would take her back. But then, hope is a stupid thing, like a cat that has lapped up a can of turpentine.

'You're not alone, Jean,' Richard says, sitting down next to her and taking a swig from the vodka bottle. 'And he'd be a fool not to want the most celebrated criminal in this weird land on his arm.'

'I know,' she says, hugging him gratefully. 'Thanks for all your help, Richard. You've been my knight in shining armour.'

'Babe, I'm just a prick in tin foil.'

The next day, the morning papers are emblazoned with Jean's headshot. Not the one with the gimp masked Ruskie, but the portrait Charlie had taken a few years before.

The headlines read: 'Jean Snow: Knows Nothing.'

Chapter Twenty-One

Most men would have run a mile upon hearing their semi-girlfriend is the half-naked mystery woman splashed all over the papers in a Commie Honey-Trap. The fact that her supposed conquest languishes comatose in hospital would strike many people as a red flag. Not Gabriel. When Jean told him the police believed her story, he offered to buy her a congratulatory 'You're Not Going To Prison!' dinner to talk things through. Jean suggested the Russian restaurant Borsht and Tears as a fitting venue. Gabriel insisted that this would be a celebration and that they should start as they mean to go on. In places they love, without shame.

He had been so understanding, so sympathetic to her plight, and took everything she said about why she attended 'The Night Of The Punter' at face value. After Charlie's betrayal, Jean had learned not to trust anyone with the whole truth. She told Gabriel her motivation was simple curiosity, not espionage. But even if she confessed all her sins, she knew he would accept her completely.

So, it is strange that as Jean exits Greenwich rail station and trudges towards their favourite sushi spot, she does not feel relief, or excitement, or gratitude. Actually, she wonders if she should call the whole thing off. Jean tries not to care about her reputation, of personal and professional revelations smeared all over the broadsheets, but she does. She has never felt so devastated, or pessimistic about the future.

And she is a woman who has spent decades convinced that whatever can go wrong, will.

Danielle tried to convince her the only way from rock bottom is up, but Jean's fear is that she will go horizontal, lounging in a pit of despair she will soon call home. Her urge to ditch Gabriel may be part and parcel of this self-destruction. Is this desire to implode their affair a symptom of nuclear shutdown? This vicious numbness, her inability to do anything but sit in the dark mouldering in a bathrobe, drinking voddy and pushing red buttons as her life leaches of joy, would pass in time.

Wouldn't it?

Jean inspects herself in a shop window. She looks like shit. It's been days since she brushed her hair and she has the locks of a demented temptress, Helena Bonham Carter at her most unhinged. Though she scrubbed and shaved her pits, when she emerged from the shower they had still smelt of B.O., the stink sunk deep into her flesh. Too exhausted to bother with makeup, her eyes are pink and puffy with fatigue, her skin as sallow as rancid butter. Wearing tattered old harem-pants, army boots and an oversized jumper full of holes, she appears to have stolen the pyjamas of a goth teenager.

It took all the strength she had just to leave the house.

Jean swings open the door to the restaurant. She stands stock-still. Gabriel sits at their usual table in the corner, but he is not alone. Although she can only see the back of her head, the long, blonde, silken locks in front of him unmistakably belong to his wife. Jean's heart fully stops for three seconds before it begins a hammering jackrabbit pump.

Of all the fucking days to look like Bellatrix Lestrange.

Jean is this close to dashing out of the restaurant and diving into a taxi to take her home, when Gabriel spots her. She gives a smile that is more akin to a grimace and drags her leaden feet towards the table.

'Gabriel! And Poppy!' Jean squeaks, hovering above their table.

Their table, their restaurant, she realises in a flash of long overdue understanding, is really *their* table, *their* restaurant. Anxiety grips her chest like a vice. Which side to sit on? Next to Gabriel, facing Poppy, like a real live unashamed woman in a consensually open relationship? Or would that look too territorial. And if she sits next to Poppy, facing Gabriel, it will be easier to shuffle her troll-like being into the shadows, to stare away from his wife's naturally flawless face. She prays she doesn't suffer one of the crying jags that come at her out of nowhere with the force of a monsoon.

'Jean! So nice to finally meet you in the flesh,' Poppy says eagerly, standing up and kissing her on one cheek. She smells like sunshine and spring flowers. 'I hope I'm not interrupting! I flew in last night to surprise Gabe, and he mentioned you two were having dinner. He didn't think you would mind?'

'Of course not! What a pleasure,' Jean tries to say with enthusiasm. She awkwardly hugs her non-boyfriend in greeting and wonders at Poppy's chill, that she is apologising for interrupting her husband's lover's dinner. 'At long last!'

That is over-egging it.

She had, of course, agreed to meet Poppy when she was next in London, but never in a million years did Jean think Gabriel would be so clueless as to spring it on her without warning. She had always thought him so sensitive to her needs. Perhaps it is more accurate to say that he is sensitive, and Jean's needs sometimes align with his own.

What is she doing here? With them. What are they all playing at, really?

'Here, sit down,' Gabriel says, pulling out a chair for her next to Poppy, across from him. 'We took the liberty of ordering some starters! Poppy was starving.'

His wife smiles at her brightly, lifting up the black bottle on the table.

'Do you care for sake?' she asks politely.

'Yes,' Jean says, staring at the alcohol being poured into her cup with the intensity of a lost soul in the Sahara at a glimmering oasis. It is unfortunate that this meeting is to occur when she is in the full swing of her first existential crisis.

'Gabe? Top up?' Poppy asks, moving towards his cup.

Poppy calling him Gabe unsettles Jean. It is a reminder of their parallel, separate, far more deep and enduring relationship. It speaks to the companionship of years, when a spouse is not only a lover but also a father, brother, best friend. What he and Jean have is so much more transient and fragile. All they have, really, is a whirlwind summer romance.

Maybe she is over-analysing this.

'No thanks, love,' Gabriel responds.

He squeezes his wife's hand on the table while his foot brushes Jean's underneath of it, in what she assumes is supposed to be a reassuring game of footsie. *I have enough limbs for two people!* his body language is trying to say.

'Such fresh fish here, no?' Poppy says as Jean stares into the menu, her mind still scrambled. Poppy leans towards her, reading it over her shoulder, her hand lightly brushing Jean's arm. 'I thought I had it memorised, but actually I haven't been here in a good six months. What's your favourite?'

'There's a new spin on the dragon roll we had last time, Poppy, but spicier and vegetarian. Wasn't that good, Jean?' Gabriel says casually, with a cursory glance at his own menu.

He is being so terribly normal. This should help Jean to relax, but it makes her even more stiff. At least her skyrocketing nerves have taken the edge off her exhaustion.

'It was very nice,' Jean says, gulping down her sake and smiling shyly. 'I liked the spicy veggie dragon roll. But I prefer tuna.'

When will she learn small talk that isn't as dry as kindling.

'I heard something funny about tuna when I was last in Japan,' Poppy says, with the air of someone who travels there frequently for work and for pleasure. 'Apparently a "tuna woman" is the word for a dead fish in bed, and also someone hit by a running tram.'

Gabriel and Jean chuckle self-consciously in tandem.

'Sorry, that didn't evoke the gales of laughter I anticipated,' Poppy says with a self-deprecating giggle, staring into her sake cup with embarrassment. 'Must be a bit nervous!'

'Don't be silly, it was very amusing,' Jean says, relieved that she is not the only one finding this dinner forced. She resists the urge to explain to Poppy that usually she is more interesting than this but is currently in the grips of a severe depression and can barely wash. She looks up as the waiter arrives, politely standing at the end of the table waiting for them to finish their conversation. 'Although I may have to reconsider my order . . .'

'I wouldn't think less of you for taking tuna,' Poppy says in a flirtatious tone, her fingers and their long shellac nails resting gently on the back of Jean's hand.

Jean giggles uncertainly, wondering if Poppy could possibly be flirting with her, dressed as she is as emo-vagrant Lorde. She requests the salmon sushi platter. Poppy orders chicken teriyaki, and Gabriel goes for an aubergine hot pot.

'Aubergine, Gabe? I thought you hated the texture,' Poppy says in surprise.

'I thought I should expand my horizons, given that Daniel kept raving about the health benefits of veganism,' Gabriel says, with a tight smile that belies the friendliness of his words. 'Although I may end up stealing some of your teriyaki.'

'My boyfriend's a chef,' Poppy explains, swinging her long fringe back and out of her eyes. They are a startling greyish blue, like the feathers on a dove. 'He started the first vegan Italian restaurant in Brooklyn.'

'Vegan Italian? How interesting,' Jean says, fiddling with her chopsticks as the starters arrive. 'I'm finding it hard to imagine what they serve . . . they don't even use eggs?'

'Sounds horrible, doesn't it?' Gabriel says eagerly, splashing more sake into his cup and finishing off the bottle. 'Pasta without butter? Pizza without cheese! *Cashew* tiramisu? What a joyless existence!'

'I wouldn't call it joyless . . .' Poppy says, her teeth gritted beneath her beaming smile.

'A different kind of joy,' Jean suggests, surprised that she can make conversation about fake dairy whilst sitting in the scorched earth of her ruined life. 'Maybe?'

'Soyboy joy,' Gabriel laughs, running his hand through his hair and stabbing a dumpling in its centre with a fork. Hot grease spurts out of it to pool on the table.

Poppy's smile turns downwards.

'I thought we talked about this . . .' she mutters under her breath, as Jean looks away into a potted plant in the corner of the restaurant.

'Talked about what?' Gabriel asks innocently around a mouthful of food.

'Micro-aggressions,' Poppy says calmly. 'I asked you not to call him that.'

'He said it himself, he eats a lot of soy! And . . . he's a boy.'

'A boy?' Jean repeats, confused by the turn the conversation has taken.

'He's twenty-two,' Poppy explains, trying hard not to sound defensive. Jean recognises her tone. It is the same one Gabriel sometimes uses. 'He's a very old soul.'

'I've never understood what that means. What the fuck is an old soul?' Gabriel says into the air. 'Is he decrepit in spirit? Does he suffer from energetic dementia?'

'Wow, twenty-two is so young to run his own restaurant, that's so impressive,' Jean interjects, astonished at this petty side to Gabriel. 'It's such a difficult business to do well in.'

'He has a trust fund,' Gabriel explains, rolling his eyes. 'Who knows how successful the business really is. He can afford to keep it afloat as a vanity project.'

'It's been featured in *Vogue* and *Harpers*,' Poppy says, popping two dumplings into her mouth in quick succession and then dumping a pile of seaweed onto her side plate with clear annoyance. 'It's always *very* busy.'

'I'm sure there's a big appetite in Brooklyn for vegan Italian,' Jean says, doing a pretty good job of someone pretending to be at ease in this situation. She looks down at the dumpling she had taken for herself, but her hunger has vanished.

She pushes her plate away from her churning stomach, her hands on the table.

'Americans love faddish nonsense,' Gabriel agrees, as he takes Jean's hand in his own and rubs his thumb over her knuckles, pointedly.

Jean looks from their linked hands to Poppy's face, then to Gabriel's, and the empty seat that hosts the presence of her rich vegan child boyfriend, haunting their banquet like Banquo. For an introductory wife-girlfriend dinner, the conversation is emotionally fraught, but in none of the ways Jean had anticipated. She feels less like a rival, threat or third wheel and more like a failed bid for jealousy. An anguished confusion descends upon her. It has become far too familiar a sensation for her to bear.

And then it hits her.

'Excuse me, I'm just going to nip to the loo . . .' Jean says, fondling her mobile in her trouser pocket. Once on the bog, she rings Tess, but her call goes to voicemail. She tries again. And again.

'Hello?' Tess answers on the fourth try, sounding cagey and out of breath.

'I've had a revelation,' Jean says by way of introduction as she urinates.

'That being a social outcast is bizarrely liberating?' Tess says with good cheer.

'Not there yet. The revelation is . . . I'm a poly pawn,' Jean says, biting her lip until it draws blood.

'Stop speaking in riddles,' Tess huffs. 'I'm in the middle of something.'

'Gabriel's wife is here. With us. At dinner.'

'LOL! OMG. Bomb emoji!'

'Can you not speak like you text please?' Jean says, farting loudly. 'I'm one "Hashtag I Told You So" away from a nervous breakdown.'

'Sorry. What the fuck is she doing there?' Tess says, more seriously this time.

'It's a surprise?' Jean whisper-shouts.

'Surprises should be gifts and trips. Not wives,' Tess says wisely.

'I think he's trying to make her jealous,' Jean says more quietly. 'She has a toyboy in Brooklyn.'

'Raaawrrrr,' Tess growls throatily. 'Get it, girl.'

'The point is,' Jean says, annoyance relieving her intense hurt. 'Do you think he *actually* is in love with me. Or is this

286

willingness to keep me in my current state of slut-shamed infamy only a reaction to his wife's waning interest?'

'I mean . . . It can be both?' Tess says after a pause. 'Is that too mean to say? I'm sure he does really love you. He just liked it better before. When he had you here and her there and no hotblooded young stallions boning his wife.'

'You make it sound so tawdry,' Jean says, wiping and flushing. 'And me so stupid!'

Maybe she was stupid. Maybe what she thought was love was all a fantasy. Maybe they were all deceiving themselves, for different reasons.

'I don't know what to tell you. Actually, I do. Can you not ring me when you're taking a shit? I know you think it's charming, but it really just isn't ever.'

'I wasn't taking a shit,' Jean whispers angrily. 'And *why* is it acceptable for you to send me photos of your weird shits, but it's somehow abnormal to speak on the telephone while I am defecating?'

'Jean?' Poppy calls out, amused, as the washroom door swings open.

'I've got to go,' Jean whispers into the phone before hanging up. 'One minute!'

The main courses arrive as the women return, Jean's face still red from mortification imagining what Poppy may or may not have overheard.

'Are you back in London for long, Poppy?' Jean asks, trying to remain composed.

'Only for one week, I'm afraid. It's hard to get much time off. The work culture there is go-go-go! But I thrive on that,' Poppy says, tucking into her piping hot chicken with the fervour of a hungry teenager. 'I like the adrenaline, and the novelty.'

'You sure do,' Gabriel says, with decided ambivalence.

All this time, Jean had been subconsciously thinking that Gabriel's wife must be a woman scorned or side-lined, as Tess and Richard implied. Really, that is all a sexist collection of stereotypes. Really, it looks like Poppy is the only truly free spirit among them.

'What about you, Jean? You're having some . . . er . . . time off, I gather?' Poppy says politely. She must have gathered more than that; Jean's name has been trending on Twitter for eight days.

'I'd like to start a new business,' Jean says with as much optimism as she can muster, as if anyone will ever hire her to represent their public face again. 'Helping women navigate the politics of the media. Sexism is so entrenched, false assumptions follow us whatever we do. I imagine you've heard, for instance, about my recent . . . exposure?'

'I . . .' Poppy trails off, clearly trying to decide whether it is more or less polite to admit knowledge of the scandal. 'I have read about it.'

'Well, as you probably know I'm no longer a suspect in the investigation, although they may call me as a witness if they ever find who poisoned him. But what interests me is the bullshit following all this: the persistent attention, the sensationalism, the TV offers. All these stupid conspiracy theories and a host of other clickbait bollocks!'

The injustice of it all lifts Jean's anguished spirits with the power of fury.

'If I'm going to have a public profile inflicted upon me, I want to be able to turn that around and use my prior expertise for good,' Jean continues passionately, feeling like herself again for the first time in a long time. 'To liberate women from the constraints of having a "reputation" if they step out of the narrow confines of acceptable womanhood. To help them navigate the dirty games that run things behind the scenes! And who better than a former spin-doctor for badly behaved men to do that?'

'That sounds fabulous! What TV offers did you get?' Poppy asks excitedly, dropping her chopsticks and giving Jean her full attention.

If only this had happened to Poppy, she would have used the notoriety to propel herself into instant fame. The kind that, with the whitewashing power of her blonde beauty and innocent smile, would soon be seen as entirely legitimate. She would probably be awarded a presenting job on primetime BBC television with an elderly male national treasure co-host. The kind of man who would never be asked to retire, but instead die on the job, his golden handshake given from God Almighty.

'*Love Island*,' Jean winces with horror. Tess had literally begged on her knees for Jean to accept it, but she can't stand the thought. 'Amongst others. There's a pilot of a show called *Made In Prison* that offered me a hosting job, but I turned it down.'

'But you could be like Emma Willis!' Poppy pouts. 'You should totally go for it!'

'I don't really want to further associate myself with crime,' Jean explains dryly. 'Also, I don't think Emma Willis would have taken that job.'

'Well, obviously not *that*, but everyone has to start somewhere.'

'Not everyone wants to be on TV, Poppy,' Gabriel says a little shortly, as he wincingly places the last morsel of aubergine in his mouth. 'That was disgusting. Slimy like intestines and tasting of feet.'

'Oh, why did you finish it?' Jean asks, as she dips a piece of her salmon in soy sauce.

'To prove some stupid point,' Poppy says, flashing him an aggressive smile.

'Mmm, look at the desserts!' Jean says with false enthusiasm as she watches the waiter pass by, armed with a plate of chocolate cake topped with green tea ice cream. She feels like a child between warring parents, trying to distract them from their barbed malice with sweets. 'I must try that cake.'

'Marvellous idea,' Poppy says with a warm smile, her leg brushing Jean's under the table. Is she imagining this, or is there a distinctly flirtatious vibe from Poppy? Maybe her tactility is down to American cultural appropriation, taking on the overt friendliness of the younger, less emotionally repressed nation. 'Excuse me, sir! I think we'd like dessert.'

'Tonight, we have still available: the chocolate torte with matcha cream, a daifuku selection, and black sesame ice cream,' the waiter explains.

'I think we'll definitely have two chocolate tortes,' Poppy says, looking inquiringly at Jean, who nods her head. 'Something sweet for you, Gabe? Or are you too sour tonight.'

'Make that three chocolate cakes,' Gabriel says with a winning, false smile.

When the deserts arrive, they all dig in, eating in silence. Jean wonders how the hell this evening will resolve itself. With the suggestion of a drink back at theirs, leading to who knows what kind of debauchery or prolonged emotional conversation? Despite Jean's best efforts to be carefree and wild, she remains a neurotic control freak at heart. The logistics haven't been dealt with, and she is getting the fears.

'Gabe and I were talking,' Poppy starts suddenly, seeming to read Jean's anxious mind, 'about what happens next. Obviously, you can take your time to think things through! I know I am an unexpected, er, addition to your evening. In hindsight, maybe I shouldn't have come tonight.'

'Not at all,' Jean mutters weakly, sipping her sake. 'This has been . . . great . . .'

'The thing is, we had quite a bit of therapy when Gabe was in New York. We've both recognised that having our dual relationships, me with Daniel and you and Gabe, far from tearing us apart are what make our relationship *work*. Gabe is still working on his compersion skills, which even if unnatural at first, can be learnt—'

'Compersion?' Jean asks, confused. She recognises the word from Danielle, but she can't remember the exact context.

'The feeling of joy in seeing a loved one love another,' Poppy explains, surprised at her ignorance. 'Even when they've just returned from making love to another.'

She must have assumed Jean had researched this poly-amory stuff, bought the sex positive manual *The Ethical Slut* and got down with the lingo. But making rules and regulations on how to love is, again, rather American. In Jean's experience, British people tend to wing it on a prayer, with a healthy dose of 'looking the other way' and 'discussing finer details never'. This way, you can ignore problems for as long as humanly possible, while also retaining the right to feel self-righteous betrayal when things implode.

It is a good system.

'Ah yes,' Jean says with a rising blush, remembering Gabriel's possessiveness and jealousy when he barged into the shower and fucked the life out of her after she told him about her threesome date. While Jean doesn't feel jealous of Poppy at this very moment, she's not sure how she would react if they started necking in front of her. She reckons there is a 97 per cent chance she would feel seething rage, a 3 per cent chance of joy for their joy. 'That.'

'Anyway, we'd like to propose we officially try out a transatlantic Triad arrangement. That way things are less "making up the rules as we go along". We can use Google Calendar to stay updated with each other's plans, spend more time getting to know each other as friends and . . . who knows what else? Maybe some group holidays, as we go forward more seriously. What do you think?' Poppy asks eagerly, staring into Jean's blank face with angelic sweetness.

Jean looks at Gabriel. He smiles at her warmly, taking her hand over the table.

'Wouldn't it be more of a transatlantic . . . quadrangle than a triad?' Jean asks, pushing her hair out of her face and stalling for time.

'Well, I think that would imply that Daniel is also up for grabs, which he's not.' Poppy laughs thinly. It seems Poppy also has to work on her compersion skills. 'I mean, it's not a free for all.'

'That's called a pod,' Gabriel explains.

'Right,' Jean says, feeling overwhelmed. 'Free, but not a free for all. Got it.'

Rules and calendars are usually her fucking jam, but this time Jean has to admit that perhaps, these are not the boundaries she wants for herself. She takes a deep breath, closes her eyes and uses one of the biofeedback tools she had learnt at the retreat.

'Unwanted emotions, bad feelings, icky hurts, are here to *guide* you,' Aadarshini had explained, as they imagined filling up their lungs with love and exhaling old toxins and wounds. 'Pain is a mechanism for self-correction. It cannot be avoided, unless you cut off the joyful part of yourself, too. Embrace pain. Lean into it! Then let it steer you in the *right* direction. Or at least, in *a* direction. Imagine you are a horse, and misery is your rider. A rider with the foresight to see the path ahead! Trust your rider. *Trust* your pain.'

Jean looks deeply inward to assess how her body is reacting on a physical level, to better follow her intuition. She has a knot of heavy, bittersweet dread in her stomach. Perhaps it is stupid to turn down love after a nanosecond of reflection, when literally nothing else in life is going her way. But she doesn't know any other way to be.

'I can't.'

'What?' Gabriel says, gobsmacked. It is clearly not the reaction he had anticipated. 'Jean, you don't have to answer now. Springing all this on you tonight was a bad idea, I didn't think it through . . .'

'Yes, take your time!' Poppy says hurriedly.

'No, I really can't. I'm sorry Gabriel. And Poppy, you seem lovely . . . it's not a matter of needing time,' Jean says slowly, gathering her thoughts.

'Then what is it?' Gabriel insists, rather desperately squeezing her hand. 'I care so much about you, Jean. What we have is special and it will only get better, I know it. You need to have faith that we can find a way to give you what you need. Whatever you need!'

Jean looks down and away from him, unable to meet his gaze.

'You really can't,' Jean says, admitting the horribly boring truth about herself to herself. 'Because what I need is . . . boundaries. The thing is, I know I'm on the brink of something here. On the precipice of something extraordinary. If I cared less, I could happily share you. But I want to love with my whole heart, not holding back out of fear.'

'You don't think you could do that with an "us" rather than a "we"?' Poppy asks, pushing around a piece of chocolate on her plate with a spoon.

'I'm afraid I'm just not cut out for it. Tess was right,' Jean admits. 'For me it can only be love, *Highlander*-style.'

It is Poppy's turn to look confused by bizarre terminology.

'"There can only be one",' Gabriel explains to her, with a pained twitch of a smile.

'Even apart from all that, the timing is all wrong. At my core, what I need right now is to work on myself. To focus on my own ambitions, to look inwards for the source of my joy. To transform myself. Maybe then I can think about sharing my life with other people in a way that's healthy. You see, I don't need a boyfriend, a girlfriend, or a pod,' Jean concludes, her eyebrows knitting together as she is struck by yet another pathetic *Eureka!* 'What I need is . . . *very* intensive therapy.'

'Your bill, monsieur,' the waiter says sympathetically, sliding a black leather case towards Gabriel.

'Well, I can't say I'm not disappointed, but I understand,' Poppy says, looking at Gabriel with an apologetic shrug of her shoulders. 'And I wish you the very best of luck in your journey, of course.'

Gabriel says nothing, staring away from the table as he shifts in his seat to remove his wallet from his back pocket.

'I can give you the number of an excellent holistic therapist I used here before I moved to New York?' Poppy says enthusiastically. 'You might find her helpful.'

'That would be great, I would appreciate it,' Jean says, as Poppy refers to her contacts list, gets out a pen and scribbles down a number on a napkin.

Jean takes it and slips it into her bag. She has been looking everywhere but at Gabriel's face. Finally, she looks up. His expression hits her like a harpoon to the gut. Her throat seizing up, tears springing to her eyes, Jean stands abruptly and dashes out the door onto the street.

Gabriel follows her.

Hearing his footsteps catching up behind, Jean slows down and stops beneath a lamp-post, stranded in a pool of light in the dark empty street. She shivers in the cold, looking at him wordlessly. So much remained to be said, and yet so little. They know it all. It is expressed in poignant silence, as clear as a bell. They are not broken-hearted, not yet. One last kiss, one last longing embrace before parting. It makes her head spin, everything they have shared together and everything they will not.

It is enough.

Jean pulls away from Gabriel's arms, smelling the warm scent of his neck one final time, before spinning on her heel and walking away. Her mind is clear and sharp, her shoulders light and unburdened. Outside Greenwich rail station, she looks up at the sky, lit by a moon as achingly full as her heart. And as alone. If there is such a thing as euphorically forlorn, then she is that. The paradox of joy and pain, melding together inseparably. She is strong, capable, vulnerable, wounded. She knows she is ready to meet whatever the future has in store for her, as she has already met and overcome so much.

Walking down her train platform, Jean smiles brilliantly as she watches the drawn, bored faces of the people surrounding her. She feels like a store mannequin brought suddenly to life, looking at her plastic compatriots in confusion that they are still stuck in place. Taking a long breath again and going deep, she feels it. Relief with no regrets, for anything that has come to pass.

And for once, Jean Stevenson knows that she has made the right choice.

Chapter Twenty-Two

Six months later

'The banana bread? Is for who?' Bjorn asks, holding a platter full of delicacies fresh from the oven in his gigantic arms. His biceps look like leavened loaves of bread, if baking were the chosen art form of Eros.

It is amazing how quickly a village will overlook almost-cat-murder when you install your superhero gorgeous boyfriend as the chef in your re-opened café flower shop. Women of all ages come from far and wide to watch him. Oftentimes, a small crowd gathers to leer through the windows when they cannot get a table, because it is fucking rammed. In his leather apron with the new Pussy Willows icon engraved upon it, with the back of his tight white T-shirt emblazoned with: 'This Is What A Feminist Looks Like', Bjorn has become Insta-famous.

'Stop. Perving!' Tess hisses in Jean's ear, as Jean silently accepts the banana bread, her mouth hanging open, all agog. Jean manages an enraptured smile, but still no words.

'For you, dear,' Bjorn says to Tess, as he kisses her full on the lips and passes over the slice of homemade apple pie with cinnamon and cream. 'Is new concoction from my mother's recipes. Less sweet, but just as good. Enjoy!'

They both watch him turn around, spellbound.

'I hate to see him go, but I love to watch him walk away!' Jean laughs maniacally. 'Those are the only type of guns I support! He's like the cast of *Magic Mike* in a sex blender!'

'Stop objectifying my Swedish toyboy manny-chef,' Tess says, with the magnificent smugness of a woman madly in love with an absurdist caricature of masculine perfection.

On the same night that Gabriel had sprung his wife on Jean, Bjorn had suddenly quit his job, confessing to Tess that it was too difficult for him to work for her when he was head over heels for her. Tess didn't even need to compromise her principals as an employer to get her happy ending. By day two, he had moved in, and by week two, they were partners, staging Pussy Willows' resurrection.

'I can't help it. He's like a Beatle, if the Beatles were emissaries from Valhalla,' Jean says, stabbing the moist banana bread dripping with butter with a fork. 'Listen to your clients! Hysterical giggling has drowned out Blondie.'

Jean puts the forkful in her mouth.

'Nectar of Thor!'

'I know, right?' Tess smiles, digging into her apple pie as Fynn runs up to her with a bouquet of fallen flowers. 'Oh, how beautiful! Thank you, sweetheart.'

As her son wanders off to the kitchen, where he is child-labouring as Bjorn's little helper, Jean looks around the redesigned shop with admiration. Without all the kittens and pet playpens, it is much less cluttered. The vibe is not so much 'quirky-cool' as what Tess likes to call 'cool-cool'.

'How did you manage to stumble into the perfect life right when you thought your dreams were going down the toilet?' Jean asks wonderingly. 'This time last year you were stuck in a job you hated, single, and living with your mother. And now . . .'

'I have no idea. Faith. Hope. Karmic dividends!' Tess laughs, throwing up her hands into the air and doing a 'make it rain' shimmy. With her fresh undercut and a new roaring tiger tattoo gracing her forearm, she is every inch a boss bitch. 'I don't survive, I *thrive*.'

'I'm as jelly as 1970s party food,' Jean says, sipping her coffee and staring into the kitchen at Bjorn manhandling a rolling pin.

'You aren't doing so badly yourself,' Tess says, leaning back in her chair with the satisfaction of a woman for whom everything is right in the world, down to the success of her friends. 'I keep seeing you in the Daily Mail papped behind Chablis M., wearing a very serious expression and amazingly unnecessary Tom Ford spectacles.'

'Aren't they great?' Jean grins, brushing her new chocolate brown, chin-lengthbob away from her face and fake peering through her clear-lensed frames. After the furore died down and her name had been completely cleared, a change of style was in order. She has started to wear a lot of very dramatic eyeshadow, for an intellectual Theda Bara look. 'I swear they bump up my IQ ten points.'

'How's the case going?' Tess asks, as Richard swings open the door of Pussy Willows to join them, wearing a hangdog expression. 'Hello, love! Why so blue?'

'Good! It's—' Jean starts to explain, before being interrupted.

'Valentina broke up with me,' Richard says, his eyes watery with tears as he flings himself into the corner seat next to Jean.

'Is it possible to "break up" with you?' Tess asks. 'I thought you were still casual.'

'Technically no promises were made. But she caught me on a date with another woman at The National and threw a drink in my face and stormed out. So emotionally, it was like being dumped,' Richard says, his lower lip trembling as he takes a sip of Jean's latte. 'Of course, it was at that exact moment that I realised I really, truly love her. Do you serve anything stronger than this?'

'I have a bottle of Jameson in the back. Ask Bjorn to add a splash,' Tess offers.

'Are you OK?' Jean asks sympathetically, sad for him but also totally unsurprised.

'As well as can be expected. I'm devastated. Heartbroken. Distraught. I've lost the best thing that's ever happened to me and may never recover,' Richard says through a thin, self-pitying smile, helping himself to a portion of Jean's banana bread. 'But don't let me bring down brunch.'

'You brought this on yourself,' Tess shrugs, sipping her mint tea. 'By acting like a heartless cad for nearly a year. What were you saying, Jean?'

'That Harlotte Public Relations is doing very well indeed! Chablis M. has raised our profile hugely. I'm getting a great deal of interest from other celeb women who have been slandered, abused or otherwise dragged through the mud,' Jean says with enthusiasm. 'She loves that I know what she's going through, in my own small way. And she's got such a ballsy, unapologetic, take-no-prisoners attitude that I have high hopes she'll win in court!'

Harlotte Public Relations started as a kitchen table operation four months ago, and in that time has already grown to a tiny office in Highbury, with a staff of one and two interns. All going well, soon Jean will be able to take on a personal assistant. She is getting the best kind of positive referrals: word of mouth.

'What happened to her again?' Tess asks through knitted brows as Richard, annoyed at being side-lined, mutters, 'Seriously? That's all the sympathy I get?'

'She refused to sleep with the CEO of her record label, so he stalled her album for nearly a year,' Jean explains to Tess, ignoring Richard entirely. 'And *then* when he heard she was speaking to other companies, a mysterious smear campaign began, including personal information only he was privy to. Plus, a load of creepy stuff that makes it sound like he's been having her followed.'

'God, how appalling,' Tess says, shaking her head. 'Stalking, as well as blackmail and sexual harassment!'

'I'm getting an Irish coffee with a side of humiliation and regret. Anything else from the bar?' Richard asks as he stands up to walk towards the bakery counter.

Jean and Tess shake their heads no.

'Yeah, she's been really strong about it, but it's been extremely traumatic. When all this is over, she wants me to take her to the OhhhM retreat for some yoni magic. Hex the bad juju and rebirth her as Botticelli's Tripping Venus,' Jean says, waggling her eyebrows at Tess. 'Want to come? We could make it a yearly thing.'

'I'm not sure Bjorn would approve . . .' Tess says coyly.

'One perfect boyfriend and you act like your yoni is all magicked up.'

'My yoni *is* all magicked up,' Tess grins.

'I have news!' Richard says as he returns, looking perkier.

'Has Valentina forgiven you already?' Jean asks, finishing off the rest of her cake.

'I doubt it. She's blocked me on all apps. But! I have decided to change careers. I am getting out of divorce law,' Richard says, sitting down with a flourish. 'I'm worried that in some "Law Of Attraction" way, it's ruined my chances at true love.'

'I think your behaviour has more to do with that,' Tess says, exchanging an amused look with Jean. Richard makes a face of mortal offence. 'Just saying . . .'

'So! I am going to retrain as a marriage councillor,' Richard says, a world of pain beneath his toothy smile.

'Richard, you've never been married. If I were to go to marriage counselling, I'd want someone with an enduring relationship of their own. Marriage might be, like, the *one thing* you absolutely need to experience to understand,' Jean explains in as kind a tone as possible. 'Apart from giving birth and death.'

'I can think of no one who would hire a single dude in his thirties,' Tess agrees.

'Women still go to male gynaecologists and take the word of priests! And surely people also like to learn from those who have done everything wrong. I'd be a cheerleader for love, Jean,' Richard says, starry-eyed, stubborn and full of hope. 'That's the sort of energy I want to put out into the universe. You see, I got it all wrong before. I was channelling young, feckless, gorgeous, lad-about-town Tom Hardy. When I *should* have been embodying the late thirties, settled, dadly Tom Hardy.'

'Right. Well, good luck with that,' Jean says, trying to disguise her doubt as Bjorn arrives with Richard's Irish coffee.

'And how's therapy?' Richard asks Jean pointedly.

'Well, Magda is still completely bonkers, but fantastic. Last night I dreamt I was Prince Harry and I caught a fish, which is apparently a very powerful sign in Jungian analysis. I think this will be a good year for work!' Jean says with a laugh.

'And has she reconnected you to "the power of the Divine Feminine in your sacramental space of inner sorcery"?' Richard says, mimicking Magda's thick German accent.

'I still don't understand what that means,' Jean says. 'But I hope so.'

'Maybe we should start a coven!' Tess suggests.

'Oooh, I am *so* down,' Richard says, crossing his legs and sipping his hot bev with Hollywood panache. 'Shotgun Jessica Lange.'

'I don't think that's how shotgun works,' Jean says. 'Not when it comes to taking on the personae of fictional Ryan Murphy characters. You'd be more likely to be her weird jazz-playing serial killer ghost lover. Or the mute butler obsessed with dolls.'

'So gender-normative Jean,' Richard pouts. 'Not to mention, both of you look shit in hats.'

'Let's not get personal,' Tess says.

'Oh, I have good news!' The entrance of a strawberry blond man into the shop makes Jean's heart temporarily flutter like mad, before settling when she realises it isn't him. 'I'm finally over Gabriel. In fact, the only time I ever think of him, is when I think of how over him I am.'

'And how often is that?' Richard asks cynically.

'A few times a day,' Jean admits.

'Still, progress!' Tess says, lifting her tea in a toast. 'I'm proud of you, babe. Repeat after me. Here's to you!'

'Here's to you!' Jean repeats.

'Here's to me,' Tess adds.

'Here's to me,' Richard and Jean respond, raising their coffees.

'Friends forever,' Tess says, lifting her mug again, higher.

'Friends forever!' Richard and Jean chime in, smiling at each other.

'We shall be,' Tess says.

'We shall be,' they laugh.

'And if one day,' Tess finishes, 'we disagree . . .'

'And if one day we disagree . . .'

'Then fuck you!' Tess laughs and gives a saucy wink. 'And here's to me.'

'Then fuck you! And here's to me,' Jean and Richard repeat with a raucous cackle.

They clink and drink, a contented silence descending.

'Oh my god is that the time?' Jean says, as she takes her phone from where it has been charging underneath the table to see several missed calls. 'I need to meet Danielle for a post-interview, pre-meeting catch up. She's very in demand these days.'

'Is this the interview on Capital Breakfast?' Richard asks, impressed despite himself.

'Yeah! Since that episode of *Have Your Cake* . . . went viral, she's gotten way more press opportunities. She's even in talks with the BBC to do a cleaned-up act for Radio 4.'

'Isn't she a bit too outrageous for Radio 4?' Tess asks doubtfully.

'You mean cruel?' Jean laughs. 'I don't know. Now she's experienced her first true heartbreak, she's stopped calling people shitcunts and actually sympathises with their pain. Which is kind of weird, but nice.'

'That's good she's evolving,' Richard says. 'It's never too late to grow in kindness and flourish in love!'

'I wouldn't go that far. She's still Danielle Sauvage! Solo captain of her sex-ship.'

'Oh, I have a bouquet for you to give to her,' Tess reminds Jean, standing to source a minimalist Bird of Paradise arrangement from a shelf. 'By way of congratulations.'

'How unwieldy,' Jean says, poking herself in the eye as she takes the gift.

'I have nothing to give her but my love,' Richard says.

'Good, that's easier to transport. See you later!'

Danielle waits outside the Capital building in Leicester Square, smoking her roll up and pacing back and forth in black pleather trousers, kitten heels and a snakeskin blouse.

'Nice threads,' Jean greets her sister in surprise. 'And is that lippy I detect?'

'Meeting with the BBC after our coffee,' Danielle reminds her. 'You're late.'

'Still debating whether or not to take that sweet, sweet government propaganda money?' Jean takes Danielle's arm as they walk towards Covent Garden. 'You are getting on a bit for relentless bohemia.'

'Never too old for relentless bohemia!' Danielle says in a gravelly voice, lowering a pair of sunglasses over her eyes on the sunless spring day as if Jim Morrison. She takes the Bird of Paradise from Jean's arms. 'I assume this is for me.'

'Tess and Richard send their love. So how was the show!' Jean asks, combing her fingers through her roots. 'Were you nervous?'

'Not at all,' Danielle says in the flat tones of Margot Tenenbaum, a cool apathy so pronounced Jean knows it is put on. Her excitement soon reinstates itself. 'It was great! We talked about my opportunities since the "Carnivore Hearts" episode went viral. There's such an appetite for toxic family dynamics, cynicism and fear of intimacy, which everyone seems to suffer from. It's a modern disease!'

'True,' Jean agrees as she points to a quiet café on the corner of an alleyway. 'What about there?'

'Sure. And how I've been a lot more vulnerable and intimate, that it's fostered a different relationship with my audience. The host described the episode as Harold Pinter meets *EastEnders*, which I loved.'

'Yes, I mean, Pinter is known for the "comedy of menace" isn't he, in the Theatre Of The Absurd. Your whole life has been a comedy of menace in the theatre of the absurd.' Jean laughs as she opens the door for her sister.

'And I've got more Kat Slater in me than I'd like to admit,' Danielle agrees, before ordering a flat white from the barrista.

'Make that two!' Jean adds. 'And a croissant. What advice did you give to cure toxic fear of intimacy then?'

'I think I said we need more delusion in relationships. That delusion is imagination plus ego and it's what makes dreams a reality. And it's what makes a relationship bearable! Believing the best of your person, having them believe the best of you, having faith it will work out. Most don't, most relationships end. What do we call dreams that aren't realised? Delusions.'

'So, delusion is what comes before the relationship both does or doesn't work,' Jean says slowly, trying to understand her sister's thought process.

'Exactly! Like Schrodinger's love affair,' Danielle says. 'Relationships are in such a constant state of unknowable flux that they are both alive and dead at the same time.'

'I thought you said your brand has moved beyond cynicism?' Jean asks as she collects their coffees. 'How is this helpful life advice?'

'This is recognising the transience of all things, you know. That life is precious. Life is unexpected. Life is sweet. Love is all those things and more, but you can't count on it enduring. So, you've just got to grasp it, in that moment. Cherish what you have when you have it, with all your heart,' Danielle says, her smile sadder this time as she sits down at a table outside. 'I guess my cynicism is the sort that goes so far round the bend of sentimentality, it turns back into cynicism.'

'I take it you haven't told Harry you're still in love with him,' Jean surmises.

'I mean, I sort of told the world I'm still in love with him,' Danielle hedges, exhaling as she stares into the distance.

'Not really. You said you *were* in love with him six months ago on your show, which I doubt he listens to any more. He might not know!' Jean points out.

'It went viral. He must know,' Danielle mutters.

'Why don't you tell him, to be sure?' Jean asks, her brows knitted in confusion.

'I'm a coward, I guess,' Danielle shrugs, mouth twisted in a little half smile.

'Fortune favours the bold,' Jean says through a mouthful of croissant. 'Nothing ventured, nothing gained!'

'Oh, it wouldn't have worked out anyway. We're so different,' Danielle says wistfully. 'Although I admit, I have got a taste for a degree of social normalcy since dating him. Maybe I am reaching my "After The Orgy" decade.'

'Never,' Jean laughs. 'Have you spoken to Door at all?'

Jean doesn't ask about their father. She doubts they will ever communicate again.

'She's under strict orders not to speak to me, but I did receive a congratulatory box of anonymous chocolates from Fortnum and Mason. As she's the only person I know who shops there, I think this is her way of saying I'm still her daughter, or something. You?'

'Radio silence. It's great! My therapist Magda says they will never change and the only way for me to healthily endure their dynamic is to radically accept them as they are. Which I can sort of do, but only if I don't see, speak or think about them. Ever.'

Danielle knocks back the rest of her latte with one eye on her watch.

'Fair. After the BBC, I'm off to a Russian banya in Hoxton to naked sauna before being whipped by men with bundles of birchbark,' Danielle says, as if this is what regular proles do. 'It's highly invigorating. Want to join?'

'I think I'll go to the National Portrait Gallery and then do some window shopping instead,' Jean says, finishing off her coffee. 'But I'll walk you to the station.'

'Love you!' Danielle shouts out as she is swallowed by the elevator doors of the Tube. Jean always knew she did, but it is the first time Danielle has said it aloud in many years.

'Love you, too!' Jean blows her sister a kiss, as her eyes mist with tears.

Epilogue

As Jean wanders through Covent Garden, the lilac beginnings of sunset replete with the scent of honeysuckle, she passes the pub strewn with flowers where she and Gabriel had gone after their first date. Her feet slow as she stares through the window. She hallucinates that she sees him through the glass. A nostalgic pang of half-forgotten longing hits her.

Her feet come to a pause, then to a halt. It is not a vision. It is him.

He is talking to a second man, younger and very handsome, with a Roman nose and short curly black hair. Gabriel is more animated than usual, as if to keep up with the boy's nervy energy. A third person joins them, returning from the bar with two pints of beer and a bottle of Perrier, a jaunty yellow straw stuck in it. It is an unmistakably glowing, luscious, tanned and tall Poppy, who must be about six months pregnant.

As Poppy sits in between them, the younger man pushes over a plate of food, what appears to be pesto pasta. He feeds her a bite. Gabriel grabs a fork, and spins it in the verdant sauce, taking it to his lips. Poppy says something, and they both laugh. Gabriel's head turns as if he can feel Jean's gaze upon him.

Jean smiles brightly, and waves. After a moment, his eyes soften with recognition and that look she remembers from lazy mornings they spent together in bed, when she thought yes, he truly adores me. And her heart fills wildly, and she turns and walks away. She knows that if nothing else, she has truly learned the meaning of compersion.

Joy for your loved one's joy.

Acknowledgments

An enormous thank you to my parents, grandparents, and my sisters Leila and Anna, without whose unfailing support, humour, wit, kindness and love I never would have completed this (or any) book. Your influence is ever-felt and cherished.

Thank you to my brilliant editor Katie Brown, whose enthusiasm, sense of fun and excellent eye for the heart of a character pushed me to draw out truths and vulnerabilities I wanted to skate around. Thank you to my fantastic agent Becky Thomas, for having stuck by me all these years and read way too much of my fiction! Always returning with generous advice and fresh ideas. And to the Trapeze team, for bringing *Strings Attached* beautifully to life!

I feel so privileged to have so many amazing, spirited, hilarious, loving sisters and queens in my life, who have helped me through the best and worst of times, supported my writing and fed into my characters. I wouldn't have got through this year without you. Hanako Whiteway, Deeba Syed, Olivia Spring, Isabelle Gill, Maggie Li, Jane Hoffman, Kathryn Azgard, Ana Li-Mraovitch, Zoe Pilger, Emma-Jane Unsworth, Anna Barr, Eve Clark, Golan and Fyodor Podgorny-Frydman. To many years of laughter, tears and laughing through our tears.

And finally, thank you to all the loves, and losses, and heartbreaks, and joys.

Credits

Trapeze would like to thank everyone at Orion who worked on the publication of *Strings Attached* in the UK.

Agent
Becky Thomas

Editor
Katie Brown

Copy editor
Sophie Wilson

Proof reader
Loma Halden

Editorial Management
Charlie Panayiotou
Jane Hughes
Alice Davis
Marleigh Price

Audio
Paul Stark
Amber Bates

Contracts
Anne Goddard
Paul Bulos
Jake Alderson

Design
Lucie Stericker
Joanna Ridley
Nick May
Clare Sivell
Helen Ewing
Charlotte Abrams-Simpson

Finance
Emily-Jane Taylor
Jasdip Nandra
Afeera Ahmed
Elizabeth Beaumont
Sue Baker
Victor Falola